DEMONS
OF THE
PAST

SHIFTERS OF CAERTON : BOOK 3

BY
H.B. LYNE

Published by Weaver of Words Press
UK

Originally Published in 2015
as Echoes of the Past: Tides of Spring
Published as part of the Shifters of Caerton Series 2019

This edition published in 2020

2

Book Cover design by Olivia Pro Design
Interior Formatting by Evenstar Books Ltd.

ISBN 978-1-913673-04-8
(paperback)
ISBN 978-1-913673-05-5
(ebook)

hblyne.com

Are we a Perfect Match?

Demons of the Past is dark urban fantasy. In these pages you won't find sparkly vampires or teenage heroines with perfect hair.

I write dark, gritty, emotionally compelling stories filled with flawed protagonists, anti-heroes and deliciously dark villains.

There will be plot twists that bring out your most colourful language and yes, I write in British English.

If any of these things bother you, turn back now.

If however, darkness is your poison, then read on and lose yourself in the shadows for a while.

Acknowledgements

Many thanks to my family for their unending support; to my editor, Zoe Markham; and cover designer, Olivia at *Olivia Pro Designs*. Thanks to Julia at *Evenstar Books Ltd* for her stunning formatting and uber patience! Thank you to the world's mythologies for their inspiration.

Also, thanks to my Patrons, whose continuing support has enabled me to continue doing what I love; thank you to Andy, Linzy, Richard, Monika, and Emé.

Author's Note

Imbolc *(pronounced "Imelk")*: a modern pagan festival, based on an ancient Irish festival that symbolised the first stirrings of spring. Today, it is celebrated on 2nd February; a month traditionally associated with the first spring flowers, the first lambs and lighter mornings. Modern seasonal changes may differ, but the traditions are deeply rooted. It is on this date that this book begins.

Danegeld: a tax paid by ancient Britons to their Danish invaders to protect the land from being ravaged.

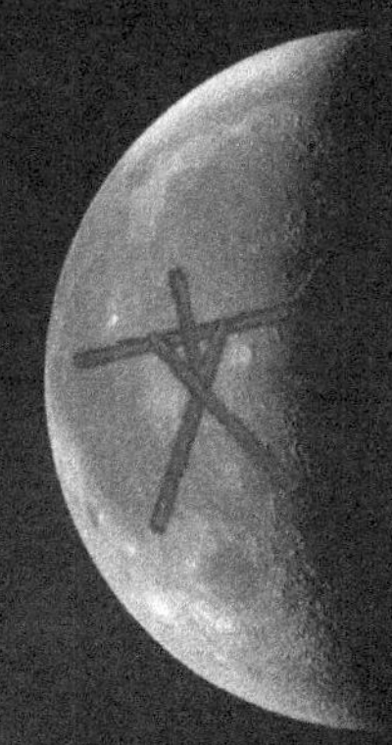

PROLOGUE

JESSICA CARTER

SHE PULLED HER LONG, BLOND HAIR BACK and tied it in a sloppy pony tail. Examining her face in the grubby mirror the Alpha observed her tanned and lined skin. Her lips were far thinner than they had been in her youth. Two teenage daughters, well, one now, and a lifetime of fighting were evident on her face. When she thought about it, maybe she was just unusual for a shifter and looked her actual age, rather than ten or more years younger.

With a snort of laughter, Jessica turned away and swept down the stairs and into the small room in the basement of the shop, where Spinner-of-Crystal was trying to calm the thrashing, frantic girl on the metal table.

'Hold still,' Jessica snapped. She climbed up on the table and wedged her knee against her daughter's chest to pin her down. The girl would not stop bawling. You would have thought that being brought up around shifters she would have been prepared for the change, but Victoria had completely lost control; unlike her twin sister, Angela, who had handled the change like a pro and embraced her true nature. Victoria was just one big disappointment and always had been. But blood was blood and initiation into Megaira was mandatory for all Witches.

'It will hurt less if you hold still,' Spinner-of-Crystal whispered. Victoria's eyes darted between the two women who were holding her down; gradually she relented and went limp. Jessica sneered as she pushed the needle through her daughter's earlobe. Victoria winced and let out a whimper, but she held steady. Jessica was surprised, half impressed and half disappointed. If Victoria toughened up and came through for her she would be a credit to her; but that would leave her no one upon whom to take out her anger.

The worst was still to come, however, and Jessica carefully picked up the silver claw. It burned her fingers but she hardly noticed. Victoria's eyes latched onto the small piece of jewellery as Jessica moved it slowly towards her ear and she began to thrash about again.

'You will wear this with pride,' Jessica said, her voice low and threatening. 'You are one of us now, for better or worse and you will wear the mark of our kin and our Patron, Megaira.'

Jessica pressed the delicate silver claw against the girl's ear while Spinner-of-Crystal held her face and shoulders still. Victoria shook violently as the silver burned her skin, and Jessica had to contend with the jerky movement. She sighed and bent lower, gripping her daughter's ear and the claw more tightly. She pressed on, forcing the claw through the new piercing. It broke through the flesh and fresh blood spilled down her neck and into her hair. Victoria screamed and managed to wrench an arm free.

The Alpha released her grip on the girl. Spinner-of-Crystal followed her lead and Victoria leaped from the table and threw herself against the wall of the little room. She shrieked and tugged at her ear. 'If you pull it out we will only have to put it back in again,' Jessica drawled.

Victoria began to calm down as she got accustomed to the sensation. She pressed her back flat against the wall and took deep breaths. Jessica watched her carefully, she doubted the girl's strength of will, but was seeing a hint of the girl's sister in her now. She wasn't going to hold her breath, the apparent calm could be fake or fleeting.

Jessica's phone rang and she left the room with a backward glance and roll of her eyes. She glanced at the caller ID and stopped dead. She drew a deep breath before answering the call. 'Your Grace.'

'I hear congratulations are in order.' The voice on the line was sombre.

'Indeed, thank you, Your Grace,' Jessica replied.

'I hope this compensates somewhat for your loss.'

'Thank you, it remains to be seen.' The scorn in her voice couldn't be hidden and her remark was met with awkward silence.

'Well, are you nearly ready?' the caller asked after a long pause.

'I believe so,' the Alpha replied with a slight tremor to her voice. An uncharacteristic lump rose in her throat and she coughed to clear it.

'You had better be, I need you to settle this vendetta quickly so as not to interfere with my plans.' The voice dripped with bitterness.

'Of course, Your Grace. It will be dealt with swiftly and decisively.'

'Good. I will know when it is done. If you succeed, the Blue Moon will finally be eradicated and their scourge ended. You will be rewarded.'

'Thank you, Your Grace.' Jessica allowed herself a small smile.

'If you fail, however, you will feel the heat of my blade.'

'Of course, Your Grace.' The smile fell from her lips. The line went dead and Jessica slowly lowered her phone. She wouldn't fail. She *couldn't* fail.

She returned to the room to find her daughter sobbing in a heap on the floor, blood all over her face and in her hair. The silver claw lay in the middle of the floor. Jessica sighed and stooped to pick it up. 'Put her back on the table,' she ordered Spinner-of-Crystal. 'Let's start again.'

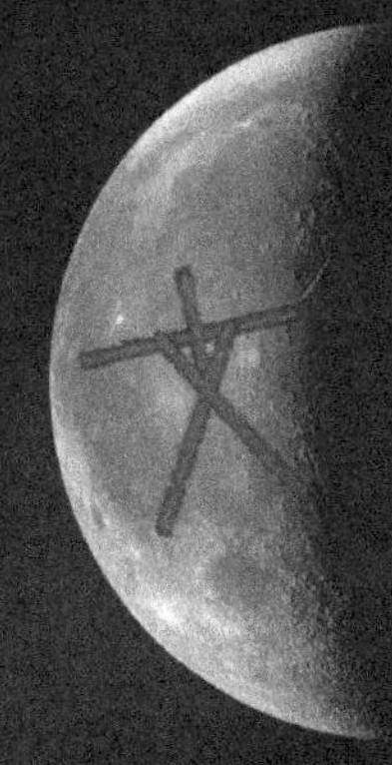

Chapter One

Stalker-of-Night's-Shadow

—·   2nd February   ·—

Stalker watched him sleeping. His breathing was deep and rhythmic and his eyelids fluttered softly. She leaned in and kissed him gently on the lips. His dark skin was hot and his neck and chest gleamed with sweat. He stirred slightly with her kiss and she slowly pulled away and slid to the edge of the bed. She felt the cool wooden floor against her feet. Her clothes were scattered all over his bedroom and she started to stand up to reach for her underwear when his hand caught her wrist.

'Where are you going?' he asked, sleepily.

'I have to get back, we have preparations to make for tonight,' she said, looking back at him.

First Strike pulled her roughly back onto the bed and into his arms. She giggled and played at struggling to get free.

'No, you have to stay here with me.'

'I thought you were asleep, I didn't want to wake you.'

'So you were going to sneak off while I slept?' he said, his eyes wide with pretend shock. 'What do you think I am?'

'Oh, don't go there,' she scolded. 'You might not like what you hear.' They both pulled faces and First Strike wrestled his way on top of her amid laughter. Stalker let him pin her to the bed and enjoyed his kisses on her neck.

He slid over to one side and propped himself up on his elbow to look at her.

'I'm crazy about you. You know that, right?' he asked, staring at her intently.

Stalker felt heat in her cheeks and chewed on her bottom lip. A warning voice in her head reminded her that wolves mate for life.

'Yeah, I do,' she whispered, stroking his arm. 'I have to go but I'll see you tonight. It's only a few hours.'

'I have to walk you out,' he said, sitting up and searching for his jeans.

'There's a taxi rank twenty yards from your front door,' she said, a little resentment creeping into her voice.

'Crimson is really strict about this stuff. I know you have that sneaky ability to suppress your trail, but it doesn't bear thinking about if any of my pack pick up your scent without mine right beside it.'

He was right. Stalker sighed and quickly got herself dressed.

'Does she know? I mean, has she smelled me on you already?'

'Maybe. Probably. But she hasn't mentioned it. What

about your pack?' he asked as he pulled on his clothes.

'Weaver knows, she knew that very first night,' she said with a grin.

'Oh god,' he groaned. 'I'll have to try and look her in the eye tonight. I wonder who will crack first.'

Stalker chuckled.

'It won't be that bad, besides, it will be crazy tonight. Everyone's coming, you might not even see her.'

They left the house and walked slowly to the taxi rank holding hands. The shut shops and still houses on either side of the street were as grey as the slate clouds above. There was the faintest threat of snow in the air, hopefully the last snow of winter. Tonight would usher in the spring and signal the New Year for their kind. A chance for fresh starts. A single taxi sat in the rank, the driver glanced up at their arrival and put his newspaper aside.

'I'll see you tonight, then,' First Strike said. He leaned in for a kiss and Stalker welcomed it. His breath was hot against the cool air and she sank into his kiss. She pulled away slowly and opened the taxi door.

'See you tonight,' she said with a smile.

She watched him out of the window as the taxi drove away, a small smile on his full lips. Stalker sighed and pulled out her phone to check for messages. She had a missed call and voicemail, from *him*.

She dropped her head back against the headrest and dialled in to listen.

'Hi, how are you? I woke up feeling weird today. Spring is coming, change is in the air, I guess. Anyway, I thought of you and wondered if you were okay. I hope you'll call me back, but totally understand if you don't. It's been weeks now and I haven't heard from you. I just want to know you're okay. I worry, you know? Anyway, I hope you're okay and hope to hear from you soon. I... Bye.'

His last, unfinished sentence clung to Stalker's thoughts as she hung up the phone and closed her eyes. Rhys's messages were few and far between now, but each one brought renewed regret and sadness. She knew that First Strike was a rebound. Part of her wanted it to be more, but her thoughts always came back to Rhys. Caerton sped past, half asleep in the early morning stillness. Stalker gazed unseeing at the window as a solitary snowflake landed on the glass and instantly melted.

She arrived back at 32 Grove Street and found most of the pack busy in the living room, making their costumes for the festival. Fights-Eyes-Open was with his family for what had become his usual Saturday-family-day.

'Dirty stop out!' Weaver-of-Sky's-Loom called, glancing up from her sewing.

Stalker laughed it off and made her way to the kitchen to get some breakfast. She peeked out into the garden. The glowing cocoon in the corner was getting brighter and throbbing more each day. Unchained Lightning was sure to hatch out of it soon, but what was he going to have changed into? It made her nervous; it made all of them nervous.

The house was becoming increasingly more homey and comfortable. A quiet winter since the destruction of the Plague Doctor had afforded them the chance to finish getting the garden fixed up and furnish the house with more than the basics. They had reupholstered the sofa, added lamps and stocked the kitchen with china and plenty of food. It was truly home now. Stalker still kept her flat, mainly as somewhere to meet First Strike, but also so that she still had something of her old life.

Stalker spent the day finishing off her outfit, and helping the others with theirs. They played music and ate together. Weaver made no more digs about Stalker's escapades, and her thoughts drifted away from Rhys's message. A brief flurry of snow caused a ripple of excitement, but didn't amount to anything.

Eyes arrived at 6.30pm looking mildly flustered and nervous.

'Why aren't you ready?' Wind Talker asked him.

'I couldn't change into my costume at home,' Eyes replied. 'What on earth would Chloe think of this?' He held up his expensive, black suit and pulled his accessories out of a bag. He had platinum cufflinks and a tie pin emblazoned with glimmering lightning bolts. The finishing touches were silver spray in his hair and sunglasses with little blue lights all around the rims.

Soon, they were ready to set off, dressed in all their finery. Wind Talker had made himself a grey cloak with a huge, silver dragon printed on the back which bore an uncanny resemblance to Unchained Lightning. Weaver had threaded tiny, flashing blue and white LEDs into her hair and wore a black skinny t-shirt with a flashing lightning bolt and the words "Power, bitch" on the front. Claws-of-Lead was dressed in casual jeans and t-shirt, but had fitted white lights into the heels of his boots and wore dozens of glow sticks around his arms and neck.

Stalker had on huge black boots with silver lightning down the sides and flashing lights in the soles. She wore a long skirt with splits up the sides and a silver vest with glowing blue studs forming a power symbol. Her hair was growing out now and was just brushing her shoulders. She had dyed it bright blue and also threaded it with LEDs, like Weaver. She had her two dha strapped to her back and had added blue tassels to the hilts with little steel lightning bolts hanging off them. Like Claws, she also had glow sticks all up her arms and around her neck.

The Lightning Lords left 32 Grove Street and climbed into Eyes' shiny new four-wheel drive. He had opted for something a bit more robust and practical when the insurance cheque for his luxury saloon had turned up.

The sun had set over the city, and orange street lights cast their eerie glow over everything. The morning's dark clouds had cleared and the clear sky was pricked with stars. A waning gibbous moon shone over Caerton as the Lightning Lords sped through the bustling streets of St. Mark's, into the almost deserted business district of Burnside and then out into Fenstoke.

It was a bizarre mix of old and new; bits of Fenstoke had their origins in an outlying village that had been absorbed into the city as it grew, while others were new developments. A college that had been built twenty years ago had a sprawling campus and there was a huge leisure development with the city's biggest mall, as well as a multiplex cinema and over a dozen restaurants. They drove further out, almost to the city limits. Fenwick, the territory of the Witches, lay to the north, just out of sight beyond big, detached houses.

Stalker directed Eyes to the venue, Fenstoke Lodge, an eighteenth century mansion built of sandstone. It stood within vast grounds, high on a hill, overlooking the whole of Caerton. This was the seat of power of The Hand of God, First Strike's pack. His house was back towards the city centre. Stalker had never been invited here with him; but had come two days previously for the final planning meeting with Odin's Warriors. Tonight the mansion was floodlit and stood out against the black forest behind it.

Eyes pulled up in front of the house, at the end of a row of parked cars. Another car arrived right after them and parked alongside. Stalker glanced at it, it was an old hatchback that had been tinkered with and added to. It had blacked-out windows, a custom paint job and big spoiler on the back.

'Everyone ready?' Eyes asked. Apprehensive nods rippled around the car.

Next to them, five young men were piling out of the other car. They were all dressed in tracksuits, one was wearing a backwards cap. Several of them sneered at the Lightning Lords as they slowly stepped out of Eyes' car, all done up to the nines.

Eyes held the pack back to let the others go ahead, which suited Stalker just fine.

'Who were they?' Weaver whispered once they were out of earshot.

'At a guess,' Stalker replied, 'The Factory Boys, from Shalebrook.'

'You've seen the whole guest list, haven't you?' Wind Talker asked as they made their way past the sweeping steps up to the entrance of the house and around the side.

'I have,' she replied with a wink.

Very large, very well-dressed men were positioned

every few yards, indicating the path into the grounds that they were to follow, hired human bodyguards, there to keep humans away from the site. The Lightning Lords were led to the mouth of a cave, set in the side of the hill behind the house. Torches burned inside the cave, not just normal, yellow flames, but flames of red, green, blue and purple lit the way deep into the hill.

Eyes led the Lightning Lords quickly through the tunnel, which was wide enough for them to walk two abreast. Stalker felt the moment when they crossed the veil in between worlds, straight through with no choice in the matter. Her navel was wrenched and the world spun quickly around in a dizzying blur. She was used to the sensation and her feet landed solidly on the crystal floor.

In Hepethia, the hidden realm of shifter kind, the tunnel opened up into a vast cavern lit with more of the brightly coloured torches and a million sparkling fairy lights wrapped around the many crystalline stalactites that clung to the ceiling. All of Hepethia was made of these incredible crystal structures and the cavern shone in a rainbow of colours.

The cave was filled with shifters, approximately sixty altogether. They were assembled roughly by pack, each adorned with costumes representing their uniqueness, though there was some intermingling going on already.

There was a collective intake of breath at the sight and Stalker grinned at her pack mates, pride swelling in her chest.

'Greetings,' a deep voice said from just beside them. Stalker knew it at once and turned to give First Strike a warm smile. 'Welcome to the Danegeld.'

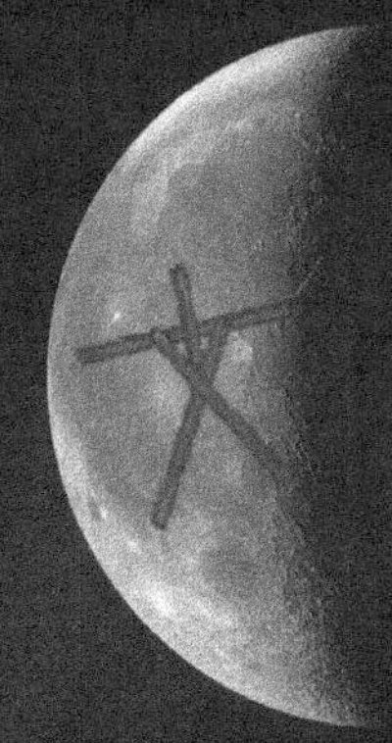

CHAPTER TWO

STALKER DISCREETLY TOUCHED FIRST STRIKE'S HAND, their fingers gently brushing, and they exchanged mutually appreciative grins at one another's attire. He was topless, wearing a heavy, ornate gold cross around his neck on a thick chain. Stalker saw Weaver trying to hide a grin as she pointedly looked away from the couple.

'I'll catch up with you later,' she said to him quietly, and led her pack down the roughly carved steps into the cavern. There was a large fire burning in a pit at the head of the cave, behind it, on a dais was a huge stone throne with two ravens carved into the arms. Below the dais stood Crimson, dressed in a deep red dress that left very little to the imagination. Her long, red hair was loose and adorned with flowers. She carried a tall sceptre with a cross upon the top, and a shimmering black satin cloak lay across her shoulders with a glittering red crown emblazoned on the back. She was speaking with another female shifter that

Stalker didn't know, but judging by the similar crown and cross motifs in her outfit, she must have been another member of The Hand of God.

Around the cave were several smaller fires, the smoke drawn out by the many narrow cracks and passages of the cave. Elementals of fire, wind, and shadow danced in the firelight, largely ignoring the shifters. The Danegeld was giving them life, feeding them, so they participated willingly and caused no problems. Ravens perched on many of the higher-up platforms, observing silently.

Stalker spotted Scribe-of-the-Fallen and Last-Breath-Echoes talking together near the dais. Echoes was dressed in loose, black clothing, as she so often was, but like her pack mates, she was wearing the symbols of crown and cross in gold and silver-coloured jewellery all over her body. She had a carved wooden mask perched on top of her head. Stalker caught her eye and they exchanged smiles and small waves. Scribe was in his typical Goth garb: big boots, black clothes and long black leather coat. His shoulder-length hair, however, was hidden by huge synthetic extensions of red and white. He too wore a mask, a partial skull of a fox that perched on his nose and covered his eyes and forehead.

The rest of the Hellsclaws stood out from the crowd too. Like the Lightning Lords, they were all wearing flashing, glowing accessories commonly seen in cyber-goth clubs like their own, The Dragon's Den.

On opposite sides of the cavern were two tight-knit groups of shifters, eyeing each other carefully: The Watch on one side, all bearing the insignia of Caerton, that of a raven; and the Glass Wolves on the other, each decorated with tiny glass ornaments. Theodore Harris, their Alpha, was wearing a striking helm of glass cut to resemble the top of a panther's head. The Alpha of The Watch, Warden-of-Stones, looked very different from the only other time Stalker had seen her. That day she had been dressed for work in a neat suit with her hair tied tightly back. Tonight she was dressed in the ornate robes of a warrior priestess, adorned with shining black raven feathers, and her long black hair was intricately braided around golden ribbons. She wore a huge broadsword across her back.

Many of the shifters present were armed, particularly Odin's Warriors. Huge swords, axes and hammers were in bountiful supply. One member of the Glass Wolves had a shotgun strapped to her back and Stalker pointed her out to Claws. He grinned at her and dashed away from the pack to go and introduce himself. He returned a few minutes later looking humbled.

'What happened?' Stalker asked him quietly.

'Not much,' he replied with a shrug. 'She didn't seem interested in talking. I recognised her when I got closer though, it was Vengeance-of-Steel, the police officer.'

'Not exactly Officer Friendly, then?' Stalker asked with a wink.

'Not remotely.'

The cave was filled with noise from shifters talking and the fires roaring, but somehow, over the din, a voice rang out calling them to order. Stalker looked towards the dais and saw Red Scythe standing beside the throne, his huge scythe in hand. He was wearing robes of blood red with a golden, rising sun embroidered on the chest. Crimson was at his side and Warden-of-Stones had made her way up there too.

'Welcome!' Red Scythe called out. 'We come together tonight to participate in the Danegeld, the paying of tribute to Odin and the Gods to whom we owe fealty.' There were a few shouts of agreement and several murmurs of dissent and Stalker looked around anxiously, trying to identify which shifters had spoken.

'We owe no one fealty, nor tribute.' A clear, loud voice echoed around the cave. All eyes turned at once to the entrance, above the gathered shifters. Five newcomers stood on the ledge, the coloured torches at their backs casting eerie shadows. Stalker could just about make out that they were all wearing mail armour and ornate, Anglo-Saxon helmets that covered the whole face.

'We acknowledge The Fyrd,' Red Scythe called out. 'It is your right to refuse to pay the Danegeld. In so doing, you are offered no protection.'

'We need no protection,' the Alpha of The Fyrd replied. The newcomers strode down the steps and took up a position beside one of the fires.

'What was that about?' Eyes whispered, close at Stalker's ear.

'It was ceremonial,' she replied, not taking her eyes off the mysterious newcomers. 'Ragged Edge explained it to me. The same exchange has been recited at every Danegeld, every five years since they began, however many hundreds of years ago.'

'Who are they?' Claws whispered to Stalker.

'A pack from outside Caerton,' she whispered back. 'They have territory in the middle of some packs of Furies and are on our side against them. But they don't bow to

Odin.'

'Each pack will come forwards with their tribute,' Red Scythe announced. 'Beginning with The Watch.'

Warden stepped down from the dais and her pack strode forwards to join her by the huge fire at the front. She held up a large knife, cut into her palm and held it over the fire for the blood to drip into it. The fire elementals were whipped into a frenzy and some of the sparks turned bright red. Warden went to each member of her pack and cut all of their palms. Once their tribute was paid they returned to their positions.

Red Scythe called on the Glass Wolves next and Theodore repeated Warden's actions. Crimson Dawn's Blood were next, followed by The Hand of God. Both Red Scythe and Crimson paid tribute with their packs, as did the other members of Odin's Warriors. They were mere messengers, not the recipients of the tax. 'The Storm Riders,' Red Scythe called.

Stalker's head whipped around to see these curious shifters, whom they knew so little about. Her friend, Fire Talon from Odin's Warriors was among them and he fell into step behind his Alpha as they made their way forwards. The Alpha carried a trident and Fire Talon wore a cloak with a storm printed on it. They all wore trinkets rescued from the sea, lots of green copper and nautical symbols. The knife that the Alpha used was encrusted with precious stones.

Next were the Hellsclaws, led by their Alpha, Voice-of-Truth. They were followed by The Savages. The cavern was utterly silent as they made their way to the front to pay their tribute. Stalker watched this small pack carefully.

There were only three of them, but they were dressed in furs. The Alpha wore what appeared to be a bearskin, complete with a head that covered his own, and one of their number was wearing antlers. They wore bones on their belts and carried vicious, handmade weapons. Stalker felt a sudden stab of recognition when she laid eyes on the third member of the Savages, it was Hunter, the shifter she had once tracked across Blue Moon territory, and her fellow member of the Path of Night. He was wearing a fox pelt across his shoulders and she gave an involuntary shudder at the thought of him acquiring it himself.

'Where's their territory?' Eyes whispered.

'Elmswood,' Weaver replied. 'South of the city.'

Red Scythe called on the Factory Boys next, who seemed mildly bored by the proceedings; and then the Wrecking Crew. Rust led his pack and Stalker noticed that they were all dressed in quite clever costumes made from bits of cars and machinery. They must have spent a great deal of effort on them and she was impressed. She caught Fury's eye and her rival sneered at her maliciously. Stalker ignored her and promptly dismissed any positive thoughts about the pack.

'We welcome Caerton's newest pack,' Red Scythe announced. 'Come forwards, Lightning Lords, and pay your tribute.'

Stalker's palms were sweating and she felt the apprehension of each of her pack mates through the empathy granted to them by their patron, Unchained Lightning. Eyes led them to the fire and took out Wind Talker's ritual knife from his own belt. He cut each of their palms and they added their blood to the mix. Stalker watched the fire fae reacting to their blood, just as they had done to all of the shifters who had gone before them. She felt a mixture of awe and trepidation. When they were finished they returned to their place by a smaller fire.

'Tribute is paid. We call upon Odin Allfather and his pantheon to recognise the fealty of Caerton and grant us fortune and favour in return.'

The fire that contained all of their blood suddenly flared up even more; a burst of heat filled the vast cavern and the fae were stirred into a frenzied dance to the beat of drums, though Stalker could see no drummers. Goose bumps popped up all over her arms, despite the heat, and the ravens all around the cave suddenly rose up as one and soared around over the heads of the gathered shifters. They cawed, the sound echoing off the walls and sending chilling vibrations through the floor. Black feathers dropped on the crowd as the birds made their course around the cavern and out through a narrow crack to the outside world.

A cheer rose up among the crowd and the sound was deafening. Stalker joined it, but the rest of her pack looked a little surprised.

'With that business taken care of,' Crimson said, stepping forwards and the crowd fell quiet at the sound of her melodic voice. 'We call now upon the Olympian deities. We welcome Persephone back from her time in Hades as winter draws to a close, and entreat Demeter to return life to earth and bring spring forth.' She plucked several of the flowers from her hair and threw them into the fire.

A great plume of smoke rose up and the flames erupted to form a beautiful flower shape with petals unfolding. The effect resembled burning paper, curling and blackening at the edges, with glowing embers and tiny sparks emitting from the blazing flames. Stalker gasped, along with several others. It was one of the most incredible things she had seen.

Crimson stepped away from the fire as it settled back into normal flames and Red Scythe returned to the front of the dais.

'We have endured winter, though it was not without loss. But spring approaches now and with it the threat of war. The Furies rise around us and are preparing themselves. The main assault could begin at any time. Many of us have experienced border skirmishes and flash raids.' Stalker flinched and she felt her pack mates tense up with her. 'But winter is not a time for open warfare. It is our strong suspicion that they have been saving their resources for a summer campaign. All of Caerton's shifters must be prepared.'

There were mutterings throughout the cavern as the shifters heard this news and felt compelled to discuss it. The Lightning Lords exchanged worried glances but remained silent. It felt to Stalker like Red Scythe was talking explicitly about the Blue Moon, but from the reactions of some of the packs, and with her new knowledge of The Fyrd, it seemed that her pack mates were not the only ones to have been hit by Furies recently. 'Odin's Warriors declared war on the Furies some months ago, but we too have been biding our time. Some of our number fulfilled their oaths early.' He caught Stalker's eye and she felt a ripple of heads turn her way. She felt a little embarrassed to be singled out and extremely uncomfortable with the memory of killing the young Witch. It hadn't been a deliberate act to fulfil her oath, it had been a brawl gone too far and a terrible mistake. It was a miracle that the Witches hadn't come marching to her door for retribution. She had to assume that they didn't know who was responsible for the murder. 'But,' Red Scythe went on. 'Now is the time for all to make good on that oath and for the wider community to also pledge their service in this war.'

The cavern erupted with shouts and dozens of fists pumped in the air, including Eyes and Wind Talker, which caught Stalker slightly off guard. Yet some held back and the war cry died prematurely.

'How can you be so sure?' a voice called out. Everyone searched the crowd for the speaker and Stalker's eyes fell upon Theodore Harris, standing with his arms crossed near the front of the crowd. 'There's no evidence to suggest that they're planning a full scale assault. They've never attempted such action before. Why now?'

'The signs all point–' Red Scythe said, a little reticently.

'To what?' Theodore interrupted. 'To more of the same minor squabbles that have irritated us for decades.'

Stalker felt a stab of insult at his words and beside her Eyes flinched. She glanced at him and placed a calming hand across his chest when she saw that he looked ready to pounce across the cave towards Theodore.

'We must be prepared!' Red Scythe insisted.

'Prepared to defend ourselves, of course. But not for war. We are not the aggressors. You would make warmongers of us all.' Theodore's pack mates patted him on the back as he stepped back and relaxed a little. He had said his piece. Red Scythe looked taken aback and stood silently. Crimson stepped forwards and raised her hands.

'You are all welcome to remain here and feast. Enjoy the celebrations, partake in the glory of our spring celebration and all of the diversions available. We thank you all for coming.'

The gathered shifters immediately burst into animated conversations and the cave was filled with noise and movement. Stalker stood still amidst it all and looked around at her pack mates, who were equally stunned.

'Did Red Scythe just try to unite the packs for war?' Eyes asked.

'And failed,' Wind Talker replied.

'That's what it will take though, isn't it?' Eyes asked. No one replied. 'I'm going to talk to him.'

'Careful,' Weaver warned. 'You work for Theodore now, remember that.'

Eyes stopped mid stride and considered her carefully. He gave a curt nod and strode off towards Red Scythe. Stalker watched him and heaved a great sigh. She had never seen any elder get shot down like that and it stung that it was her own leader from Odin's Warriors. Her eyes narrowed as she watched Theodore enjoying the attention of various other shifters and she wondered, not for the first time, where his loyalties lay.

Stalker looked around the crowd for a familiar face. She saw Fire Talon heading straight for her and greeted him with a warm smile and brief hug.

'How are you?' she asked him.

'I'm very well, thank you. You?' he replied.

'I'm great, thanks.'

Fire Talon took her by the elbow and led her to one

side.

'It's been a hard winter, I can't lie,' he said quietly. 'Something dark is coming. We've been fighting back hordes of walkers from the sea, the chosen of Poseidon and it's been getting worse all winter. The storms have been unusually severe and I know that might be something your pack might understand.'

Stalker listened attentively. She could see how worried he was and up close she saw that the harsh winter had aged him.

'Yes, of course. I can look into it; perhaps The-Lord-of-Storms-and-Rain can give us some information.'

'Thor? Thor is on your territory?' Fire Talon asked.

'Yes, at the top of the telecoms tower.' She saw the expression of stunned disbelief in his face and suddenly worried that she had revealed something that she ought not to. 'Best keep that one to yourself, I assumed others would know, but if not then it must be for a reason.' Fire Talon gave her a reassuring smile.

'I won't mention it. But look, seriously, Iron Sky has tried to warn the other Alphas, but no one is listening to him. They all think he's lost his mind. But these creatures from the sea are real and they are dangerous. But more worryingly, we're sure they are just the first wave of the offensive. There are worse things to come and without the King-of-Glass-and-Steel, well, I don't fancy our chances.'

Stalker nodded solemnly.

'Okay, I absolutely take your caution seriously and I'll talk to my Alpha. Thank you for talking to me about it.'

'No problem. I honestly hope we're wrong by the way.' He tried to smile and she gave him a pat on the arm before he headed back to his pack.

Stalker felt his warning gnaw at her insides. Everyone said the Storm Riders were crazy, distracted and deluded. But she knew Fire Talon and knew that his head was screwed on right. He had been genuinely afraid, she had seen it in his eyes. What did it mean for Caerton if they were facing war from the sea as well as the Furies?

'Stalker!' She turned at the call of her name and saw First Strike waving to her. He was standing with a cluster of other Berserkers and she went over to greet them. He pulled her into his arms and lifted her off her feet. She laughed but felt embarrassed and patted him as a signal for him to release her. She awkwardly fiddled with her hair and he looked at her quizzically.

'This isn't the place,' she mumbled under her breath and he gave a slightly hurt nod.

'This way,' Ragged Edge said, his voice low and serious. He led them across the cave to the fire nearest the back. All of Odin's Warriors gathered together. They were a formidable sight, all decorated for the Danegeld and armed to the teeth. Red Scythe stood at the centre of the circle, looking angry enough to cause severe harm to the next person to cross him.

'We have business to discuss,' he said gruffly. 'Regardless of Mr. Harris's doubts, we are at war. Clydeswell and Arlston in the west have been lost to the Furies and Odin knows what happened to Gyllas Dig, no one has heard anything out of there for weeks.'

A ripple of surprise and anger ran around the circle. Stalker listened carefully, determined not to let her emotions cloud her judgement. 'The rats that were driven out of St. Mark's in December surfaced in Thornton in the south, taking it from the Factory Boys.'

Stalker swallowed hard and felt eyes on her from all around the group.

'The north coast is vulnerable too,' Fire Talon said. Everyone looked at him. Stalker noticed Crimson roll her eyes. 'Trust me, we are being flanked. Someone is organising Poseidon's Chosen to mobilise and come ashore.'

'The Spiral Hand?' Ragged Edge asked, his voice deadly serious. Stalker was relieved that someone was taking Fire Talon seriously.

'Maybe,' Fire Talon replied with a shrug.

'There is certainly someone of that cult moving in Caerton,' Ragged Edge said. 'We've known for some time. The signs are all there. There is almost always one of them in a large shifter community like ours and you never know who it is.'

'We thought when we exiled Father Ash that we would have stamped out that threat,' Red Scythe continued. 'But it only lay dormant, and it does seem that the perpetrator is becoming active again.'

Stalker kept her nerves, but her mind was racing over Rhys and what she knew of Father Ash. There was some evidence that Father Ash was perhaps not keeping to his exiled state, the photographs of Last-Breath-Echoes in his house suggested that he had been sneaking into the city and spying on her. But Stalker didn't want to mention it and incriminate him when he could easily have hired a private investigator to take those pictures. Rhys was a whole other matter. She had believed him when he denied being Spiral Hand, but he was a Fury and her judgement was most definitely impaired when it came to him.

'The seers are reporting visions with a common theme,' Ragged Edge said. 'Death and bones. This is almost certainly related to an increase in incidences of the dead not moving on properly.'

'That's right,' First Strike said. 'There have been reports across the city of an increase in ghosts and a problem with the veil not correctly closing around cemeteries and so on. There are gaping doorways to the Underworld in places.'

'With the loss of the King-of-Glass-and-Steel, the city is barely held together,' Red Scythe said. 'We have seen an enormous amount of chaos since his disappearance. Last October a large section of St. Catherine's disappeared for several days.'

Stalker almost laughed, but the serious faces and low mutterings around her stopped the laugh from escaping her lips. The elder was entirely genuine and she mused over the idea of an area of the city disappearing. What happened to the people? Did they vanish too? Did they come back? Did they remember anything? 'There's one other thing,' Red Scythe continued, his voice low. Everyone fell silent and leaned a little closer to listen. 'There seems to be a cannibal cult in the city.'

Stalker felt her stomach lurch and she glanced around to see the collective reaction of shock and revulsion.

'We don't know much, yet,' Ragged Edge went on. 'It's been reported that some humans are turning up dead with certain organs missing, livers mostly. Just keep your eyes open.'

There was a pause in which it seemed no one knew

quite how to respond. Red Scythe waved a hand, as if swatting away the discomfort.

'Go and enjoy yourselves,' he said in his gruff voice.

The group dispersed and First Strike walked in step with Stalker away from the fire. She felt bad about knocking him back before and took his hand. He smiled down at her.

'So a chunk of St. Catherine's just disappeared, huh?' she asked with a bemused grin. He nodded.

'Sort of a shame it came back really,' he replied and they both laughed.

'Seriously though, were the humans aware of it?'

'No, there were some cases of amnesia but it was mostly just us that knew anything was out of the ordinary. If you asked a random member of the human public where such and such was, they just had no idea what you were talking about.'

'Like it just never existed?' she asked, coming to a halt and looking at him with a frown.

'Yeah. That sort of thing has happened before. There's this wonderful old story about a shifter called Howl-of-Elsewhere, who tried to trick the city by stealing the concept of direction.' First Strike lit up with excitement and Stalker had to laugh at him. He suddenly surprised her by capturing her lips in a passionate kiss and lifting her off the ground. She allowed him this time, enjoying the feel of his lips on hers and his strong arms holding her up. He carried her to a dark corner, away from prying eyes. She caught glimpses of figures moving around the fires, minor brawls breaking out, all good natured, probably, and she was aware of drumming and music and people dancing. But it was all a blur, background noise that seemed a thousand miles away while she was in his arms.

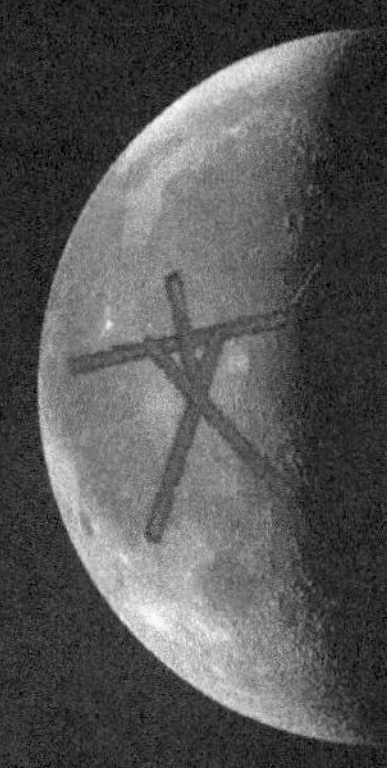

CHAPTER THREE

FIGHTS-EYES-OPEN

THE CROWD WAS DISPERSING RAPIDLY and Red Scythe was climbing down the steps from the dais with Crimson at his side. He looked old suddenly, having seemed so strong up on the dais until Theodore had stuck his oar in. Eyes rushed forwards to help the elder down but he brushed the young Alpha aside with a scowl.

'I can manage.'

'Of course,' Eyes said with a slight bow of his head. 'Forgive me. I wanted to tell you that I agree with everything you said up there. The packs must unite against the Furies if we're to hold Caerton. I want to help.'

'Ah, the enthusiasm of youth,' Red Scythe said with a sigh. Crimson smirked and took her leave. 'How do you think you can help?'

'I don't know yet,' Eyes admitted. 'Is there a precedent for the packs working together?'

'Not these packs,' the elder said, glancing around at

the revelry erupting around them. 'But in ancient times, yes of course. In times of great need it has been done. But I fear we will never get the Watch and the Glass Wolves to cooperate with one another.'

'Why not?' Eyes asked, his curiosity piqued.

'A long-standing rivalry, a clash of ideologies. The Watch represents everything old and traditional. The Glass Wolves represent progress and reformation.'

'The Glass Wolves worry that the Watch will side with the Furies if they turn up with the heir, don't they?' Eyes asked, his glance flickering briefly to the empty throne on the dais, an ominous reminder that Caerton's shifters were supposed to have a single leader. Red Scythe nodded solemnly. 'Do you share that concern?' Eyes probed.

'The Watch have only ever served the city of Caerton, I fully expect them to continue to do so. Now if you will excuse me, I have business with my people.' Red Scythe dipped his head to Eyes and Eyes returned the gesture. He watched the old man stride away, leaning heavily on his huge weapon, like a staff. Odin's Warriors were seemingly drawn to him, like moths to a flame. His ambiguous answer left Eyes with no more clue than he had previously.

Eyes turned his attention to locating Theodore. He was standing on a slightly raised section of the vast cave, surrounded by his pack and a few other shifters, including a few of the Hellsclaws, the Factory Boys and the Alpha of the Wrecking Crew. Eyes made his way through the crowd and eased himself into the tight little circle around Theodore.

'Trust me, what we really need to worry about are the demons that are threatening to overrun the city in the absence of the King-of-Glass-and-Steel,' Theodore was saying. 'Decay and entropy have completely devoured Camwell and I doubt St. Catherine's will ever be quite the same. The Fyrd bring us these terrible warnings, but they aren't city dwellers, they haven't seen what it's like here.'

'But they are out there, amongst the Furies,' Rust called out, a deep frown of concern on his brow. Eyes watched him carefully. 'They say they've seen the Furies mobilising, preparing for war.'

'They *say* they've seen this. How do we know this to be true?' Theodore replied.

'What about the Blue Moon?' Eyes asked, raising his voice over the noise all around them. The little group turned their attention to him. He held firm, he didn't let his hesitation show. 'What happened to my pack was a big, bold strike. Not some minor border skirmish. We have those on a regular basis with the Wrecking Crew, yet here we stand, facing each other.' He gestured to Rust, who gave him an appraising nod.

'Don't get me wrong, Eyes,' Theodore said. 'What happened to your old pack was devastating. We were all shocked and saddened by it. But isn't it possible that it was entirely focused on the Blue Moon rather than part of a bigger campaign?'

Eyes didn't reply. He tried to wrap his head around the idea that the attack may have been personal. It hadn't really occurred to him before. He had assumed that it was the first move in a war, part of some bigger strategy. Why else would a pack other than their neighbours have been involved? Had it just been the Witches who attacked, then maybe it could be put down to a border row or personal attack. But the main perpetrators had been the Phoenix Guard, a pack from well outside the city limits, specialists who had been brought in to take out the Blue Moon.

'What were you saying to us about the ley lines?' Vengeance-of-Steel asked Theodore as Eyes' attention came back to the present.

'Something has been walking them, changing them. I'm certain of it. There are megaliths and standing stones throughout Caerton, connecting the ley lines and something is very wrong with them. The area of St. Catherine's that disappeared contained one of these ancient stones.'

A knot formed in Eyes' stomach. Something about what Theodore was saying nagged at his memory.

'Walking the lines?' he repeated. Theodore looked at him carefully for a moment and then nodded. 'A while ago? Or recently?'

'Both. Why?' Theodore's shrewd eyes locked onto him and Eyes felt deeply uncomfortable.

'My pack dealt with a demon in the winter who said he had been walking the lines. We didn't know what he meant at the time.' Everyone looked at him, their eyes hard and accusing.

'I see,' Theodore said slowly. 'But you dealt with him?'

'Yes,' Eyes replied. 'Decisively.'

'Well, what's done is done. I'm working on a plan to restore the ley lines. I hope I can count on some of you to cooperate.' There were nods and murmurs of assent among the group.

Rust began to move away and Eyes quickly went after him.

'He's wrong about the Furies,' Eyes said quietly. Rust kept walking but threw him a brief glance.

'I know,' he snapped.

'Look.' Eyes caught his arm and pulled him to a halt. Rust looked down at Eyes' hand and Eyes promptly released his grip. 'I know we've had our issues, but I think it would be in both of our packs' best interests if we agreed to at least warn each other if either of us notices the Witches making an offensive move.'

'I suppose,' Rust replied grudgingly.

'I want you to know, if you call on us for aid in a fight, we'll come.' Eyes waited expectantly for the offer of reciprocity. Rust cocked his head and looked hard at Eyes for a moment, then rolled his eyes and walked away. Frustration rose in Eyes' chest.

'Hey!' The shout came from close behind him and he turned away from Rust's retreating back to see Lightning Claw of the Hellsclaws running after him. She stopped and grinned at him. 'Passionate speech back there.'

'Thanks,' he said, giving her a brief smile. She had the biggest hair extensions he had ever seen. Far too much of her skin was visible and he didn't quite know where to look.

'Do you want to join me for a drink?' she asked, with an inviting smile on her full lips.

'I think that would be an error in judgement,' he said, stepping back. Lightning Claw looked at him shrewdly, a glint in her eye.

'On whose part? Yours or mine?'

'Both,' he said with a snort of laughter. 'I'm married.'

'I know, I've seen your ring. She's human though,

right?'

'Yes. What difference does that make?' He was puzzled and intrigued.

'Secrets, lies, deception, putting her in great physical danger every time you leave the house, not to mention when you're in it. That doesn't exactly make for a healthy marriage. It won't last. You should be keeping your options open. When you're ready you should call me.' She gave him a seductive smile and turned to walk away. He watched her go and some particularly carnal thoughts popped into his head but he pushed them aside.

He strode off to locate his pack. He spotted Wind Talker talking with the Storm Riders, while Weaver and Claws were engaged in an animated discussion with the Scroll Keepers. Stalker was nowhere to be seen. The cluster of Odin's Warriors had broken up and dispersed amongst the other shifters and he saw many of them around the cavern, but not his pack mate. He needed a friendly face, someone to save him from himself. He fought back the image of Lightning Claw's curvaceous frame sashaying away from him and went in search of alcohol.

There was a huge table at the back of the cave, filled with food, and next to it were several huge barrels of beer and mead. He poured himself some mead and turned to watch the crowd. Music was pounding out, drums and flutes mainly but there was chanting too. He watched people dancing, their bodies silhouetted against the fires. It was a sea of sweat and he thought he could make out more than one couple writhing together erotically amongst the moving crowd.

Lightning Claw was in there, dancing with her twin

sister in a way that was perfectly tailored to tease the onlookers. She caught his eyes and beckoned him to join them. For a split second he considered it. She had a point about his relationship with Chloe. Maybe the right thing to do would be to leave his family, to protect them. It was what Fortune had wanted him to do. *Damn it, Fortune.* Why did he have to enter his thoughts?

Eyes knocked back his drink and strode over to Weaver and Claws.

'Hey there,' Claws said, patting Eyes on the back. 'You okay?'

'Great, thanks,' Eyes lied, badly. 'Where's Stalker? I think we should be making a move.'

'What's wrong?' Weaver asked.

'I don't think it's a good idea to leave the entire city unguarded while we all get drunk. Come on.' He strode towards the exit, full of frustration and felt the two of them falling into step behind him. He led them past Wind Talker and indicated for him to follow. 'Where *is* Stalker?'

'Don't worry,' Weaver said. 'She's a big girl, I'm sure she can find her own way home, or a place to crash here if necessary.' There was an annoying smirk on her face and Eyes rounded on her.

'What's the joke?' he snapped.

'Sorry, Alpha,' Weaver said, sarcastically. 'I thought you knew by now. Stalker's involved with First Strike. She's probably with him now.'

'Great,' Eyes barked. He was struck by Stalker's freedom to do what and with whom she pleased compared to his own attempts to wrestle with temptation. 'Fine, let's go.'

A few other shifters were making their way out at the same time, apparently most packs were sending home a designated driver, of sorts, now that the formalities were out of the way, so he felt less guilty about the lie he had told to get out of there. For a moment he considered sending the others back to the party, but he wasn't sure he could trust himself to go home to his wife without an escort. Besides, their territory was on the front line. They had to defend it.

He dropped the others off at various points along their border with instructions to patrol briefly before turning in for the night and then drove quickly home. He crept into the shower to wash out the ridiculous silver hair spray and then slid into bed next to Chloe. He nuzzled up close to her, drinking in her scent and stroking her beautiful curves. She stirred and made suggestive noises, her eyes fluttered open and she greeted him with a smile and lingering kiss. He made love to her that night with more intensity and passion than he had in a long time and as he drifted off to sleep in her arms, Lightning Claw was almost entirely forgotten.

Eyes woke slowly, he could hear Amy laughing downstairs and felt the warmth of sunlight spilling across the bed through a gap in the curtains. He rolled over and looked at the clock, it was already late in the morning and he let out a low groan. He had slept more deeply than he had in months, so he must have needed it, but he hated to feel like he had wasted any of his precious time with his family before needing to go to the pack. They would need to debrief from the night before and share what they had each learned from speaking to different shifters.

He stared across the room for a while, as the sleep lifted from his eyes. Movement in the mirror on the wardrobe door caught his eye and he saw Perfection-of-Flesh reflected there, admiring his muscular physique. It was a strange sight, a glimpse across the veil that didn't normally happen. It was reassuring to see the envoy of Heracles still there, keeping his family safe and healthy. Chloe had recovered from the rats' infection quite quickly, thanks to the fae's help and Eyes was extremely grateful.

Chloe's voice reached him, along with the sound and smell of frying bacon. His stomach made a sudden rumble and he rolled from the bed, pulled on some pyjama trousers and wandered downstairs to find food and his family.

Amy ran to him as he reached the bottom of the stairs, squealing and lifting her arms for him to pick her up.

'Hey there, munchkin,' he called as he scooped her up into his arms. 'What are you up to?'

'Mummy's making brekkie. I had cereal and spilled milk! Look!' She pointed at the stain on her pyjama top and Eyes chuckled. He carried her to the kitchen and plopped her onto a stool at the breakfast bar. Chloe was cooking, her hair still ruffled from the previous night and the smile she greeted him with told him she was still thinking about it.

'Hi,' she said.

'Morning. Did you sleep okay?' he asked, giving her a gentle kiss on the cheek.

'Hmm, yes thanks. You slept late. You must have needed it.' She gave him a wink and he chuckled as he nuzzled into her neck.

'Daddy, when is my birthday?' Amy asked as she

carefully coloured in a colouring book.

'Next Saturday. Nana and Grandad are coming for lunch.'

'Yay!' she squealed, bouncing on the stool. 'Is there cake? I want a monster cake, with sprinkles.'

'We'll see,' Chloe said. 'Do you have to go to work today?' she whispered as she dished up his breakfast.

'Yeah, I really do. I'm sorry.'

'Will you be home tonight?'

'Of course.' He pulled her against his chest and kissed her lips softly.

When Eyes arrived at Grove Street early in the afternoon the rest of the pack were gathered around the kitchen table deep in serious discussion. Stalker was back and Eyes tried not to think about what she had been doing all night.

He went to the kitchen window, as he did every day, to check on Unchained Lightning. His cocoon throbbed and glowed, it was getting bigger and brighter by the day.

'Eyes.' Wind Talker got his attention and beckoned him over to the table. 'From what we learned last night, I think we need to seriously consider doing whatever we can to weaken the Witches. We're working on a plan now.'

Eyes looked down at the table and saw the sheet of paper that they had been brainstorming on; most of the ideas had been crossed off.

'We know they own a new age shop,' Weaver explained. 'We can probably do a few things to mess up their business, cause them some trouble so that they get distracted from coming after us.'

'We don't know that they will come after us,' Eyes said. 'It's been two months since the Alpha's daughter was killed.' He glanced at Stalker, she barely flinched and he took that as a positive sign that she had come to terms with what had happened.

'They might not know we killed the girl,' Wind Talker said. 'But they will certainly be part of the campaign against Caerton. Whatever we can do to interfere with them will benefit everyone.'

'Okay, so which plan is looking most favourable?' Eyes asked.

Claws tapped a note on the paper.

'This one, plant drugs on the shop premises and call the police.'

'We thought we could mug a drug dealer and steal his stash, plant it at the Witches' shop so that it looks like they are dealing drugs out of the place,' Stalker said.

'And you're okay with this plan?' Eyes asked her warily.

'Fine, as long as no one gets killed.' She shrugged.

'Okay,' Eyes said, though he wasn't sure about the plan at all. 'Let's do it tonight. Destroy this.' He indicated the paper and Claws ripped it up without hesitation.

The pack spent the afternoon exchanging stories from the Danegeld. Wind Talker, Weaver and Claws were curt with him and cast him resentful glances. He shrugged it off. He really didn't want to have to justify his actions to them, he couldn't tell them the real reason for wanting to leave and he didn't want to have to lie to them too. His life was already too full of complicated lies.

It seemed that a few other shifters shared Theodore's scepticism about the Furies, but largely the rest of the city's shifter population was deeply concerned. There had been a lot of talk of defending territory, but none of cooperation between the packs and no one but the Berserkers wanted to go on the offensive.

Stalker relayed much of what was said among her fellows and Eyes struggled to take it all in. He wondered how Fortune had juggled all of this. Maybe he hadn't had to. Red Scythe had implied that things were getting worse, that all of this activity was unusual.

Eyes returned home for dinner and helped put Amy to bed. He kept one eye on the clock as it got dark outside and he dreaded having to broach the subject of going out to Chloe. They emerged from Amy's room and Chloe snaked her hands around his waist.

'Last night was a nice surprise,' she whispered. He kissed her gently, his thoughts flashing back to what she was talking about and briefly wandering to Lightning Claw before he stamped out that particular image. 'I may be wearing my most sexy underwear.'

Eyes groaned in frustration and pulled away from her reluctantly.

'I'm really sorry about this, but I've been asked to schmooze some new clients and take them out tonight.'

Chloe shoved him hard, her face furious.

'Oh no you don't,' she hissed. 'You can't do this to us any more. You can't be gone all hours of the night and day, then swan in here, fuck me like a demon and disappear again. What do you think I am?'

She stormed down the hall and slammed their bedroom door. Eyes winced and hovered by Amy's door to listen for her waking up. There wasn't a peep out of her so he slowly approached the slammed door. He opened it and saw Chloe sobbing on the bed.

'Chloe,' he whispered. She sniffed and then lay still, ignoring him. He sat down on the bed and placed a gentle hand on her hip. 'I'm really sorry.'

'Prove it,' she snapped, turning over to face him. 'Call your boss and cancel tonight.'

'I really can't do that,' he said quietly, hating himself. 'I've been spending a lot more time at home lately, you know that.'

'You were out late last night.' She scowled at him and he nodded reluctantly.

'I was, and I came home as soon as I could.'

'I just don't want things to go back to how they were before Christmas. You were hardly here.'

'I changed jobs, it was awful and crazy and I walked away from my career as a barrister for you, for something with less hours. It won't go back to the way it was.' He was telling the truth, but he couldn't tell her that it wasn't his job that was keeping him away from home, his job had hardly consumed any of his time in months. If war really was on the horizon then there was a very real chance that pack business was going to keep him from his family just as much as it had done before, if not more.

'Why do I not believe you?' she said quietly.

'I have to go now. We'll talk about this again later. I am really sorry.' He stood to go and left with a very heavy heart.

Eyes met the others back at Grove Street. Claws had found them all balaclavas to wear, just like the Knights of St. Catherine's. Eyes participated half-heartedly, his mind still on Chloe. He felt terrible and just wanted to get back home to her.

'I know of a guy who deals near the Circle,' Claws said. Eyes was loathe to go anywhere near that place, after his last experience there against the Red Minister who had swarmed them, but he didn't have a better suggestion so he went along with it. They went on foot, so as not to allow either of their cars to show up on CCTV in the area, and Claws led them to where this drug dealer was normally to be found.

The area surrounding the Circle was poorly lit and extremely deprived. The roads were wide and lined with empty shops, disused offices and cramped houses filled with squatters and illegal immigrants who had nowhere else to go. Cars drove through quickly, often not risking stopping at red lights, as carjacking was rife.

The railway passed close to the Circle, raised high on a viaduct and in one of its arches, away from prying eyes, the Lightning Lords stopped to finalise their plan. A quiet road ran under the blackened bridge and a solitary figure stood illuminated in the pale light of a lit bus stop.

'That's him,' Claws said, under his breath.

'We shouldn't all go right in there,' Wind Talker said.

'Right,' Eyes agreed. 'Stalker and Claws, you two see if you can handle it, the rest of us will wait here as backup.'

Stalker rolled her eyes at him before pulling her balaclava over her face. Eyes grabbed her arm as she spun away and she glared back at him. 'I want you in there to make sure it doesn't go too far,' he said in her ear. Stalker considered him carefully for a moment and then nodded in understanding. He released her arm and watched her and Claws slip quietly towards the guy leaning against the bus stop. The rest of them watched from the shadows down the street.

His pack mates approached the dealer swiftly and silently. There was a surreal moment as the human's face was caught between amusement and horror. Eyes felt tension in the pit of his stomach as he watched from a distance.

There was a small scuffle as they forced the drug dealer into the shadows and pinned him up against the wall and Eyes listened carefully for any hint of a problem. He caught a glimpse of Claws' gun pressed against the scumbag's temple. Eyes considered the possibility that he ought to fiercely oppose this plan, but he just couldn't. He mostly felt numb about it, it was a means to an end and if it paid off then it could land the Alpha of the Witches in jail, where she could do relatively little harm. It also took a drug dealer off the market for a while, at least.

Stalker and Claws came pounding down the pavement towards them, snapping Eyes out of his thoughts.

'Run!' yelled Claws and they all set off at a sprint away from the scene. Eyes cast one quick glance back at the drug dealer in a heap on the ground. Once they were several blocks clear they ran up a side street and into a small, covered car park behind a row of shops and came to a stop.

'What happened?' Eyes asked, only a little breathless.

'We got it,' Stalker said, holding open her hand with about a dozen little baggies, some filled with pills, others with white powder.

'What about the man?'

'He'll live.' Stalker shrugged.

'I had to knock him out,' Claws said.

'Right,' Eyes said, nodding. 'Stalker, how do you feel about taking it from here? You're the only one of us who can sneak onto their territory with even the faintest hope of going unnoticed.'

'Fine,' she said with a slight smile and a sparkle in her eyes.

'Good. Get it done. I have to go home, I am not popular tonight.'

'Trouble in paradise?' Wind Talker asked and Eyes ignored the dig.

'Good luck, Stalker. Text me when it's done and let me know you're okay.' He fixed his eyes on her and she gave him a reassuring nod.

'Piece of cake. I hope you and Chloe are okay,' Stalker said quietly. Eyes gave her a small nod and watched as she shifted into her fox form and ran off down the street.

The others got back to Grove Street safely and Eyes drove home, half worrying about Stalker and half worrying about how he would be received. The house was dark and quiet when he got home; it was nearly midnight so he had expected it to be so. He crept into his room and found Chloe asleep in the middle of the bed, naked. She hadn't slept naked in years and he watched her for a minute, trying to decide what to do. Was she inviting him to wake her again, or taunting him? He stripped off his clothes and climbed into the bed beside her. He rested a hand on her back and nuzzled close to her, but decided not to try anything.

'I love you,' he whispered before he fell asleep.

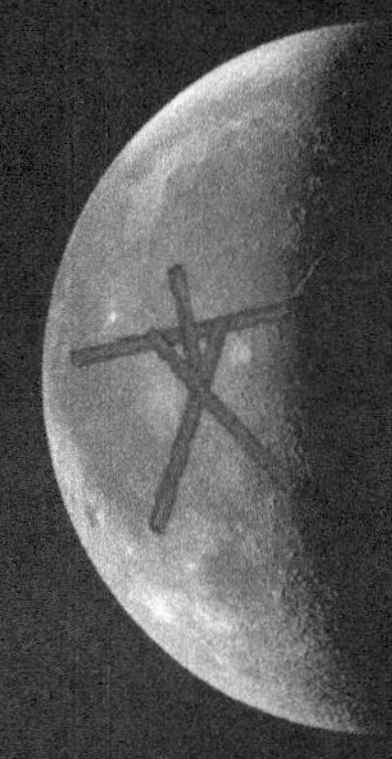

Chapter Four

Stalker-of-Night's-Shadow

Her paws padded lightly on the ground. She ran through the quietest back streets and kept her nose to the ground. Her breath was visible as little puffs on the cool night air. She rounded a corner and caught the Witches' scent in the air. It was a few hours old and she proceeded cautiously along the street. A sign caught her eye hanging over a doorway in the middle of a long parade of shops. There was a sombre-looking Green Man on the sign and the name of the shop was The Witching Hour. This had to be it.

Stalker doubled back and found the narrow road that the shop backed onto. The windows on the back of the building had bars on them and the back door had a mesh security door across it. The scent of the Witches was all over the place but the building was dark and silent.

Looking up at the back of the building, she noticed an air vent above the door. She quickly glanced around, it was almost pitch black and the narrow back street was empty. Stalker drew a breath and slowly forced her body to shrink. Her limbs disappeared, her body withered away to almost nothing and wings erupted from her back. In moth form, Stalker fluttered up and crawled in through the dusty vent and emerged in the back hallway of the building. Flying around the back of the shop, she found an office with an inviting desk. She shifted back into her human form and stretched her limbs briefly, shaking out the stiffness from their confinement.

The office was shrouded in darkness, with just a hint of light from the hazy orange sky casting a faint glow across the floor. She held still for a moment, waiting for an alarm or some supernatural security device to be triggered. But the room remained still and peaceful.

She went to the desk and glanced over it. There were stacks of invoices and all of the mundane trappings of an orderly office. She carefully opened the desk drawer and peered inside, flipping through a few files and papers, but found nothing of interest. There was a small, metal cash tin with the key in the lock. Stalker clucked her tongue and suppressed a smirk. She lifted out the tin and unlocked it. Inside was a small amount of cash. She lifted the black coin tray out and put the little bags of drugs inside, then replaced everything just as she had found it.

She took one last look around, then left the same way she had entered. She shifted into the form of an owl and flew all the way back to Grove Street, enjoying the air rushing past her feathers and the elation from successfully completing her mission.

She sent a message to Eyes, just as he had requested

and then turned in for the night.

The following morning, Claws left an anonymous tip with the police and they went about their business as usual.

Stalker was on her way to work when she got the text from Rhys. It had become unusual for him to reach out to her more than once a week, so twice in a few days took her by surprise.

> Hi, I hope you had a good weekend. I'd really like to talk to you, if possible.

She automatically deleted it and stowed her phone in her locker as soon as she arrived.

Work had become routine in the month since returning after Christmas. Stalker greeted her familiar students with smiles and mundane chatter. The little vial of water against her chest felt pleasantly cool as she worked, filling her with calm. When it came time to show her class a new block and throw combination she had a handful of volunteers eager to partner with her for the demonstration.

She grinned as she picked Joey, and he scurried forwards. He came in for an attack and she easily blocked his arm, hooked one foot behind his knee and brought him to his back without so much as winding him. He grinned up at her and she grabbed his hand to help him up.

'Easy,' she said, flashing a smile at the assembled class. They broke up into pairs to practice and she moved among them, helping the weaker members of the group.

As her last class of the evening filed out Stalker released a satisfied sigh.

It was gone 8pm when she got back to the house. Eyes was there, pacing the kitchen and running his hands through his hair repeatedly.

'I can't stay long,' he said. 'I just wanted to thank everyone for getting the job done last night. Hopefully we'll hear in the next day or so what happened with the police.'

A sudden crackling sound from the garden yanked all of their attention and they piled out through the back door. Unchained Lightning's cocoon had split open and bright light was spilling out of it. Fine forks of lightning flashed out and struck the house and garden wall, leaving the scent of burning stone, but mercifully doing no real damage.

'Great Artemis,' Weaver gasped. 'Can we get it across the veil before it attracts any attention?'

'No time,' Stalker said as the fae pushed its way out through the crack. His snout came first, complete with formidable pointed teeth. His front legs emerged, widening the crack in the cocoon for his thick body to push its way out. The cocoon disintegrated around him, disappearing completely, and the garden was drowned in blinding white light. Stalker shielded her eyes. The light began to fade and she lowered her hand. Unchained Lightning was uncurling himself and he stretched to his full height, which was now almost as tall as the house. He still resembled a dragon, but he was bigger and had enormous muscles bulging under his almost translucent skin. He was no longer a wingless Chinese dragon, but now had great leathery wings sprouting from his silver back and he spread them, filling the garden. Stalker gasped as she looked up at him.

Up on the high wall of the garden, two huge, black birds perched, watching them. As the great elemental stretched out his wings the birds squawked and took flight, but they circled steadily overhead. A memory came back to her of identical birds watching them when they fought the Plague Doctor. But it was a worry for another time and she dismissed it.

Unchained Lightning looked down on the pack and opened his mouth. Sparks flew out, showering down on them like hot rain, but they didn't burn. His voice was like thunder when it rumbled out from his cavernous chest.

'I need a throne.' In a flash, he disappeared across the veil and back into Hepethia, leaving the Lightning Lords in stunned silence.

'A throne?' Stalker said after a few moments.

'That's what the big man said,' Wind Talker replied nonchalantly. He turned and went back inside. Stalker watched him, bemused by his reaction.

'What kind of throne? Is this normal?' Stalker fired her questions at Weaver, who blinked at her for a moment.

'I'm not sure,' she said slowly. She followed Wind Talker back inside and left Stalker, Eyes and Claws looking at one another with no answers. They traipsed back inside to find Wind Talker jogging down the stairs with a box from the attic.

'Ah, research mode,' Stalker said, nodding in approval. It was not her forte, so she cleared out of the house and let Wind Talker and Weaver crack on with it.

A few blocks from the house, Stalker sensed the presence of Pursuit-of-Midnight-Solitude, at first just a prickling up her spine but then a twitching shadow at the corner of her eye. A wide grin lit up her face and she sprinted along the dark street after the slippery shadow, eager for the thrill of running wild through the city. She chased it across St. Mark's to Red Bridge, which she traversed without her feet even touching the ground. She ran along the concrete wall, a sheer drop into the river below to one side and fast flowing traffic to the other. She swung around each rod that she came to that connected the deck of the bridge to the vast red towers that bore the load of it, flying out over the river, the air rushing past her grinning face. At the end of the bridge, she leapt down onto the bank and scrambled up it and into St. Catherine's. She powered through the unclaimed territory, climbing up buildings, leaping across rooftops and vaulting fences with ease. Always chasing the elusive spirit that had led her to her true name.

She eventually abandoned the hunt and resumed a more careful patrol in fox form around the northern and eastern borders of Lightning Lord territory. Northgate chugged on, spewing endless smoke into the sky. Redfield hustled and bustled with late night activity and Stalker had to skirt south towards the park to escape the humans spilling out of the pubs and bars. The smell of the Wrecking Crew clung to the edge of the park as she trotted along the boundary. All was quiet and she headed back to the house for some sleep.

She dreamed of Rhys, powerful dreams featuring the demon that cloaked him and Rhys's dark eyes feasting on her the way they had when they first met. When she woke she was in her human form, having shifted in her sleep. She was covered in a fine layer of sweat and her pulse raced.

'Bad dreams?' Weaver asked as they got up and got ready for the day.

'Yeah,' Stalker replied. It wasn't a total lie, the dreams had been disturbing, but not bad in the traditional sense. A secret part of her was excited by them.

The morning was uneventful and Stalker spent it trying to shake off the vivid dreams. At lunchtime, the pack gathered together for lunch. As they ate and chatted Stalker felt a ripple in the veil and her hackles rose. She looked around for the source.

'What's wrong?' Eyes asked, watching her carefully.

'Something's crossing over,' she replied. She stood from the table and went to the window. Stalker squinted and caught a glimpse of light reflected off shining metal. She went to the door and flung it open, hoping to scare off the intruder. 'Who's there?' she called out.

The rest of the pack gathered behind her and she stepped out into the garden carefully, allowing them to follow her. Movement caught her eye and she whipped towards the source, her hand on the hilt of one of her swords.

'Calm down.' The silky voice slid across the veil, along with the rest of its owner, Scourging Agony, a slippery demon ally of the Witches who had turned spy for the Lightning Lords. 'It's only me.'

Stalker relaxed a little, but didn't let go of her sword.

'What do you want?' asked Eyes, stepping around Stalker to face the demon.

'The little trick with the drugs was clever, a bold move,' the demon said, clicking his blade-like fingers together. 'It put their organisation into a little disorder. However, Jessica Carter is no fool and has spent years developing relationships with the police and various other authorities. She also has ways of persuading them to her point of view. She convinced the attending officer that the drugs had been planted and he assured her that they would investigate the matter.'

'Does she know who it was?' Stalker asked, suddenly very nervous for herself.

'She suspects but has no proof. She was very curious as to how someone got onto the premises without forced entry. As am I.' The demon looked around at them, his eyes narrowed to slits. Stalker tried to mask her extreme discomfort. Of all the demons in the world, this was the one she most wanted to conceal her true nature from.

'Curiosity is a peculiar thing,' Weaver said from the doorway. Scourging Agony's black eyes turned on her. 'You know what it did to the cat, don't you?'

The demon gave her an appraising nod, then raised a hand and gave them a strange wave before turning and disappearing back across the veil.

'Thank you,' whispered Stalker.

'Don't mention it,' Weaver replied with a smile and they filed back inside.

'So that didn't really work, then,' Claws said, dropping down into a chair at the table.

'No, not really. Back to the drawing board,' Eyes replied.

Stalker felt frustrated that she had risked her life and wasted her time for no reason, but didn't say anything, it wasn't her pack's fault.

It wasn't until Thursday that Unchained Lightning reappeared. The television suddenly flicked on and skipped between channels erratically, the microwave began beeping repeatedly and all of the lights flickered on and off rapidly. Stalker and the others leaped to their feet and looked around in alarm.

'Unchained Lighting?' Stalker asked. Wind Talker nodded and they crossed the veil to find the enigmatic fae circling the garden. He soared up into the cloudy, grey sky as soon as he spotted them and disappeared over the house. They ran through the house and out of the front door to find him circling in the street.

'We're so glad you're okay, after the fight with the Plague Doctor,' Wind Talker said, his voice earnest.

'You've grown more powerful and we thank you for your continued patronage of the Lightning Lords,' Weaver said, with a bow of her head.

The fae was weaving in between lamp posts, leaving a slight glow in the air behind him. Stalker watched him carefully, unsure what he was going to do. She had never had reason to mistrust him before, but his behaviour had become erratic and alien.

'You asked us to find you a throne,' Claws said, stepping closer to him. 'What did you mean by that?'

'Power,' the elemental crackled. 'I am Power and I crave it. I want a seat of Power and underlings to do my bidding.'

Stalker thought of his father, the Lord-of-Storms-and-Rain, perched on his sky-high throne, conducting a choir of weather elementals. This idea had to have come from him while Unchained Lightning was with him recuperating after the fight. As far as she knew, the Blue Moon's ally, Grins-Too-Widely, had no such choir. But he had been very different and was an ancient shifter with an affinity for stealth and secrecy, working in the shadows was his forte, not soaring through the sky in broad daylight and electrocuting enemies.

'Do you have a suitable location in mind?' Eyes asked, his voice wary.

'I do,' the elemental replied with a hiss like static. 'Unfortunately, it is currently occupied. You will need to evict the current tenants.'

Stalker and Weaver exchanged troubled glances.

'I see,' Eyes said. 'Where is it?'

Unchained Lightning sped off along the street. The pack automatically ran after him with no need for words. Stalker shifted into a cheetah so that she could keep pace with the dragon-like fae and Eyes and Weaver also took their animal forms. Claws and Wind Talker ran along behind and Stalker soon lost track of them. Their ally didn't lead them far, just a few blocks from Grove Street to a power substation, comprised of a couple of small buildings behind a high wall in the middle of a residential area. Stalker recognised it immediately, having passed it a hundred times. In the human world it was a real substation, sitting at the end of one of terraces of St. Mark's, a road called Legion Way; and on this side of the veil it had been styled to look very similar.

Stalker skidded to a halt as soon as she saw it. The fae was weaving in a figure eight across the wide street. In Hepethia, the substation had huge red brick walls that were topped not just with barbed wire like in the human world, but big black iron spikes. The others caught up with her and they stood staring at the larger of the two buildings inside the fortified walls. Ripples of electricity rolled up the prongs on the top of the building and sparks flew off the tops of them. She couldn't see any actual fae or demons, but the whirring sound of machinery, sparks and that steady hum of electricity told her the place was alive.

'Shall I try to get in and check it out?' Stalker asked. The place made her uneasy, but if they were going to secure it as a throne for Unchained Lightning, they would need to get inside and see what they were dealing with.

'Okay, but take Claws with you, in case there's trouble,' Eyes said, his voice ringing with finality. Stalker wanted to object, her pride hurt, but knew there was no point.

Claws glanced up at the high walls, a worried crease on his brow.

'Come on,' Stalker said encouragingly. She leapt into the air, shifting mid-jump into a snowy owl. Claws followed suit, shifting into his barn owl form and flapped heavily up into the sky beside her. They hovered just outside the fence, looking in on the hub of power. Inside was a courtyard with machinery dominating the centre. Four tightly coiled spirals of metal stuck out of the concrete floor, jutting up and out at a precarious angle forming a square around a huge iron throne. Cables overhead spread out like a vast spider's web and pale blue ripples of electricity flowed along them from the coiled pillars.

The throne was empty, but the courtyard was patrolled by a large, lumbering construct of sheets of metal and grinding cogs. All around it were tiny imps, some bright blue, others black as coal, all with jagged claws and gnashing teeth.

The two shifters exchanged glances and flew back down to the ground, shifting back into their human forms and landing beside the others.

'There's certainly a throne in there, currently unoccupied, but there's a whole court of minions,' Claws explained.

'Right,' Eyes said with a sigh.

Stalker felt that creeping unease that could only mean there was someone watching her. She looked around and on the other side of the street a bizarre demon stood watching them. It had a human body but the head of a hawk and its eyes darted from one pack member to another. The rest of the pack followed her gaze. The demon suddenly sprouted wings on its back and it flew off into the sky.

'Vigilant Justice,' Wind Talker whispered. 'We're being watched.'

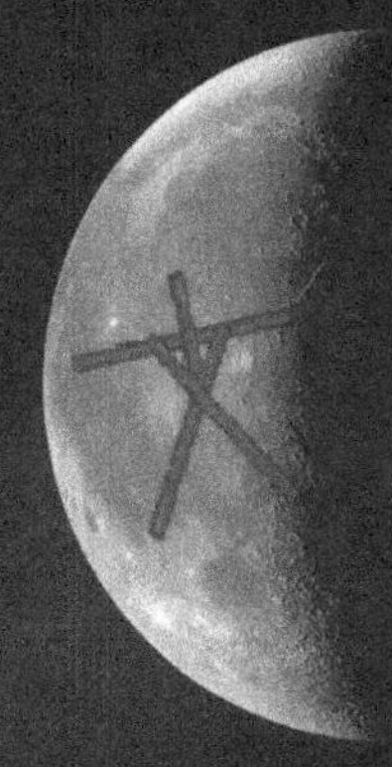

Chapter Five

Fights-Eyes-Open

——. 9th February .——

It was a chilly, grey day and Eyes would have loved nothing better than to stay curled up in bed with Chloe. She had softened to him again after a week of him making every effort to be at home as much as possible. They were woken at the crack of dawn by a rather excited four-year-old jumping on their bed.

'Happy birthday to me!' Amy squealed before running off to find her presents and cake. Eyes and Chloe reluctantly left the warmth and comfort of their bed. Eyes sat in the window seat in the living room, nursing a hot mug of coffee in his hands and watching Amy rip paper off the presents that Chloe had picked out and wrapped for her. Each gift was a surprise to him too, as he had had barely any involvement in choosing them, and he felt a stab of regret.

He was sipping his coffee when he caught a glimpse of movement on the pavement opposite the house. He looked outside but couldn't see anything out of place. He felt a tingle up his spine, something just didn't quite feel right. He turned back to his coffee, but there it was again, in the corner of his eye, a flicker of movement. His eyes darted back to the street but whatever it was, it was invisible to direct sight.

'Just one more,' Chloe chided. 'Save the rest for when Nana and Grandad get here. I know they'll want to see you open some of your presents too.'

'No!' yelled Amy. 'I want to open more now.' She crossed her arms over her chest and stuck out her bottom lip. Eyes bit back a snigger.

'How about pancakes for breakfast instead?' Chloe asked. She didn't wait for an answer, instead she scooped Amy into her arms and marched to the kitchen.

Eyes couldn't shake the feeling that something was amiss, the sensation clawed at his senses and kept him at the living room window instead of following them to the kitchen. He resented the distraction on such a special day and nipped into the study to call Wind Talker.

'I have a situation at my house,' he said, without bothering with small talk or pleasantries.

'Isn't it Amy's birthday today?' Wind Talker asked.

'Yes, but it's not that. I think there is someone watching the house. I can't be sure. I thought I saw something but then it was gone, twice.'

'It could be something just the other side of the veil, only visible when a small gap opens, like someone standing behind curtains blowing in a breeze,' Wind

Talker suggested. 'Would you like me to send someone over to watch the place for you?'

'Yes please. Thank you.' Eyes hung up the phone and returned to his family.

An hour or so later, the doorbell rang and Amy ran excitedly to the door. Eyes ran after her, his nerves on edge, but the warm sound of his parents' voices filled the air.

'Hello, birthday girl! Oh, what have you got there?'

'Hi, come on in,' Chloe's voice rang out and the hallway was filled with people, coats, bags and beautifully wrapped parcels. Eyes greeted his parents warmly, but his mind was out in the street and he made sure he manoeuvred his way to the door to close it, taking a quick look outside as he did so. He caught sight of an urban fox behind the bushes opposite and it calmed him significantly to know that Stalker was there. When he closed the door he slid the chain across it, not that that offered much protection from the things in the world that might really threaten his family.

After Amy had opened yet more presents, Eyes helped Chloe make lunch and for a short while, he forgot about the strange activity outside. Everyone called him Martin and he felt almost normal. Amy ran around the house with her new toy pony and the soft dinosaurs that her grandparents had bought her, delighting everyone with her joy and causing equal frustration by getting underfoot in the kitchen.

Lunch was a noisy affair and as they were finishing, Chloe disappeared into the kitchen to prepare the cake. Eyes turned the lights off and closed the curtains, unable to hide the smile from his face as he watched Amy bounce up and down on her chair in anticipation.

'Happy birthday to you,' Chloe sang as she entered the room, the monster-shaped cake in her hands, topped with four bright candles. Everyone joined in the singing and Amy grinned as the cake was laid before her. She drew a great big breath, puffed out her cheeks and blew the candles hard. Eyes was the first to clap and cheer as the candles were blown out and smoke wafted up from them, filling the air with its distinctive fragrance.

While everyone was cheering a sudden noise outside caught his attention and his own delight was cut off abruptly. No one else had heard anything, but he was sure he had heard a howl. He walked briskly to the window and gently parted the curtain. Nothing seemed to be amiss at the side of the house, so he dashed quietly into the front room and strode to the window. Before he reached it there was an explosion, shattering the entire bay window. Eyes leaped back, shielding his face with his arms. His heart sprung into his throat and instantly memories of the attack on the betting shop swamped his mind. For an instant he was frozen, trapped in time. He heard screams from the dining room and snapped out of his paralysis. He scurried through to the dining room, stooping low.

'Get under the table, everyone!' He scooped Amy off her chair and covered her head as he crawled under the table with her. Chloe was shaking and his parents stared around with petrified, wide eyes.

'What's going on?' Chloe asked in a frightened whisper.

'I don't know,' he replied. 'I'm going to go and take a look. Stay here, all of you, and keep quiet.'

Eyes passed Amy to Chloe and ran quietly to the kitchen, staying low and keeping away from the windows until he reached the back of the house. He looked carefully out through the window in the back door and saw movement in the garden. A badger shuffled out from the bushes at the back of the garden and shifted into Wind Talker. Eyes moved silently into the hall and approached the living room cautiously. Broken glass and plaster covered the floor and crunched under his feet. There was thick smoke drifting into the house and it stung his eyes. He couldn't see a thing, but he could hear feet pounding on the tarmac and there was a shout.

He ran to the back of the house and stepped out through the back door. Wind Talker was approaching the house and Eyes ran to him.

'Witches,' Wind Talker hissed and the two of them ran to the side of the house and pressed themselves against the wall under the dining room window. Eyes led them towards the front of the house. His ears were still ringing from the explosion and his heart was hammering in his chest. He had never been so frightened in his life, not even when the Blue Moon were attacked. This was his vulnerable, human family and it was like a knife straight to his heart.

He reached the corner and peered carefully out into the street. He was practically blind, the smoke was so thick. There were shadows moving all around and scuffling feet.

'Stalker's here,' he whispered to Wind Talker. 'Who else?'

'We're all here,' Wind Talker replied. 'Claws took up a position at the end of the street and Weaver was making circuits of the block. Stalker was covering the front and me the back.'

'How did they get past you?' Eyes snarled, fury welling up inside.

'Maybe they crossed the veil right here?' Wind Talker said, like it was the most obvious thing in the world.

'Where are they? Why aren't they making their move? We need to find the others, come on.' Eyes kept low and ran swiftly through the smoke, Wind Talker right behind him. He nearly tripped on the kerb opposite the house but quickly found his footing. Stalker almost ran right into him.

'What are you doing out here?' she hissed at him. 'They know, they're here for your family. An eye for an eye.'

He looked at her blankly before everything clicked into place. He turned to go back to his house, which was just visible through the smoke. There was a dark figure on the roof, where the smoke was thinner, and indistinct movement all around the base of the house. Eyes ran towards the front door and to his horror, saw thick vines snaking their way up from the foundations over the windows and door, rapidly covering the entire house.

'No!' he yelled and ran to the door. He began pulling at the vines, but they were covered in thorns and tore the skin from his hands. Stalker was at his back, tugging on his arm.

'You won't get through there,' she said. She pulled his arm hard and his head snapped to her, he went to strike her, blind rage filling his senses. She leaped back and he realised what he was doing.

'Sorry,' he muttered. There was movement all around

them and a shot rang out from down the street. 'Get down,' he cried and dropped to the floor.

'It's Claws,' Stalker said, running off into the smoke.

Eyes half stood and ran back into the street, keeping low. He looked up at the house, it was completely covered in living, vicious plant life and on the roof stood the conductor of this sick orchestra. He could just make out her long, lean body and long, thick hair blowing in the wind. As he watched her, she erupted into black flames and then transformed into a murder of crows that dispersed and flew up into the sky above the smoke. He knew her names, they came to him like a whisper from the shadows: *Jessica Carter, Gaze-of-Purity. The Alpha of The Witches.*

Hate swelled in his chest and a snarl escaped his lips as she disappeared out of his reach.

Wind Talker and Weaver emerged from the smoke, running straight for him, their feet pounding furiously on the road. Right behind them were two huge beasts, bounding along on two legs, the knuckles on the ends of their long forearms thumping the road too, like gorillas. He shifted form as his pack mates ran past him on either side and he strode forwards to meet The Witches. A strange stillness oozing from inside him seemed to slow everything down, giving him ample time to plant his feet and ready himself.

He struck one of them full in the face, using her momentum to drive the impact and she flipped over backwards and sprawled on the floor for a moment before scrabbling to her feet. The other came at him with huge talons, but he dodged and spun around her. Wind Talker and Weaver shifted form and joined the fray. It was a bloody and vicious brawl, fur flew and the air was filled with ripping, snarling and snapping jaws. Eyes struck one of the attacking beasts full in the face, sending blood splattering from her nose onto the grey tarmac.

Out of the smoke a van suddenly appeared, skidding to a halt right next to the five fighting shifters. The side door slid open and the Wrecking Crew piled out, tooled up and ready for a fight.

Two more enemy Agrius shifters emerged from the smoke, racing towards them. The Wrecking Crew laid into them, holding nothing back. Eyes watched in stunned silence as Speaker-of-Steel, one of Rust's crew, strode over to a parked car and ripped the bonnet off like it was paper and rolled it into a huge tube. He turned and sliced through the smoke with it, knocking down one of the Witches and rendering her unconscious in the road.

'Eyes! Get inside! We've got this.' Claws' voice rang out through the smoke, which was beginning to clear and in the distance Eyes heard a siren. He tore himself from the fight, leaving the others to deal with the monsters in the street. He charged to the living room window and began ripping at the plants. Stalker appeared next to him, one of her swords in hand and she sliced through the vines like they were butter. He could hear screams inside and fear coursed through every vein in his huge bestial body.

He roared as he ripped a hole in the vines and clawed his way in through the window. He slammed into the floor, glass digging into his palms and knees. Stalker deftly leaped in behind him, her feet crunching lightly on the broken glass. Eyes strode through the house, still in his Agrius guise and headed straight for the dining room. The table was overturned, his family were gone. Panic flooded his head and the Agrius threatened to take control of him.

There was a scream from upstairs and he charged for the smoky hallway, his senses rapidly returning to him as his instinct to protect his family overrode the beast. He took the stairs four at a time and emerged on the landing, panting. Amy's bedroom door was open and he caught sight of movement inside. He strode to it and took a split second to assess the scene. A young Witch in human form was standing just inside the doorway with a silver knife clutched in her hand. Chloe was huddled in the corner, wrapped around a crying Amy and Perfection-of-Flesh had crossed the veil and was standing over them, protecting them. Eyes had arrived a second too late to save the fae, his chest was cut open and gold liquid was pouring out of him. His eyes caught Eyes' own and he mouthed something that Eyes couldn't make out before exploding in a shower of golden sparks.

Without a second thought, Eyes grabbed the Witch by the throat and yanked her out of the room. She made choking noises as he tossed her like a rag doll down the hall. He leaped through the air and landed on her chest, crushing her ribs under his massive legs. He plunged his teeth into her neck and her blood filled his mouth. She lay still under him. He pulled away and looked at her, his head cocked on one side, blood dripping from his open jaws. She looked almost identical to the girl they had killed in St. Catherine's. He felt absolutely calm, almost as if he were watching from somewhere above himself, detached from the situation. The girl had a silver claw through her ear, it looked raw, like it was still healing. Silver was harmful to their kind, especially those born under the full moon, like him. He climbed off her and stepped back.

His senses began to return to the present, he could hear gunfire and a police siren in the street outside and his wife and child whimpering in the room behind him. He shook his head and shifted into his human form. He ran in to them and knelt down in front of them.

'Are you both all right?' he whispered. There was no reply, they simply shook and sobbed. Amy's face was buried, but he looked into Chloe's eyes. They were somewhere far away, tears streaked down her red face. He gently checked them both over for physical injuries, but could find none. 'Thank Artemis,' he breathed.

'Martin,' a quiet voice reached out from behind him. He turned to see Stalker in the doorway, the sword in her hand at her side dripping with blood. 'You need to come downstairs with me. Teri will sit with them for a minute.'

Weaver appeared just behind her and nodded solemnly. Eyes looked down at his family and shook his head. He didn't want to leave them.

'No,' he said firmly.

'It's your dad,' Stalker said, quiet but insistent.

Eyes felt something horrible lurch inside him and in a sudden panic he tore from the room, pushed past Stalker and leaped down the stairs in just three strides. He ran down the hall and into the kitchen. His mother was shrieking and sobbing, her face stained with tears and blood all over her clothes. She was clutching her husband, who was slumped against one of the kitchen cupboards, his throat had been torn out and his face was white, his eyes lifeless.

'Dad?' Eyes croaked and walked slowly over to him, dropping to his knees. He was dead, undoubtedly, but Eyes didn't want to accept it. He tried to find somewhere to check for a pulse, but there was nothing left of his throat, so Eyes lifted his wrist. Nothing.

'Martin,' Stalker spoke softly behind him again. 'I know this is absolutely terrible and I know you need to deal with your family, but I just need one minute of your time out here, please.'

Eyes scowled at her, he saw the urgency in her face and grudgingly followed her down the hall to the front door. It stood wide open, the vines had been roughly hacked back, and the smoke was almost clear outside now, just a fine layer hung in the air. A police car stood idling at the kerb, its blue lights flashing silently in the haze and Vengeance-of-Steel was leaning against it, a shot gun slung over her arm. When she saw him she strode over to him.

'They've fled,' she said, her voice cold and hard. 'Theodore is aware of what's happened and is sending a cleaning crew now to process the scene before my colleagues arrive. I have to call this in now, shots were fired, if I don't report it questions will be asked. It's best if your pack leaves now. You and I will stay.'

'Where are the Wrecking Crew?' Eyes asked, scanning the street. Curtains twitched in almost every window and a few doors were starting to open as his neighbours dared to seek answers.

'They chased The Witches away,' Stalker replied.

'It was really good of them to come, I didn't think they would from my last conversation with Rust.' Eyes spoke softly, he was numb. 'You too,' he addressed Vengeance-of-Steel.

'Not by choice,' she said icily. 'Just doing my job. I'm here to respond to this stuff first, before my colleagues.'

'Eyes, I'm going to take the others back to the house now,' Stalker said. 'I hate to leave you, but we can't be here when the other police arrive.'

'I know,' he replied, nodding gravely. 'I'll be okay.' He walked slowly back into the house, his mother was still howling in the kitchen but he had to check on Chloe and Amy. As he put a foot on the stairs, Weaver appeared at the top, looking worried. She jogged down the stairs to him.

'Neither of them have moved, Amy keeps crying but Chloe has gone into some sort of catatonic state. Eyes, I think she may be affected by the madness. I am so sorry.'

There was a ripple in the veil and three strange men crossed over. They were dressed in plastic overalls and all had pale skin and white eyes. They were fae. Eyes was about to leap onto the nearest intruder, but he held up his hands in surrender and Weaver grabbed Eyes' shoulder roughly, holding him back.

'Theodore sent us,' the man-like fae said quickly and firmly. 'Just leave everything to us.' The three of them dispersed and Eyes watched cautiously as they began moving around the house, examining the scene. One went out through the front door and there was a blinding flash of light. Eyes ran to the door and looked out. His neighbour opposite stood on her front step, totally frozen. A few other humans in the vicinity were equally still, their faces filled with fear and shock.

'Don't worry,' the pale man said quietly as he bent to take something out of his huge bag on the floor at his feet. 'They're fine, just frozen in time while we sort this mess out.' He began spraying something green from a white bottle onto the plants that engulfed the house and they instantly began to rot at an incredible speed, falling down off the house and disintegrating on the ground. Eyes went back inside and ran up the stairs. One of the men was crouched over the dead Witch on the landing.

'Did you do this?'

Eyes nodded. The man gave him an appraising nod, like the slaughter of this girl was something to be proud of. Eyes felt pretty cold about it, he had done what he had to but he wasn't pleased about it. He strode past him and into Amy's room. The two of them were still huddled just as he had left them. Chloe was staring into the mid-distance, her grip on Amy unrelenting. Amy was crying silently, but had managed to turn her head so that she could see him. Her eyes were wide and terrified.

'Daddy?' Her voice trembled and fresh tears spilled from her eyes.

'I'm right here, baby.'

'You left,' she said, trembling.

His lip quivered and tears welled up in his eyes.

'I'm so sorry, I'm right here now. I was just outside before, trying to stop the bad things getting in. I'm so sorry I wasn't right here with you. I'm so sorry.' The tears ran down his cheeks and he swatted them away. The guilt, fear and grief were overwhelming. How could he have run outside like that? Why didn't he stay with them?

'We're done,' a quiet voice spoke from the door. Eyes turned to see one of the cleaners standing there.

'Thank you,' he said, his voice hoarse.

'You're welcome, but it's really Theodore you should be thanking. Good luck.' The man turned and went downstairs.

Moments later, it seemed, the house was filled with police and paramedics. Someone was trying to drag Eyes away from his family, he was too numb to object strongly. Two paramedics lifted Chloe and managed to untangle Amy from her arms. Eyes tore free of the people around him and scooped Amy up into his own, protective arms.

'You left us,' she whimpered and began wailing.

Someone gently removed her from his shaking arms and he felt himself being led away. He looked down at the spot where he had killed the Witch, she was gone and there was no trace of any foul play. Downstairs the front window remained smashed in and there was blood all over the kitchen. He was led out into the street and saw Vengeance-of-Steel talking with two other police officers by her car. She glanced over at him with a blank expression and returned to her conversation. There was no trace of the vines left on his house and he saw more police stringing tape across the street and the forensics team arriving. His parents were being loaded into an ambulance together, his father on a stretcher and covered in a sheet. Eyes stared at them in numb shock.

He was helped into a separate ambulance and moments later, Amy was placed in his lap. She looked up at him and then dropped her head onto his chest. Everything was a blur, he felt that strange detachment again, but he wrapped his arms around his precious daughter and held her. The Witches had been after her, like Stalker said, an eye for an eye. The Lightning Lords had killed the Alpha's daughter, so she had come after his. Thank Artemis she had failed. But the price had been his step-father. Fresh tears ran down his face as the paramedics wheeled Chloe in on a stretcher. She lay staring at the ceiling, totally blank and it occurred to him that he might never get her back.

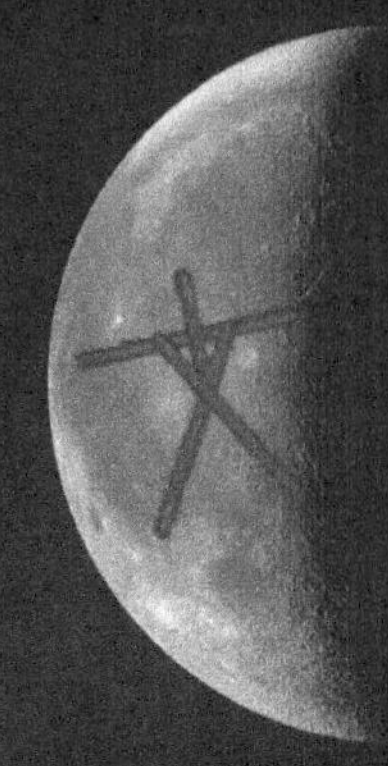

Chapter Six

Stalker-of-Night's-Shadow

They left Eyes' house quickly on foot, Stalker in the form of a collie, the others in their human forms. It was an anxious journey and Stalker picked up her pack mates' rage and fear as they made their way across Crossway and St. Mark's. The streets were buzzing with activity. Police cars and ambulances flew past them as they fled the scene. News of the event seemed to follow them like a tide chasing them up the beach. People ran from their houses and workplaces, phones clutched in their hands as they read the news on them or shared it with others.

As they reached the doorway of 32 Grove Street, Stalker caught the scent of one of the Witches. She gave a short bark to alert the others and sniffed carefully around the door. The lock had been damaged and the door swung open as Wind Talker touched it.

Stalker led the way inside, advancing slowly down the hall. The scent was stronger inside, but old enough to suggest that the intruder was long gone. Stalker stared in horror. There was graffiti on the walls, declaring the Lightning Lords to be "Luna's Bitches". It was smeared in blood; the metallic smell clawed at Stalker's throat and she whimpered softly.

Wind Talker thundered up the stairs and Stalker followed him, feeling anxiety rolling off him in waves. He bounded up the stairs to the attic two at a time and when Stalker arrived a moment later he dropped to his knees and cradled his head in his hands. Almost everything was gone, including most of the boxes of Flames-First-Guardian's notes and the map of their territory. Wind Talker's ritual supplies were smashed and scattered all over the floor.

Stalker nudged his arm with her nose in a gesture of support, then turned and ran back down the stairs. The living room had more blood on the walls, and the furniture had been knocked over. The new upholstery on the sofa had been ripped with talons, shedding the stuffing onto the floor. Stalker snarled and padded into the kitchen. The table and chairs had been overturned and Weaver and Claws were already straightening things out.

'Fucking bitches!' Claws snapped. His hands were trembling.

Stalker shifted form and yanked open the back door, the glass panels of which had been smashed. She stepped onto the broken glass, feeling it crunch under her boots. The garden had been ransacked, plants pulled up and the earth in the centre of the garden had been disturbed, though it didn't look like the culprit had had time to dig deep enough to uncover the hidden grave.

'Damn them,' Stalker cursed under her breath as she went back into the kitchen.

'Should we call Eyes to tell him about this?' Claws asked.

'No,' Stalker and Weaver said together without hesitation.

'He's got enough on his plate right now,' Stalker said with a sigh. She set right a chair and sat down at the dining table. The four of them lingered in the kitchen in silence for what felt like hours. They couldn't even look at each other.

'Why didn't I see it coming?' Weaver whispered eventually.

Stalker glanced at her, a puzzled frown creeping onto her face. Weaver usually had visions warning them of things like this attack. But Artemis hadn't seen fit to warn her this time. It did seem odd.

'I don't know,' Wind Talker said softly. He stared at the floor, utterly lost for answers for possibly the first time in his life.

'Where's Unchained Lightning?' Claws said suddenly. He was on his feet in an instant and crossed the veil before the others had even reacted. They exchanged worried glances and followed him quickly into Hepethia and out into the garden. It was empty. Stalker searched the skies, but they remained resolutely dark grey and empty of life.

'Should we try summoning him?' Stalker asked, casting furtive glances at the others.

'No,' Wind Talker replied. 'Not yet. If we haven't heard from him by tomorrow evening we will.'

Reluctantly, they crossed back into the human world

and slowly did what they could to secure the house and set things roughly right.

'We should take turns keeping watch,' Stalker said quietly. For some reason she couldn't bring herself to raise her voice much above a whisper. Their home had been defiled and didn't feel entirely safe now. The others nodded in agreement and Wind Talker moved to sit at the foot of the stairs to take first watch. Weaver and Stalker curled up together in the living room to get some rest.

Stalker was plagued by violent dreams. She saw Eyes' father slumped on the kitchen floor with his throat ripped out and the sickeningly familiar face of another dead Witch over and over again. Eventually she settled into a deeper sleep, away from the terrifying images but when she woke up in the morning she still felt exhausted.

'I'll go and patrol the border soon,' she told the others over a solemn breakfast. 'We should call Eyes and find out how he is.'

Stalker didn't wait for a reply, she immediately made the call. She waited a while and eventually he answered.

'How are you doing? How's your family?'

'Mostly alive,' he said, his voice thick with venom.

'I'm so sorry,' Stalker said. She tried not to take his tone personally.

'No, I'm sorry. I haven't slept yet. Amy's okay, traumatised, but I think she'll be okay. My mum, well, same really. Grieving. Chloe, I don't know. She's catatonic.'

'Oh Eyes, I am so sorry.'

'How are things there?'

She hesitated, unsure whether to tell him about the break in or not.

'Okay, we're all exhausted and worried. I'm about to head out to patrol the border.'

'Good idea, can you arrange shifts to keep patrolling for the next 48 hours in case there is a second attack?'

'Of course. Don't worry about us, you take whatever time you need with your family.'

'Thanks. I have to go, Amy's waking up. I'm glad you're all okay.' Eyes hung up the phone.

'You didn't tell him about this place,' Claws said, watching her carefully.

'I know,' she replied. 'That can wait. He wants a constant patrol for the next 48 hours. I'll head out now.'

She stood up and headed for the door, Weaver followed her.

'Be careful out there. I'll relieve you in a few hours.'

'Okay, thanks.' Stalker gave Weaver a hug, then shifted into the form of a grey cat. Weaver opened the door for her and Stalker jogged out into the street.

All was quiet on their eastern border, but the stench of The Witches had never been stronger. Stalker briefly considered marking their side, but now was not the time, an attack could be lurking at any point on the boundary. She patrolled back and forth for several hours, with really nothing to do but run over the events of the attack in her mind. There had been male shifters mixed in with the female ones and she knew that the Witches were all female. So they had had help. The cowards had enlisted the Phoenix Guard to attack the Blue Moon and now they had help with this attack. The Furies were clearly more inclined to cooperate than Caerton's shifters.

She thought of Rhys and felt a stab of anger and

suspicion. Could he have been a part of the attack? She paced in one spot for a few minutes, fuming over the thought, before heading a few blocks away from the boundary and shifting back into her human form in the cover of a blind alley. She took out her phone and cradled it in her hands, staring at it for several minutes, trying to decide whether to make contact with him or not.

She took some deep breaths and tried to rein in her anger. It would do no good to be too confrontational. With a little thought and a few changes as she typed, she was finally happy that her message conveyed the important information without being accusatory. She knew it was important not to put anything too explicit in a message, just in case it was intercepted, so made it suitably vague.

> We had an incident with an old adversary yesterday. It was bad. Pretty shaken up by it, esp my top bro. His family are pretty torn apart. Really trying hard not to leap to assumptions, thought you ought to know.

Stalker walked back to the main road and wandered slowly towards home, hoping to run into Weaver. Her phone buzzed with an incoming message and she opened it quickly.

> So, so sorry to hear that. I understand your feelings. Please believe that I had absolutely nothing to do with it. I've had nothing to do with any of them for years. Are you ok? Were you hurt? What are you going to do about it? Do you want to meet up and talk this over in person? Sorry for all the questions :/

She just managed to form a smile. She was glad to

have contacted him, though she had no idea if she could believe him or not.

'Hi.' Weaver's voice was suddenly right in front of her and Stalker nearly walked right into her. She looked up from her phone in alarm. 'Sorry.' Weaver chuckled and Stalker let out a relieved sigh.

'Thank goodness it was you that caught me off guard, and not one of them.'

'You all right? What has you so distracted?'

'Nothing. Don't worry about it. Everything's quiet here but be careful,' Stalker said, changing the subject.

'I will. You make sure you rest.'

Stalker nodded and set off back towards Grove Street. She had no intention of resting yet. She sent Rhys another message.

Can I meet you now? Are you at home?

The reply came immediately.

Yes of course. See you soon.

Stalker found a private place to shift into a cat again and sprinted across the city to his house, leaping over fences and running along rooftops, keeping off the ground as much as possible in order to avoid the humans and keep her scent a little out of reach in case there were any enemies prowling in unclaimed places.

She arrived on Rhys's doorstep in her human form, still unsure what she was doing. She just knew she needed to look into his eyes and see him deny any involvement in the attack.

'Hi,' he greeted her, his face serious. 'Come in.'

She went inside cautiously, but everything was still and normal. The curtains were open, daylight filled the room. On this side of the veil there really was no sign of the mystery that surrounded Rhys. 'Are you all right?' he asked, tentatively reaching for her. She twisted away from his hand and kept looking around, nervous in his presence.

'No, I'm not,' she snapped back. 'My Alpha's family was attacked. His human family, Rhys. They killed his dad and went after his wife and child.'

Rhys leaned against the back of the sofa and watched her as she prowled around his living room. She kept one eye on him at all times but she felt the anger and sadness just under her skin, barely contained and she knew she might explode at any moment. She wanted to be in a safe place to release those feelings and she was filled with frustration at not knowing if this was a safe place or not.

'Were any of your pack hurt?'

'No, not seriously. They broke into our house too!' Her voice was raised and she stood still suddenly, took a deep breath and tried to calm herself down. 'They broke in and tore the place apart, stole things, important things. They wrote "Luna's Bitches" on the walls. Why would they do that?'

'They follow Nyx, not Artemis. It's one of the bones of contention between them and the others. They believe they were here first, their mother is older, pre-Olympian. But I don't know why they would write Luna and not Artemis, that is a bit odd. It's more catchy, I guess.'

Stalker stared at him for a moment, he was providing an insight, he was betraying his upbringing by telling her about what the Furies believed. Was he trying to earn her trust? He didn't seem to be wrestling with anything, the truth just flowed easily from him.

'What about you? What do you believe?' she asked, hoping to see beneath his cool exterior.

'I don't believe in any gods or goddesses. It's all just different lifeforms, really, we're all equal with any other shifter or demon or fae. What do you believe?'

Stalker was caught off guard, she opened her mouth to speak but had no idea what to say. She had accepted everything the Blue Moon told her about what they were, who created them and had no reason before now to consider that there might be other ideologies that could have merit.

'Before I changed I was an atheist,' she said slowly, forming her thoughts carefully. 'All of this kind of blew my mind. I just believed what I saw and was told, I guess. I've met an elemental that is probably Thor in Norse myth. I can see why humans who may have glimpsed our world would think they were gods. I think we are chosen, aren't we? Something is making us different.' She wasn't about to betray her own deep secret, about being different from other shifters, but that was all she could think about. Something made her different, she had to believe it was for a reason. Artemis gave them all their own form, except her, she gave her the power to be any animal. She thought of the Alpha of the Witches up on the roof of Eyes' house, changing into a murder of crows and it suddenly dawned on her that there might be more differences between them than their religion. 'If the Furies don't believe they are chosen by Artemis, what forms do they have?'

'What do you mean?' Rhys cocked his head, his expression puzzled.

'Well, all the shifters I've met have a form based on which phase of the moon they change under. Nyx is a goddess of night but not the moon. Is it different for your kind? Are you fundamentally different from Caerton's shifters?'

'At first we just have the Agrius,' Rhys said, shifting his weight uncomfortably. 'The idea is that after we change for the first time we are taught how to control it and then Nyx grants us another form that suits our personality.'

'What happened to you?' She stepped closer to him, curious and slightly sad for him, knowing that he had fled from his dying family when he first changed.

'I think I still just have the Agrius. I endeavoured to never change again after that first time, but early on it was hard, I couldn't control it. I haven't shifted in years.' His eyes flickered up to meet hers, they were so sad, but gave away nothing from beneath the surface, he was working hard to keep his feelings locked up.

'I'm sorry,' she said softly and she meant it. She loved what she could do with her body, she loved running through the night as an animal, she loved the power of the beast, although she was cautious of it too. She never wanted to lose touch with her humanity, but she wouldn't trade what she was now for her mundane existence beforehand. Despite the bloodshed. If what he said was true, though, it might mean that she was chosen by someone other than Artemis.

'It's okay,' he replied. 'I'm trying to live a human life and keep all of that behind me. That's why I backed off when you changed. I was scared of being pulled in, of being tempted to shift and I was scared of what might happen to you now. That life is dangerous, shifters live short, brutal lives and I didn't want to fall in love with you only to lose you.'

There was a crack in his voice and it touched Stalker, hot tears stung her eyes and her lip trembled. She took a step towards him, torn between wanting to fall into his arms and run for the hills away from his potentially manipulative ways. His eyes latched onto hers and she looked deep into them, they were open to her now, he was willing her to see into his soul and believe him, to trust him. She searched his soul as she stepped closer and took his hand. The physical connection intensified her ability and she could almost feel herself stepping inside him and running through the darkness as flashes of memories flew past her. He was so afraid, that was his fundamental truth. He had been telling her the truth about that much at least.

He reached for her face and caressed it gently, bringing her back to reality. She tilted her face into his touch and closed her eyes as the tears she had been holding back spilled down her cheeks.

'I saw,' she whispered. 'I saw inside your heart.'

'I know,' he whispered back. He drew her slowly into his arms and she felt herself mould against his body, her head nestled into the crook of his neck. He breathed deeply and stroked her still-blue hair and she felt a shiver run through her. Suddenly his hands stopped and his head pulled back from her.

'What is it?' she asked, tilting her head to look at him. His jaw was set, his eyes cold and still. 'What's wrong?'

She pulled away and he let his hands drop to his sides.

'I guess I really fucked this up, didn't I?' His voice was hard.

'A little bit,' she replied, cautiously stepping back.

'There's someone else now, right? I can smell him on you.'

Stalker groaned as she thought of First Strike. She rubbed her forehead and nodded slowly.

'Yeah, kind of. But look, my pack was attacked yesterday and I only thought of him just now. It was you that I wanted to run to.' She tried to catch his gaze, after a moment their eyes met and he softened slightly. 'It was a long, lonely winter and I sought out company. It can be over in a heartbeat if that's what I decide. I need time to figure all of this out though, Rhys. I don't know what's going on here.'

'I know, I'm sorry.' He nodded. 'I'll be here for you though, whatever. I don't think I can live without you in my life.'

Stalker's breath caught in her throat. She wiped the tears from her face and took a deep breath.

'I think I know how you feel. Just give me some space to work this all out in my head. Okay?'

'Sure,' he said, his jaw set and his face strained.

Stalker turned and went to the door. She opened it and glanced back at him, still leaning on the sofa, not looking at her. She sighed as she left, sadness and confusion flooding her weary body.

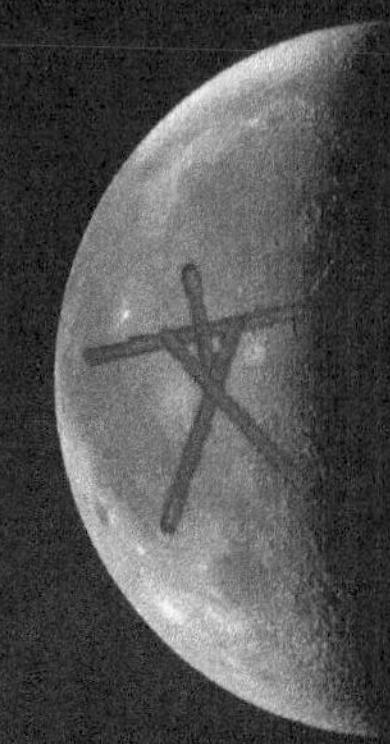

Chapter Seven

Fights-Eyes-Open

'We simply don't know yet, Mr Davison. We just have to wait and see. I recommend keeping her here again tonight and reassessing in the morning.' The kind-faced doctor left the room and Eyes sat down next to Chloe. He took hold of her hand and pressed it to his lips. Her eyes stared up at the ceiling, unseeing. He wanted desperately to take her home, perhaps being home would help her recovery, or it would if it were safe. He would have to go back there and assess the damage at some point, but it could wait. Right now he needed to be by Chloe's side. His mother and daughter were sleeping in a room up the hall, they would probably be discharged within a day or two. He had no idea where they would go.

There was a knock at the door and Eyes looked up, his pulse raced at the sudden intrusion. Through the little window in the door he could see a delivery man with a large bouquet of flowers.

'Come in,' he called out and the man entered, his face set in a suitably sympathetic expression.

'Delivery for Mrs Davison,' he said as he entered the room.

'Thank you,' Eyes said, getting to his feet and taking the flowers. 'Who are they from?'

'There's a card,' the delivery man replied. He held out a clipboard with a form attached to it, which Eyes dutifully signed. The delivery man placed the flowers in Eyes' arms and left. Eyes looked more carefully at the colourful bouquet and found a little silver card nestled in amongst the stems. He opened it and quickly skimmed the carefully handwritten message.

> *Dear Chloe,*
> *Wishing you a speedy recovery and all the best for your family at this difficult time.*
> *Martin, please let me know if there is anything I can do.*
> *Best wishes,*
> *Theodore Harris*

Eyes wrestled between gratitude and suspicion as he placed the flowers delicately on the table next to Chloe's bed. He was grateful to Theodore for his assistance in getting the house cleaned up before the arrival of the police, and touched by the flowers, but he couldn't help wondering if the man had a hidden agenda.

There was a cough behind him and Eyes turned sharply to see a police officer standing in the open doorway. He sighed, he knew this would be coming and had thought of little else since climbing into the ambulance. He knew what he needed to say, he just hoped he could make it convincing.

'Mr Davison?' the officer asked. He was a late middle-aged man with slightly greying hair under his hat, and carried a little extra weight.

'That's right,' Eyes replied. 'You need a statement, correct?'

'That's right. Is now a good time?'

'As good as any.'

The officer closed the door and took a seat in the corner of the room. He took out a notebook and leafed through a few pages. Eyes watched him carefully and waited.

'So, all we have on record so far is that your home was attacked yesterday afternoon. Your mother has so far declined to make a statement. Can you provide us with some details please?'

'Of course.' Eyes sat down and crossed one leg over the other, going into lawyer mode. This was business, he had to think of it that way in order to keep his cool and make this tale believable. 'It was my daughter's birthday, we had just had lunch when there was an explosion in the street, which shattered the front windows of the house. I did what I could to ensure my family's safety before going out into the street to investigate. I was accosted by several assailants, I believe they were members of the Knights of St. Catherine's. I was able to fight them off and when I returned to the house there were others inside. My father was…' Eyes stalled. The memory of his father with his throat hanging out shot to the forefront of his mind and he swallowed hard as he pushed it back.

'I understand this must be hard,' the officer said kindly,

pausing in his note-taking for a moment. 'The more detail you can manage the better.'

'My father's body was in the kitchen. My mother was with him and the assailant had moved on through the house. I ran up the stairs and found him in the doorway of my daughter's bedroom, she and my wife were huddled inside. He had a knife, it had blood on it. I grabbed him and threw him down the stairs. He ran out through the front door. Next thing I knew, police were there and paramedics were seeing to my family.'

'I see. Do you have any idea why a gang from across the river would come for your family?'

'I'm a barrister,' Eyes replied smoothly. 'I've prosecuted members of the Knights in the past. I'm guessing this was a grudge attack.'

'I see. One of your neighbours reported strange noises,' the officer said with a leading tone.

'They had dogs with them, Alsatians I think. I saw them in the street, they were growling.' Eyes felt beads of sweat on his forehead. This was where the lies began to strain against reality, with the other witnesses.

'Did you see dogs in the house?'

'No, but there could have been. I wasn't seeing very clearly.'

'Of course. Initial findings suggest that your father was attacked by an animal.' The officer looked at Eyes carefully, his pencil poised over his notebook. Eyes felt a ripple of relief, he had been right to mention dogs, now everything was clicking into place.

'Really? That's awful.' Eyes allowed his feelings to surface again for a moment and gaped at the police officer.

The news had to appear to be a shock. 'I didn't see his injuries closely.'

'When you arrived here you had blood on your clothes,' the officer stated.

'That's right. They were taken for evidence. It was my father's blood. I went to him once the attack was over and tried to check for a pulse but I couldn't find one.'

'But you didn't look closely at his injuries?' the officer asked, a hint of suspicion in his voice.

'Of course not,' Eyes snapped. 'I couldn't bring myself to look closely. I saw the blood and that his throat was injured. I'm not accustomed to seeing my loved ones in such a state, I averted my eyes.'

'I understand,' the officer replied hastily and Eyes reined in his temper with a steadying breath. 'I think that's all for now. We'll be in touch if we have any further questions. We should be releasing the scene by the end of today, so you'll be able to return home tonight, if you want to that is.' He looked genuinely sympathetic for a moment and Eyes let go of the defensiveness he had been exhibiting towards the officer, who was only doing his job.

'Of course.' Eyes stood up to see him out and closed the door behind him. He let out a huge sigh of relief. The worst was over, but there would be more questions. He didn't know if pinning it on the Knights was going to work, but he had no other choice. He looked back at Chloe, she was still staring at the ceiling but a single tear had fallen and left a wet track down the side of her face. Eyes closed his eyes and rubbed his coarse hands over his face, angry with himself for almost forgetting that she was conscious and must have heard every word he had told the police.

He brushed her hair and leant to kiss her forehead. 'I am so, so sorry.'

Later that afternoon Eyes went to check on Amy and his mother. His mother was under sedation, she had been cleaned up and looked peaceful.

'Hi, sweetheart.' Eyes moved over to Amy. The hospital staff had been forced to admit Amy to the same ward as her family when they arrived, she screamed and screamed when they tried to take her to paediatrics and as she wasn't physically injured the staff had finally relented. She turned her head away from him. 'How are you feeling?'

She stared resolutely out of the window and Eyes felt hot tears sting his eyes as he watched her. She would come around, she had to. 'Would you like to come and see Mummy?'

Amy turned her head, her face fearful. She nodded slowly. Eyes stepped closer and held out his hand, she took it and let him scoop her up into his arms. He carried her past the busy nurses' station, no one paid them any attention, and into Chloe's room.

'Mummy?' Amy's voice was barely above a whisper. Eyes set her down and led her to Chloe's bedside. He hoped that Amy's presence might help Chloe, that and the fact that he hated to have them separated. He just wanted to keep them all together. Amy placed her hand over her mother's and Eyes saw Chloe's fingers twitch ever so slightly. He felt his stomach flip and stifled a cry before it burst out. It wasn't much, but it was something.

He lifted Amy up onto the bed and she snuggled up to Chloe, resting her head on her mother's chest. Eyes watched with baited breath, but Chloe didn't react. He sat down in the chair next to the bed and watched them silently for a long time. Nurses came and went, no one said anything about the little girl curled up on the narrow bed. Amy didn't say one word to Eyes and barely looked at him, she just stared at Chloe until she fell asleep.

Eyes ran over and over the previous day's attack in his mind. Searched for faces, sounds and clues. He remembered Gaze-of-Purity on the roof of his house, he remembered the dead Witch and the taste of her blood. As he sat there, staring at his traumatised wife and daughter, the fury swelled within him. There would be a day of reckoning, he would have his revenge on the Witches for the slaughter they had inflicted, twice now. He would not sit idly by, waiting for them to return a third time. But he knew he had to be careful about this. Charging in there now would only get him and his pack killed. They needed strength, they needed allies and they needed to know what they were walking into.

The room began to grow dark and a nurse came in to turn on a light and check on her patient.

'Mr Davison,' she spoke softly, bringing him gently out of his vengeful thoughts. 'You need to sleep. I'm afraid that visiting hours will be over soon and you should go and get some rest. I promise you they will be absolutely fine.'

'I won't leave them again,' he said. He was determined, but he couldn't hide the crack in his voice.

'I'm afraid we can't let you stay overnight. The doctor is hopeful of being able to discharge your daughter and mother tomorrow, they will need you to be well rested before you take them home.'

'Home?' Eyes almost laughed. The nurse gave him an

apologetic smile and slipped quietly from the room. The bell rang soon after, signalling the end of visiting hours but Eyes stayed resolutely by the bed. Chloe's eyes had closed at some point and he hadn't noticed. She was breathing softly against Amy's hair.

The ward sister put her head around the door and scowled at him before moving on, but he knew she would be back and that he wouldn't be given a moment's peace if he stayed. With a heavy sigh he stood up, stooped to kiss his family gently on each of their sleeping heads and crept from the room.

They would be safe, he knew that, but he worried what further damage it might do if Amy woke up to find him gone. He went to the nurse's station and the ward sister stepped out from around the desk.

'We'll see you in the morning, Mr Davison,' she said in clipped tones with a sour smile. He was clearly not her favourite person, nor was she his.

'I'm concerned about my daughter waking to find me not here,' he said brusquely.

'If we moved her to paediatrics then you would able to stay the night with her,' the sister replied with a raised eyebrow. Eyes wanted to keep them all together, not spread all over the hospital. He gave a resigned sigh and shook his head. He trudged back to the little room and stroked Amy's hair. She stirred and her eyes fluttered open to rest on his face.

'Hi,' he whispered. She didn't reply, she just stared at him. 'I have to leave sweetheart, they won't let me stay overnight. Shall I take you back to your bed in the room with Nana?'

Amy looked at her sleeping mother and then back up at him, her face was flushed and her eyes struggled to stay open. She nodded slowly and then turned to kiss Chloe on the cheek. Eyes lifted her off the bed and carried her back to her room. His mother was still sedated and the room was dark. He laid Amy in the bed and tucked her in under the blankets. 'I'll be back first thing in the morning. I wish I didn't have to go, I really want to stay with you.'

Amy turned her face away and brushed his hand from her side. He stepped back, rejected and hurt but he felt responsible for her actions, he knew she was hurting far more than he was right now. 'Try to sleep, sweetheart. I love you very much and I'll see you in the morning.' He leant to kiss her and lingered close for a moment, hoping for a reply but none came.

Eyes left the hospital and took a taxi to Grove Street. It felt strange to be out in the real world after being in the hospital. The streets were darker than he remembered and everything moved far too quickly. He entered the house cautiously, unsure how the others would greet him. The hallway was dark but light shone under the closed living room door. Eyes flipped the switch and bright light flooded the hall. He blinked against it and covered his eyes with his hand as they adjusted. He heard movement and the living room door flew open, Weaver came bounding out and stopped still to stare at him from the other end of the hall. He dropped his hand and looked at her for a long moment.

Something on the wall caught his eye and he tilted his head to look at it. Huge red letters scrawled across the wall made his heart sink.

'We've scrubbed it but it won't come off completely,' Weaver said quietly. 'Wind Talker bought paint today, we'll decorate tomorrow.'

'The Witches broke in here then?' Eyes asked wearily as he walked slowly down the hall.

'Yes,' Weaver replied.

Eyes stepped into the living room and saw that the graffiti continued in here, more of the same profanity. The others were there, sitting around a stack of pizzas.

'Why is no one patrolling?' Eyes snapped.

'We have been patrolling constantly,' Stalker replied calmly. 'Claws just got back ten minutes ago with dinner. I'm heading back out as soon as I've eaten. The border is quiet and the Wrecking Crew are doing circuits in their van. Please don't worry. How are your family?'

'Not great,' Eyes snapped. He was angry and was not about to be distracted. 'Why didn't you tell me about this when I spoke to you?'

'I didn't want to worry you,' Stalker replied. 'What's done is done and there was nothing you could do about it. You needed to focus on Chloe and Amy.'

'Did they take anything?'

'Yes,' Wind Talker said, wiping his greasy hands on a paper napkin. 'Everything, they took everything important, except the painting and the buried bones, they didn't find them.'

A strange laugh bubbled up in Eyes' chest, a sort of mild hysteria burst out of him as he struggled to wrap his brain around the news. He strode out through the kitchen into the back garden. He was vaguely aware of someone behind him as he crossed the veil and he spun around to face the rest of the pack.

'I am your Alpha!' he roared. 'You do NOT keep me in the dark. It is not for any of you to judge what I should or should not know, what I can or cannot handle. You tell me everything that is pertinent to this pack. Those vile creatures now have everything Flames kept records on, half of which we hadn't even read yet. This is our base, our sanctuary and they desecrated it. I need to know these things!'

Stalker flinched against his rage, but he ignored her reaction. 'Where is Unchained Lightning?' Eyes asked, suddenly aware of their ally's absence.

'I don't know,' Wind Talker replied.

Eyes slammed his fist into the wall and the bricks cracked. Pain shot through his fingers and into his wrist. He flexed his fingers, ignoring the pain and oblivious to the clouds stirring overhead.

'Has he been seen since the fight?' Eyes said, barely containing his anger.

The others exchanged worried glances. Eyes felt the rage filling his muscles and bubbling dangerously close to the surface. Thick clouds rolled overhead and a few drops of rain began to fall. Eyes turned his face to the sky and felt the cold splashes on his hot face. 'We were attacked, my family ripped apart, they came here and stole our shit and our ally is missing.' His voice was low and threatening, there was a rumble in his chest like thunder and the sky above responded with his growing fury. 'And you sit around eating pizza?'

His pack mates looked utterly devastated, embarrassed and humbled. Their reactions didn't do anything to abate what was rising, in fact it only made him more angry. He prowled around the garden and punched another wall. There was a small flicker of lightning in the sky overhead. Eyes strode to the centre of the garden and turned his face to the sky again. His muscles were on fire with adrenaline and he felt his body start to change as the beast threatened to take over. He roared into the night air. 'Bring the lightning!'

At his command, a fork of lightning tore down from the tumultuous clouds and struck the Alpha's chest.

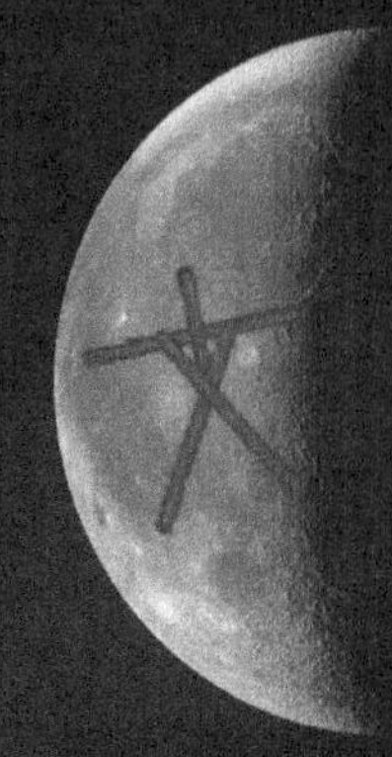

CHAPTER EIGHT

STALKER-OF-NIGHT'S-SHADOW

'HOLY FUCK!' STALKER CRIED. The Alpha's body went rigid, his fists were clenched at the ends of his outstretched arms and his hair and clothes were smoking. Unchained Lightning flew down from the sky and circled Eyes, sparks flying off him and showering the garden with their needles of electric blue light.

'Oh my god!' Claws shouted and Weaver darted forwards but Stalker grabbed her arm to stop her from getting too close. Their ally circled slowly and the sparks died down. Eyes still stood staring up at the sky, his chest heaving with laboured breaths. Slowly, his eyes opened and his head lowered to look at them. Every hair on his body was standing on end and it was only the fear in her veins that prevented Stalker from bursting into laughter.

'Are you all right?' Weaver asked, tugging her arm free of Stalker's grasp and stepping forwards. Stalker followed tentatively. Eyes was clearly alive and not seriously injured, but there was a look in his eyes that she didn't like at all and she didn't trust what he may do next.

'I'm fine,' Eyes replied, icily. He stretched out a hand and ran it slowly along Unchained Lightning's side as the elemental slithered past him. Small sparks flew from his fingers and the fae made a strange noise that Stalker could only assume was a sort of purr. Unchained Lightning moved into the corner of the garden and came to a halt, his huge, glowing eyes resting on the Alpha.

'Glorious,' the elemental said, his voice crackling.

'Thank you,' Eyes replied, giving the fae a small bow. 'I honour you and your power and wanted to display that.'

Stalker watched him, the way he moved, the way he spoke to their ally. He was very different. 'Are you well?' he asked the fae.

'I was,' Unchained Lightning paused, his head tilted to one side, 'indisposed. The Witches held me in some sort of cage. I did not like it.' His voice thundered suddenly and he raised himself up to his full height. Stalker pressed a trembling hand to her lips.

'How did you get free?' Wind Talker asked, his voice soft.

Unchained Lightning bowed his head and blinked, a low rumble in his throat. Eyes looked at him with a sad smile, his hair still smoking slightly.

'I was able to break free when you called me.' There was a crackle of static in the air and Stalker gaped at Eyes. He had known immediately that something was amiss with the fae's absence. The rest of them had dismissed it. She felt foolish and turned her face away from Unchained Lightning, not wanting him to see the guilt in her eyes.

'We have a lot to do,' Eyes said, turning his attention back to the stunned pack. 'Our ally requires a throne. We will acquire it for him and develop our strength, forge alliances and create a watertight plan of attack. Make no mistake, we are at war, but we will not be reckless. Tomorrow night we return to my house to assess the damage there. Stalker, I want you patrolling first tonight but someone must relieve you at some point. Everyone needs to be well rested.'

Stalker nodded in agreement. Eyes strode across the garden and passed through the middle of the dumbstruck pack to head back into the house. Stalker turned and watched him go, as did the others. He stepped across the veil in the kitchen and the rest of the pack turned back to each other, their faces filled with alarm and confusion.

'What the hell was that about?' Claws asked. Stalker glanced at Unchained Lighting, who was still purring in the corner, watching them shrewdly.

'He's obviously in shock after the events of yesterday,' Wind Talker said sternly, his voice full of disapproval.

'Who wouldn't be?' Weaver asked, looking surprised at his tone. 'It was terrible, them going after his family like that. We should go talk to him, ask after them.'

Weaver led the way, Stalker lingered for a moment in the garden, looking back at their ally. He blinked at her, his head tilted to one side. He somehow managed to look child-like and innocent, despite being a twelve-foot long, electric blue, glowing dragon with huge wings. She bowed to him before following her pack across the veil.

'The doctors don't know anything,' Eyes was saying as Stalker entered the kitchen. 'They can't know the truth about what happened, so they don't really know what they are dealing with. If she doesn't snap out of it herself, I doubt there is anything the human doctors can do. She'll need spiritual healing.'

'Of course,' Weaver replied, gently squeezing his arm.

'Let's give her a few days and if there's no improvement I'll see what I can do,' Wind Talker offered.

Stalker didn't feel she had much to contribute to the discussion and she passed through the kitchen towards the front door. As she reached it she heard someone behind her and turned to see Eyes approaching her looking apologetic.

'Wait,' he called out softly and she stopped to look at him. He came right up to her and pulled her into a tight embrace, which she returned. It took her by surprise but she welcomed the gesture. 'Thank you,' he whispered, his voice muffled against her hair.

'What for?' she asked, taken aback.

'For being there yesterday and for captaining the ship. I'm sorry I was such an arse earlier.'

'Don't worry about it, it's what we do for one another. We're a pack.' She pulled back and gave his arm a gentle squeeze. His face twitched like he was trying to smile. 'I'm going out on patrol now. It's Wind Talker's turn next.'

She gave him one last reassuring smile, then set off for the border. Stalker climbed a wall in the next street and took to the rooftops. She found that she could cover a lot more distance that way and she liked keeping her, albeit faint, scent off the streets. She ran along high walls, vaulted fences and traversed scaffolding with growing confidence, and as she swung and leaped her way across the territory that night she felt Pursuit-of-Midnight-Solitude leading her to the most secluded places.

When she reached Redfield Park she caught the scent of one of the Wrecking Crew and she came to a halt at the boundary, carefully peering into the darkness. There was a rustle of leaves nearby and a soft thud, Stalker spun to locate the source and saw the skinny female standing before her, brushing dirt from her hands.

'Hi,' Stalker said, breathing a small sigh of relief that it wasn't Fury.

'Hi,' the woman replied with a wry smile. 'I'm Sky Runner, by the way. I don't think we've ever been introduced.'

'No, we haven't. I'm Stalker-of-Night's-Shadow.'

'I know.' Sky Runner grinned.

'You were up in the tree?' Stalker asked, bemused.

'Yeah, I tend to patrol that way, in trees, on rooftops, you know. That's what my name means.'

'Of course.' Stalker smiled. 'Me too, rooftops, I mean, not trees. I do a bit of parkour.'

'That's so cool,' Sky Runner said with a broad grin. 'Maybe you could show me some tricks some time?'

'Yeah, that would be great.' Stalker smiled, happy to be making friends with one of their neighbours when things had been so sour for so long. A shadow twitched in the trees, Pursuit-of-Midnight-Solitude nagging Stalker to re-join the hunt, and she remembered why she was out this way. 'Have you seen anything tonight? Any movement from the Witches?'

'Nothing. It's too quiet. You know what I mean?'

'Yeah, I do,' Stalker replied, an ominous feeling

settling in her stomach. 'Thank you, by the way, for coming to the fight yesterday. It might have been a very different outcome if you hadn't been there.'

'That's okay. Rust says jump, we ask how high. You know? Is your Alpha okay?'

'More or less. I'd better head out to the border. Nice to talk to you.' Stalker gave Sky Runner a genuine smile, which she returned. Sky Runner turned and started jogging away into the park, shifting gracefully into a fox as she ran. Stalker watched her go and then set off along the edge of the park at a brisk jog. She too shifted into her fox form under the cover of the trees and emerged at the end of the park onto the lit street.

She ran the border slowly, taking in every scent, every nuance. At regular intervals the Witches had marked the border more strongly, quite recently, but they hadn't crossed it, she was certain. When she reached the place where they had been chased off by the Wrecking Crew the trail was fading but Stalker stayed there for a long time, taking in all of the different scents, noting each individual one. There were male scents mixed in with the female Witches, they could have been the Phoenix Guard again, but they hadn't used fire to attack, which was obviously the Phoenix Guard's speciality. The smoke bomb in the street had been camouflage, not intended to do any damage. No, Stalker was sure this was another pack, more Furies.

That bothered her and she paced the border restlessly for the next two hours, frustrated and confused. Wind Talker relieved her in the early hours of the morning and she returned to Grove Street to get some sleep. She didn't sleep well, the gnawing sensation of something forgotten or missing kept her from settling properly and she gave up once the rest of the pack were up and about.

Eyes left early for the hospital, Claws had to work and Weaver went out to take her turn on patrol. Stalker spent most of the day tidying up the garden, while Wind Talker slept and then worked on the inside of the house. Stalker had to work that afternoon and it was harder than it had been in a long time to hold back and not hurt her students.

She threw one girl in her judo class so hard that she tumbled across the floor into another two teenagers who were practising together.

'I am so, so sorry,' Stalker said, running over to help the kids to their feet. They looked at her warily and no one volunteered to be used to demonstrate any moves for the rest of the class.

When her Banshay pupil arrived for the last class of the day, Stalker decided it would be best to leave her own dha in the bag and focus on building some basic skills, much to the disappointment of her young student.

Stalker left the dojo at eight o'clock and walked wearily south into Crossway to meet the others. The sky was dark and there was rain in the air, though it was only light drizzle. Stalker usually liked the spring rain in Caerton, she liked the smells of cut grass and wood smoke that usually came with it, but it was still only mid-February and not much life was stirring in the city yet. Halfway there, her phone rang and she answered without really looking to see who it was. 'Hello?'

'Hi.' First Strike's deep voice caught her by surprise and she faltered in her stride.

'Hi,' she replied, immediately thinking of Rhys.

'Are you all right? I gather something went down at the weekend. I hadn't heard from you so I was a bit worried.'

'I'm sorry,' she said, guilt rushing to the forefront of her mind. 'Yeah, I'm fine, we're all okay. Just shocked really. I'm sorry, I should have let you know I was okay.'

'Oh no, don't worry about it. I mean we're not, we never said we were, you know, a couple, I guess. I don't expect you to always check in with me or anything.' He sounded flustered, which was most unusual for him.

'Okay, well I'm still sorry that you were worried. Everything okay over your way?' The Hand of God also shared a territory border with the Witches, but to her knowledge, they had never encountered one another. There was always the chance that would change, however.

'All quiet here, thanks for asking. If you need anything just let me know.'

'I will. Thanks. Best not to say too much more over the phone, but about what was said at the festival, about uniting everyone,' she glanced around to make sure she was alone. The street was quiet.

'Yeah?' First Strike said, urging her on.

'It will be necessary. Can I count on you and yours?'

'You can always count on me and Crimson, and well, if she orders it the others will obey.'

'Okay, thanks. I have to go now. See you again soon.'

'I hope so. Be careful.' His voice was loaded with caution and Stalker took it seriously. As she hung up the phone she thought about what he had said about his pack obeying their Alpha. Sky Runner had said the same thing. Back in the days of the Blue Moon, Stalker would have done whatever Fortune told her to, in part because of how new she was, but not just that. His leadership was compelling and charismatic. The Lightning Lords were different. Eyes was their Alpha, but almost only by default and they felt held together by obligation sometimes, rather than deep loyalty and commitment. She had no problem sneaking off to meet Rhys or patrol in the middle of the night when she was meant to be sleeping, she would always go her own way and speak out if she had a problem with what the pack wanted to do. She thought of her pack mates as equals and their structure as vaguely democratic; if that was unusual for shifters then maybe it would ultimately make the Lightning Lords stronger than the others. But perhaps it was their biggest weakness.

She arrived at Eyes' house to find the others waiting outside next to his car. There was police tape all over the house and the front windows were roughly boarded up to secure the place. As Stalker approached she felt prickles all over her skin and she came to a halt in between Eyes and the front door. She sighed as she felt the condition of the veil around her.

'There is a rip in the veil, I'm sorry, Eyes.'

'That's okay, I thought there might be. We can fix it.' He strode to the door and unlocked it. The five of them went inside cautiously. The smell of smoke still clung to the torn curtains and glass was scattered all over the floor throughout the living room and hallway. Eyes turned the lights on and they began a cautious sweep of the downstairs, checking to see that the house hadn't been looted and that there was no one hiding in wait for his return. Stalker was the first to move upstairs, she crept along the landing to the door to Amy's room. There was no trace of what had happened, no sign of Perfection-of-Flesh, or the dead Witch, just a few tiny pieces of glass that had found their way up the stairs on the soles of shoes, and the furniture in Amy's room was a little askew.

'We should cross the veil,' she called out softly, confident that the others would hear her but not wanting to raise her voice, doing so felt unwise or disrespectful somehow. Eyes was the first by her side, the others followed up the stairs. Stalker took Eyes by the hand and tried to give him a courageous and reassuring smile, but it faltered on her lips. 'Are you ready?'

Eyes nodded without saying a word and together they crossed through the torn veil. Stalker's breath caught in her throat. The house had bled through the veil, creating a dark copy of itself. It was dark, but some moonlight filtered in through Amy's bedroom window. The carpet was soaked in blood and tiny specks of gold hung in the air in the bedroom where Perfection-of-Flesh had been killed, a lingering echo of his sacrifice. Little demons of fear and death scurried away at the arrival of five shifters, some diving under Amy's bed and others scuttling down the hall.

On the landing where the Witch had died the blood was splashed right up the walls in a grotesque spray pattern as well as staining the light carpet. Where her body had lain was a small but hideous demon of blood, making sickening choking noises as it bubbled and oozed on the floor. Stalker approached it carefully and drew one of her dha. She drove the blade into it and the demon fell silent before disintegrating into a pool of blood.

Eyes looked at it as he passed, a cold look in his eyes,

and he led the way down the stairs. There was movement in the hallway and sounds of crunching glass and fleeing footsteps. Eyes moved into the living room and Stalker followed. The curtains billowed in the breeze but the room was almost pitch black. Eyes tried a light switch but nothing happened. Stalker gripped her dha firmly as she followed him through the living room and into the dining room.

The dining table was on its side against the wall, much as in the human world, but where it should stand in the centre of the room was a cluster of fear demons, huddled together like a frightened family, unaware that their hiding place had been overturned. The Lightning Lords ignored them and Eyes led them through to the kitchen at the back of the house.

There was a little more light here, moonlight entered through the un-boarded windows as it had upstairs, and it flickered as if shining through rustling trees outside in the garden. Where Eyes' father had been killed there was more blood and a demon much like the one upstairs, but hovering over it, almost invisible but for the glinting moonlight on metal, was something much worse. Eyes stopped dead and the others came to a halt beside and behind him, Stalker at his right hand. She could feel the power of the demon before she could even see it clearly. It seemed to shimmer with the moonlight but as it became aware of them it solidified and turned to face them.

It was a tall knight in plate mail, its helmet had a visor that covered the face, but where the eyes should be was pure darkness and Stalker just knew that if the visor were open she would see nothing.

'Greetings,' the knight said, his voice deep and quiet. 'Let's begin our work.'

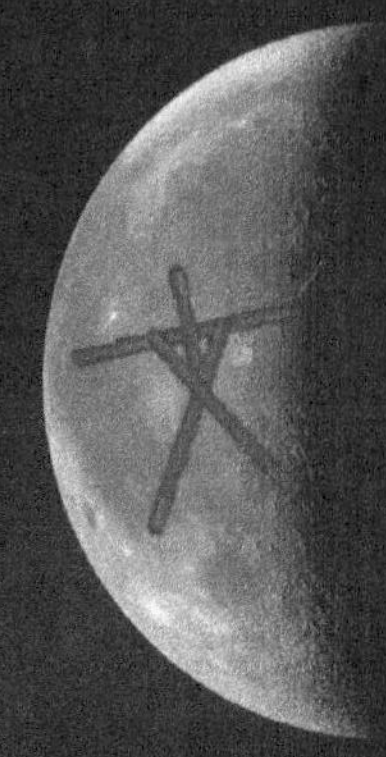

Chapter Nine

Stalker lowered her sword slightly and eyed the demon carefully. The hairs on the back of her neck were standing on end and goose bumps had erupted up her arms under her jacket.

'Knight-of-Shadowed-Fear,' Wind Talker said, his voice strong and confident. Stalker glanced at him and saw the fear in his eyes, but his voice did not betray him. 'What work, may I ask?'

'Well, more of this would be most welcome,' the Knight replied. Stalker cringed, she could hear the smile in his deep voice. Eyes tensed up by her side and she quickly placed a steadying hand on his arm.

'Not a chance,' Eyes said, his jaw clenched tight.

'The last of your kind that I agreed to work with were quite accommodating,' the Knight said politely. 'Your predecessors. I expect you to keep to the bargains I made with the Blue Moon. But if violence is off the cards then no matter, there is much that we can accomplish together that does not involve more human bloodshed, if that is not palatable to you.'

'It is not,' Claws said emphatically, stepping out from behind Eyes. 'Judging by your name, you are fuelled by the fear of the unknown danger, correct?' The Knight merely inclined his head towards Claws. 'An event like this should keep people very afraid for some time to come. How about you feed on that and then move on?'

The Knight seemed to expand before them, absorbing the darkness around him and spreading to fill the space. They all took a step back, except Eyes, he held his ground, looking up into the demon's metal face. Stalker's grip on her dha tightened as she waited to see what the demon was going to do.

'I'm afraid that won't be possible,' the Knight's voice boomed out, filled with darkness. 'There is a war brewing and I am here to assemble my forces. You do not have to help me but you will not stand in my way.'

Stalker's knuckles turned white as she gripped her sword more tightly. Suddenly her knees shook and buckled, a lump of terror rose in her throat and threatened to erupt in a scream. The terror coursing through her was paralysing and as she searched the room desperately she saw Weaver clutching at her chest, struggling to breathe; Claws had dropped to his knees and was cradling his head in his arms; Wind Talker stumbled back against the cupboards with his mouth agog; and Eyes stared wide-eyed and paralysed just like her. The Knight was doing this, inducing this dread in them all. Stalker tried to fight it, but it was futile. *Move!* she screamed at herself. Her blood was pumping through every vein at tremendous speed and her feet remained rooted to the floor.

The Knight leaned over the rasping blood demon on the floor and drew a long, rattling breath. Darkness passed from the blood demon into the Knight's metal-covered mouth and Stalker watched, transfixed. The blood demon shrank away to nothing until it was completely absorbed into the Knight-of-Shadowed-Fear.

There was a sudden gust of wind and the back door blew open, slamming back against the kitchen cupboard behind it and rattling the glass in the window panes. The Knight shimmered in the moonlight and then disappeared out through the door with surprising speed and agility, with just the faintest clinking of his metal armour. The shadows seemed to follow him, leaving the house a little brighter.

Seconds passed and the terror gradually ebbed away. Stalker slumped sideways, her knees weak with exhaustion. She looked around at the others and found them grabbing on to things to steady themselves, and exchanging worried glances. Weaver clung onto Claws and her eyes met Stalker's, they were wide and afraid.

'He was clearly here waiting to see who summoned him,' Wind Talker whispered, a tremor to his voice.

'We didn't summon him,' Eyes hissed.

'Not on purpose,' Weaver said softly. Stalker looked at her again, she still didn't quite seem herself. 'But our actions here, and those of our attackers, sent a signal throughout the realms and he answered it. The rip in the veil allowed him to enter Hepethia from his own demon realm.'

'Can you fix it?' Eyes asked, his head whipping around to Wind Talker.

'Yes, of course,' he replied. 'I need a few things. My supplies were destroyed but I am working on replenishing my stocks. I should be able to do it tomorrow.'

'Can we try to force him back through the tear before repairing it?' Claws asked, still holding onto Weaver.

'We could try,' Stalker replied. 'But all he has to do is unleash that crippling terror on us again and we'll be just as powerless against him. We need to fix the veil to stop anything else coming through, and let him go about his business for now. We'll work out a way to banish him as soon as we can.'

'Another problem, for another day,' Eyes said wearily, rubbing his brow.

The pack crossed back into the human world and drove back to Grove Street. It was a sombre night and when Stalker woke the next morning the mood hadn't changed.

'Where are we with things?' Eyes asked as they ate a subdued breakfast.

'I have to work this morning,' Claws said, swallowing his food awkwardly. Eyes shot him a venomous look and Stalker felt a prickle of tension run through the room. 'I have a case that needs my attention. A stolen mask. It's important, and should pay well.'

'Fine,' Eyes replied curtly.

Stalker was the first to finish eating and dashed from the room, eager to escape the maudlin atmosphere. She stepped into the shower and scrubbed her skin. It was her third shower since the attack, she somehow couldn't feel clean enough. The dead Witch's face kept haunting her thoughts and memories of her twin that she had killed months ago surfaced every time.

Once everyone was washed and dressed, they went their separate ways: Eyes to the hospital; Claws to work; and Weaver, Stalker and Wind Talker went back to Eyes' house to mend the veil. The house was quiet, no sign of the Knight-of-Shadowed-Fear or any other significant demons. Stalker kept watch while Wind Talker and Weaver did what needed to be done. Even in broad daylight the house seemed eerie, in part because it still looked like a crime scene. She found a broom in the cupboard under the stairs and swept up the broken glass as best she could while Wind Talker and Weaver repaired the veil the way they had at the betting shop. Stalker took the police tape off the front of the house and went at the blood in the kitchen with a bottle of bleach, grim determination and help from the others once they finished their task.

They returned to Grove Street in the afternoon and Stalker felt a little lighter, having done something to help Eyes. He arrived late in the afternoon looking tired and thoroughly depressed.

'What's happening with your family?' Stalker asked.

'Chloe is being kept in again tonight, they're running more tests and have someone coming to do a psychological assessment. They think she has severe post-traumatic stress disorder and there was talk of putting her into care. I won't accept that. I want her healed, today.' He looked pointedly at Wind Talker, who nodded slowly, his expression sympathetic.

'How about the others?' Weaver asked cautiously.

'They've been discharged and are at my mum's house.

Amy's going to stay with her for now. Chloe's sister is coming to stay with them for a while to help look after them both.'

Stalker felt tears prickle at her eyes, she felt terrible for him. She knew that Fortune had wanted Eyes to leave his family and her friend Fire Talon had been forced to abandon his family too, this was why. But she understood why Eyes refused to let them go. She had no family and few close friends, but she clung tightly to her job and the parts of her that were still human. It was impossible to let them go, to do so would be to lose something so precious. She didn't want to lose sight of herself, of all of the things in her life that had made her who she was now. Life didn't have to be all about war and the supernatural, humanity was important, otherwise they were nothing but monsters.

Wind Talker led them across the veil into the garden. There was no sign of Unchained Lightning but Wind Talker strode into the centre of the garden and looked up to the sky. He raised his hands and blew out a big puff of breath. Stalker saw the clouds above respond to him, they grew suddenly thick and dark and the wind picked up. A few spots of rain fell and then Stalker heard something soaring towards them, thunder in its wake. Unchained Lightning appeared over the roof tops and struck the ground, landing with a heavy thump and small discharge of static.

'You called?' their ally said with a crackle.

'I did,' Wind Talker replied. 'I need to summon a powerful healing fae and would greatly appreciate your help. Just being present, lending your authority and influence will help.'

'Of course,' the elemental said. He settled himself in

the corner of the little garden and watched with interest.

Wind Talker opened his bag and pulled out a thick, white candle. He passed it to Stalker and rummaged for some other supplies. He handed out peppermint oil and some first aid supplies then sat down on the earth in the centre of the garden to crush some herbs with his mortar and pestle. With his grinding motions, a protective circle began to ripple out from him, getting larger with each circle he made with his elbow until it filled the garden. Wind Talker stood up and approached Eyes with the small bowl of crushed herbs and his knife.

'May I?' he asked and Eyes readily gave him his hand. Wind Talker cut into the Alpha's palm, Eyes barely winced. Stalker lit her candle and Weaver sprinkled the oil into the circle as Wind Talker pressed the herbs into the cut on Eyes' palm. He looked at Claws and indicated for him to come across the circle with the bandage he was holding. Claws began wrapping the bandage carefully around Eyes' hand and Wind Talker returned to the centre of the circle. He looked up at the sky and raised his knife and the bowl of herbs. 'In this act of healing I honour those beings with superior powers to heal. I honour the gods of healing, especially Asclepius, and humbly request their aid.'

Stalker heard a strange hissing noise and looked around for the source. The soil around the garden began to move and Stalker twitched in alarm. The hissing grew louder and snakes began to emerge all around them.

'Wind Talker?' Stalker whispered, unable to hide the concern in her voice.

'Wait,' he whispered back.

The snakes slithered around, writhing over each

other and moving towards the centre of the circle. They merged right next to Wind Talker and began to pile on top of one another, building up into a growing mound. Wind Talker stepped back into the circle next to Stalker and they exchanged anxious glances. The snakes twisted around to form a six-foot tall pillar of green and brown rippling motion. The pillar began to take on a more humanoid form, with limbs and a head emerging.

'Is that fae or a demon?' Stalker whispered, leaning close to Wind Talker.

'Fae,' he replied softly. 'All nature spirits are fae. We greet and thank you for attending us, Whispering Iasis.'

'What healing do you require?' the creature asked, its voice a low hiss. 'None of you is seriously injured.'

'My wife,' Eyes spoke, his voice strong. 'She suffers with the madness that humans are afflicted with when they see our true form. She is broken. I need her whole, I need her happy and healthy. Please, can you help?'

'The madness of which you speak is the price and protection granted by Artemis. It cannot easily be undone.' The envoy of Asclepius writhed and shifted its form as it spoke.

'I must have her back as she was, please. The price is too high and inflicted upon the wrong person in this case. She has done nothing wrong.' Eyes' voice trembled and Stalker looked at him, wishing she could take away his pain.

'It is not her paying the price, it is you,' the fae rattled.

Eyes opened his mouth to reply, but no sound came out.

'Can we pay another price?' Stalker asked quickly.

The fae turned towards her, a face forming out of the writhing snakes. She tried not to flinch. 'If this is the price for allowing our nature to be revealed, can we make an exchange? We'll do something for you if you can remove the madness from her.'

Whispering Iasis seemed to consider this for a moment, it turned slowly on the spot, looking at each of them.

'Very well,' it said at last. A tail flicked out of the pillar and lashed out towards Wind Talker, catching him in the chest with alarming force. He staggered backwards and clutched his chest, a cry sticking in his throat. He tugged his t-shirt off over his head to examine himself. There was a bright red sting on his chest and it was spreading rapidly, dark lines appearing as the poison filled his veins and discoloured his blood.

'No!' Stalker cried out and everyone ran forwards to support Wind Talker as he struggled to stand.

'There is a house,' the fae hissed. Stalker glared at it, her arm around Wind Talker. 'The map will show you the way. Heal the house and I will heal your Alpha's wife.'

Stalker looked back at Wind Talker's chest. Sure enough, the dark lines on his skin had formed a street map and at his heart was a shimmering red mark indicating the location of the house. Wind Talker touched his skin and took a steadying breath.

'I'm okay,' he said, standing up and moving out from the pack clustering around him. 'Claws, can you memorise this before it fades?'

Claws nodded and took a good look at the marks.

'Very well,' Eyes said, staring at the fae. 'We will do

this. Thank you.'

The fae rattled and then sank into the ground, breaking apart into a hundred snakes again, who quickly slithered away and buried themselves back into the ground.

'How on earth do we heal a house?' Stalker asked.

'Let's go and find out,' Eyes replied, setting off across the veil without hesitation.

The house they had been instructed to heal was to the north of Grove Street, about halfway to the telecoms tower in a leafy little area tucked in between faceless rows of terraces and a more commercial area. The streets were broader and lined with trees, the semi-detached houses had front gardens and driveways. The house they had been led to stood on a corner and looked perfectly normal. The pack sat in Eyes' car, idling across the street, peering at the house. Stalker felt nothing unusual from the veil, but more subtle effects would only be felt up close.

'It'll be dark soon,' Stalker said quietly. 'We should cross the veil and check it out in Hepethia.'

She willed her body across the veil and her feet dropped to the ground as the car disappeared from around her. She stumbled but quickly corrected herself. The others shimmered into Hepethia one by one and Stalker looked around at them, a smile tugging at her lips. Hiding in Eyes' car, behind tinted windows, was an excellent way to cross the veil unseen.

She looked around them and saw that they were in a relatively untouched area of Hepethia, its raw crystalline beauty winked at them in the late afternoon sunlight. A few yards away, right where the house they had been sent to heal had stood in the human world, was an almost identical house, sat amongst the quartz rocks. The house was covered in small birds, all along the rooftop, the garage and the swing set in the garden. They preened and bobbed their heads and looked perfectly mundane, except for their number. 'What the hell?' Stalker murmured.

'Witches?' Eyes whispered, panic in his voice.

'I don't think so,' Weaver said, heading slowly towards the front door. The birds watched them advancing, but didn't do anything. Weaver reached the door first and carefully opened it just wide enough to peer inside. She glanced back and gave a nod and then pushed the door wide open. Stalker slipped inside first, followed by Wind Talker and Eyes. Weaver and Claws remained at the door to keep watch.

'Wind Talker,' Stalker whispered. 'What do you see on the other side?'

He had his talisman in contact with his skin under his shirt and was able to see both sides of the veil at once. They moved silently down the wide hallway, past an open door into the living room.

'A little girl, watching television,' he replied softly.

They moved towards the kitchen at the back of the house, everything looked fairly mundane, but Stalker sensed the presence of something lurking out of sight. She moved to the stairs and crept up them cautiously, the others just behind her. On the narrow landing there were several doors, but only one stood closed, it had purple flowers on it. Stalker moved directly to it, there was a scratching sound from inside and she opened the door slowly.

The room was flooded with the red light of sunset

and it poured out onto the landing. There was a caw and the fluttering of wings and Stalker stepped into the room quickly. Perched on the end of a white bed with a pink canopy was a big black bird, bobbing its head and ruffling its feathers. Paper fluttered all over the walls, reminding Stalker vividly of the Blue Moon Betting Shop. These sheets, however, were covered in brightly coloured sketches. Rows and rows of a child's drawings of birds.

There was a wardrobe in the corner and the doors were banging gently, like something was shuffling about inside. Stalker drew one of her dha and moved silently to the wardrobe. She flung open the door and saw a black shape twirling around, but it seemed to not be aware of the intrusion, it just kept spinning, like a small child turning in clumsy circles and it muttered indistinguishable words. 'It's a minor fear demon,' Wind Talker whispered. He reached past Stalker and closed the wardrobe door.

'What does this room look like on the other side?' Stalker asked.

'Almost identical, not quite as many drawings, but a lot of them. No black bird. The mother was up here but has just gone downstairs.'

They left the room and crept back downstairs to the kitchen, which was now filled with the smells of cooking and little motes of life bobbed around the room. Sitting on one of the worktops was a small, gnarled demon of worry, chewing its nails and glancing around with big eyes. It saw them and looked momentarily alarmed, recoiling from them, but it seemed to decide they were not worth worrying about and its big eyes dropped to the floor.

In the centre of the kitchen floor was a large, heavy-looking rug and Stalker looked at it with suspicion. It was an odd sight in a kitchen and she glanced at Wind Talker with raised eyebrows. 'There's a covered trap door on both sides,' he said without her needing to ask.

Eyes stooped down and tossed the rug aside, revealing a big wooden door set into the floor.

'We have to open it, don't we?' Stalker said. Eyes grasped the round, metal handle firmly, glancing up at Stalker and Wind Talker briefly before tugging on it. The door opened with a loud creak and Stalker could see how heavy it was from the strain on Eyes' face. The door fell from his grasp as soon as it reached the tipping point and slammed into the tiled floor with a deafening *thunk* that shook the floor. There was a staircase leading down into a pitch black basement and with only the briefest hesitation, Eyes set off down it. 'Wait,' Stalker called out quietly but he went on. She glanced at Wind Talker, wearing the worry she felt on her face. He gave her a resigned shrug and set off down the steps into the darkness.

Stalker followed and willed her eyes to adjust to the darkness; she drew upon the power of her darkness allies and they allowed her just enough light to see where she was placing her feet and make out Wind Talker just ahead of her. He came to an abrupt halt and she drew level with him. Eyes had reached the bottom of the stairs and in front of them was a door. It was like a bank vault door, but black; it had a huge wheel on the front of it and thick black chains strung across it.

A strange sensation prickled at Stalker's senses as she looked at the door, something about the veil was unsettling her. It wasn't a tear, like the ones she had encountered before, it was more like the absence of veil at Crescent Park. She didn't like it.

'It's not quite like this on the other side,' Wind Talker whispered, his face was ashen, Stalker could just make out in the dark. 'It's a plain wooden door with a padlock. No one would think anything of it if they came across it.'

Stalker watched Eyes as he placed a hand on the door. He let out a small guttural noise of strain and then dropped his hand heavily to his side.

'Well, we're not getting through it on this side of the veil any time soon, I can't change it,' Eyes said, his voice laced with frustration. Stalker turned and moved quickly back up the steps into the kitchen. The last rays of sunlight were casting their eerie red glow into the room. They covered the trap door and went back to the others at the front of the house.

'This place is very wrong. How is it like this?' Stalker asked. 'How are the humans shaping it like that?'

'What?' Weaver asked sharply.

'There were drawings on the wall in the little girl's room and when the mother was cooking we could see it changing the kitchen.' Stalker explained.

'I've never heard of that before,' Weaver said, a deep frown etched on her brow.

'There was something wrong with the veil,' Stalker said slowly. 'Like a hole or a doorway or something. Could it be causing some sort of bleed-through?'

Wind Talker and Weaver glanced at each other.

'Maybe,' Wind Talker said slowly. They moved around to the back of the house to find a secluded spot, and Wind Talker checked the other side of the veil to see that the coast was clear. They crossed over and dashed quietly to the car. 'The mother was ill,' Wind Talker said as they drove home. 'She was pale and thin.'

'That worry demon must have belonged to her,' Stalker said. 'The one in the kitchen. The stress is making her ill.'

'It's something to do with the girl,' Eyes said, a grim look in his eyes. His hands gripped the steering wheel a little too tightly, turning his knuckles white. 'She may be supernatural or have some sort of insight. Perhaps there is something buried in that basement and the mother knows and is keeping it from the girl.'

'We don't know enough yet. We can't even think about getting through that door until we've done some more scouting and research,' Stalker said. 'I know you want to get this done quickly and get Chloe healed, but we have to do it right.'

Eyes nodded but said nothing and she felt his resentment pouring off him like radiation. She didn't want to be the cause of his frustration, but she had to stick to her guns on this. They couldn't put theirs and this family's lives at risk by barging in and releasing goodness knows what terror into the world. That door was well-secured for a reason.

Eyes dropped them off at Grove Street and drove away to be with his family. Stalker looked up at the dark sky, basking in the lack of light. She felt the call of the night drawing her out to hunt like an impatient child tugging at her hand. 'I'm going out patrolling,' she called to Weaver, who stopped inside the door and looked back at her with a curious expression.

'Okay, that's probably a good idea. Want company?'

'No thanks, but do you want to take a turn after you've had some sleep? We should keep patrolling regularly from now on, just in case.'

'Of course. Stay safe,' Weaver said with a nod and Stalker smiled in reply before turning and setting off at a jog towards Crossway.

She took a different route every time she went out now, covering as much of the territory as she could, getting to know all of its back alleys, green spaces and dead ends. There were precious few dead ends to her now, even in her flightless, human form. She could scale almost any wall, with her developing parkour skills, but she noted each potential trap for enemies and good escape routes for herself and her pack mates.

As she vaulted a fence and dropped fifteen feet from a bridge onto the road below, Stalker felt Pursuit-of-Midnight-Solitude at her heels and grinned as the demon rushed past her and drew her into the chase. She shifted into her fox form and sprinted after the rapidly moving shadow, leaping from cover to cover, clinging to the darkness. It was exhilarating and made her feel more alive than anything else in her life. She was free from all doubt or worry, free from conscious thought, totally enraptured by the thrill of the chase. It was addictive, she was spending more and more of her nights like this and getting less and less sleep, but she was barely aware of it. The compulsion was blinding and she was its slave.

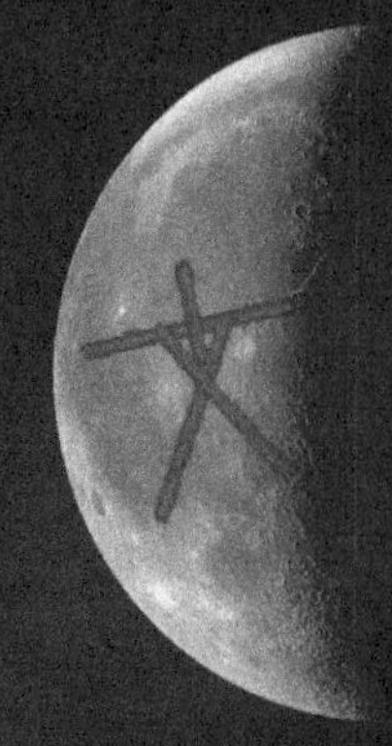

CHAPTER TEN

FIGHTS-EYES-OPEN

'MUM,' EYES CALLED OUT GENTLY AT THE BEDROOM DOOR. There was movement inside but no reply came. 'I have to go to work. Rebecca's making breakfast. Do you want to come down for something to eat?'

'In a minute,' she replied, her voice muffled through the door.

'Okay. I'll see you later.' He placed a hand on the door and paused for a moment, listening to her moving around. He reluctantly moved away and went down to the dining room where Amy was slowly eating cereal. Chloe's sister, Rebecca, was buttering some toast and passed him a plate with a frosty glare. 'Thank you,' he said as politely as he could manage.

'I'm taking Amy to see her mum later,' Rebecca said as she returned her attention to the breakfast.

'Thank you.'

'It is ridiculous that you are working already. Can't

they give you compassionate leave?' She flashed those cold eyes at him again. She had been like this ever since she arrived. Clearly she blamed him for what had happened and thought he wasn't doing enough. She had no idea and Eyes fought the frustration bubbling up inside and slapped on a fake smile in order to keep things civilised.

'They gave me two days and will give me more for the funeral, but this morning is a really important meeting. They can't delay a meeting with all of the city's most important politicians, businessmen and city planners just for little old me.'

'Why can't someone else go in your place?' she snapped.

'Because no one knows the job like I do, Rebecca.' Eyes sighed. He quickly finished his toast and moved over to Amy. He kissed the top of her head, she didn't react. 'I'll see you later, munchkin. I love you.' His hand lingered on her hair, he could feel her tense up at his touch and he reluctantly pulled away.

He left without another word and drove into the city centre on autopilot. He would have given anything not to be going into Free River Tower, but Theodore had insisted that his presence was required and when Theodore beckoned there was really no way of saying no.

He arrived and made his way to the top floor. The building was buzzing with activity. He got out of the lift on the brightly lit top floor, opposite the double doors into Theodore's office, they were closed and his assistant appeared at his side with a cup of coffee and an eager smile.

'Can I take your coat?' the young man asked and Eyes passed it to him with one hand while taking the coffee with the other. 'Would you like to wait down here?' The assistant indicated a seating area just down the hall, where his own desk was located, and Eyes followed him. There were a few other people waiting, some of whom Eyes recognised from his other meetings over the last few months.

'Is Theodore going to be long?' Eyes asked. The assistant checked his watch.

'I think he's hoping to start in a few minutes, he was taking a call.'

The phone on his desk rang and the assistant answered it swiftly. 'Yes, Mr Harris?'

Eyes glanced at him and moved to take a seat, keeping one ear on the conversation, though he couldn't hear Theodore's side. 'Yes he has. Of course.' The assistant replaced the phone in its cradle with a click. 'Mr Davison?' Eyes stopped in his tracks and turned back to face him. 'Mr Harris would like to see you now.'

He put his coffee down untouched and followed the assistant back to Theodore's office. He could get used to having someone scurrying about taking his coat, bringing him coffee and opening doors for him. Theodore had a good thing going on here and Eyes wondered if it would ever be possible for him to achieve all of this for himself.

'Martin,' Theodore greeted him warmly at the door and opened his arms wide. Eyes moved awkwardly into his embrace and felt Theodore's hands pat him firmly on the back.

'Theodore,' he said stiffly, pulling out of the embrace as soon as was polite.

'How are you doing?' Theodore asked, his voice filled with apparent compassion. The assistant closed the door behind him and Eyes was able to relax a little.

'Not great, obviously.'

'Is your wife going to be all right?'

'Yes, she'll be fine, thank you. Thank you for the flowers.'

'Not at all.' Theodore waved a hand dismissively and indicated for Eyes to take a seat.

'And for the help on Saturday, at the house. Thank you.' Eyes held eye contact and let the nod of his head impart the depth of his gratitude.

'You're welcome. It's in everyone's interests to get these messes cleared up as swiftly possible. Now then, I wanted to show you this before the meeting.' He slid a large piece of paper across the huge desk and Eyes leaned closer to look at it.

'Are these the subway schematics?' Eyes asked, looking at the neat lines sprawling across the paper, a street map faintly visible underneath them.

'Indeed.'

'I haven't seen them before,' Eyes said, his curiosity piqued.

'Take a close look,' Theodore said. Eyes glanced up at him and saw a gleam in his eye and an eager smile on his lips. Eyes stood up and leaned on the desk so as to get a good look at the plans from above. He didn't know what he was looking for but he cast his eyes over the lines and tiny writing. He recognised place names and took note of the locations of stations. As he stared at the lines criss-crossing their way from one side of the page to the other a shape began to emerge from the precision and detail. He stopped looking at close details in order to see the bigger picture.

'Huh,' he uttered as he realised what he was looking at. The pattern was neatly hidden in the detail, you needed to layer the underground tunnels with the street map to see it. Even then the criss-crossing roads hid the shape from casual glances. 'The tracks and roads form a pentagram. Why is that, Theodore?' He looked up to see Theodore grinning at him, his fingers steepled in front of his face. He dropped his hands and leaped up from his chair.

'Ley lines,' he said. 'They follow the ley lines.'

Eyes looked back at the map and bent close to see what lay at the centre. He stood up and stared Theodore straight in the eye, unable to hide the shock and apprehension from his face.

'Why is this building at the centre?' he snapped.

'It's all part of the plan,' Theodore said, glee in his voice, his eyes wide. 'The plan to strengthen the city and form a powerful flow of energy so that we can summon him.'

'Summon who?' Eyes asked, edging away slightly.

'The King-of-Glass-and-Steel, of course,' Theodore said, as if it were perfectly obvious. Eyes let out a relieved sigh, though a warning to remain cautious still flared up in his mind.

'Of course,' he said, almost laughing. 'You're sure that he isn't dead, then?'

'Yes, The Watch would have felt it if he had been killed. They didn't, or so Warden swears. I don't believe she would lie about this. It's too important.'

'It's going to take years for the subway to be completed,' Eyes said, raising a sceptical eyebrow.

'We don't need it to be complete. We need these tunnels to be dug.' He pointed at the map and traced the sections of track that made up the pentagram. 'The ritual will take place on the roof here, at the centre. I'll need Wind Talker; all of Caerton's adept ritualists will be required to participate.'

'I'm sure that won't be a problem,' Eyes said with a smile as he thought of how Wind Talker would react to being invited to participate in such an epic ritual.

'I needed to let you know about this plan, it's why I brought you in on this. I need your support in the meeting, you need to back my proposals for order of completion.'

'Of course,' Eyes said, nodding solemnly.

Theodore rolled up the plans and slid them into a tube.

'Let's go to the conference room, it's time.' Theodore held out a hand for Eyes to go ahead and Eyes drew a deep breath. Right now, he had to switch on his best lawyer face and schmooze the hell out of Caerton's most influential humans in order to make this plan work. He felt the pressure acutely but couldn't let it show. This was really happening, he was working for one of the most powerful and least trustworthy shifters in Caerton and doing his bidding in what may be exactly what he claimed, but may also be a Spiral Hand plot to raise evil. *Luna, guide me and give me strength,* he thought as he stepped into the conference room.

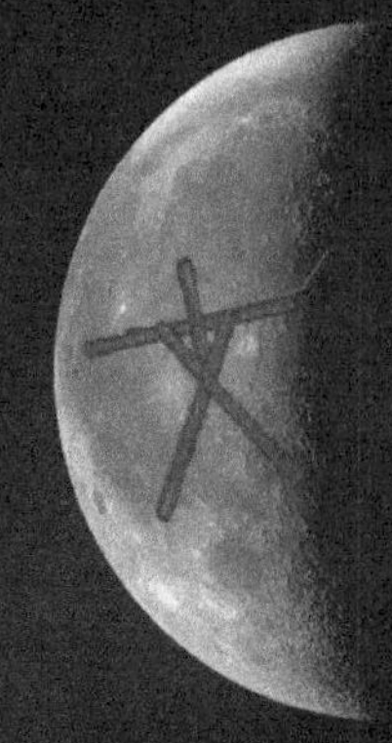

Chapter Eleven

Stalker-of-Night's-Shadow

Stalker was just applying the last few strokes to the third coat of paint in the living room when the front door opened and slammed shut. She put down the roller and wiped her hands on a rag as Claws blustered into the room, his face red and sweating.

'What's wrong?' she asked as he dropped down onto the dust sheet-covered sofa, which billowed up on either side of him and settled slowly.

'The only lead in my case is dead.'

'Oh no, what happened?' she asked, sitting down next to him.

'Washed up in the river. Stabbed.'

'Oh right.' She grimaced. 'So, murdered then. Is it connected to your case?'

'Probably. Maybe. I don't know. He was a shady character, to be honest. A number of people may have wanted him dead for various reasons. But whether it's connected to my case or not, the trail has gone completely cold.'

'Is this the missing mask case?' she asked.

'Yeah.' He sighed. 'I can't talk about it really, client confidentiality and all that. I came up with an idea about the house though.'

'Oh yeah? What's that?'

He turned to her, his face lighting up with an enthusiastic smile.

'Asbestos!' he said, grinning.

'Okay. Am I supposed to fill in the rest of the plan myself?'

'We tell the family that the house is filled with asbestos and they have to move out while we sort it out. Then we have total access to the place on both sides of the veil and they are moved out of harm's way while we sort it out. I'm sure Eyes can acquire some convincing paperwork.'

'That is a really excellent plan,' Stalker said, beaming with pride.

'Thanks,' he replied. His smile faded though, the moment passed and she guessed that his thoughts had returned to the mask and the dead lead.

Wind Talker strode in through the back door and tossed something small through the air. Claws reached out and caught it easily.

'I just finished it for you,' Wind Talker said, sitting down in the chair opposite.

'What is it?' Stalker asked, leaning closer to Claws to see it as he turned it over in his hand. It was a gold ring, like a wedding band. 'Oh Wind Talker, how romantic. But you know there are rules about what pack mates can do with each other, right?' she said, teasing him with a smirk.

'It's an instant blackout,' Wind Talker replied, glaring at her. He turned to Claws. 'You can wear it all the time but when you press it against an electronic device it will cut the power to it. Just be careful how you answer your phone.'

'Thanks,' Claws said, smiling and placing the ring on his right ring finger. 'Don't want to confuse the ladies, do I?' he said, winking at Stalker. She laughed and covered her face.

'Did you ask for it?' she asked him.

'Yeah.'

'I'm not sure Unchained Lightning will be too fond of it. Be careful when and where you use it.'

'I didn't even think of that,' Claws said, looking crestfallen.

'I did,' Wind Talker said. 'It doesn't break anything when used, it just temporarily pauses power flow. It should be okay.'

'How long does it last?' Claws asked.

'No more than a minute. So if you use it to shut off lights or security cameras you have to be quick.'

Stalker wasn't convinced that their ally wouldn't take great offence to the ring, but she didn't want to put a downer on things so she held her silence.

A little while later Weaver emerged from the bedroom, having caught up on her sleep, and the pack set about cooking dinner. Eyes walked in with a flurry of wind and strode into the kitchen looking ready to hit something.

'What's wrong?' Stalker asked, looking up from the tomatoes she was chopping.

'Theodore is using the underground railway to change the flow of energy around Caerton in preparation for summoning the King-of-Glass-and-Steel.' He dropped down into a chair and they all stared at him in stunned silence.

'Don't hold back, mate, give it to us straight,' Claws joked uneasily. Stalker felt a smirk tug at the corner of her mouth but she pressed her lips together to suppress it.

'Are we sure he isn't Spiral Hand?' Weaver asked, her face grim.

No one replied. Stalker wiped the knife she was holding and put it down carefully.

'If this is true, then isn't it a good thing?' she asked. Weaver looked at her and shrugged.

'Yes, of course,' Eyes replied. 'We need the city's soul back, we need to know where it's gone and why. There is just the overwhelmingly huge suspicion that Theodore is not what he claims to be and that this is a much more sinister plot.'

'Well, it's a good job we have you on the inside, keeping an eye on things,' Stalker said, trying to find the bright side.

'True,' Wind Talker said stiffly. 'That will be a very difficult summoning.'

'He wants you there to help,' Eyes said, glancing at Wind Talker. Stalker watched Wind Talker as he looked surprised and then puffed out his chest importantly and cleared his throat.

'Well of course, it would be an honour.'

Stalker laughed, the others cracked smiles too.

They ate and talked, they even laughed a little, which

was nice, and when the meal was done Stalker left the house quietly to patrol. No one questioned or challenged her, it was so normal now for her to slip away after dark.

She returned to the house after an uneventful run, it was well past midnight and the house was dark and quiet. She crept into the front room and eased her feet out of her boots. Wind Talker was absent, already out taking his turn to patrol, but the others were sleeping in their favourite spots: Claws in his human form on the sofa, Weaver curled up on a cushion by the heater and Eyes in his wolf form under the window. Stalker shifted into her fox form and lay down next to him, hoping to comfort him. He stirred, lifting his grey head slightly and made a quiet snuffling noise.

Stalker replied with a gruff little sound from her throat and the two of them settled down to sleep.

When she woke up the others were already getting breakfast and she shifted form to join them.

'I have to go to my house today,' Eyes informed them.

'Do you want me to come with you?' Stalker offered. He shook his head.

'No, human business. I rang around insurance companies and the like yesterday. Someone's coming out to assess the damage today and then I can go ahead and get the work done. The police are releasing my dad's body, so I can arrange the funeral.'

Everyone went quiet and Stalker didn't quite want to look at Eyes.

'Will you want us there?' Weaver asked quietly.

'I'm not sure yet,' he replied. 'I'll let you know. I'm going to set things in motion for getting those asbestos clearance orders sorted out today but it may take a day or two. In the meantime, I want the Legion Way substation thoroughly scouted. We can't let other pack business be forgotten, our patron is waiting for his throne.'

'Of course,' Wind Talker said. 'We'll do that today.'

'Thank you.' Eyes gave Wind Talker an appreciative smile, though Stalker caught a glimpse of tension between them. The awkward tension was broken by Eyes' phone ringing loudly on the table. He scooped it up. 'It's Last-Breath-Echoes,' he said softly. He answered the call and put it straight onto speakerphone. 'Hello?'

'Hi. I thought you should know that I filed a report on your father. It says he was killed by a large dog, probably an Alsatian.'

'Okay,' Eyes replied, closing his eyes and tipping his head back. Stalker let out a slow breath of relief. 'Thank you.'

'No problem,' she replied in her dreamy tone. The line went dead and the Lightning Lords exchanged partial smiles.

'Very handy having her in the morgue,' Claws said softly.

Eyes got up and put his plate by the sink without a word, before heading out of the house. They watched him go and Stalker looked to Weaver for some reassurance that their Alpha would be all right. Weaver shrugged, instinctively knowing Stalker's unasked question and unable to answer it.

Once they were all ready, the rest of the pack crossed the veil and set off for the substation. The streets were quiet, as they usually were in Hepethia, and the pack moved carefully in formation with Stalker in the lead and Wind Talker covering the rear. As they approached the substation, Stalker could hear the hum of electricity and felt the throbbing in the air of the flow of power into the place.

Stalker led them all the way around the block, checking out the substation from all sides. There was only one gate in the high, red brick wall and it was well fortified. The cables overhead all led into the complex and pulsed with electricity flowing through them in and out of the substation.

They made a few circuits of the place, taking it all in and observing what little activity there was. Stalker was a little frustrated. She wanted to get in there and find out what they were really up against. She felt the hairs on her arms stand up and heard a rushing sound approaching. Unchained Lightning flew towards them and circled them; the air all around was suddenly charged with static.

'We're scouting, we were trying to keep a low profile,' Stalker said to the glowing fae with a resigned sigh.

'My apologies,' the elemental said softly.

'Have you been in there?' she asked, pointing at the substation. He nodded slowly.

'I can come and go freely, I am Power.'

'I see.' Stalker drew a slow breath and turned to Wind Talker. 'There was me thinking that we would have to sneak about to find out anything about the tenants.'

'Who occupies the throne now?' Claws asked.

'Let me show you,' the elemental said and flew over the wall into the substation. Stalker looked at the others expectantly and was met with confusion and curiosity. The four of them moved towards the gates into the substation and Wind Talker cleared his throat before lifting his chest and banging his fist on the wood. The knock reverberated around them and a moment later the gates clunked and lurched slightly and the Lightning Lords stepped back out of their way as they swung out towards them.

The gates opened onto the courtyard that Stalker and Claws had seen from the air. In the throne sat a shining blue construct of cables, his eyes were closed and his hands rested lightly on the arms of his throne. The courtyard was filled with activity, tiny motes of energy skipped around the place and electricity elementals scurried in and out in a blur. They moved as if they were carrying small bundles and their figures were hunched in supplication as they dashed towards and backed away from the throne. Stalker watched in awe, it was like a strange electrical tide around a tiny island. As she watched, she noticed that with each influx the elementals deposited their tiny bundles at the feet of the throne before flowing away.

Unchained Lightning was floating above the wall to one side, watching the scene with unreadable eyes. The building at the back of the courtyard was emitting clunking and whooshing noises at regular intervals and through a window Stalker could make out machinery moving inside.

'That's Glimmering Wires,' Wind Talker whispered and nodded towards the peaceful-looking elemental in the throne. 'He's strong. Can you feel it?'

Stalker nodded slowly. There was radiation flowing from the elemental and she felt in her core why the minor elementals entering the substation were stooped in a permanent bow.

'There are others,' Unchained Lightning crackled as he swooped down to stand beside them. 'Charge-of-Power and Sparking Clank. They call themselves the Sparkblood Conglomerate. They share the throne.'

'Nice,' Stalker said, her insides churning with the visceral images of congealing blood that the name evoked.

Glimmering Wires opened his eyes and looked directly at the Lightning Lords, unsurprised to see them. Stalker got the impression that he had been aware of their presence and was now, finally, granting them audience.

'What do you want?' His voice jingled like wind chimes and caught Stalker off guard.

'Forgive us,' Claws said, stepping forwards from their huddle. 'We have come to pay our respects. We claim this territory for our kind and thought it was about time we acquainted ourselves with the most powerful residents.'

'Ahh.' Glimmering Wires sighed and nodded slowly. 'You are Unchained Lightning's pets.'

Stalker shot a sideways glance at their patron and wondered if that was how he had described them, or if the word came from Glimmering Wires.

'That's not quite how we would phrase it,' Wind Talker said slowly. 'But yes.'

'You will serve us, as he does. Bring us more power, children of the lightning, and we shall get along just fine.'

Unchained Lightning flickered slightly and a small charge of static rippled through the air. Stalker sensed anger brewing inside him but he seemed to have it under control.

'We shall see what we can do,' Claws said with a slight bow of his head. 'Many thanks for allowing us entry.'

There was a sudden movement behind the throne and the ground shuddered. Stalker grasped hold of Weaver's arm and they looked at each other anxiously. A shape rose up from the metal, seeming to separate itself from it and its heavy feet thudded as it moved around the throne to face them. The construct was made of plates of metal that ground against each other, showering the ground around it with friction sparks. Bits of the construct clunked and clanged about inside its cavernous body. It wasn't humanoid, it took the form of a small tank on four lumbering limbs and its head bobbed slightly as it moved; its yellow lamp-like eyes shone with wisdom.

'Sparking Clank, I presume?' Claws said, a slight tremble in his voice as he squared up to the eight-foot tall construct. It nodded its head and there was a low rumble in its chest. 'We are honoured to meet you.'

Stalker watched the construct move slowly around the throne. Glimmering Wires watched it carefully too, his eyes narrowed to slits. There was a rivalry there, she could sense it and she wondered if that would prove to be a weakness that they could exploit. Curious to see if her ability to see others' inner truths could be extended to such alien entities as elementals and constructs, Stalker locked her gaze onto the glowing gaps in Glimmering Wires' face that were his narrowed eyes, and probed with her mind. She rooted through miles and miles of compact cabling, a jumble of thoughts and existence that made no sense to her. He was so different from human or shifter and his innermost being reflected that. She focused hard and continued to probe without him seeming to notice. She caught glimpses of images and flashes of light that stung her mind. She persevered and suddenly stumbled across a hidden secret, buried deep within his mind. It was obvious really but she was glad to confirm it, rather than having to work on a hunch, and she quickly pulled her mind out of his and back into herself with a gasp.

Weaver and Wind Talker glanced at her and she quickly looked between their worried faces and tried to brush off their concern. Nobody else seemed to be looking at her strangely so she hoped that it was only her pack mates who had noticed anything odd.

'Prove your worth,' Sparking Clank said in an ominous, deep rumble. A hatch on his belly opened and several car batteries thumped to the floor. Claws inched forwards carefully and picked one of them up.

'What would you like us to do?' he asked.

'Burn,' the construct replied.

Stalker looked around in alarm and Claws glanced uncertainly back at Wind Talker, who remained calm and nodded once. Stalker watched as Claws dug his fingernails into the join along one edge of the battery and ripped it open with a grunt. The acid spilled out over his hands and arms with a ferocious hiss and smoke billowed up from his skin. His body shook and back arched and Stalker tensed herself, ready to grab him and subdue him if the beast took over. Claws took a slow, shaking breath and tossed the battery onto the floor as his temper settled.

Sparking Clank shifted his weight and seemed to tilt his head thoughtfully for a moment. A strange noise issued from his metal jaws, a sound like nails spilling onto the floor and Stalker realised the construct was laughing. 'I like you,' he rumbled and turned to leave.

Claws looked down at his smoking hands and Stalker stepped cautiously to his side to give him a reassuring pat on the shoulder. His skin was badly burned and there was a hint of an un-shed tear at the corner of his eye.

'Let's head back to the house,' Weaver urged, her eyes darting around anxiously.

'Good idea,' Stalker replied.

Claws bowed to Glimmering Wires and the elemental waved a lazy hand to dismiss them. They backed out through the gate, Unchained Lightning floating along with them and once they were out in the street the gates swung shut.

'Are you all right?' Stalker asked Claws. He nodded and gave his hands a shake.

'Let's go,' Wind Talker said gruffly and they set off at a jog. Stalker kept her eyes peeled for trouble. As they reached the end of Legion Way, Stalker caught sight of the two huge, black birds that they had seen watching them several times. They cawed and took flight from their roof-top perch. As the pack turned the corner Stalker stopped in her tracks at the sight of a man hanging by his neck from a road sign on the other side of the road. The others came to a halt, Wind Talker bumped into her and she flung out a hand to hold them all back. The body turned slowly, limp and lifeless, and yet the bulging eyes were alive and focused on the Lightning Lords.

'That's Reeve-of-the-Condemned, an agent of something called The Hundred Court,' Wind Talker whispered.

'That doesn't sound good,' Stalker replied.

Unchained Lightning flew overhead, circling the pack

and then dipping down into the street just behind them. He watched the hanged man carefully and crackled with static as if waiting for instruction.

The hanged man raised a grey, withered hand and pointed at them with one bony finger.

'You will be judged,' he said, his voice a hoarse whisper.

'Oh good,' Weaver said with a loud sigh and Stalker looked at her sharply, confused. 'Well the name and appearance rather suggested that we had already been judged and found guilty. If the judgement is yet to happen then maybe we can prepare a defence,' she explained quietly.

'What crime are we accused of?' Claws called out to it.

'Sins of the father,' the demon croaked cryptically. 'You must attend the hearing on the next half moon.'

'When is that?' Stalker whispered.

'Monday,' Claws replied, a crack in his voice. That was his moon, he was as attuned to the half moon as Stalker was to the new moon.

'How do we prepare for this hearing?' Wind Talker called out.

'Arrive alive,' the demon replied, a sickening rasp to his voice. The body slowly rotated again and seemed to grow thinner until it had vanished.

'Do you know where this Hundred Court is held?' Claws asked Unchained Lightning.

'The Court House,' he replied. His eyes rolled in their huge sockets. He rose off the ground and took off back towards Grove Street. Stalker caught Weaver's eye and they exchanged small smiles.

'Obviously,' Stalker mouthed and Weaver started to

laugh but quickly stopped herself. They moved quickly and quietly through the streets back to the house and only crossed the veil once safely inside. Wind Talker stomped through the house, his face red and temper obviously frayed.

'What's wrong?' Weaver asked him.

'It was probably on the map,' he snapped. 'The Hundred Court was probably on the map but it was stolen. St. Mark's doesn't have a court house, it's not as simple as our patron would have us believe.'

'Maybe it used to have one, like the Watchtower, it's not a Roman look out now, it's Claws' office building, but in Hepethia it's still the Watchtower,' Weaver said, her optimism undeterred by Wind Talker's bluster.

'It wasn't on the map,' Claws said with a nod of certainty. He tapped a finger to his temple. 'Photographic memory.'

'Eyes might know,' Stalker suggested. 'Perhaps he came across the history of the judiciary in Caerton in his law education.'

'Good point,' Wind Talker said, his temper beginning to settle. 'We'll ask him later. We only have four days until the half moon, we can't sit on this.'

'We won't,' Stalker said, firmly.

Eyes didn't return to Grove Street until late that night, having spent the day sorting things out at his house and then spending time with his family.

'I snuck out after they were asleep,' he explained. 'I feel dirty.'

Stalker gave him a hug and made him a cup of coffee.

'Do you know if St. Mark's used to have its own

courthouse?' she asked him. Eyes frowned.

'Yes it did, it was knocked down in the fifties when everything was centralised. Why?'

'The birds and weird demons that have been watching us are envoys of something called The Hundred Court,' Weaver told him. 'One of them spoke to us today and told us we have to attend a hearing on Monday.'

'What are the charges?' Eyes asked, his eyes wide with surprise.

'We don't really know, all we were told was that it was to do with "the sins of the father",' Stalker said. 'So, I think it must be to do with the Blue Moon.'

'Remember the Knight-of-Shadowed-Fear said that he expected us to keep the bargains he made with the Blue Moon?' Weaver said. 'I'm sure he isn't the only one who expects that. Demons are tricky like that and elementals are too primal to be able to distinguish easily where one pack ends and another begins.'

'Do you know where the old court house was?' Stalker asked Eyes.

'No, but it'll be public record,' he replied.

'I was thinking about the house we need to heal,' Claws said. 'We should research it, check the news archives, investigate the family. See what we can find. I was going to go to the library tomorrow to do that, I could look up the court house too.'

'Good idea,' Eyes said, his face lighting up. 'Stalker, you go with him and help.'

Stalker blinked at him, research was hardly her forte. She wasn't about to question his orders, however and she simply nodded in agreement.

The following morning, Stalker and Claws set off for the library in Caerton city centre, taking his car and parking right by the central plaza. It was a sunny day, though there was still a distinct chill in the air and the streets bustled with workers and shoppers, while buses and cars sat chugging out fumes in the sluggish traffic. One of the major roads that surrounded the plaza was closed and traffic was being diverted away from it. Stalker glanced at the sign tied to a lamppost informing people of the road closure.

'It's for the underground,' she muttered to Claws as they hurried past the cordoned off area. Deafening drilling shook the ground and filled the air with dust.

'Oh?'

'Looks like there'll be a station right here in the city centre.'

They walked briskly across the plaza to the library and Claws led the way upstairs to the computer room.

There were a couple of students working quietly and an old man sat at a desk reading a newspaper, the room was quiet but for the hum of a dozen computers. Claws shrugged off his jacket and flung it over the back of a chair. Stalker sank down into the chair next to it and opened a browser on the computer.

'I don't even know where to look,' she whispered.

'Here.' Claws leaned over and typed an address in, a digital news archive site opened up and he gave her a wink. 'I use it a lot for work. You see what you can find about the house. I'll check the electoral register for the name of the family and go from there.'

Stalker nodded and started putting in search terms

that might yield results. She was still scrolling through useless articles a few minutes later when Claws let out a little "whoop" and leaned over. 'Got them. Just one adult registered at that address, Julia Bennett.'

'Great, thanks, that should help me here.'

She added the surname to the search and immediately got some likely-looking results. She scanned the headlines and clicked on one that read "Murder in St. Mark's".

Local entrepreneur, George Bennett, was found dead in his home yesterday morning following a burglary. His wife, Julia Bennett, and their two-year-old daughter, were away visiting family and discovered the body upon returning home.

This is not the first time such a tragedy has befallen the occupants of this property. Shortly after its construction in 1937, the owner, Leonard Finchley, was brutally stabbed by an escaped convict.

Stalker stopped reading and took a few notes. She slid the note paper across the table to Claws, who looked down to read it. They exchanged nervous glances and Stalker went back to the search results to look for more. The pair of them spent several hours digging up everything they could find. Between them they managed to plot out a timeline for the house and noted many of its previous owners. There was a record of planning permission acquired for a nuclear bunker in the fifties and Stalker thought of the door in the basement with a shiver. In the sixties, the owner who had had the bunker built was killed by a pack of wild dogs. Stalker read over the article that mentioned this several times, a hard knot forming in her stomach.

The property was later auctioned off and bought by the

B. M. Development Consultancy, who promptly renovated it and sold it on. The company folded shortly after this. 'No prizes for guessing what the funds were used for,' Stalker muttered. Sure enough, the Blue Moon Betting Shop officially opened for business three months after the development company went under.

'I think we've got everything we need here,' Claws said as he shut down the browser. Stalker did the same and followed him out of the computer room. He led her to another room on the top floor of the huge city library, where paper archives were kept. The assistant greeted them as they entered. 'We're looking for old maps of the city, specifically St. Mark's from about seventy years ago.'

The assistant showed them where to look and soon they were rolling out an old, yellowed street map of Caerton. Stalker leaned over it, intrigued. It was huge, covering a large table and the assistant helpfully placed paperweights on the corners for them and then left them to it.

'Look,' Stalker said, pointing to a spot just over halfway up the map. She had immediately looked for the most obvious, familiar place: Grove Street. That would orient them. The city had changed enormously in the last seventy years. On this map there was no telecoms tower, in fact, Redfield wasn't there at all, it was still countryside. Most of Northgate was still rural too, with the industrial area of the city confined to the docks on the coast and riverside. There was even some of the old Roman city wall still standing there, including the north gate that the area came to be named after. 'I wonder what happened to the wall.'

'Probably damaged in the blitz,' Claws replied, also

scanning the map carefully. 'Or torn down afterwards in the name of progress.'

Stalker ran her gaze down the river, looking for the courthouse. To the west of Grove Street she found St. Mark's church, marked by a cross on the map and just opposite it was a small, slightly smudged black crown.

'There!' She jabbed the paper with her finger. In tiny, faded writing under the crown were the words *Arlow Crown Court*. 'What's there now?'

'A car park,' Claws replied.

'Shame,' she said. Historical landmarks being torn down and replaced with concrete monstrosities should be illegal, she thought.

'Why is it called Arlow Crown Court do you think?' she asked.

'I guess that's what the area used to be called.' Claws gave a shrug.

They packed up the map but before leaving Claws got the most recent street map of the city and made a copy of it on the library's special printer for large copies.

'We can start fresh, make our own map,' he said as he rolled it up. Stalker thought it was a good idea and a nice thing to do for Wind Talker.

As they walked back to the car Stalker found her thoughts running over everything they had pulled up on the house. She felt a bitter taste rise in her throat. It seemed like the Blue Moon were haunting them, their legacy was the bane of the Lightning Lords. How were they supposed to move on when they had constant reminders of their fallen pack? Could the mentors that she had trusted so much when they took her in really be behind so much death? She didn't want to think about it but she was going to have to confront the answer to one question, at least. What secret were they hiding in that bunker?

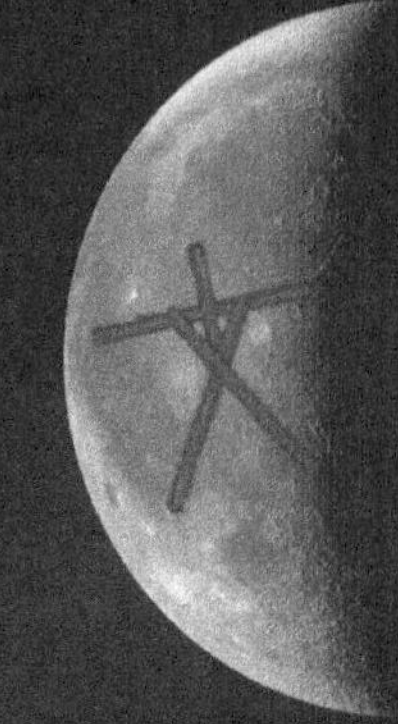

Chapter Twelve

Fights-Eyes-Open

—. 18th February .—

Monday morning rolled around and Eyes drove slowly across St. Mark's, his palms sweating and his gaze flickering frequently to the legal documents folded neatly in an envelope on the passenger seat. It was a stretch to describe them as "legal" and now he owed his shady solicitor contact two significant favours.

He pulled up outside the house and took some deep breaths before picking up the envelope and making his way from his car to the door. His hand shook as he raised it to ring the bell. He could hear movement inside and a woman called out to someone else as she approached the front door. It was flung open and a slightly flustered woman stood in the doorway, a child's lunch box in one hand and hair brush in the other.

'Mrs Bennett?' Eyes asked, though he knew instantly

who she was.

'Can I help?' she asked, her voice cracking with stress and a deep frown on her brow.

'I'm afraid I have to serve notice that your property has been red flagged as containing asbestos.' He held out the envelope and she took it hesitantly. 'You and your family will need to evacuate the property within 24 hours and allow access to workers to remove the asbestos.'

Mrs Bennett glared at him and she ripped open the envelope. She skim read the documents, flicking through the pages. Eyes glanced around her cautiously and saw a young girl, a few years older than Amy, standing a little way up the hall looking at him with curiosity. She had dark circles under her eyes and chewed on her finger as she watched him through her bushy brown hair. He felt a flutter in his gut and couldn't help but be reminded of his own daughter. Resolve planted itself within him and he drew himself up to his full height. If this plan worked, he would not only be healing his own family but this one too. They were doing a good thing and he was not going to waste any more hesitation or guilt on the matter.

'This is ridiculous,' Julia Bennett snapped. 'We can't just evacuate our house at a moment's notice.'

'It's a court order, I'm afraid,' Eyes said stiffly. 'We need to ensure the property is safe for your family, Mrs Bennett.'

He seemed to have said the right words as the harassed-looking woman closed her eyes and breathed deeply before nodding.

'Of course,' she whispered. 'I'm just about to take my daughter to school. I'll make the arrangements today.'

'Thank you. I do apologise for the inconvenience.' He meant it sincerely and she nodded in acceptance of his apology. 'I'll return tomorrow morning with the crew to collect the keys.'

She nodded again and closed the door. Eyes turned and walked briskly to his car, his hands were trembling as he got behind the wheel. He sighed with relief that the worst was over and set off for Grove Street.

The rest of the pack were finishing breakfast and getting ready. Claws had his suit on and sat nervously on the sofa waiting for the others.

'How did it go?' he asked as Eyes sat down next to him.

'Fine. She seemed to believe it anyway, we can start tomorrow.'

'Good. Do you think this hearing is going to be much like a human one?'

'I highly doubt it,' Eyes replied with a slight smile.

Wind Talker came jogging down the stairs and into the living room. Eyes tried not to laugh at the sight of him in a suit, his broad shoulders and chest stretching the fabric at the seams and one of Claws' ties tied badly at his throat. 'Very nice,' Eyes said with a barely hidden smile.

'It's symbolic,' Wind Talker said, adjusting the tie.

Weaver and Stalker came in from the kitchen, chattering nervously and finishing their breakfast, both dressed in smart clothes and looking nothing like themselves. The blue had nearly washed out of Stalker's hair now, but she had it scraped back in a short pony tail and a shiny black Alice band on her head.

'Are we all ready to go?' Eyes asked, standing up.

There was a jumbled chorus of affirmative replies and

Eyes led them out to his car. He drove them the short distance to St. Mark's Church. It stood on a raised mound, surrounded by neatly cut grass and a road ran all the way around the base with other roads leading away from it like a huge wheel. Opposite the eastern side of the church was a small multi-storey car park and Eyes pulled into it and found a space on the ground floor.

'What do we do?' Stalker asked quietly. Eyes looked at her in the rear view mirror and took a deep breath.

'I think we just cross over and see where we end up,' he replied.

Like at the house, the five of them crossed the veil in Eyes' car, hidden from view in the dark car park behind tinted windows. Their feet found the floor and Eyes looked quickly around. He drew a sharp breath as he came face to face with a vast construct in the small lobby that they had emerged in. The demon had hundreds of tentacles that rifled through thousands of sheets of paper and tiny creatures scuttled around it collecting and delivering documents. The construct stopped and peered at him with its eyes, all twenty of them.

'What do you want?' Its voice was like the rustling of paper.

'We're here for a hearing,' Eyes replied. 'We're the Lightning Lords.'

'Ah, yesssss,' the demon hissed and smiled, showing rows of sharp teeth. Eyes leaned away in alarm and felt his pack mates against his back. Claws put a hand on his shoulder and patted it, Eyes stood tall and glared at the demon. 'This way.' It moved aside and held out a dozen tentacles to indicate the hall behind it. Eyes squeezed through the small space into the corridor and he looked back to see the pack follow him.

'Thank you,' Claws said as he passed the construct and it gave him a small nod.

They made their way down the dimly lit, panelled corridor, their footsteps loud against the wooden floor. The smell of polish filled Eyes' nostrils and he wrinkled his nose. He could make out a wooden door ahead but it seemed to take an age to reach it, the corridor kept expanding and keeping the door out of reach. He walked briskly, determination driving him forwards, through the frustration that rumbled beneath the surface. The gap gradually closed, and finally he grasped the handle and pushed the door open.

Bright light met him and he blinked against it as he stepped out into the open space before him. The others followed close behind and spread out to stare up at the courtroom around them. Eyes felt sand beneath his feet and as he took a few cautious steps he felt it seep into his shoes. All around them were tiered wooden benches and the court was open to the blue sky. Straight ahead was a sheltered platform with large chairs and a red and gold banner hanging over a judge's bench, on it was emblazoned a golden lion, the Lion of Saint Mark. It was all rather like a gladiatorial arena, which didn't give him the greatest confidence that this was going to be a fair trial.

Behind the bench was a tall, thin figure, shrouded in shadow from the canopy over its head. Eyes squinted, hoping to make out more detail, but the demon blended perfectly into the shadows. All around them on the seats were dozens of figures, all chattering eagerly and watching the shifters carefully. Eyes saw the hawk-headed demon and the hanged man that his pack mates had described to him. There was a beautiful woman sitting close to the judge, she shimmered silver and blue and Eyes felt serene as he looked at her. All around the arena were crows and ravens and at the edges of the pit were dozens of small, black imps wielding sharp implements. They twitched and jabbered in croaky voices. Beside the judge stood a towering figure with long, serrated blades hanging from its shoulders all around its body instead of arms.

Unchained Lightning flew down from the clear, blue sky and landed with an impressive thud in the sand beside Eyes. Behind the Lightning Lords, the wooden door slammed shut and Eyes flinched. The small imps suddenly rushed forwards and Eyes felt something sharp stab his leg and searing pain in his hand. He yanked his hand up and the pain was blinding. His eyes re-focused and he saw that a black, iron poker was sticking straight through his right palm and another dug into his calf. He snarled and kicked at the imp on the other end of the pokers but it merely cackled at him.

All around him his pack were similarly impaled, the smell of blood reached his nose and snapping, snarling sounds issued from the other shifters as they struggled to retain their composure.

'Test their guilt,' a commanding voice boomed out from the judge's bench and Eyes began to convulse; he dropped to his knees, feeling the coarse sand beneath him. Memories flooded his mind, of every pain and hurt he had ever inflicted on anyone he cared about. The two dead Witches' faces, almost identical as they were, jumped out at him as clear as day. His family were there, bleeding, broken and traumatised and Eyes began to sob. The convulsions became worse and he felt a hard knot in his stomach begin to pulse and rise into his chest. His throat felt tight and wet and he knew what was coming just a second before he vomited on the sand beneath him.

He dropped face down to the floor next to the contents of his stomach, his breath short and sharp in his aching throat and chest. His body fell still and his vision slowly returned to normal. He heard the groans of his pack around him and lifted his head enough to see Wind Talker collapsed in a heap nearby, his face pale and clammy and the residue of vomit on his chin.

Eyes made himself sit up, even though his body ached. He looked around and saw that he and Wind Talker had fared far worse than the others. Weaver knelt down beside him and placed a tender hand on his shoulder.

'Are you all right?' she whispered. He nodded and Weaver hastily helped him to his feet. He dusted the sand from his suit and cleared his throat. Eyes winced as the imps withdrew their implements and retreated to the edges of the pit. The figures on the benches cackled with glee, fingers were pointed and noisy chatter filled the air.

'Silence!' a booming voice commanded and the crowd obeyed.

The figure behind the bench leaned forwards into the light. The judge wore a black gown and had at least six arms protruding from its sides and its face was an iron mask. 'You stand before the Hundred Court to be judged for your crimes. How do you plead?'

'We cannot possibly enter a plea without knowledge of

specific charges,' Eyes called out.

'Failure to uphold bargains,' a silky voice said. Eyes looked for the source and saw the creature with bladed arms drifting down from the seats and landing softly on the sand in front of the judge.

'Jagged-Knives-of-Guilt,' Wind Talker said, his voice hoarse as he addressed the demon approaching them. 'Which bargains?'

'Many,' Jagged-Knives replied. 'Ancient and recent.'

'We don't have any ancient bargains,' Eyes said, confusion gnawing at him. 'We're a new pack.'

'There are ancient bargains that we all have to uphold, like the Danegeld,' Wind Talker said, a slight edge of scorn to his voice. Eyes glared at him for a moment but knew that this was not the time or place to address his attitude.

'They are not here to be judged,' Unchained Lightning boomed and Eyes glanced at him with uncertainty and appreciation in equal measure. 'They are here to seek clarification and came of their own free will.'

Jagged-Knives scowled and backed away slightly as the court erupted into shouts and jeers.

'It's true, your honour.' Eyes searched for the source of the soft voice. It was the shimmering woman, she was standing up and almost iridescent. 'They came willingly.'

'We did,' Claws called out, emitting his calming presence and authority. 'We have no wish to break any bargains and seek to clarify the matter so that we can rectify any wrongdoing and clear any unfounded charges.'

'That's right,' Eyes said, spurred on by his pack. 'We petition the court for a full body of evidence so that we can prepare a defence.'

'There are those who have reason to complain about your pack's conduct of late,' the judge stated. 'Those who claim to have collaborated with the Blue Moon in the past,'

'We are not the Blue Moon,' Eyes interrupted.

'You are a continuation of their line and must answer for their crimes, as well as your own.'

'I won't accept that,' Eyes said, his patience strained.

'We are not a complete continuation,' Claws said calmly. 'I was never a member of the Blue Moon, nor was our patron, Unchained Lightning. We make this pack a new, separate entity who happens to now claim some of the same territory as the previous pack.'

'They are the Blue Moon,' Jagged-Knives snapped. 'Half of the Blue Moon perished but half of them stand here today.'

The crowd erupted again in renewed shouts both for and against the Lightning Lords. Eyes tried to pick out the friendly voices in the crowd but the demons and fae were in many cases so alien that it was impossible to read them. The shimmering woman was enigmatic, she had spoken up for them, but she was keeping her counsel now, watching calmly from her seat. 'The survivors of that pack must pay for the crimes of their fellows.' Jagged-Knives clicked his blades together ominously and paced the floor.

'I cannot ignore the fact that they have a new pack mate and patron,' the judge said calmly, drawing the crowd to order with his hypnotic voice.

'We are a unit,' Claws said. 'A balanced pack at that, blessed by Artemis herself. We cannot be separated out as former-Blue-Moon and never-Blue-Moon. We are simply the Lightning Lords. If you were to convict and punish my pack mates then you would also have to punish myself and Unchained Lightning, whom are undoubtedly innocent of any crime you care to find. You cannot punish the innocent or there is no justice.'

There was a ripple around the gathered audience, a murmur of agreement, even from those who had a moment ago opposed them so fiercely and Eyes allowed himself to hope.

'I accept your argument,' the judge said slowly and clearly. 'Let all of Hepethia know that the Lightning Lords are not the Blue Moon. They shall be judged independently from their predecessors and must make their own way in the world, free of the Blue Moon's debts but also their protections.'

There were cries and shouts from the crowd and Jagged-Knives looked ready to slit throats over the judgement. 'You will still be judged, though,' the judge finished.

Eyes narrowed his eyes and felt frustration pounding in his temples.

'Judged for what crime?' he called out over the din and the court fell quiet, all eyes upon him. 'I have made mistakes, I have done things that I wish I could undo and people that I love have been hurt. I feel responsible for the loss of my sires. I feel the guilt. I don't need a judge to find me guilty, I must bear my guilt myself every day. Those whom I have wronged may judge me.'

'Wrong!' bellowed the judge. 'I may judge you.' One of his arms lashed out and stretched across the space between them. At the end of the arm was a deformed hand with only three thick fingers and a piercing blue eye in the centre of the palm. The hand planted itself firmly on Eyes' forehead and sent searing pain through his head as the eye probed his memories. He stumbled and bent forwards as the pain filled his veins. The hand remained fixed to his forehead.

His step-father's face came first, pale and splattered with blood and his mother's screams punctuated the memory. This was the man who had raised him and loved him as his own, dead because of Eyes. But then there was Fortune, whispering in his ear, telling him to get out and keep the others safe before being ripped to pieces and burned. Eyes' composure cracked and tears began to streak down his face. Fortune had sacrificed himself so that his son might live, the son he had been forced to leave as an infant, the son he hadn't seen again until the day he had shifted for the first time. Two fathers lost to the same foe.

The tentacle-like hand withdrew and the dark eyes inside the iron mask of the judge looked at Eyes shrewdly. 'Case dismissed,' the judge hissed.

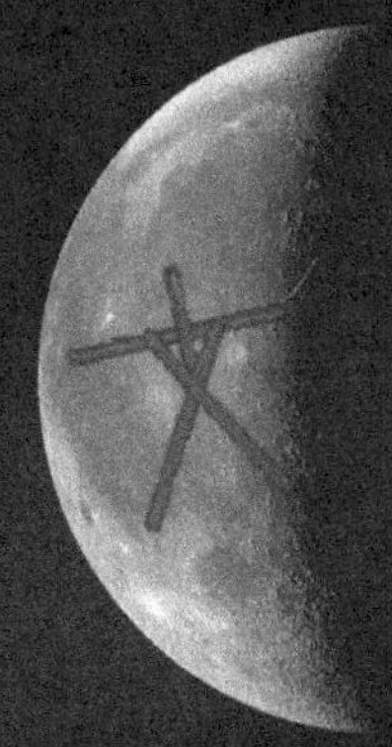

Chapter Thirteen

Stalker-of-Night's-Shadow

The Lightning Lords hurried from the court before the judge changed his mind or Jagged-Knives took issue with the outcome. Unchained Lightning took off into the sky and the shifters made their way to the end of the hall where they had crossed over, right in front of the administration construct, who was still busily filing papers.

Wind Talker used his talisman to look across the veil and indicated that it was safe to cross. They arrived back in the Alpha's car, roughly deposited into their own seats. Stalker closed her eyes for a moment and ran over the events of the hearing in her mind. Something Eyes had said stuck out at her, about his "sires", and the judge had evidently found something in his head to convince him to dismiss the case. She opened her eyes and observed him carefully. He looked exhausted as he sat in the driver's seat next to her, his eyes closed, catching his breath and running his hands through his hair, just like Fortune.

Stalker blinked and cocked her head as the cogs clicked into place. He had said "sires" in the courtroom, multiple fathers. She gasped in realisation and questions popped into her head and almost tumbled out of her mouth.

'Let's get out of here,' Claws said quietly, breaking the silence and preventing her from blurting out anything about Fortune.

'I know a place we can go to unwind,' Weaver said softly from the middle of the back seat. They set off, Eyes paying at the exit. It was nearly dark as they pulled out into the lit street. It had felt like they were in the Hundred Court for no more than half an hour but an entire day had passed.

'What was the name of that blue fae back there?' Stalker asked, twisting to face Wind Talker.

'Nicaea,' he replied. 'Some sort of Naiad, a water nymph.'

'I wonder why she spoke up for us.' Stalker sat straight in her seat and stared out of the front wind screen. No one replied.

Weaver directed Eyes north through St. Mark's towards Northgate. They turned off the main road onto a wide, leafy avenue of relatively new houses and Weaver instructed Eyes to park.

'Where are we going?' Stalker asked as they all climbed out of the car.

'You'll see,' Weaver replied with a grin. She led them up a narrow side street and took a sharp right up an alley that ran along the back of the terrace and came to a halt in the dark. She looked back and caught Stalker's eye, giving her a wink before stepping across the veil. Stalker glanced over her shoulder to check that the others were with them and then followed Weaver.

She emerged in a beautiful wood, with no houses to be seen. The half moon overhead shone through the tree branches, dappled silver moonlight covered the floor. The trees were covered in leaves and as Stalker looked more closely, she saw fruit on them.

'Wrong time of year for apples, isn't it?' she asked, her voice edged with curiosity.

'This is The Orchard, it's always autumn here, the fruit is always ripe.' Weaver smiled and led them along the narrow path between trees. They arrived in a small clearing with a wooden barrel in the centre, bathed in moonlight. The trees around them whispered in the wind and Stalker strained to hear what they were saying.

'I think we're supposed to pick the apples,' Wind Talker said softly, gazing around.

Weaver reached for the nearest low hanging branch and grasped one of the small apples. She glanced at the rest of the pack and Stalker gave her an encouraging nod, eager to see what would happen. Weaver tugged the apple and it came away from its branch easily. A sigh rippled around them and sweet music drifted into the clearing.

Stalker took an apple and the music grew a little louder. As the others picked more fruit the melody gradually filled the air, a merry jig urging them on. Stalker laughed and began picking the apples more quickly, tossing them into the barrel and the others followed her lead. She threw an apple to Weaver but she missed the catch and it fell to the floor with a soft thud and rolled over to the barrel. As

Weaver stooped to pick it up she stopped and Stalker ran over to see that she was all right.

'Look,' Weaver said with wonder in her voice. Rising out of the ground around the base of the barrel were five wooden goblets.

Stalker picked up a goblet and stood up to peer into the barrel. The apples that they had thrown into it were gone and a shimmering pale liquid filled it instead. She grinned and scooped up the juice into her goblet. She took a big swig, expecting it to be apple juice but the sweet tang of alcohol met her tongue instead.

'It's cider,' she said after swallowing. The others eagerly filled their goblets and drank and the music around them picked up even more, pounding a relentless and infectious rhythm. Stalker moved to the music, a feeling of euphoria filling her body and mind. Weaver began to dance and Stalker grabbed her hand to dance with her. They burst into laughter and Stalker glanced at the men, who were watching with smiles. 'Come on!' she called. 'Join in!' She ran to Eyes, grasped his hand and dipped under their joined hands in a little spin. He laughed and started dancing, though with rather less grace than her or Weaver. Reluctantly, Claws and Wind Talker joined the dance too and the five of them formed a chain and danced around the clearing, weaving between the trees at the edges and filing past the barrel to refill their goblets every once in a while.

The music began to slow and the dance wound down as the shifters grew tired. Stalker dropped to the floor and lay down, staring up at the starlit sky; the ground was crisp and cool beneath her.

'Eyes,' Weaver said softly. 'What was that about in the court?'

Eyes sighed heavily and one by one the others sat in a loose circle. Stalker sat up and propped her heavy head on her hand. Her vision was a little fuzzy from the cider and she blinked to try and clear it.

'Fortune was my real father,' Eyes said quietly.

'Ha!' Stalker burst out, sitting abruptly to attention. 'I am not surprised!' Everyone ignored her, all attention on Eyes.

'The man in my kitchen was my step-father, he raised me from when I was a little boy. I never knew Fortune until the day I changed and he took me into the Blue Moon. After a few days he told me the truth.'

Stalker sobered a little. She thought of how fatherly Fortune had always been and how much that had mattered to her. It must have been amplified a thousand times for Eyes. She understood better now his intense need for vengeance.

The Orchard sighed and the music turned sombre.

'I think we're supposed to each share something personal,' Weaver whispered, looking around at the trees and up at the moon overhead.

'Claws,' Wind Talker spoke up quickly. 'Why haven't you embraced your inner beast?'

Stalker watched Claws carefully, she had a little understanding of his anthropocentric nature from their one-on-one chats but as far as she was aware, none of the others had talked to him about it. He took his time, choosing his words carefully.

'It took me a long time to get comfortable in my human

skin. I grew up with self-esteem issues and had to work hard to overcome them. I was really only just happy with myself when I changed, so learning how to love myself again after such a massive change is just as difficult, if not more.' Claws took a long, slow drink of cider. No one spoke. Stalker wanted to say something reassuring, but was at a loss for words.

'What are you scared of, Weaver?' Eyes asked, his eyes dark.

'Drowning,' Weaver replied quickly. Stalker looked at her quizzically and wondered if she was using a euphemism. Weaver took a drink from her goblet and didn't meet Stalker's gaze.

'Is that all?' Stalker asked gently.

'No,' Weaver replied with an enigmatic smile. 'I guess I'm pretty scared of losing any of you lot too.' Stalker nodded and tried to catch Weaver's eye to give her an encouraging smile, but Weaver's gaze was fixed on the fallen leaves in front of her.

'Stalker?' Claws asked hesitantly. 'Have you ever been afraid to tell us something important?'

She glared at him, he wouldn't meet her eyes. She knew full well that he knew exactly what he was asking and she fought the urge to leap up and smack him around the head.

'I don't believe so,' she replied, her teeth clenched. 'I wasn't too keen on telling Eyes about the vandalism at the house, but that wasn't fear.' She was not going to say anything about Rhys, that was her own, private burden and she didn't appreciate Claws trying to prise it out of her. The Orchard rustled around them and she glanced anxiously up at the quivering branches. It seemed like it knew that she had not been honest and she chewed her tongue as she wrestled with conflicting obligations. 'I guess there is something.' She paused, thinking furiously for an alternative, equally truthful secret. 'I am scared of losing my temper at work and hurting a student. That worries me a lot actually and I've never spoken to you about it because I was afraid of looking weak or burdening any of you with my own stuff.'

Claws rolled his eyes but didn't press the issue. She lifted her chin and looked at him defiantly. 'Wind Talker?' she said quickly, not allowing anyone else a chance to quiz her. 'Who do you most want to kill?'

'The Alpha,' he replied immediately. Stalker nearly choked on her cider and spat it out in a dramatic spray into the circle. Her gaze switched rapidly between him and Eyes, gauging what was going on. Eyes was impassive, his gaze lowered to the ground, his fingers caressing the rim of his goblet. It seemed this was not a surprise to him. She knew there was tension between them and Wind Talker had wanted to be Alpha when they first formed their new pack, but she hadn't realised he wanted it that badly.

The Orchard sighed again, leaves rustling all around them.

'Thank you.' A soft voice emerged from the gentle rustling sound, it was more like a quiet chorus of voices. 'The last time the Blue Moon were here they shared their secrets too.'

Stalker looked up into the trees, surprised to hear them talking and alarmed by their words.

'We aren't the Blue Moon,' Claws said quietly but

firmly.

'No, I suppose not,' The Orchard replied.

'What were their secrets?' Stalker asked, unable to contain herself.

'Ahhh.' The Orchard sighed with an audible smile. 'They are not mine to share.'

'It was worth a try,' Stalker mumbled and Eyes patted her knee gently.

'When were they here?' Eyes asked, looking up into the leaves.

'Many, many cycles ago,' replied The Orchard. 'I do not know how to tell you in terms you would understand.'

'Years? Seasons?' Weaver whispered, glancing around.

'Lunar cycles?' Stalker asked out loud, looking up.

'They had a fae of the moon with them, Caeruleum Lunulam.'

'Why did they have a fae of the moon with them? Was she their ally?' Eyes asked, looking around at the trees with a deep frown on his brow.

'Yes.'

Stalker looked at her pack mates, confused by the significance. Weaver's eyes were wide in surprise and Wind Talker looked deep in thought.

'So Grins-Too-Widely wasn't always their patron?' Stalker asked.

'Apparently not,' Wind Talker replied. 'What happened to the lunar fae?'

'I don't know,' The Orchard replied. A heavy silence hung in the air for a moment. 'Thank you for wassailing with me, it was nice to have company but I must sleep now.'

'Could we come again?' Weaver asked.

'Yes,' the trees rustled. The Lightning Lords got to their feet, Stalker stumbled slightly, her head still foggy from the alcohol. 'Beware Crimson Thorns,' the Orchard sighed sleepily. Weaver grasped Stalker's hand to help steady her and they looked around at the rustling leaves.

'What does that mean?' Wind Talker asked, raising his voice almost to a shout.

'Redfield Park plays host to a troubled fae, Crimson Thorns. She will block your path on your way to defeat your greatest foe.' A breeze blew through the woods scattering fallen leaves across the floor and Stalker felt a shudder run right through her.

'That was cryptic,' Eyes growled as they made their way back along the path they had entered from.

'The Orchard is a thousand years old,' Weaver explained. 'She has great insight but is not the most direct fae in Hepethia.'

Weaver led them back across the veil. Stalker kept hold of Weaver's hand, her head gradually clearing and she tried to make sense of what they had learned. She wasn't sure how much of it was useful, but she knew one thing for certain, she would have to have Eyes' back.

Stalker woke the following morning feeling groggy. The pack was stirring to life around her, even though it was early. They had to collect a van and some equipment that Claws had arranged to hire and then get over to the house they were to heal by 9am.

'Morning,' Stalker said to the others as she emerged from her sleepy state. The others murmured in reply and Wind Talker simply gave her a curt nod. Stalker couldn't quite bring herself to look at him, the memory of his revelation in the Orchard stirring in her jumbled and slow mind. It seemed no one wanted to discuss it, and Stalker eyed her pack mates carefully, unsure if she should bring it up or not.

Eyes arrived as they were eating breakfast, having gone back to his mother's house for the night.

'How's your family?' Weaver asked him as she passed him some orange juice.

'Could be better,' he shrugged. 'I'll be glad when we get this over with and get Chloe healed. She's been moved to a psychiatric unit now, which is not where I want her.'

'Of course,' Stalker said quietly. 'Let's go, shall we?'

They rolled up to the house just after 9am in a big white van, all of them clad in blue overalls, except Eyes, who was in a suit. He went to the door and exchanged a few words with the mother and returned with a set of keys. Stalker watched the house, waiting anxiously for the mother to vacate.

'I wish we knew what we were going to find in there,' she whispered. Weaver placed a hand on her shoulder and squeezed.

'It'll be fine,' she replied.

The mother came out of the house with a large bag over her shoulder a few minutes later and went to her car in the driveway. She nodded to Eyes before getting in and driving away.

'Where's the girl?' Stalker asked, her brow furrowed.

'At school,' Eyes replied as he swung out of the van and marched up to the front door.

Stalker slid gracefully out of the van and went around

to the back to open the doors. Claws gave her a brief smile and passed her a tool belt, which she dutifully put on. He and Wind Talker lugged a large drill to the edge of the van and together the three of them hoisted it out of the van and carried it up the path and into the house. They put it down in the living room on a huge dust sheet. This was all for show, for now at least. Eyes was waiting in the kitchen for the rest of the pack, his face set in a grim expression.

'What's the plan?' Stalker asked.

'We break open the door on this side and take a look around. Wind Talker, you check across the veil and tell us what you see.'

Stalker glanced between Eyes and Wind Talker. There was an edge to Eyes' voice and she just knew that he was wishing he had the talisman that allowed the bearer to look across the veil, rather than having to trust Wind Talker with that task.

Claws pulled back the rug on the floor and lifted the trap door open. Stalker pulled a torch out of her tool belt and flicked it on. She pointed it down the steps and glanced around at the others.

'Who's going to do the honours?' she asked.

'I will,' Eyes said brusquely. He snatched a crowbar from Claws' tool belt and set off down the steps.

'Wait,' Stalker called and Eyes stopped and looked back up at her. 'We should search the house for a key for that padlock.' Eyes blinked at her for a moment, confusion in his eyes. 'For one thing, we might want to be able to lock the door again and for another, this trap door and stairwell are well used. Look, there's very little dust, the door opened easily and that padlock is in good condition, not rusted or anything. The family uses this, they must have a key. It might help us to understand.'

'Stalker's right,' Claws said firmly. Eyes nodded and returned to the kitchen. 'Let's spread out. Check every drawer, every nook and cranny.' Claws turned and started rummaging through the kitchen drawers. Wind Talker headed out to the pantry and Weaver set off for the dining room.

'Let's go upstairs,' Stalker said to Eyes and grudgingly he followed. 'I know you want to do this quickly, but we must be careful too. We have no idea what we're going to find in there.'

'You're right,' he said quietly as he followed her up the stairs.

'You check the mother's room and I'll check the girl's,' she said gently, trying not to sound too bossy. He nodded again and headed off to locate the mother's room. Stalker went straight for the girl's room and looked around in the doorway. Drawings lined the walls and fluttered slightly in the breeze from the open window. Stalker crossed the room and pulled the window shut. A black bird landed on the sill outside and squawked at her before flying off. Stalker stepped away from the window and looked around at the drawings on the walls, they were nearly all of birds, but mixed in were some darker, more mysterious images. Black circles and something that looked like a well were repeated in several drawings.

She heard Eyes muttering to himself in another room up the hall and was snapped from her curiosity. She looked around the room and went to the wardrobe that they had seen the worry demon in when they visited the house in Hepethia. She opened the doors and looked at the clothes hanging there, everything looked normal. She pushed the clothes aside and ran her hand over the back of the wardrobe, right into the corners and carefully over the whole surface. Nothing. There were stacks of shoes lining the wardrobe floor and she stooped down to root around amongst them. Right at the back was an old pair of ballet slippers that looked much too small for the pre-teen girl who lived here. Stalker grabbed them and shook them. A small key dropped out of one of them onto the thick carpet, making almost no sound. A gasp escaped Stalker's lips and she quickly picked up the key. 'I found it!' she yelled and tore from the room.

Eyes came bursting out onto the landing and stared at her in disbelief. Stalker ran down the stairs two at a time and leaped down the last four at once without breaking stride. She floated gently to the ground and ran into the kitchen. The others appeared from their respective corners of the house and gawked at her as she held the tiny key up in her fingers.

'Where was it?' Claws asked.

'In the girl's wardrobe.'

'The girl's?' Wind Talker asked, jerking his head in surprise.

'Yeah. The drawings on her wall were strange too. Not just birds, but there was a well too.'

'Let's get down there,' Eyes said, his voice firm. He took the key and went first again, into the blackness. Stalker shone the torch over his shoulder and heard the small click as he unlocked the padlock. He glanced up at them and lifted his eyebrows, a look of "this is it" written on his face. Stalker followed him down the steps, the others trailed after and Eyes wrenched open the door. It evidently wasn't as heavy as it looked as it flew open quickly and banged against the wall.

She followed Eyes inside and shone the torch around the basement. The space wasn't vast, but bigger than expected. The walls and ceiling were lined with corrugated iron and empty metal shelf units lined two of the walls. Along the far wall were a set of fold away bunk beds. It was a totally normal air raid shelter and it was gathering dust.

Stalker felt a vaguely familiar prickling sensation crawling all over her skin and now that the door was open the source was clear to her. She was reminded vividly of the Danegeld.

'I don't get it,' Weaver whispered. 'If someone was coming down here regularly, why does it look like no one has been in here in decades?'

'Can't you feel the doorway?' Stalker replied absently, staring into the space. She shone the torch at the floor and noticed scuffled tracks in the dust and a little patch just inside the entrance to the shelter where there was very little dust and a few crumbs of food. She bent down and pressed her fingers to the floor, picking up some crumbs on them. She sniffed and darted her tongue out to taste one.

'Don't,' Weaver said loudly, her voice reverberating off the walls.

'It's okay,' Stalker replied, standing up. 'Fresh bread crumbs, no more than a day old.'

'What's the state of play in Hepethia?' Eyes asked, glancing at Wind Talker.

Wind Talker shook his head slowly.

'It's pitch black, I can't see anything.'

'We'll have to cross over blind,' Eyes said quietly. Stalker felt her stomach lurch at the prospect. Her pulse was racing. Eyes took a step into the shelter and disappeared in front of her. Weaver and Wind Talker were quick to follow, leaving her and Claws facing each other in the dark basement. They exchanged worried glances and then crossed over together.

There was no tug at her navel, no spinning sensation. Just another step, straight through the open door that anyone could enter.

Stalker raised the torch and shone it over her head. They were in a very different space. The ceiling was impossibly high and just behind them was an open door with a little daylight filtering down a very long staircase. At her feet was a circle drawn in white chalk as perfect as if it were brand new and Stalker looked carefully in the little pool of white light from the torch to see footprints in the dust leading away from the circle. She double checked the floor between the circle and the door and confirmed that the footprints originated in the circle, the doorway in the veil.

The vast cavern stretched out ahead of them and cautiously, Stalker led the way, following the tracks. The walls were stone and as she shone the torch over them she noticed graffiti covering them. Faded red spray paint warned them to "stay away", "keep out" and "turn back" but interspersed were smaller declarations of "feed me" and "hide me". A shiver went up Stalker's spine and she felt movement in the dark around them. She stopped still and felt the others halt right behind her.

'What was that?' Eyes whispered. He had felt it too. Stalker closed her eyes and focused on the darkness, welcoming it, inviting it into her. When she opened her eyes she could see more clearly and she sensed Pursuit-of-Midnight-Solitude somewhere just out of sight, urging her on.

'It's okay,' she said firmly. 'We have to go on. Nothing's going to hurt us, it's just darkness elementals.'

'There are no demons here, it feels like there should be,' Weaver said, her voice floating away into the black.

'I'm guessing the graffiti is mostly doing its job,' Eyes said dryly.

Stalker shone the torch on the floor just ahead and set off walking again. An unpleasant smell crept up on her as she walked, at first stale air but then the distinct smell of urine and faeces.

'Oh god, what is that?' Claws asked, clamping a hand to his face.

No one answered, there were no words. Stalker caught sight of silver glinting in the torchlight and edged slowly forwards. She could feel the space open up ahead of her before she saw it clearly, that feeling of being on a precipice. She shone the torch into the empty space. It was a huge well in the floor, easily fifteen feet wide and it was lined with silver. The others gathered at her sides to peer into the pit and she heard movement inside it. She lowered the beam of the torch into the well, it was deep, but not so deep that she couldn't see the bottom.

'Hello?' a distorted voice croaked up out of the darkness.

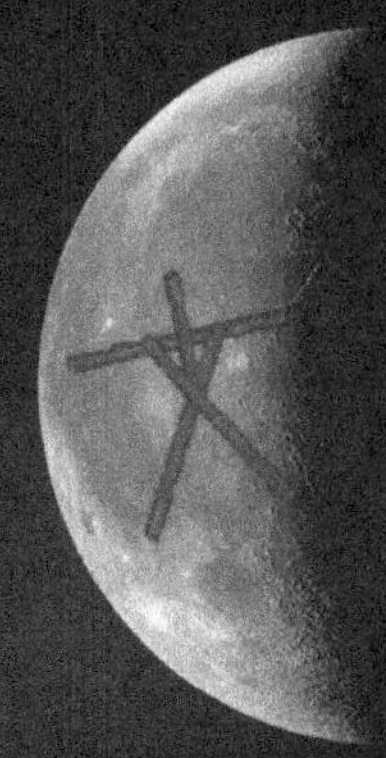

Chapter Fourteen

'Oh my god,' Stalker breathed, her hand shaking and making the torchlight shudder over the man's filthy and fragile body. His bearded face was turned towards them and he held a trembling hand up to shield his eyes against the bright light.

'Who are you?' the man croaked feebly. 'Where is she?'

'She?' Stalker asked, turning to look at Eyes beside her.

'The girl? Has she been feeding him?' Eyes whispered. He crouched down and looked into the pit.

'What do we do?' Stalker asked.

'We have to get him out, obviously,' Weaver said firmly.

'How? The sides are silver, it'll fry any of us that touch it,' Claws said, stooping to gently tap his fingers to the silver rim of the well. He yanked his hand back as his skin hissed and smoke issued from his singed fingers.

'What's going on?' the frail old man called up and then

burst into a fit of coughing at the strain of raising his voice.

'It's all right,' Stalker called down to him. 'We're going to figure out a way to get you out.' She turned to Eyes. 'Get me a rope from the van. I'll go down there.'

The others looked at her in alarm. Stalker lifted her chin defiantly and glared at Eyes. He was the first to relent and gave her an appraising nod. He looked over at Claws, giving a single jerk of his head and Claws was off, sprinting back the way they had come.

'What's your name?' Weaver called gently into the pit.

'Hidden Voice,' Eyes replied. Stalker's gaze darted to the Alpha. 'I seem to be able to tell any shifter's name. It started recently when the Witches attacked my house,' he explained.

Stalker swallowed hard. It was an interesting ability.

The shifter in the pit croaked something in reply but it was impossible to make out.

'This is horrific,' Stalker murmured. 'How long do you think he's been down there?'

'Years,' Wind Talker replied, his voice steady, his face impassive.

'How is he still alive? Even if people have been feeding him?' Stalker whispered. Her head was spinning.

'He's a tough old shifter,' Weaver replied with a small smile.

Stalker shone the torch around the pit. There was a concrete box at the edge on the far side that had a hole in the top. The stench of waste was issuing from it and a small pile of roughly torn scraps of fabric sat beside it. Roughly in the middle there was a filthy pile of rags that seemed to serve as a bed. Right below where the Lightning Lords stood were the traces of crumbs and thoroughly chewed bones. The girl must have been feeding him leftovers, tossing them into the pit for him.

Pounding footsteps and a bobbing white light down the tunnel caught Stalker's attention. Claws skidded to a halt a moment later and held up a coil of rope. He quickly tied it around his waist, skilfully choosing the best knots.

'Are you sure?' Eyes asked her quietly. Stalker nodded in reply, resolute but still nervous. Her eyes met Claws' and he gave her a reassuring nod as he grasped the rope tightly in both hands and planted his feet firmly in the dirt. Wind Talker was at his side, ready to help take the strain if necessary. For a brief second that made Stalker more nervous, unsure whether she could trust him or not. She had to do this, though, so she took a deep breath, stepped carefully to the edge and jumped.

Her talisman kicked in after a second of free fall and she floated gently the last few feet to land with a soft thud on the dusty, dirty floor. A second later there was a slight flapping sound and the rope landed next to her, bouncing gently against the wall a few times before coming to rest. Stalker swept the torchlight across the bottom of the pit and settled on the confused face of Hidden Voice, huddled next to his bedding. He looked so old and frail, he was little more than skin and bones and his watery eyes implored her to explain who she was.

'I'm going to get you out of here,' she said quietly as she approached him slowly.

His hands flew up to shield his eyes from the torchlight and she immediately lowered it away from his face. 'How long have you been down here?'

'I don't know,' he croaked. 'Who are you? Where is the girl?'

He was shaking as she drew close to him, his eyes were wide with fear.

'Who put you in here?' she asked softly. His eyes darted to meet hers, they were ice cold and his face twitched with fury.

'Blue Moon,' he hissed through clenched teeth.

Stalker sighed. Well, now they knew. She looked him over carefully. He had too much bare skin to try walking up the rope and nowhere near enough muscle to pull himself up either.

'I'm not Blue Moon,' she said gently and slowly reached a hand to touch his arm. 'They're gone. I'm going to have to change form to carry you up. Is that okay?'

His eyes widened even further and his lip trembled slightly but he nodded his head. Stalker stood and moved back a few paces. She looked up at the high walls all around them and located the rest of the pack peering over at her. 'We're coming up, get ready with the rope,' she called out.

She looked back down at Hidden Voice and tried to give him a reassuring smile, but realised that he couldn't see her face in the dark. She wasn't going to be able to hold the torch once she shifted so she knelt down beside him again and held the torch out to him. 'You take this.' Slowly, he took it and his arms shook with the weight of it.

She backed off again and willed her body to shift, forcing the bones to lengthen, muscles to expand and thick hair to sprout all over her body. She stood over him, an extra foot tall and unable to speak softly; the torchlight shuddered and flickered across the floor and over her feet.

She couldn't see his face, but she heard him sobbing. She approached him slowly, carefully and as gently as she could manage in her Agrius form, she lifted him and hoisted him onto her shoulder. He whimpered and remained rigid in her grasp but was light as a feather.

Stalker held her free arm out to find the rope and grabbed it tightly, wrapping it around her forearm, and gave it a firm tug to signal the others. The slack disappeared and Stalker felt her shoulder wrench slightly as her pack mates began to pull. She swung her feet up and planted them on the wall. Pain shot through the balls of her feet and there was an angry hiss from her skin as it burned, but she took a deep breath and braced herself against the pain. Every step was agony and she winced each time her huge paws made contact with the silver. Hidden Voice trembled and moaned as they moved gradually upwards.

Finally they approached the top and Eyes and Wind Talker grabbed Hidden Voice and dragged him up first. Stalker flung up her free arm and grabbed Weaver's offered arm and bounded out of the pit easily. Claws let out a massive sigh and Stalker shifted form swiftly and flung a thankful arm around him.

'You are covered in shit,' he hissed at her ear and she pulled quickly away from him. He was smirking and she gave him a friendly shove. They moved over to Hidden Voice, who was collapsed on the floor, shaking. Wind Talker had taken the torch away from him and was shining it carefully over his body.

'Look,' he whispered and the others drew closer. In the white light of the torch, faded and covered in filth, were markings on the frail old shifter's skin. Old tattoos were all over his arms and across his shoulders where his rags had slipped down. Runes telling of fire, phoenix and fury. On the back of one shoulder was an even more chilling tattoo, that of a small spiral. Stalker gasped.

'Oh my god,' she whispered. Her body shook with shock and fear. 'He's a Fury, Phoenix Guard and Spiral Hand. That's why they locked him away down here.'

'What do we do?' Claws asked.

Wind Talker flipped the torch around and swiftly smacked Hidden Voice on the back of the head, rendering him unconscious.

'What the hell did you do that for?' Stalker snapped at Wind Talker.

'He's a Fury and Spiral Hand,' he replied bluntly.

'He's a hundred years old and half dead. I don't think he poses any threat to us.'

'We don't know that,' he replied, a little more softly. 'We can't risk him hearing what we say now.'

'How on earth is he ever going to trust us again now that we've knocked him out?' Stalker hissed, crossing her arms tightly across her chest.

'Stalker,' Eyes said gently. 'We need to formulate a plan and it would be prudent to do so out of earshot of him. For now, at least, he is still our prisoner.'

'Prisoner?' Stalker glared at him. 'You mean we're taking him into protective custody. We need to fix him. That's what we're doing here.'

'No, it's not,' Eyes replied coolly. 'We are here to heal the house. Not him. It is the human family that need saving, not this wretch.'

'What do we do with him?' Weaver asked, her voice

soft and unreadable.

'We should kill him,' Wind Talker said, his voice absolutely void of any emotion. He may as well have been suggesting what they eat for lunch. Stalker was speechless.

'No,' Eyes said firmly. 'We need to find out if anyone knows him and we need to know why the Blue Moon kept him alive, rather than just killing him,' Eyes replied.

'Let's take him to Father Ash,' Wind Talker suggested, his voice calm.

'Father Ash?' Stalker asked.

'He's the only expert on Spiral Hand that we know and he may be able to help extract all the information we need.' Stalker gawked at him. She knew he meant torture.

'Good, let's do it,' Eyes said, his voice ringing with authority.

Wind Talker scooped up Hidden Voice and slung him over his shoulder. He and Eyes set off along the passage but the others held back.

'I don't like this at all,' Stalker whispered.

'Neither do I,' Claws agreed as he coiled up the rope.

'It's the only plan we have,' Weaver said gently. 'We need answers before we know if we can trust Hidden Voice enough to rehabilitate him. *If* we can rehabilitate him. Like it or not, he may be too far gone.' She cast Stalker a furtive glance and set off after the others.

'She's right, you know,' Claws said quietly and Stalker nodded in the dark. He grabbed her hand and they set off together, walking cautiously in the pitch black towards the two bobbing torch beams ahead.

Eyes covered Hidden Voice with a dust sheet and they locked the basement, putting everything back as they found it. They left the house and piled into the van. Stalker got in the back with Claws and Wind Talker to watch over their charge. She took off the filthy overalls that she had been wearing and thanked Artemis for her clean clothes underneath. She still stank of faeces and rot though and she felt suddenly self-conscious about seeing Father Ash in such a state.

Eyes drove far too quickly, the urgency evident in his cornering that had them lurching about in the back, and Stalker was relieved when they screeched to a halt on gravel. She opened the van doors and Wind Talker picked up Hidden Voice and clambered out awkwardly as Eyes ran ahead and rang the doorbell.

Father Ash answered looking calm and cool as always and looked them over with a curious expression, his head cocked to one side.

'Oh my,' he said, staring at Hidden Voice's filthy form. 'You'd better come in.'

They filed inside and stood awkwardly in the huge hallway as he closed the door. He signalled them to follow him down a passage that led under the grand staircase to a small spiral staircase leading down. Stalker supported Hidden Voice's head as they climbed down the steel stairs and they emerged into a kitchen that was almost entirely stainless steel.

Wind Talker rested Hidden Voice carefully on the huge island in the centre of the kitchen and Stalker allowed herself to be touched by his apparent care and concern. 'So, what do we have here?' Father Ash asked as he perched on a high stool next to the island.

Wind Talker tugged back the rags to reveal the tattoos

and Father Ash nodded and briefly made eye contact with Wind Talker.

'We found him on our territory,' Eyes said calmly. 'He had been locked up, we presume by our predecessors. His name is Hidden Voice. Have you heard of him?'

'Oh yes,' Father Ash replied slowly, no trace of surprise to his voice. 'I helped hunt him down. I always wondered what happened to him.'

Stalker's breath caught in her throat and she gaped at him. 'He was an absolute master of disguise, an expert in infiltration, the perfect spy.'

'How did you catch him?' Wind Talker asked, his voice laced with curiosity.

'With difficulty,' Father Ash replied with a small smirk.

'Why didn't you execute him?' Eyes asked.

'It wasn't up to me, he was found on Blue Moon territory and it was up to them what to do with him. They took him away.'

'Was that on Fortune's watch?' Eyes asked, his face set in a hard expression, his teeth clenched and Stalker wished she could make this easier for him.

'Yes,' Father Ash replied, observing Eyes shrewdly. 'It was about fifteen years ago.'

Stalker tried to make eye contact with Eyes but he stared resolutely at Hidden Voice. 'I did oversee him being branded with the spiral tattoo, however,' Father Ash added. 'We used to do that to all the Spiral Hand that we uncovered, just in case.'

Stalker bit back the urge to ask him if he had that tattoo.

'We need to get information out of him,' Wind Talker

said, clearing his throat.

Stalker felt her stomach lurch. She couldn't think what they could hope to get out of him. He'd been hidden away for years, any information he'd acquired was irrelevant now, even if he was sane enough to recall anything.

'I see,' Father Ash said, his eyes narrowed. 'And you wanted to do this at my house?'

'We thought you might be able to help, we thought you would know something about him, which you do.' Wind Talker was very calm and business-like, not allowing himself to be drawn into a disagreement with this extremely powerful elder.

'Well, I've told you all I know. I have to admit that I am curious myself as to what he might have to say after all these years.' Father Ash swept away, moving to a steel cabinet on the far side of the kitchen. Stalker watched him carefully as he opened a drawer and pulled out a syringe, needle and small bottle of clear liquid. She glanced around again and saw that there was no oven in the room, just cupboards and two large fridges and on one wall was a display of knives that didn't look like typical kitchen knives. She swallowed hard, acutely aware now that this was not a kitchen.

Father Ash returned with the loaded syringe and set about locating a vein.

'What is that?' she asked before he could insert the needle.

'Adrenaline, to wake him up,' Father Ash replied, looking her up and down. She shrank under his gaze and shuffled her feet uncomfortably.

He stuck the needle into Hidden Voice's arm and

slowly pushed the plunger. Hidden Voice's arm twitched and his eyes flickered under their closed lids. Slowly he began to regain consciousness and Stalker held her breath. His eyes opened and squinted against the glaring light over the table.

'He's been in the pitch black for years, this is too bright. Can we turn the lights down?' Stalker implored, her eyes meeting those of Father Ash. Hidden Voice followed her gaze and looked up into the face of the elder.

His entire body went rigid for the briefest moment and then he began to shake violently. He scrambled frantically on the steel counter, his nails scratching at the edges as he shuffled away from Father Ash. 'Calm down,' Stalker called out. 'It's okay, you're safe.' Everyone stood back in surprise as Hidden Voice convulsed violently and moaned in distress. His eyes met Stalker's and for just a second she saw on his face as clear as words "No, I'm not".

His body suddenly jerked and thick, black fur erupted all over his skin.

'He's shifting,' Father Ash said calmly. 'Hold him down.' The Lightning Lords rushed forwards and grabbed Hidden Voice, pinning him down on the table. Stalker had her hands on his right leg and it shuddered violently under her grip as his muscles and bones shifted. His Agrius form was wiry and lean, not bulky like most shifters, but his muscles hadn't completely atrophied from lack of use and he struggled hard against them. Father Ash moved quickly back to the drawers and returned a moment later with another syringe. He jabbed Hidden Voice in the neck and the poor wretch fell suddenly still. Slowly his body returned to its human form and he lay still, breathing softly. 'I don't think you're going to get anything coherent out of him,' Father Ash said coolly as they all stepped back.

Stalker glanced at him with concern in her eyes. Hidden Voice had been okay until he laid eyes on Father Ash. It seemed likely that he remembered Father Ash bringing him down and remembered what he was once capable of. That terrified him, to be back in his captor's company and he had completely lost control.

'Let's take him elsewhere,' she suggested quietly. Eyes nodded in agreement.

'Thank you for your help,' Eyes said, squaring up to Father Ash and offering him his hand. Father Ash took it and they shook hands firmly. Wind Talker lifted Hidden Voice again and they left the house, returning quickly to the van. Stalker looked back at Father Ash in his front doorway as Claws slammed the van doors shut. What was that glint in his eye?

'Where are we going to take him?' Claws asked. 'We can't go back to the healing house and we really shouldn't take him to Grove Street.'

'The beach,' Wind Talker said. 'There's a cave not far from here, it should be pretty private.'

Eyes nodded solemnly.

'And we're going to wake him and question him, right?' Stalker asked, her voice unsteady. She looked from one worried face to the next, only Wind Talker's remained impassive.

'Yes,' Eyes said firmly. 'I have to go to a meeting with Theodore now, though.' He looked at his watch and a pained expression crossed his face.

'Can't you cancel?' Stalker asked, frowning.

'Not really, we're meeting with members of the city council.'

'Right,' Claws said steadily. 'Not to worry. We'll get back to Grove Street and drop you off with your car then head back to the beach and you can meet us there later. We'll keep him sedated until then.'

Stalker nodded, feeling reassured by Claws' calm authority.

Eyes drove the van back to St. Mark's and pulled up outside 32 Grove Street. Stalker clambered out of the van after him and caught hold of his arm, halting him on his way to his car.

'You okay?' she asked quietly. He looked down at her hand gripping his arm and raised his eyebrows. She released him, feeling chastised by that one look.

'Yeah,' he replied. 'I'm good. Frustrated about having to leave, some things never change, eh?'

'Yeah. Don't worry, we've got this. See you later. Good luck with the meeting.'

Eyes got into his car and sped away. Stalker went back to the van and climbed inside.

'Claws, Weaver,' Wind Talker said firmly. 'You should patrol, make sure everything is as it should be here and check over the family's home too, make sure there are no negative side effects of us removing him.'

Weaver glanced anxiously at Stalker, then nodded at Wind Talker.

'Of course,' she said softly. She moved to the back door of the van and started to climb out.

'You okay?' Claws asked Stalker as he moved past her towards the door. She nodded in reply and he left with no further word. Claws slammed the van door shut and Stalker climbed into the front to sit beside Wind Talker.

'So,' she said as he started the engine. 'Just you and me with this guy then?'

He glanced at her and then set off without a word. Stalker kept looking in the back to check on Hidden Voice as Wind Talker drove them back to the beach. The ancient, broken shifter didn't even stir. When they arrived, Wind Talker drove the van down a crooked track that went almost all the way down to the beach from the road above. The last few meters were just narrow enough for people on foot, but not for a vehicle, but below the bank of soft sand and long grass the van was out of sight from the road. They were at the very end of this stretch of golden sand, the tide was out and a high cliff rose above them.

Together, Stalker and Wind Talker pulled Hidden Voice out of the back of the van and carried him down onto the beach. Wind Talker led the way to a cave in the cliff. It had a huge opening facing the sea and small rocks littered the entrance. Wind whipped her faded blue hair around her face and stung her eyes, and the waves crashed against the cliffs just around the sweeping bend. She didn't know how long they had until the tide came in and that made her stomach flip.

They laid Hidden Voice down on the moist sand and he stirred slightly. Stalker paused over him, watching and waiting to see if was about to wake up. He lay still and she breathed a heavy sigh of relief. Wind Talker moved away and started picking though the rock pools, so Stalker sat down next to the sedated shifter.

He began muttering and she leaned close to listen,

only the odd word was audible over the wind and waves but she clung to those few words, those clues.

'No..... not me.... crazy fae.... traitors!..... fools.'

'Who?' Stalker urged, gently. 'Who are fools?'

'Blue Moon,' he whispered, his eyes popping open. They latched onto her and his hand darted out and grabbed her wrist. Her breath caught in her throat and she was paralysed. 'You have to stop them.'

He passed out again, dropping his hand to the wet sand. She released her breath slowly and gingerly rubbed her aching wrist. What had that been about? She looked up to see Wind Talker still picking his way through the rocks. A few minutes later, he made his way back to her, his hands full of shells.

'I need seaweed,' he called over the noise of the beach. 'I want to try a ritual to extract some information from him. Can you go and see if you can find some down the beach?'

'Sure,' she said, getting to her feet. She paused, unsure whether to tell him what Hidden Voice had said. The words stopped in her throat and she wasn't sure why. She brushed sand off her jeans and set off towards the shallow water. As she gathered the soggy seaweed, she struggled to think of a good reason not to have told Wind Talker. Ultimately, she simply didn't trust him and the awful, sickening feeling that settled in the pit of her stomach at the conscious acknowledgement of that fact was the worst thing about it. He was her brother. It was devastating to carry these feelings and worst of all to know that he would sense them through the empathy they shared. He was ruthless, cold even, but he had only ever served the pack.

She should trust him with her life.

Her arms were full of seaweed now and she turned to head back to the cave. She looked up and was surprised when she saw how far she had walked. She set off at a brisk pace, the wind at her back, urging her onwards. As she neared the cave she felt something strange, a tingling sensation all over and for a moment she thought she heard footsteps, dozens of marching feet. She looked around but the beach was deserted. Her pulse was racing though and she drew her lower lip between her teeth as she strode towards Wind Talker. He was hunched over Hidden Voice and there was something odd about the way he felt through the bond. The very empathy she had been so conscious of a few minutes before now seemed to be setting off an internal alarm. He was satisfied. He had been anxious all day, but now he felt still and calm and it was only the sudden contrast that drew her attention to it.

She quickened her pace and ran into the cave. Wind Talker looked over his shoulder at her, his face pale and resolute. Then she saw the knife in his hand, the blood running down it, and Hidden Voice's throat neatly cut.

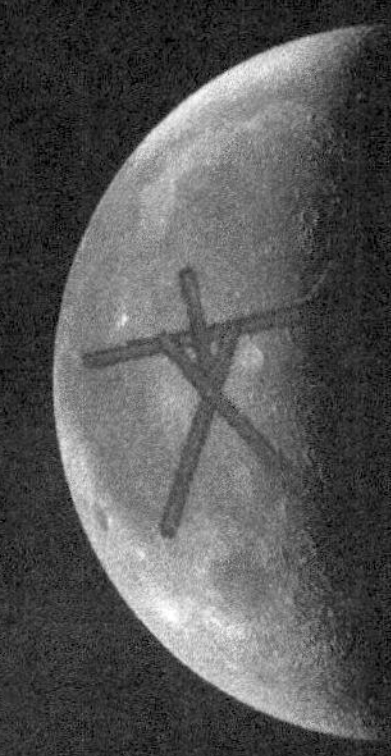

Chapter Fifteen

'WHAT THE FUCK HAVE YOU DONE?' Stalker screamed. Her voice echoed around the cave.

'What had to be done,' he replied coolly.

'I thought we were going to get information out of him?'

'He was insane, there was no ritual, there was nothing we could do.'

'He was talking,' she yelled, throwing the seaweed to the ground. 'He spoke to me right before you sent me off. He was muttering in his sleep and he woke up just for a second and told me to stop the Blue Moon.'

'Why didn't you tell me?' he snapped. He got to his feet and squared up to her, his face red and furious.

'I don't know,' she said, her voice falling away. Hot tears of rage stung her eyes.

'Well, what's done is done and it was for the best. I stand by my actions.'

Stalker's pulse was racing and her hands balled into fists, her nails digging into her sweaty palms. She felt the beast inside fighting to break free and the vial of calming water against her skin getting hot. She turned and strode away from him, knowing that if she stayed she might kill him.

She walked right into the rising tide, the salt water filled her boots and she felt the spray on her face. Seagulls circled overhead, cawing against the wind. After a few deep breaths, Stalker felt back in control and she trudged back up the beach. She pulled out her phone and called Claws. It was Weaver who answered.

'Everything okay?' she asked.

'Where's Claws?' Stalker asked, rubbing her eyes with her free hand.

'Driving. What's up?'

'You need to come to the beach, now. Wind Talker just executed Hidden Voice.' She hung up. She couldn't bear to hear Weaver's reply. Next she called the Alpha. His phone rang to voicemail and she paused, not wanting to say too much. 'We have a situation, it's urgent. Please meet us at the appointed place as soon as possible.' She hung up and put her phone away.

Stalker looked up and down the beach, they would need wood for a funeral pyre. There was no hope of finding dry driftwood here, but back up the hill and across the road was the start of the woods that led up to Father Ash's house so she dragged her heavy feet in that direction.

Time seemed to slow to a crawl as she wandered through the trees picking up sticks. Each time her arms were full she trudged down to the beach and added the wood to a slowly growing pile as close to the road as possible, with the tide creeping in towards it. Wind Talker began to help after a few trips, though they didn't exchange a word, and as the sun touched the horizon they had a substantial pyre ready. Stalker's rage had abated somewhat but she was left feeling heavy and filled with self-blame. If she had only stayed with Hidden Voice this wouldn't have happened. She heard a car pull up on the road behind them and turned to look up the beach.

The car belonged to Claws and he, Weaver and Eyes all climbed out of it. No wonder it had taken so long for them to arrive, if they had waited for the Alpha. The three of them came striding down the slope onto the beach to meet them.

'What happened?' Eyes barked, his face full of thunder.

'Wind Talker killed him, slit his throat.'

'How did he get the opportunity?' Eyes asked, glaring at her. She felt a sudden rush of fury and had to hold herself back.

'He tricked me, he told me there was a ritual and that he needed seaweed. While I was collecting some he did it. Don't look at me like that. Don't you think I feel terrible enough about this?'

Weaver was staring at the pyre but Claws caught Stalker's eye and gave her a sympathetic look.

'Any of us could have been in your position,' he said softly. 'Where are they now?'

Stalker pointed to the cave where Hidden Voice's body remained, with Wind Talker standing sentinel over it. The tide was rising rapidly now and they didn't have long before the beach would be covered. Eyes and Claws marched over to the cave and Stalker was left alone with Weaver.

'I feel like I let you all down,' Stalker whispered.

'No,' Weaver replied quickly, reaching out to touch her shoulder. 'You mustn't feel like that. You weren't wrong to trust your pack mate.'

'But I knew, I knew he wanted to kill him. I shouldn't have left them alone for even a minute.' Hot tears stung as they built up and she could contain them no longer. Weaver grabbed her and pulled her into a tight embrace and Stalker sobbed against her shoulder. Crunching footsteps in the sand signalled the arrival of the others, carrying Hidden Voice between them. They placed the body on the pyre and Stalker noticed the frosty glares between the Alpha and Wind Talker.

'Is there anything we can do first?' Weaver asked, her face and voice desperate. 'Some shifters can extract information from bodies, can't they? Last-Breath-Echoes, the Witches?'

'I don't have that knowledge,' Wind Talker replied stiffly.

'I really don't want anyone else knowing about Hidden Voice,' Eyes said, his voice dark and dangerous. 'We have to keep this between us. It's bad enough that Father Ash saw him. This shifter was dangerous and whatever he knew was dangerous too. That's the only possible reason for the Blue Moon locking him away like that.'

'I want to know why they didn't kill him,' Stalker said, some strength returning to her voice. 'He was the only one who might have known that.'

'Light the pyre,' Eyes ordered and Wind Talker bent to

light some kindling around the base.

Weaver put an arm around Stalker's shoulders as they watched the wood catch fire. Slowly, the fire spread throughout the pyre and the Lightning Lords watched in silence as the flames snaked up to meet the body. Wind Talker raised his arms and summoned a fae of flame to stoke the blaze. The heat prickled Stalker's skin.

Waves crashed onto the beach, inching ever closer and a purple, velvet cloak of night began to spread across the sky, fading to dusty pink where the sun had gone down over the sea.

As Hidden Voice burned, Stalker began to feel a creeping, uncomfortable feeling, like someone was watching them. She looked around but couldn't see anyone. A few minutes later an odd sound seemed to reach out from the sea, hard to identify over the sound of the waves, but irritatingly familiar. She strained to hear it and looked around for the source. Footsteps, it was the sound of marching boots on the sand, muffled and distant. She pulled away from Weaver and stepped away from the pyre, searching it out.

'What's wrong?' Weaver asked.

'I can't believe you did this,' Eyes hissed under his breath, but the wind carried it to Stalker's ears and she turned to see Eyes glaring sideways at Wind Talker. 'You disobeyed me. I told the four of you to guard Hidden Voice until I got back from my meeting.'

'I did what you wouldn't,' Wind Talker replied, venom in his voice.

'Guys!' Stalker shouted across the blaze. 'This isn't the time.'

'Something's wrong,' Weaver added. 'What is it Stalker?'

'Can't any of you hear that?' She looked around desperately. The sound of marching was growing louder, almost as loud as the sea and the goosebumps all up her arms told her they were still being watched. She looked around desperately but it was getting so dark.

'You killed a man without my permission. How can I ever trust you again?' Eyes snarled at Wind Talker, oblivious to Stalker's distress.

'You would have us playing babysitter, instead of taking action,' Wind Talker replied, his voice rising. 'You are weak.'

'It's not weakness to prepare properly before a confrontation,' Eyes snapped back. 'What do you think my true name means?'

'Your human family keep you shackled to a morality that has no place in our world,' Wind Talker said, a dangerous edge to his voice.

'Not now!' Stalker yelled. The footsteps grew louder still. 'Please, can't anyone hear that?'

She searched Weaver and Claws' faces, but they looked confused and scared, they glanced at each other and looked at Stalker as if she were mad.

There was a caw and Stalker's head whipped around to see a raven perched on the top of the bank, its head bobbing as it shifted its weight on its spindly feet. The marching was deafening now and all around them.

'Wind Talker!' Stalker screamed, planting her hands over her ears, desperate to escape the maddening sound. 'Look across the veil! Something's coming through.'

But Wind Talker hadn't heard her. He was squaring up to Eyes now, their faces glowed orange in the light of the fire.

'You have overstepped the line, Wind Talker.' Eyes was puffing out his chest and bearing down on his pack mate now and Stalker watched, paralysed and unable to act.

'I haven't even begun to overstep the line!' Wind Talker roared and his body suddenly erupted in thick, brown fur, vicious talons sprang from his gnarled hands and his face morphed into the bear-like muzzle of his Agrius form.

'No!' Stalker screamed.

Eyes was only a split second behind, shifting to match Wind Talker. Weaver and Claws stood stock still, stunned expressions on their faces. The raven cawed again and took flight and the marching pounded in Stalker's ears.

'Now is not the time!' she screamed, still covering her ears. 'We have to get out of here!'

Eyes shoved Wind Talker back and he stumbled across the sand. He quickly righted himself and lunged at Eyes, a terrifying roar issuing from his foaming mouth. Wind Talker grabbed Eyes around the middle and they locked together in a frenzied grapple. Spitting, snarling and snapping sounds filled the air, along with the crackling fire, crashing waves and deafening army about to descend on them all. Stalker couldn't bear it, something inside snapped and she shifted form against her will. The Agrius took control of her and everything became a blur of noise and confusion.

She bounded around the fire towards Eyes and Wind Talker, blind fear and rage fuelling her, her conscious mind was somewhere else. As she neared the brawl something heavy hit her from the side, sending her bowling over and splashing into the rising tide. Another shifter pinned her down, another Agrius stared down at her with bared teeth and deep green eyes. It was Claws. She struggled against him, desperate to rip the fight apart and get them all off the beach away from the approaching army; but she was pinned tight to the ground and water filled her ears, muffling the terrifying sounds around her.

Slowly, very slowly, as she stared up into the green eyes of her pack mate, the beast abated and she was able to return to her human form. Claws shifted with her, his face suddenly full of apprehension. She gave him a shove and scrambled to her feet.

Wind Talker and Eyes were rolling around on the sand, biting and clawing at each other and Weaver stood nearby, watching with a worried expression and biting her nails.

'Why did you stop me?' Stalker snapped at Claws.

'You were out of control, you might have killed one of them,' he replied angrily. 'You made me shift.'

'You didn't have to,' she snapped back. 'We have to break this up, something's very wrong and we can't have those two fighting.' She took a few steps towards the fight but Claws grabbed her arm and held her back. She flashed him a dangerous look and he released her but followed close behind as she strode towards the others. Weaver dashed over and put a steadying hand on Stalker's chest.

'No we can't, we have to let them settle this.'

Stalker gaped at her. Suddenly she realised that the marching had stopped. All she could hear was the fire, the sea and the fight before them. She looked around anxiously, but there was no sign of anything being wrong. The bottom of the pyre was in the water now, but the flames continued to burn, blackening the body on top. Her eyes settled on Wind Talker and Eyes as they scrambled about in the wet sand. It looked like Eyes was hurt, blood was pouring from his leg and side and he was struggling against Wind Talker. Stalker felt a hard knot in her stomach as she watched Wind Talker raise a huge fist and slam it hard into Eyes' face, breaking his jaw. He grabbed Eyes' shoulders and lifted them, then slammed him hard into the ground as a wave rushed up over them both. When the water receded, Eyes was lying limp in human form, his hands raised, with Wind Talker still in Agrius form sitting on his stomach and gripping his shoulders with his clawed hands.

'I yield,' Eyes cried out, blood trickling out of his mouth. Wind Talker tossed Eyes down like a doll and stepped away from him. He shifted form and wiped blood from his own face where it had trickled from his nose.

'I am the Alpha now,' he snarled and strode away to the van.

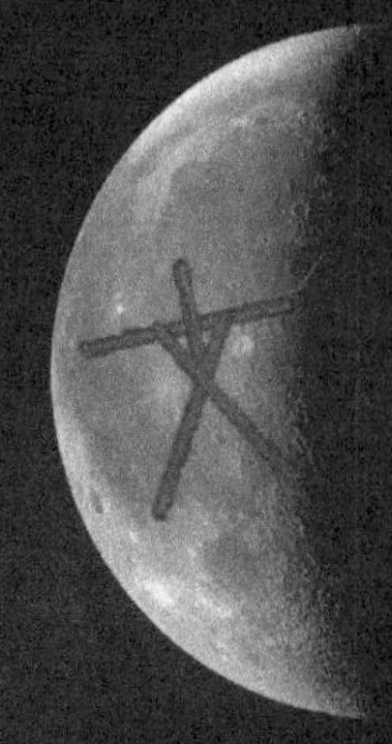

Chapter Sixteen

Fights-Eyes-Open

He sat up slowly and watched Wind Talker stomping up the sandy slope to the van. He was in indescribable pain and he winced as he tried to move. In an instant, Claws and Stalker were at his sides, helping him to his feet.

'What just happened?' Claws asked quietly.

'He challenged me and won,' Eyes croaked. He felt blood in his aching mouth and spat it into the shallow water at his feet. 'He is now our Alpha.' His eyes met Weaver's. She had watched the fight and allowed it to unfold and he felt the guilt pouring from her. She looked at him for a moment, her mouth twitched slightly and she turned and followed Wind Talker up the bank.

'Can we leave the body? Is it safe?' Stalker asked, glancing over her shoulder at the blackened body on the pyre.

'The fae should see that the fire is hot enough to destroy it,' Eyes replied, looking resolutely ahead. He limped across the sand with his arms around Stalker and Claws' necks and they helped him into the back seat of Claws' car.

'I won't obey him,' Stalker said quietly as she buckled herself into the front passenger seat.

'Yes you will,' Eyes replied firmly.

The van reversed up the track onto the road and its lights swept across Claws' car as it turned and moved past them. Claws set off after it, his eyes fixed on the road. Eyes clung to his bleeding side and felt every muscle scream in pain with each breath he took. He gently moved his jaw from side to side, which sent spasms into his temples and down his neck.

'What was going on with you?' Claws asked quietly, his eyes glancing at Stalker beside him. Eyes watched with interest, he had no idea what Claws was talking about.

'Something else was there. But it seems I was the only one aware of it. There was a raven watching and an army marching on us, I could only hear it, not see it.'

Eyes frowned and pinched the flesh between his eyes. Stalker was more intuitive than the rest of them, she always knew when something was wrong and he felt a fool for not paying more attention to her. Now he had lost leadership of the Lightning Lords, as well as Hidden Voice and quite possibly the trust of the others. He had allowed Wind Talker to develop those feelings, rather than addressing them sooner, this was all on him.

His eyes drifted closed as the car sped past street lamps and his mind seemed to be void of anything. He felt the car stop and his head jerked up, his eyes struggled to open and he felt the residue of blood in his mouth. Someone was opening the door and he looked up to see Stalker leaning into the car. She helped him out and he leaned heavily on her as she walked him to the door of 32 Grove Street. He looked at her in alarm, he didn't want to be here, he wanted to go home to his bed and his family. The thought of his beloved family stuck suddenly and the panic ebbed away, replaced by grief.

'We couldn't take you back to your family in this state, even if we knew your mother's address,' Claws said softly, as if reading his mind. Eyes nodded slowly and allowed them to lead him inside. The van was already there and he heard Wind Talker banging about in the kitchen once they entered the poky hall. Stalker and Claws got Eyes to the sofa in the living room and sat him down gently. He had spent an unfair amount of time on this sofa like this, physically and emotionally broken.

He let his head drop back against the cushions and he fell into a deep sleep.

The next morning, Eyes woke slowly to the sounds of movement all around him. He had slumped sideways in his sleep and felt an uncomfortable ache in his neck, though his injuries from the fight seemed to have healed. He opened his eyes and tried to sit up, he felt stiff but mostly all right. He heard Wind Talker's low voice in the kitchen, and Weaver and Stalker were stacking up the cushions that they normally slept on in the corner of the room.

'Morning,' he croaked. His throat throbbed and his lips were dry and caked in blood. The women looked at him and both tried to rustle up smiles. He stood up slowly and pointed towards the door. 'I'm going to go and freshen up.' He limped from the room, his left leg still not quite healed and dull from the position he had slept in. Climbing the stairs took great effort, each step seeming to get higher and higher, but eventually he made it to the bathroom and shut the door. He stripped off his stiff and sand-covered clothes and ran the shower, stepping into the cubicle carefully. The water pressure was terrible, but it was hot at least and he welcomed the spray on his face and in his hair. He rinsed out his mouth and spat blood down the drain; dirt and dry blood ran off his body and swirled grotesquely in the shower tray. He planted his palms on the cool tiles and felt the water pounding on the back of his neck, easing the aching muscles. Time drifted by and he had no idea how long he had stood there when there was a quiet knock on the door.

'Are you all right?' Weaver asked softly from the other side. Eyes cleared his throat.

'Yeah, fine. I'll be down in a minute.'

'Can I come in and talk to you?'

'Just a minute.' He moved slowly, still aching all over. Once the shower was off and he had a towel secured around his waist, he opened the door. A blast of cold air entered the room and cleared away a little of the steam that hung in the air. Weaver looked awful, her eyes were all puffy and red and her fingernails were bleeding in places. 'Come in.' He held the door wide for her and closed it again behind her. She sat down on the toilet seat and he leaned against the sink, afraid to sit down in case he couldn't get up again.

'I'm so sorry,' she whispered. 'I feel like I let you down.'

'Hey,' he said, leaning towards her. 'No, no you didn't.'

'I should have counselled you better, been there for you more, shared more of the burden. I let it get to the point where Wind Talker had just cause to challenge you. Once he did that it had to play out and now...' Her voice cracked and she covered her lips with her bloody fingers.

'I should have done what Fortune wanted me to do,' he said softly. As the words left his lips he felt as though a weight had been lifted. Tears ran down his face and he hurriedly brushed them aside. 'If I hadn't been so distracted I could have led this pack properly from the start and they wouldn't have been hurt.'

'You don't know that,' she said, looking up at him with wide eyes. 'The Witches might have attacked them anyway, even if you had left them. They would still have seen your daughter as a valid target for revenge after we killed their Alpha's daughter.'

'And now we've killed another one, as well as our only lead in potentially figuring out why this whole vendetta started in the first place.' He sighed and closed his eyes. What had Hidden Voice found out while he was spying on Caerton's shifters? Was it still relevant? Could he have known what started this bitter enmity between the Blue Moon and the Witches?

'Will you bow to him?' Weaver asked, her voice barely audible. He looked at her carefully.

'Of course,' he replied. 'That's the way it must be. He won the challenge.'

Weaver nodded slowly.

'Okay then.' She stood up and moved to the door. She looked back at him over her shoulder. 'If you ever decided to challenge him back, I would support you.' She slipped out of the room without another word and Eyes stood still, his gaze fixed on the door.

Eyes dressed himself in some spare clothes that he kept in a bag in the bedroom, one in a little line of such bags tucked under the bed, even Wind Talker hadn't unpacked any belongings into the wardrobe. Despite all they had done to make the house feel like home there was still a feeling of this being temporary, or the niggling warning that it may be necessary to abandon the place at a moment's notice.

He went back downstairs and approached the kitchen warily, not quite ready to face his new Alpha. Wind Talker was leaning against the kitchen sink, his arms crossed over his chest.

'It should be simple enough, we'll go as soon as everyone's ready.' He stopped and looked hard at Eyes as he entered, his face went rigid and he gave Eyes the curtest of nods. Eyes inclined his head slightly and went to pour himself some coffee. He couldn't look at him, anger flared up inside and the glass coffee jug clinked against his cup as he poured with shaking hands.

'What's the plan?' he asked through gritted teeth.

'We're going back to the healing house today to repair the veil,' Wind Talker replied stiffly.

Stalker got up from the table and crossed the kitchen, placed a plate of fried food in front of Eyes and gently patted his shoulder.

'Have mine, I'm not hungry,' she said. He nodded in thanks and she moved away. 'I have to work later.'

'Fine,' Wind Talker and Eyes said together. They exchanged awkward glances and Eyes felt everyone looking at him. He picked up the plate and moved swiftly to the table to eat, not looking at anyone. Stalker gave his shoulder another squeeze then left the room.

After a hurried breakfast, with everyone waiting for him, Eyes followed the others out of the house and into the van. Claws drove with Wind Talker up front and the others sat in the back. There was the unmistakable odour left behind by Hidden Voice and Eyes wrinkled his nose. They sat in silence as the van rocked on its way to the other house and Eyes' thoughts drifted away, scanning everything that had happened in his life since he found out what he was.

'It's weird,' Stalker said softly as they stood around the small bunker. 'It's like a deliberate doorway, not a tear.'

'It will have had to have been,' Weaver answered. 'For the girl to get through. Humans can only cross the veil if there's a doorway.'

'I'm guessing she's under some sort of hypnosis,' Claws suggested and everyone looked at him. 'I mean it's not conscious is it? None of it. The mother is worried, but doesn't know why. There's no way she would have just accepted us coming in here if she knew what was hidden. The girl's drawings suggest she's retaining some of it, but doesn't understand it, she probably thinks it's a recurring nightmare, coming down here.'

It made perfect sense, Eyes gave an appraising nod.

'Let's cross over and see if we can change things in Hepethia now, shall we?' Weaver suggested. Together they crossed through the doorway into their own world, back into the pitch black cavern. A shudder ran through Eyes, he felt the darkness clawing at him and was disoriented by having his sense of sight removed. Weaver grasped his hand and squeezed it tight. 'Focus,' Weaver urged.

Eyes looked upwards and imagined the blue sky breaking through the darkness above. A tiny crack appeared in the darkness and slowly it spread, growing longer and wider. He was vaguely aware of the distant walls crumbling and turning to dust. Light spilled into the space from all around, and beneath their feet bright green grass sprouted. He looked around and saw huge crystalline forms bursting up out of the ground, surrounding them with struts of pink and white. On the grass, in the centre of their little circle, was a white circle, like paint on a football pitch, the doorway was still there. All around them was unrecognisable and when Eyes peered into the distance, towards where Hidden Voice's well-prison had been, the ground was smooth and flat.

The small birds that had covered the house on this side of the veil were still circling overhead and some landed on the crystals and watched the Lightning Lords. Eyes looked around, wondering what they needed to do.

Claws suddenly clapped his hands and then waved them at the birds.

'Shoo,' he shouted. 'You don't belong here anymore.' The birds took flight and joined the ones that were soaring overhead and gradually they all flew away.

'Guys,' Stalker said, her voice breathless. 'It's amazing.'

'Nice job,' Wind Talker said, looking around with something that might have been awe. His attention snapped back to the task in hand and he began rummaging through his satchel. He pulled out a small bottle of water and some herbs. Eyes watched as Wind Talker crushed the herbs between his fingers and sprinkled them onto the small white circle on the ground. He then dribbled some water over the top and knelt on the floor, placing his hands just outside the circle. 'It is our will that this doorway be closed forever.'

The ground sizzled slightly and then the grass gave way to smooth crystal and the circle was gone. Eyes looked up and found Stalker's face. She was looking around, her expression expectant. Her eyes settled on his and she smiled.

'It's done. The door is gone and the veil is perfectly normal now.' Stalker looked around at everyone, beaming. Weaver grinned too and finally released Eyes' hand.

Movement on the ground nearby caught Eyes' attention and the circle of shifters broke up as he moved towards it. There was a strange hissing noise and suddenly the ground quivered and a tower of snakes rose from the short grass. Eyes stepped back reflexively before he realised that it was Whispering Iasis. The fae formed before them and let out a long hiss.

'It is done, you have paid the price. Your wife will be released.' The fae looked at Eyes and he let out an enormous sigh of relief.

'Thank you, thank you.'

'Please,' Weaver spoke from just behind Eyes. 'If you don't mind, you knew there was a problem here. Do you know how it came to be?'

The fae trembled and hissed again. Eyes took a small step back, remembering the sting it had inflicted upon Wind Talker.

'Yesssss,' it hissed.

'Can you tell us?' Weaver urged.

'The price for such information would be too high for

you.'

'Try us!' Claws yelled. But it was too late, the tower of snakes had disintegrated and disappeared back into the earth.

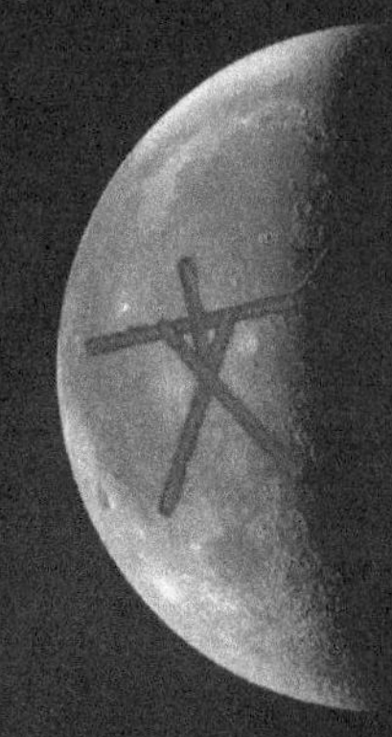

Chapter Seventeen

Stalker-of-Night's-Shadow

The Lightning Lords crossed the veil, back into the little bunker in the basement of the house. It was suddenly dark again, a stark contrast to the bright sunshine in Hepethia. Wind Talker tipped some water onto the floor and scrubbed out the chalk circle with the sleeve of his jacket. The veil was totally healed and the tomb on the other side was no more. Stalker felt relief wash over her, though it was tinged with frustration at Whispering Iasis's parting line.

'Do you think we need to do anything about the girl?' Claws asked.

'I suspect she was receiving messages through the doorway,' Wind Talker said, more certainty in his voice than Stalker felt was appropriate. 'Now that it's closed nothing can lure her across.'

'Let's get rid of the key to this room anyway, just in case.' Stalker held up the little key and stuffed it into her pocket. 'I'll throw it in a bin on the other side of the city.'

'We'll check on the family in a week or so and make sure they're okay,' Eyes said, looking pointedly at Wind Talker. 'Won't we?'

Wind Talker smiled awkwardly and nodded. The five of them filed out of the bunker, Weaver coming last and locking the padlock on the door. They quickly tidied the house, leaving it as they found it and went out to the van.

'I have to go to work now,' Stalker said, breaking the tense silence.

'I have to go to Chloe,' Eyes said, suddenly perking up as if he had just realised that she should now be herself again. He set off to collect his car without a second glance back. Stalker caught sight of Wind Talker looking irritated, his tongue between his teeth. It was going to be hard for him to get control over the pack, none of them seemed pleased with what had happened and Stalker remained fiercely loyal to Eyes. Anger at Wind Talker's betrayal stirred again in her chest and she knew she had to leave before it spilled out of her.

'See you later,' she said, mainly to Claws. She grabbed him and gave him a hug, which he reciprocated. She turned to Weaver and embraced her next.

'Hang in there,' Weaver whispered into her ear and Stalker patted her pack sister on the back in acknowledgement. She released Weaver and looked furtively at Wind Talker. He wasn't getting any warmth from her any time soon. She lifted her chin defiantly and walked away.

Stalker arrived at the dojo feeling agitated and bustled about in the locker room for as long as she could, changing into workout clothes and securing her dha in there while she taught her classes. She could hear her students arriving and with a deep breath, she went across the corridor into the studio to join them. Her first class was beginners' judo and Stalker relied heavily on her vial to keep her temper at bay. The class flew by quickly, her pulse rarely settling but there were no major incidents. Her next class was sure to be more challenging, as it was her Jieishudan class, a more advanced self-defence class, frequented mostly by older teenagers and young adults. Things tended to get more heated as there was a lot more contact in this discipline.

Her judo kids left and the next class filed in while Stalker was getting a drink and wrapping her fists up ready for the class. As she was diligently winding the strip of fabric around her knuckles, with her back to the room, she felt a familiar prickle up her spine and caught a faint whiff of the shifter's scent. A snarl rose in her throat as she identified the intruder and she turned slowly to see Fury strolling in with her normal students. Stalker glared at her and she glared right back, a smirk playing on her lips.

Stalker shook her head in disbelief and chose to ignore Fury's presence for the time being. This was not the time or place for a turf war, Fury must know that. Stalker wanted to let this play out and see what Fury wanted, besides to rattle her.

'Warm up drills,' Stalker snapped. 'Now.' The students, nearly a dozen of them, started doing sprints back and forth along the length of the studio, some of them casting wary glances at Stalker as she paced near the door. Her eyes never left Fury, who was joining in half-heartedly. 'New girl!' Stalker shouted over the pounding of feet on the floor. Fury scowled at her. 'Pick up the pace.'

Fury started running faster, occasionally shoving another student in passing. After a minute of sprints, Stalker whistled and the class came to a halt and gathered around her. 'Pair up and spar, please folks.' She caught Fury's gaze and beckoned her over as the rest of the class hurriedly paired up and spread out. Fury ambled over and stood with her arms crossed over her chest.

'Hi, then,' she said in a lazy drawl.

Stalker raised her fists and bounced lightly on the balls of her feet. Fury rolled her eyes and copied her. 'Are we really going to do this?'

'What the hell are you doing here?' Stalker hissed, ignoring Fury's question. She threw a punch, which Fury easily blocked.

'Delivering a message,' Fury replied, returning the attack. Stalker dodged and weaved around behind her. Fury whipped around, her long, thin braids streaking through the air, the beads at the ends of them smacking together. They circled each other, occasionally throwing punches with ever increasing strength, but neither one of them landed a hit. Stalker was only half aware of the rest of the class, mostly they were getting on with what they were meant to be doing but a nearby pairing were only vaguely following instruction and were watching the two shifters warily.

Stalker lunged in for an attack, one eye still on the watching humans and Fury grabbed her right arm and twisted it up behind Stalker's back, holding her firmly in an arm lock. She yanked Stalker close and snarled in her ear from behind. 'Get control of your territory,' she hissed.

Stalker pulled hard against the grapple, but she was held fast and her felt her arm straining in Fury's grasp. She winced and held in a cry of pain, aware of the class gradually turning their attention to her.

'What are you talking about?' she snarled under her breath.

Fury grabbed hold of her hair and yanked her head back. Stalker whimpered as pain shot through her forearm and up into her shoulder. If Fury pulled any harder she would break her arm.

'Runmead is swarming with fear demons, thanks to you lot. They're spilling over from St. Mark's and Crossway. Sort it out, bitch.' Fury's voice was low enough that only Stalker could hear, but everyone was watching them now. Stalker struggled in vain against Fury's hold, frustration mounting and threatening to overflow. There was a way out of this, but it was absolutely unacceptable in front of a room full of innocent humans.

'Ah, ah,' she whimpered, the pain in her arm growing even stronger. 'Okay, message received loud and clear.'

Fury's grip loosened ever so slightly, it was enough for Stalker to wriggle her good arm free and she grabbed hold of Fury and threw her hard over her shoulder. She landed with a heavy thud on the mat and jumped quickly to her feet. She stalked from the room without looking back. Stalker gently cradled her arm and looked carefully around the studio at her students. Every eye was on her and confused, fretful expressions met her gaze. She felt utterly humiliated, to be so thoroughly bested in her own specialist class in front of everyone. Her cheeks burned and her arm throbbed; it was probably sprained.

'Are you all right, Ariana?' a nearby student asked, his voice full of concern.

'Fine, thanks,' she replied, unable to hide the embarrassment she felt. 'Carry on.'

She held back tears of anger that threatened to spill as she barked orders to her class for the next forty minutes and the moment the class was over she bolted from the room and went to hide in the staff locker room. Her arm ached and she felt grief, rage and humiliation in equal measures. Hot tears spilled from her aching eyes and she covered her mouth with her good hand to conceal the vocal sobs that she couldn't halt. Her shoulders shook as the huge emotions spilled out of her.

She took a sharp breath and wiped her face on her sleeve, determined to shake off these feelings enough to get out of the dojo. She grabbed her things from her locker, strapped her dha across her back, where they instantly disappeared from sight, and slammed her locker shut. She dashed from the building without saying goodnight to Ron and set off at a sprint into the chilly night. The sky was clear and stars pricked the orange-tinged sky.

It was only when she was almost in Burnside that she even realised that she wasn't heading back to Grove Street, or even her own flat. She veered west, careful not to enter the Glass Wolves' territory and headed for the city centre. The run would normally clear her head, but tonight she couldn't freerun for the pain in her arm, so she had to stick to the ground and veer around obstacles, rather than scaling them. A red mist of hate for Wind Talker and Fury seeped through every synapse, and when she skidded to a halt on Rhys's doorstep her heart was racing and her head pounding. She knocked hard on the door and pressed her forehead against the cool wood.

She heard movement inside and lifted her head. The door opened in front of her and Rhys stood back to let her in.

'I had a feeling it would be you,' he said softly. She moved past him into the living room and heard the door close softly. She turned and saw him looking at her with his dark, intense eyes, much as he had feasted on her the very first time they met. She crossed the floor quickly and grasped his face in both of her hands, capturing his lips in a passionate kiss. He took hold of her and lifted her off her feet, he carried her easily to the sofa and they dropped down onto it with barely a pause in their frenzied kissing.

Stalker couldn't think straight, her feelings were so strong that they drowned out all conscious thought, and she gave herself willingly to them. She pulled off Rhys's shirt and tossed it aside, she gasped for air and felt his hot breath on her face. As they tugged and grabbed at each other's clothes, clumsily stripping one another, all of the drama seemed to fade away. Stalker had been driven into his arms by events utterly unrelated to him, but now all she knew was his smell, his hard body pressing against hers, and his full lips all over her own.

Finally, Stalker had what she had wanted since she first met him, and it was as incredible as she had imagined it would be. They seemed to know one another's bodies instinctively, and as fast and frenzied as their love making was, it wasn't clumsy. Their passion peaked, and gradually the rest of the world came back into focus. Stalker's breathing was heavy and her skin was coated in sweat as

Rhys laid gentle kisses on her neck. She stroked his hair and allowed the darkness to creep back in, she couldn't fight it, she was too vulnerable. The euphoria faded and she felt her cheeks sag.

'What happened?' Rhys whispered, looking deep into her eyes. 'Or can't you tell me?'

'I shouldn't tell you, but I have to talk to someone, and I can hardly spill my guts to Ben.'

Rhys gave a snort of laughter and shook his head. He rolled carefully onto his side and lay beside her on the sofa. He pulled her close against his body and wrapped her up in his strong arms. She suddenly felt safer than she had in weeks. 'A rival from a neighbouring pack came to my class tonight to make trouble. She nearly broke my arm.' She held up her arm, which was absolutely fine now, but Rhys took hold of it and rubbed it with his soft fingers.

'That's not good. But that's not everything, is it?'

'No.' Stalker closed her eyes, she could feel tears threatening to spill again. A small one escaped and rolled down her face. Rhys kissed away the tear, and cradled her head.

'It's okay, you can tell me anything. But if you don't want to I will just hold you for as long as you need.'

A whimper escaped her lips and more tears fell. The relief was enormous.

'One of my pack mates betrayed us all. He killed someone that we needed to question and who I wanted to help. Then he challenged the Alpha and took control of the pack. I hate him. I hate him for it. I won't kneel to him. He's no Alpha of mine.'

'Fuck, that's really awful.' Rhys continued to stroke

her arm but his body tensed briefly and she could hear the shock in his voice.

'I have to go back soon and tell them about what happened in my class. But I don't want to, I wish I could just stay here with you.'

'How do the rest of your pack feel about what happened with the Alpha?'

'I don't know, but I get the feeling I'm not the only one who feels like this. Claws and me tend to be on the same wavelength. My Alpha, the real Alpha, and Weaver, they're big on the rules. Weaver especially. So she'll do as she's told, she'll follow Wind Talker and Eyes will too, for now at least.' She didn't care that she was sharing names, she no longer worried about what Rhys knew. Either he was an enemy in disguise or not, it didn't matter. All that mattered was that right now he was here for her.

'Don't go,' Rhys whispered, pulling her tightly against him. 'Stay here with me tonight and make love to me again.'

And she did.

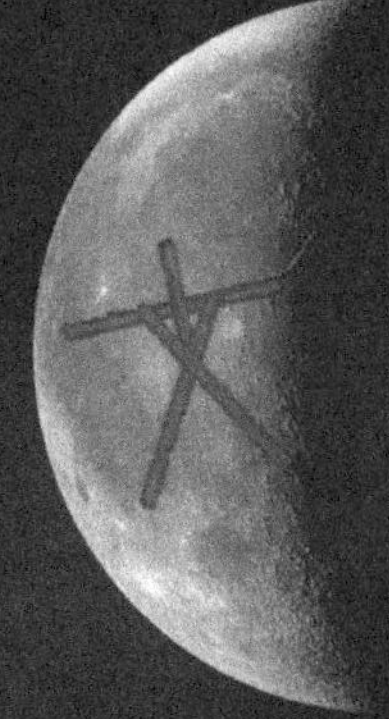

CHAPTER EIGHTEEN

FIGHTS-EYES-OPEN

EYES WAS ALMOST AT THE HOSPITAL when his phone started to ring. He glanced at it and recognised the number of the psychiatric ward. He felt a rush of excitement that lit up his face, knowing exactly why they would be calling, but ignored the call as he was driving. He parked his car in a drop-off space, not caring if he got a ticket. He ran into the hospital and up to the ward, taking the stairs two at a time. His pulse raced furiously and peopled stared at him as he brushed past them. In record time, he skidded to a halt at the locked door of the ward. He pressed the buzzer and tapped his foot impatiently as he waited for an answer. The voice of the duty nurse echoed in the empty corridor.

'Hello, can I help?'

'It's Martin Davison,' he said sharply and the door was buzzed open for him without another word. He threw it open and ran towards Chloe's room. The duty nurse met him halfway down the brightly lit corridor and held up her hands to halt him.

'Mr Davison,' she said firmly. He brushed past her and burst into Chloe's room. She was sitting up in bed, her face red and blotchy from crying, her wrists restrained to the bars on the sides of her bed.

'What's this?' he shouted. 'Get those things off her.'

Her eyes met his and they were terrified. The hope and joy he had allowed himself to feel on the way here evaporated.

'Martin?' Chloe's voice croaked and he moved quickly to her side. 'What's going on? Why am I here?'

'You were in a bad way, we didn't know what else to do. But it seems like you're feeling better.' He stroked her hair gently as he spoke and pressed his lips to her forehead. 'Take these restraints off now, she's not a danger to anyone.' He looked imploringly at the nurse and she gave a brief nod before moving over to undo the straps.

'What happened at the house? Where's Amy?' Chloe asked, her voice shaking. Eyes cupped her cheeks and looked into her eyes.

'Amy's fine, she's with my mum and Rebecca. I'm going to get you to them as soon as possible. We'll talk about the house later, it doesn't matter right now. All that matters is that we're okay.'

Chloe's eyes searched his and her lip trembled. She was scared of him. Eyes felt a lump rise in his throat as the reality struck. Chloe may not be afflicted with madness, but she was far from whole. He held her, pressing her head against his chest.

It seemed like hours before the consultant came to check on her.

'I think we should keep you here overnight, Mrs Davison, just to make sure you're all right.' The doctor was well-meaning and kind, but she had no idea what she was dealing with and Eyes shook his head firmly.

'No, we're going home. You can discharge yourself,' he reminded Chloe. 'I know Amy really misses you, and so do I. Let's go home.' He needed her to agree, he was desperate. He needed to get her away from the hospital and back in familiar surroundings. He couldn't actually take her to their home, but he thought it best not to mention that just yet.

Chloe nodded slowly and looked from Eyes to the doctor.

'I want to go home.'

'Okay,' the doctor said, obviously a little disappointed. 'You haven't been sectioned, so I can discharge you into the care of your family. I'll get the paperwork and the nurse will take your IV out.' She nodded at the nurse, who immediately did as she was told.

Eyes waited while everything was done, he couldn't bear to let go of Chloe's hand, but she didn't squeeze his back and hardly looked at him. The nurse left and returned later with a bag of Chloe's things that she was wearing when she was brought in.

'Do you want me to help you change?' he asked softly. Chloe shook her head.

'Can you give me a minute?' she asked, not meeting his eyes.

'Of course,' he replied. He left the room, a heavy weight on his shoulders. He stood outside and kept a watchful eye on her through the window in the door. She dressed slowly, looking at each item of clothing carefully before putting it on. Eyes couldn't raise a smile, he had been through hell to heal her, but now he had so much more work to do to fix things between them. He doubted a fae could help with that. There were no short cuts, nor should there be, he knew that.

Finally they were ready to leave and he took her arm to lead her to the car. There was a parking ticket wedged under his wiper and he pocketed it before settling Chloe into the front passenger seat. She had a glazed expression on her face the entire drive across the city to Eyes' mother's house in the north of St. Mark's. It was nearly dark as he helped her up the driveway and into the house.

'I can't believe it!' Rebecca called as she met them in the hall. She pulled her sister into a tight embrace, leaving Eyes to close the door. He watched as Chloe sank into Rebecca's arms, giving herself to the warmth of her family in a way she hadn't done with him. He was a mere spectator as Chloe was reunited with the others. Amy was delirious with joy and even his own mother greeted his wife as if she were her own daughter. His mother had been withdrawn and a shadow of her former self since the attack, she had lost her husband and was obviously traumatised by it all, but she hadn't asked a single question, so he had avoided confronting the truth with her. He had dodged Rebecca's inquisition, feeding her the same lies that he had told the police. She obviously didn't believe it, but he refused to be drawn into an argument.

They ate dinner together, though hardly anyone spoke. Chloe stared at her food and idly moved it around her plate with her fork, not eating more than a couple of small bites.

Rebecca took Chloe to the bathroom to wash and get ready for bed and Eyes was tasked with doing the same for Amy.

'Thank you for bringing Mummy home,' she said softly as he brushed her curly hair.

'That's all right, munchkin. I wanted her home too.'

'When are we going *home* home?'

Eyes sighed.

'I think we'll probably find a new home. Would that be okay with you?'

'Yes.' She nodded and smiled at him. It was the happiest he had seen her in days. A glimmer of hope stirred that perhaps he might get some of his family back.

Once Amy was asleep he tip-toed into the adjoining room that he had been nominally sleeping in, not that he had been here much. Chloe was lying in the bed and he curled up next to her, pulling her against his body.

'I love you,' he whispered. She shuffled away from him and stifled a sob.

'I don't even know you anymore.' Her voice was little more than a hoarse whimper.

Eyes rolled onto his back and stared hard at the ceiling, hurt, rejected and drowning in guilt.

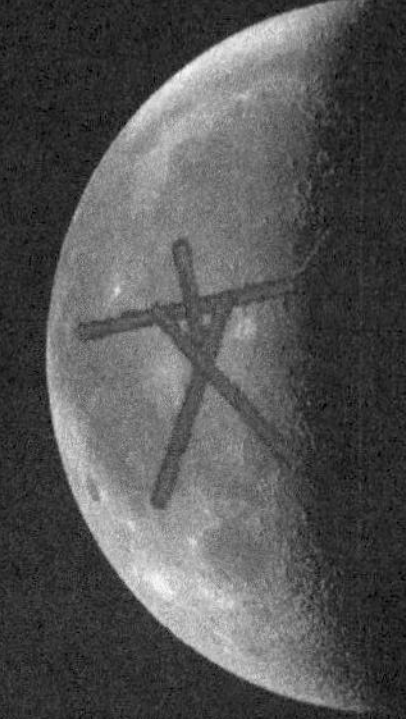

Chapter Nineteen

Stalker-of-Night's-Shadow

It was mid-morning when Stalker quietly entered 32 Grove Street, her chest felt tight and she tugged at the neck of her top, as if that would help ease her breathing. She heard voices in the kitchen and made her way up the dark hall to join the others. Eyes wasn't there, but the others were talking quietly and looking over the map that she and Claws had got from the library. Stalker stood in the doorway, hugging her arms across her chest.

'Hey there stranger,' Claws said, without looking up. 'Everything all right?'

'So-so,' she replied and moved into the room.

'Heard any more weird stuff?' Weaver asked, not quite meeting Stalker's eyes. Suddenly she had the feeling they had been talking about her.

'No,' she replied slowly. 'But I would like to try and understand what that was.'

'It was a very heightened situation,' Wind Talker said,

his eyes resolutely on the map, his voice emphatically innocent.

'I was not imagining it!' Stalker snapped. 'Frankly, it's insulting that any of you would insinuate such a thing.'

She turned and stormed into the living room. She went to the window and looked out onto the street while she took some deep breaths. She felt someone enter the room behind her and closed her eyes, hoping not to hear Wind Talker's patronising voice.

'I know you didn't imagine it.' It was Weaver and Stalker felt her shoulders relax. 'I think we should investigate, I mean, after all the warnings from the Storm Riders, we can't ignore something like this.'

'Back to the beach then?' Stalker asked as she turned to face Weaver. 'See if it happens again?'

'Sure. I'll call Eyes, see where he is.' Weaver left the room as she pulled out her phone and lifted it to her ear. Stalker wiped her clammy palms on her jeans and walked back to the kitchen. Wind Talker glanced up at her, an odd look on his face.

'Sorry,' he mumbled.

'It's okay,' she replied, not really meaning it, but she wanted to get on with everything they had to do and couldn't stand another argument. 'Fury turned up at my dojo last night. Apparently fear demons are spilling out of our territory and causing them problems.'

Wind Talker nodded solemnly.

'That's understandable, given the arrival of The-Knight-of-Shadowed-Fear. We'll let the border incursion go, this time, and see to the fear demons in due course.'

Stalker nodded in agreement. She didn't like the idea

of letting Fury get away with her actions, but she wasn't going to debate it with Wind Talker now.

'Chloe's not doing so great,' Weaver said from the doorway. 'Eyes needs to stay with his family today.'

Wind Talker clucked his tongue and stood up, his chair legs scraping across the linoleum. Stalker watched him warily, waiting for more. He slammed his coffee mug down on the table and brushed past her and Weaver as he strode to the door.

'Come on then,' he snapped. 'Let's get back to the beach and find out what the fuck is going on.'

Stalker exchanged trouble glances with Weaver and Claws, before the three of them filed down the hall and out of the house after him. They had the van until the following day, so Wind Talker drove and the other three sat in awkward silence in the back. Stalker couldn't shake the memory of Hidden Voice lying on the floor of the van, unconscious and unknowingly riding to his death. A cold, hard lump formed in her throat as she stared at the floor.

Twenty minutes later, the van ground to a halt on the soft sand track down to the beach and the Lightning Lords climbed out of it. As Stalker climbed around the van, careful not to slide down the sand bank, she looked down to see Hidden Voice's funeral pyre disintegrated and scattered around the beach. The tide was very low, the beach smooth and stretching out away from the dark cliffs to her left. Something caught her eye though, marks in the sand. She scurried down the bank and heard the others following her. She ran to where the pyre had stood and stooped to examine the sand.

'Tracks,' she said, calling over her shoulder to the

others. They gathered around her.

'Has the body been washed out to sea?' Weaver asked, anxiety evident in the tremble in her voice.

Claws followed the tracks towards the cliffs and Stalker ran along beside him. The wind whipped her hair around her face and gulls cried as they circled overhead.

'These footprints are too deep, too erratic. Whoever it was, they were carrying something heavy.' Claws rubbed his face and stared up at the cliffs. The footprints were just visible for a few paces once their owner had climbed onto the rocks but once the sand had been stomped off the shoes, there was nothing that Claws could track. 'I'm good, but not that good,' he said sheepishly.

'Hey, don't worry about it,' Stalker said, patting his shoulder. She glanced around to make sure they were alone and on seeing the deserted beach, shifted into the form of a bloodhound. She sniffed carefully around the tracks and the wet rocks. All she could smell was the salt of the sea and sand, and the faintest trace of the corpse that had been carried away, tinged with smoke and firewood. She shifted form again, heaved a sigh and shrugged. 'Nothing.'

They headed back to Wind Talker and Weaver, and Stalker shook her head as they drew level. 'Looks like someone took the body.'

'Shit.' Wind Talker kicked a piece of charred wood and it skidded across the damp sand.

'Maybe it was Father Ash?' Weaver suggested, hopefully.

'Maybe,' Claws nodded. 'I'd guess it was a man, from the size of the footprints.'

'I don't see that there is anything we can do about it

now,' Wind Talker said shortly. 'Do you hear anything unusual?' He looked pointedly at Stalker and she shook her head. She looked around, suddenly remembering the raven that had been watching them. There was no sign of it now.

'Can I borrow your knife?' she asked Wind Talker. He opened his bag and passed it to her. 'Thanks.' She held out her hand and pressed the blade to her thumb. She had once summoned a raven to carry a message to Ragged Edge, maybe it would work again. Ravens were Odin's messengers, his eyes in the world of humanity and they were bound to his Berserkers. She held her bleeding thumb up and felt the salt spray from the sea sting as it made contact with the cut. She searched the grey sky but saw nothing. Suddenly, the gulls cried and swept away, heading for the cliff top and flying inland. Stalker spun to face out to sea, something moved a short distance down the beach, a shape formed in the sand.

'What is that?' Claws asked, taking a few steps towards it.

'It's a wind fae,' Wind Talker answered. Sand whipped up from the ground in a rapidly shifting spiral and it moved swiftly up the beach towards them.

'What are you doing here?' a soft breath reached out to them from the column of sand.

'Please,' Claws said, holding his hands up. 'Can you tell us what happened here?'

'You know,' the fae hissed.

'We burned a body and now it's gone. Who took it?' Wind Talker asked, his voice a little more soft than Stalker had heard it in a while.

'No idea,' the fae replied. The wind dropped slightly and then whipped up again. 'Maybe it was him.'

'Who?' Stalker urged.

'The shifter who visits here every day at moonrise.'

Stalker and Weaver looked at each other, Weaver's eyes were narrowed.

'Was he here when we burned the body?' Claws asked.

'No,' the fae replied, spinning frantically. 'But the others were.'

'Who?' Stalker snapped, her patience waning.

'*Your* people.' The voice on the wind sighed and then disappeared.

'My people or our people?' Stalker cried, but the fae was gone. She kicked the sand and it sprayed up into the blustery air.

'It's only a couple of hours until moonrise. We could hide the van and keep watch.' Weaver suggested. Stalker looked around the desolate beach and then back at Weaver.

'Okay,' she said sulkily.

'Yes, excellent plan,' Wind Talker huffed, straightening his shirt. They returned to the van and Wind Talker drove it half a mile up the road away from the city and towards Father Ash's house. He pulled off the main road up a track that led into the woods and parked under the cover of the trees, out of sight of the road. Stalker led them away from the van, back towards the beach through the woods. She walked quickly, the others trailing along behind her. Dry twigs and leaves crunched under her boots and she was faintly aware of the living creatures in the woods scurrying away from the four intruders.

The trees were starting to show signs of life again,

with small buds appearing and as she walked, Stalker saw snowdrops by the roadside. She wondered who would be moving into the Watchtower now that spring was upon them.

As she drew level with the beach, Stalker moved deeper under the cover of the trees, away from the road. They could see some of the beach from here, and had a good view of the road in both directions. She leaned heavily against a tree and closed her eyes, feeling the warm sun on her face through the tree branches above. She felt movement around her as the others caught up to her, the heavy footfalls of Wind Talker and Claws moved past her and came to a halt a few yards away, but Weaver's almost silent footsteps stopped beside her.

'Are you all right?' Weaver asked softly. Stalker opened her eyes and looked at her as she shrugged.

'Not really. You?'

'I'm okay. I'm curious about something.' Stalker cocked an eyebrow at her and waited for her to elaborate. 'You were gone all night and came back this morning smelling of, you know.' Weaver tried to hide a smile. Stalker allowed a small smile to grace her lips.

'Yes,' she whispered.

'But it wasn't First Strike, was it?'

Stalker's smile dropped. She hadn't even thought of him. She swallowed hard and shook her head.

'No, it wasn't. I'm not seeing him anymore.'

'Stalker.' Weaver hesitated. 'Be careful, I can tell he's human.'

Stalker's breath caught in her throat and she let out a guttural noise.

'I will, it's fine. Don't worry.' She couldn't tell Weaver. She had come this far without mentioning Rhys to anyone but Claws. She knew what Weaver and Wind Talker would make of the secrets and lies and demon shrouds.

She turned her attention to the road and beach, waiting for the stranger to appear. It could be the Spiral Hand that they needed to uncover. Stalker couldn't think of a reason for any of Caerton's shifters to come out here every day at moonrise.

Weaver checked her watch every few minutes and threw furtive glances around the quiet woods. Stalker cast her gaze around, checking all directions for movement. As moonrise approached, Stalker felt her pulse begin to quicken and she paced the soft ground. A caw above her in the trees caught her attention, and she looked up to see a big raven sitting on a branch, bobbing its head. She stopped and looked at it. Another one joined it. 'Something's happening,' she whispered. The others looked at her, Claws stood up from his squatting position at the base of a tree and looked up at the birds.

Stalker moved cautiously to the tree line, so as to get a better view of the beach. In the far distance she saw someone walking a dog, throwing a stick into the sea for it to chase. The tide had crept up the beach and there was now only about half as much depth to it as when they had arrived, but it was still wide open. There was no sign of anyone else approaching.

Weaver shifted just a part of her face, thanks to her pendant, and sniffed around with her sensitive cat-nose and Stalker looked imploringly at Claws. He rolled his eyes and then cleared his throat before leaping into the air and shifting mid-jump into a scruffy-looking barn owl. He swept off into the trees and she watched him soar overhead to scout from the sky. The ravens startled and took flight too, gliding away towards the cliffs.

Stalker's pulse pounded in her temples as she waited anxiously, trying to ignore Wind Talker checking his watch as he leaned against a tree. She moved right to the edge of the road and stared out onto the beach. Where was he? Had he sensed them? Her pulse was really racing now and she rubbed her temples, trying to ease the tension. *Thud, thud, thud, thud.* She closed her eyes and took deep breaths. But it was no good, the pounding was relentless.

'What is that?' Wind Talker whispered behind her. She looked his way and saw that he was alert and looking about anxiously. *Thud, thud, thud, thud.* It wasn't her pulse and he could hear it too this time.

Stalker looked back toward the beach and saw three ravens circling. The dog walker was fading into the distance. She glanced both ways to check for cars, and seeing none she ran across the road, breaking cover completely. 'Stalker!' Wind Talker hissed from behind her. She ignored him and ran down the bank onto the beach.

The footsteps were heavier now, getting ever closer. Even without the chaos of a pack brawl it was maddening. She spun in circles, searching for the source. Wind Talker and Weaver were running down the bank towards her and a fourth raven had added to the circling overhead.

'What is it? Is this what you heard before?' Weaver called out over the thundering noise.

Claws swooped down from the sky and landed on his human feet at a run in between Weaver and Stalker, looking from one to the other.

'What is that?'

Wind Talker fumbled with something around his neck and Stalker watched him as he grabbed his talisman in his fist and his eyes slipped out of focus.

'Nothing, there's nothing here on the other side,' he called.

Stalker felt the veil rippling just a few feet from her, between her and the sea. She raised a hand and pointed.

'Right there, Wind Talker!'

'There is no one there, I swear!' he yelled back.

Stalker watched the spot, unable to move or speak. The veil opened and she caught a glimpse into another world, it was almost pitch black, in contrast to the early afternoon sunshine here, it certainly wasn't Hepethia. A figure moved in the darkness, marching towards the gap. She was vaguely aware of the others close behind her and she heard Weaver gasp.

'The Underworld.'

'Who's there?' Claws called out.

The shadowy figure crossed the veil and marched towards them. He was a soldier in battered, leather armour, red hand prints covered his eyes and most of his face. He was faint, almost translucent, but growing more and more solid with every step he took. He stopped right in front of Stalker, fully solidified. He raised a hand and struck her hard across the face. Stalker stumbled and reflexively reached for her bruised cheek. The pain coursed through her face and she felt supportive hands on her from her pack mates, helping to steady her.

'What the hell was that?' Claws shouted. Stalker

glanced at him and saw the rage in his face.

'Stalker-of-Night's-Shadow,' the ghost said in a voice that echoed off the bare sand. 'You have forgotten your purpose.'

'W-what?' Stalker stammered, looking at him through narrowed eyes.

'You swore a vow to Odin's Warriors because you felt the call of battle. I am Hands-and-Face, you are my descendent, and a grave disappointment.'

'I'm sorry,' Stalker said, unsure what else she could say to that.

'You're distracted and undisciplined. You have failed to take advantage of all of the gifts offered to you by Artemis and Odin. You let your enemies grow in strength and evade you, and you have forgotten where you come from.'

'I don't know where I come from!' she cried, frustrated tears stinging her eyes.

'You have forgotten!' Hands-and-Face roared. With that, the ghost turned and strode back across the veil into the Underworld, leaving Stalker open-mouthed and nursing her aching cheek.

Stalker turned on her heel and marched back to the van without looking at anyone. She heard them scurrying behind her, whispering frantically, but she tuned it out. Her ears seemed to still be ringing with the marching footsteps of the invisible, undead army. She climbed into the back of the van with Claws, while Weaver sat up front with Wind Talker, and Stalker got the distinct impression that they were trying to give her space, which she supposed she ought to appreciate, but mainly it just made her more angry.

She stared at the floor and wrung her hands, her thoughts racing. Her cheek had stopped throbbing, but the emotional pain of the encounter was still tangible. Claws sat in silence opposite her, radiating his calming aura. If it was working and this was how she felt under its effect, it didn't bear thinking about what she would feel like without him there.

The words of Hands-and-Face stung so much because she knew he was right. She had neglected to investigate why she was different, or where she had come from. Shadow's Step had dangled the thread in front of her right from the start. He had asked her about her biological parents and told her that at least one of them would have been a shifter, but she wasn't ready to face her past when her present was so confusing.

Her new world had exploded so soon and so spectacularly, that she had barely had a moment to slow down and consider her past. But she couldn't hide behind excuses, the winter had been quiet after the defeat of the Plague Doctor. She'd had a chance to dig into her origins, but had chosen not to, on some level.

The van pulled up on Grove Street and Stalker climbed out of the back without looking at any of the others. She set off at a jog towards the dojo, she had classes to teach, though how she was going to manage, she didn't know.

Mercifully, Fury was absent and although it was challenging for her to keep her cool, nothing eventful happened during her classes. As she left the dojo at six o'clock, Stalker called Eyes. He answered after a few rings and she could hear shouting in the background.

'Hello?' he snapped, short of breath.

'Hi,' Stalker replied. 'Everything okay?'

'Not really. What can I do for you?'

'Have you spoken to any of the others today?'

'Not since Weaver called this morning. Why?'

'Typical, I'm sorry no one updated you. We went back to the beach and found that someone had taken Hidden Voice's remains.'

'What?!'

'I know. I tried to track it but the sea and—'

'Fine, fine,' Eyes interrupted. 'That's fine.'

'A fae appeared and told us that a shifter visits that spot on the beach every day at moonrise, so we waited for them to show up but they didn't. Something else did though.' She stopped and took a deep breath.

'What? What happened?' His voice was softer, like he could sense her anxiety.

'A ghost of my ancestor crossed over from the Underworld and berated me for neglecting my ancestry and told me I was a disappointment to him.' She felt a hard lump in her throat as she stumbled over the words in a torrent.

'I see,' he said quietly. 'How do you feel about that?'

'Hurt, but it's true. I need to follow up on it. I need to be excused from pack duty while I sort some of this out.'

'I'm not the Alpha anymore,' he reminded her, a reluctant sigh in his voice. 'You need to ask Wind Talker.'

'What's going on with you? How's Chloe?' Stalker asked, ignoring his suggestion. She wanted to tell him about Fury too, but there was only so much she could burden him with.

'Angry.' There was another shout in the background and Stalker flinched as she heard something smash. 'I have to go. Take care of yourself, don't do anything rash. Okay?'

'Yes, of course. Same to you.' She hung up the phone and looked up and down the darkening street. Cars swept past and music was coming from a nearby flat. Stalker stood, almost hypnotised for a few minutes, gathering her thoughts. She had to go back to Grove Street. Her pack would be worried about her and she needed to reconnect with Weaver and Claws at least, even if she still couldn't look at Wind Talker.

She set off at a run and crossed St. Mark's quickly. She vaulted fences, ran up walls and jumped down from precarious heights with ease, her talisman protecting her from dangerous falls. It barely registered in her mind that she might be seen floating to the ground and when the thought did flicker into her consciousness she found she didn't care. When she ran like this she was free.

She burst through the door and walked briskly through to the kitchen, short of breath and glowing pink. The three of them all stared at her as she entered.

'Everything okay?' Claws asked, a slice of toast in his hand.

'Yeah. Sorry for running off earlier,' she replied, looking down at the ground.

'Totally understandable,' Weaver said, nodding sympathetically.

'Tomorrow we need to wrap up the healing house business, and return the family to their home,' Wind Talker said stiffly. 'Eyes has the keys and has been the face of this operation, so we'll need him to join us.'

'I'll tell him,' Stalker offered. She didn't think Eyes would welcome a call from Wind Talker and got the feeling Wind Talker knew that too. She typed a text message, relaying the request to Eyes. She looked up to see Claws buttering some more toast and he slid the plate along the kitchen worktop to her.

'Eat,' he ordered. She smiled and tucked in, suddenly acutely aware that she hadn't eaten all day.

'Get some rest,' Wind Talker ordered. 'All of you.' He looked pointedly at Stalker and any thoughts of disappearing out into the night were promptly squashed. Wind Talker left the room and trudged up the stairs.

'We need Eyes back,' Stalker whispered.

'He'll be back,' Weaver replied, tidying away her own dinner plate. 'He just needs room to process what happened.'

Stalker glanced at Claws. He returned her furtive look, he understood what she had meant. Whether Weaver had misunderstood, or was deliberately ignoring Stalker's meaning wasn't clear.

'What do you want to do about what happened today?' Claws asked her, keeping his voice casual. Stalker looked at him carefully, he avoided eye contact by busying himself with tidying the kitchen.

'I don't know,' she admitted, passing him her empty plate. 'I can talk to Ragged Edge about my role in Odin's Warriors. But I don't even know where to begin in finding my birth parents.'

'I can probably help you with that,' he said, glancing at her and pausing the washing up.

'Really?' A spark of hope warmed her inside.

'Of course,' he said with a smile. 'Work's been agonisingly slow since that lead of mine died. I had to let that case go.'

'That's a shame,' Stalker said softly. She couldn't feel too bad about that, her mind was still on his offer to help her. Weaver approached and placed a warm hand on her shoulder.

'We all want to help. Even Wind Talker.'

Stalker scowled and Weaver removed her hand. She gave an unapologetic shrug and left the room.

'Don't shoot me,' Claws whispered. 'But he does. He's worried about you.'

Stalker gawked at him. He held her gaze. He wasn't going to back down, he was challenging her to accept what he had said.

'I couldn't shoot you if I tried,' she said, shaking her head and breaking the tension. 'You're the gun-slinger.'

'Let's get some sleep,' Claws said, a small smile on his lips. Stalker grabbed him and pulled him into a tight embrace, which he returned. 'It'll all be okay. We'll work it out,' he whispered against her hair. She was trembling slightly and tears threatened to spill. She sniffed and stayed locked in his brotherly arms.

'Thank you,' she whispered. She pulled away and wiped her eyes. They followed Weaver to the front room. Wind Talker had not come back downstairs, which was a relief to Stalker. The three of them settled down to sleep, though Stalker was disturbed by frequent vivid dreams of Hands-and-Face. It was a relief when dawn arrived and the others started to show signs of waking. Stalker leaped up, shifting back into her human form and was the first into the kitchen.

She had a reply from Eyes, agreeing to meet the rest of the pack at the house at 9am. She started making breakfast as the others gradually joined her. Wind Talker had slept upstairs all night and was the last to emerge. They got ready with barely a word, changing into overalls to maintain their cover story.

They set off in the van, an uneasy silence filling the air. When they arrived at the house, Eyes was already there, leaning against his four-wheel drive. He had dark circles under his eyes, was showing at least a day's growth of beard and his hair was unkempt. Stalker approached him cautiously, struck by the difference.

'Are we ready to do this?' Eyes asked, not bothering to greet any of them.

'I don't see that there is anything left to do here,' Wind Talker replied stiffly. 'Have you contacted Mrs Bennett?'

'Yes, she's due here in ten minutes.'

'Let's just make a quick attempt to make it look like we carried out work in there, shall we?' Stalker suggested.

'Agreed,' Wind Talker replied and he led the way.

They went straight to the bunker and hurriedly cleaned some of the dust and cobwebs off the breeze block walls and empty shelves, and swept the floor.

'Hello?' a voice called from upstairs. Eyes jogged up into the kitchen and Stalker followed, while the others finished putting things in order.

'Mrs Bennett?' Eyes called out. Stalker followed him out of the kitchen and saw the woman standing in the hallway, twisting the strap of her handbag in her hands.

'I hope your family is well. We're just finishing up here.'

'Where was it? The asbestos?' she asked, her eyes darting over his shoulder towards Stalker and beyond.

'In the basement,' Eyes said, his voice steady as a rock. 'We were able to remove it and replace the original walls over the cavity.'

'Oh,' she said, nodding. 'I haven't been down there in years. I'd almost forgotten it was there.'

Stalker heard footsteps behind her and turned to see Claws approaching. He caught her eye and gave a discreet nod, indicating that the woman was telling the truth.

'Well, everything is fine now,' Eyes said kindly. 'No more need to worry.'

Stalker felt the weight behind his words and from the way Mrs Bennett finally seemed to relax a little and settle her gaze directly on him, she got the impression she felt it too. A curious expression flickered over her features, a hint of a frown and then a relieved and appreciative smile. Stalker smiled and gently eased past Eyes and Mrs Bennett, and out through the door, Claws right behind her. They went to the van and waited. Weaver and Wind Talker emerged, carrying a dust sheet and a tool box. Eyes followed a moment later and they all gathered by the van.

'Everything okay?' Stalker asked Eyes. He nodded.

'Fine.' There was an uncomfortable silence. 'It's my step-father's funeral tomorrow. I wanted to ask you all to come, for the support, you know? But it could be awkward, people might ask questions.'

'You can't go alone,' Claws said, his voice full of concern. 'You're right about it not being a good idea for us all to go, but maybe just me?'

Stalker glared at Claws. If only one of them was going to go, she wanted it to be her. But maybe Claws was the best choice, he had his calming aura and she had enough of her own baggage right now. Eyes nodded and looked relieved.

'Thanks, that'd be great.'

Wind Talker gave a curt nod, then moved around the van and opened the door, a signal for them all to leave. Stalker caught Eyes' arm and he looked at her.

'I'm here for you,' she said, fixing her eyes firmly on his. 'You don't have to do anything on your own.'

'I know,' he sighed. 'Thank you. But you have your own issues to deal with. Find your own truth, Stalker, don't worry about learning everyone else's.' He gently pulled his arm free and strode to his car. Stalker reluctantly turned and climbed into the back of the van. She took out her phone and wrestled with competing desires. Part of her wanted to run and hide in Rhys's arms, but she knew that she had work to do in order to appease her ancestor. Finding her resolve, she typed a text message to Rhys.

> Hi. How are you? I miss you. Something big happened. Feels like I say that every day. I wish I could come see you and tell you about it, but I have to deal with it, not hide. Can I see you in a couple of days? You could come to my place for a change. Love S x

At last she could use her real initial with him, he was one less person to lie to. It was a relief. She knew he'd be working and didn't wait for a reply. She leaned back against the side of the van and closed her eyes. The uneven rocking stopped her from falling asleep, as desperately tired as she was. They stopped at Grove Street to empty the van and change out of their overalls, then dropped the van off at the rental place. Tensions gradually seemed to ease, but Stalker was itching to get back into the garden, and she resented the easy banter between the other three as they walked back to the house.

She was the first to reach the door and burst into the house, crossed the veil and charged into the back garden. It was empty and she scanned the sky for a sign of Unchained Lightning. Thick, white clouds drifted across the sky and she stared hopelessly up at them. She felt the others cross the veil behind her and slowly turned to face them.

'What's going on?' Weaver asked, obviously concerned.

'I wanted to speak to Unchained Lightning.'

Right on cue, the elemental soared over the roof and landed with a thud in the garden.

'Where is my throne?' the fae boomed. Stalker flinched.

'We had urgent matters to attend to,' Wind Talker said, stepping forwards.

'You are Alpha now,' Unchained Lightning said with a crackle.

'I am.'

'My throne is the most urgent matter you have. If you do not secure it I will revoke my patronage.'

Stalker noticed Wind Talker's face drain of colour and concealed a grin of satisfaction.

'We need more information before we move against the Sparkbloods,' Weaver said. 'But we will make acquiring it our top priority. You have our deepest apologies for being so easily distracted.'

Stalker's smile drooped. There was that word again.

This was what Hands-and-Face had meant, she was distracted from the truly important things. Honouring their pack ally should be one of their most important duties, alongside protecting the humans on their territory.

'I wanted to ask you something,' she said, stepping forwards and looking up into his big, blue eyes.

'Yes?'

'I once helped you realise what you were.'

'Hmm, yes?' The fae tilted his head and watched her with narrowed eyes.

'Well, I wondered if you could do the same for me. It was recently pointed out to me that I haven't been as proactive in figuring out why I'm different as I should have been. I have to believe that I am this way for a reason and if I knew that reason I might be better able to live up to your expectations.'

Unchained Lightning nodded his head slowly and let out a purr-like rumble.

'I cannot help you, all I know about you is that you are not using all of your power. There is a poor connection, preventing the rest from being accessed.'

Stalker frowned at him, confusion dizzying her. She trusted him to understand the flow of power, that was his nature, but this raised more questions when what she wanted was answers.

'Okay,' she replied hesitantly. 'Is it blocking my memories too?' The memory of Hands-and-Face bellowing at her on the beach resurfaced.

'Possibly.'

'How do I fix it?'

'An injection of conductive material.' Unchained

Lightning abruptly launched himself into the air and flew away, leaving Stalker staring after him, nonplussed.

'Well that was helpful. Not.'

'We'll help you figure it out,' Weaver said. She moved into the centre of the garden and picked up a twig. She changed her right index finger into a sharp claw and scratched her left thumb with it, drawing blood. She wiped the blood onto the twig and began whistling. Stalker watched in bemusement.

A shadow fell over the garden and Stalker heard the beating of wings overhead. She looked up and saw a murder of crows circling against the white clouds. A single crow broke away from the group and flew down to greet Weaver. It landed on the outstretched twig and bobbed its head. 'Thank you for answering my call,' Weaver said. 'We need information on the Sparkblood Conglomerate. Can you help?'

The crow cawed and bobbed its head.

'We need to know about their weaknesses, how they interact with each other and others around them, what motivates them.' Wind Talker quickly rattled off the list, and the crow looked at him with its head cocked to one side. It croaked in confirmation and took flight, re-joining the murder, and swooping away with them.

'I didn't know you had an affinity with crows,' Stalker said. She was surprised and a little saddened by her own ignorance of her sister's powers, but tried not to let the latter show.

'It's a new development,' Weaver said with a shrug and crooked smile. She led them back across the veil into the human world and as they entered the kitchen, Stalker's phone began to ring. She pulled it from her pocket and saw First Strike's name on the display. There was an initial wave of disappointment, quickly followed by guilt.

'I'd better take this upstairs,' she mumbled. She brushed past the others and ran up the stairs two at a time, answering the phone as she reached the top. 'Hi, sorry, I was on the other side. Everything alright?'

'I was going to ask you the same thing,' he said, frustration in his voice.

'Yeah, everything's fine. Why?'

'I hadn't heard from you in a while and there are rumours...' His voice stalled and Stalker felt a cold sensation run down her throat. She thought she had been careful not to reveal anything about Rhys to anyone. The thought that another pack might know anything was instantly alarming.

'What rumours?'

'That there's been a change of leadership in the Lightning Lords,' he snapped.

'Oh.' Stalker couldn't hide the relief. Her whole body loosened as she stepped into the little bedroom, and she leaned against the door as she closed it. 'Yeah, that. It was unexpected, but it'll get straightened out.' She instantly regretted her words, and drew her lower lip up between her teeth.

'Right,' First Strike said, an edge of confusion in his voice.

'How did the rumour circulate? And does everyone know?' Stalker suddenly felt paranoid.

'Oh you know, whispers on the wind.' She knew he meant that fae or demons had carried the news. She realised they could hardly prevent that sort of information exchange, they relied on it often enough themselves.

'Right,' she replied. 'Look, about us.' She drew a breath, this was going to be hard. She heard a noise from his throat at the other end of the line. 'I can't see you anymore.'

'I know,' he said with a sigh. 'I knew that was coming.'

'I'm sorry.' Stalker closed her eyes, holding back the guilt.

'It's okay, it is what it is. We had a good time, but it's hard to build a relationship with the lives we lead.' There was tension in his voice and Stalker listened carefully, unsure just how much he meant what he said.

'I hope we can still be friends,' Stalker said after a long silence. She hated the words as they left her mouth.

'Yeah,' he replied.

'I'll see you around,' she said, her cheeks aching.

'See you later.' His voice was suddenly cold and distant. He ended the call, and Stalker slowly lowered her phone from her ear, looking at it sadly. She took a deep breath. She had done the right thing and could now see Rhys with a clear conscience. She tried to dismiss the little voice that told her that First Strike had accepted it too easily, and that the tension in his voice should be a concern. He was hurt, but he'd be okay. Wouldn't he?

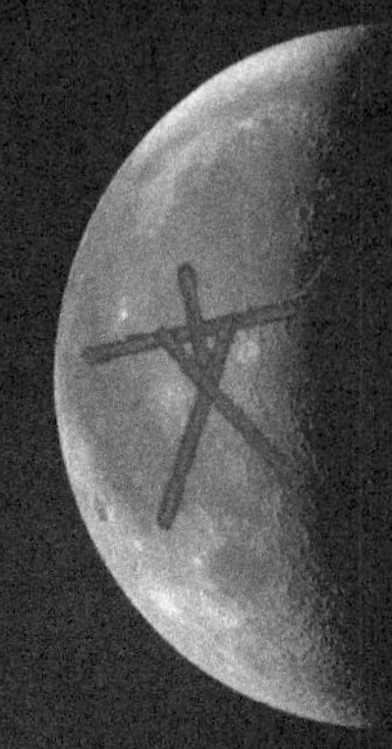

CHAPTER TWENTY

FIGHTS-EYES-OPEN

HE LOOSENED HIS BLACK TIE and unbuttoned the neck of his shirt. His mother sat with Chloe, her eyes were red but no tears fell now. She had sobbed her way through the morning, but for the funeral itself she had remained quite stoic. Chloe had cried, but when Eyes tried to put his arm around her she shrugged it away. The house was full of people, neighbours had brought sandwiches and cakes and come to pay their respects. Eyes stood in the living room doorway, detached from it all, but with Claws at his side.

He glanced over his shoulder at Amy sitting on the stairs with her aunt. They hadn't been at the funeral, Chloe hadn't wanted Amy there.

'She's so young,' Eyes whispered. Claws followed his gaze.

'Yeah, she is.'

'She'll forget him.' A hard lump formed in his throat.

'She might not, if people talk to her often about him and show her pictures of him.'

'I'm worried that she'll remember what happened but not remember who was lost. I don't even know where to begin with making her next birthday a joyful occasion.'

'Don't worry about that,' Claws said gently. 'It's a year away. Just keep putting one foot in front of the other, one day at a time.'

Eyes looked at him, about to protest, but the look on his friend's face stopped him; it was an expression of kind resolve. Claws was right and there was no sense arguing.

'I feel like if we slipped away now, no one would miss us,' he whispered.

'Me maybe,' Claws replied. 'But not you. I know you feel rejected right now, but they do need you to be here, to be strong for them.'

Eyes nodded. His gaze drifted back to Chloe and his mother. Other people busied around them, fetching them food and drink, offering them comfort and condolences. No one approached him, they treated Chloe like the one who had lost a parent, but not him.

Gradually, the house emptied. Claws lingered, clearly reluctant to leave him.

'I'll be fine,' Eyes reassured him. 'Thank you for coming.'

'I'll touch base with you later, update you on pack business.'

'Thanks,' Eyes said with half a smile. He showed Claws to the door and watched him go. The last guests filed out after him and Eyes shut the door quietly. He found Amy curled up in his mother's lap in the living room, while

Chloe and Rebecca began clearing up. He went to help them and rolled up his sleeves to wash up. A heavy silence hung over them, and the tension was crippling. Eyes focused on productivity, and tried to ignore the scathing looks that Rebecca kept throwing his way.

When the kitchen was clean, he set off back to the living room, and heard Chloe and her sister immediately start whispering behind him. He shrugged it off and continued through the house. His mother sat stroking Amy's hair, silent tears falling down her cheeks.

'Amy, sweetheart, are you tired?' He knelt down in front of her and she looked at him. She nodded and rubbed her eyes. He reached out to take her and his mother flinched, her startled eyes met his and she instantly looked apologetic. 'It's okay,' he whispered and scooped Amy into his arms. He carried her to bed and quietly got her into her pyjamas. 'Would you like a story?'

'No,' she said, her voice soft and sad. 'Stay with me?'

'Of course,' he replied. He tucked her under the blanket and lay down next to her, stroking her hair. He closed his eyes and remembered his father chasing him around the garden in summer and helping him build model aeroplanes at the dining table in this very house. He had never known Fortune when he was growing up, he had only ever had one real father and now he was gone. A tear escaped his eye but he was too tired to lift a hand to brush it away. His mind slowly went quiet.

He woke with a start, disoriented in the darkness. His phone was buzzing, and he carefully eased his arm out from under Amy's head before tugging it from his pocket. Claws' name showed on the display. He crept quickly from the room and answered as he closed the door.

'I strongly urge you to come here as soon as possible,' Claws whispered hurriedly.

'What's going on?'

'We've got a lead and Wind Talker wants to act on it now. I know the timing is terrible, but you need to show your face here. I'm sorry.'

Eyes could hear the concern in Claws' voice. He heaved a sigh and ran his hand through his hair.

'Okay. I'll be there soon.' He ended the call and looked at the display, it was nearly 11pm. The house was quiet but he could just about hear the TV downstairs. He jogged down to the living room. Chloe sat alone, a cushion in her lap, her eyes glazed over as some American sitcom replayed on the screen. 'Are you all right?'

Her head slowly turned to him, her face blank, then turned back to the TV.

'Are you going out?' she asked, her voice wavering slightly. He didn't reply. There was no way he could get out of the room without an argument. 'You're always disappearing.'

'I know,' he said quietly. 'I'm sorry.'

'I have these memories that I don't know what to do with,' she croaked. Eyes felt his heart skip a beat. He didn't want to have this conversation at all, never mind when he had been called out to join the pack. He didn't know what to say. 'A girl with a knife, that no one else remembers and a golden light shielding us from her. Then there are the monsters.' Tears poured down her pale cheeks and she twisted the corner of the cushion in her hands. 'It wasn't Knights with dogs.' Her head snapped to him and her face was cold and hard, accusing.

'No, it wasn't,' Eyes whispered. His hands were shaking.

'You know exactly what it was, don't you?'

'Yes.'

'Were you one of the monsters?' Her voice was thick with venom. 'The one who snatched the girl from in front of us?'

Eyes flinched, his jaw trembled and he felt pressure on his heart and lungs. He struggled to breathe and thought furiously of how to answer. Chloe stood up, tossed the cushion aside and strode over to him. 'If you walk out of that door tonight, don't you ever think about coming back.'

She walked past him and stomped up the stairs. Eyes was paralysed. He watched her go and when she was out of sight his eyes went to the door.

'Arghh!' He held back the roar, containing it in his throat, as his hands curled into fists, and he punched the living room door frame, splintering the wood. He grabbed his coat and car keys, and strode from the house. He just about had enough wits about him to lock the door behind him and paused for a moment, resting his forehead against the glass. Then he turned and walked away, he had no choice.

Eyes parked his car outside 32 Grove Street and sat for a moment, gripping the wheel so tight that his knuckles turned white. He took a few deep breaths, trying to sort out the muddle of thoughts competing for his attention. He would be civil with Wind Talker and help with whatever needed doing. Chloe would sleep off some of her grief and anger, she hadn't meant what she said, it had just been a very emotional day and they could sort all of this out in the light of day. He told himself what he needed to hear.

He climbed from his car and entered the house. All was quiet and dark as he moved through to the kitchen. He crossed the veil and found the rest of the pack in the back garden. Unchained Lightning stood on one of the high walls, his wings folded neatly against his shimmering body.

Weaver sat on the soil in the middle of the garden, her hands palm up on her knees and her eyes closed, in some sort of meditative state, with crows perched on her shoulders and arms. He stared at her and blinked hard several times.

Stalker caught sight of him and moved swiftly to his side. She grabbed his hand and dragged him closer. Strange images started flickering into his mind, disorienting him. He looked down at their joined hands in alarm and looked into Stalker's eyes.

Can you see?

It was her voice, projected into his mind, just like the telepathy they had shared when they were Blue Moon. He closed his eyes and focused on the images she was sharing with him. Once they came into focus he nodded his head and he felt her relax beside him.

He tried to make sense of what he was seeing. It was like looking through one of those fish-eye lenses, a strange panoramic view that was curved at the edges. The image bobbed and switched back and forth sharply, like the moving head of a bird. He was seeing through a crow's eyes. He was looking down on the substation in Hepethia, Glimmering Wires sat on the throne in the centre as electricity elementals whizzed in and out, feeding him. Suddenly, the elemental rose up out of the throne and dispersed into the pylon around him, every cable glowed bright blue and pulsed rapidly. The fae had transported himself into the power lines, he could travel along them.

Once he had vacated the station, something else took his place. A flickering white fae rushed forwards to take the throne. This must be Charge-of-Power, the one member of the Sparkblood Conglomerate that they hadn't yet met. As the smaller electricity elementals scurried towards the throne to deposit their offerings, Charge-of-Power stretched towards them and grabbed the packages of power from them, shovelling them into his mouth greedily.

The crow suddenly took flight, soaring over the substation and off over raw Hepethia, in all its crystalline glory. It flew north, Eyes recognised the tangled maze of red brick houses beneath him, the one that the Blue Moon had created to entrap rogue demons escaping from St. Catherine's. The factories of Northgate loomed and the bird swooped down to fly over them. It landed on a tall fence and bobbed its head, giving Eyes a view of a vast car park that had deep trenches dug into it. A bright, full moon hung in the sky, shining blue over the war zone and Sparking Clank lumbered about at the factory doorway, his followers scurrying under foot.

Eyes yanked his hand away from Stalker's and his eyelids popped open, he glared at her in alarm.

'What was that?' he hissed. Stalker looked at him, her eyes wide with surprise.

'I don't know.'

'What's going on? How did you do that?'

Stalker looked anxiously at Weaver, who still sat peacefully. The others stood over her, looking around at Eyes, confusion on their faces.

'I'm not sure. I figured out a while ago that I sometimes shared Weaver's visions when she had them in her sleep and when we came out here to commune with the crow fae she decided to try and bring on a vision in meditation. It worked and I shared it. Somehow I was able to project it onto you three as well.'

'It must be part of your growing abilities. Weaver's getting stronger too, she's never had a vision while awake before,' Wind Talker explained in a gentle whisper.

'The connection's gone now, though,' Stalker said, frustration lacing her voice. 'I need to be focused.'

'Sorry,' Eyes mumbled.

'Are the crows giving her this vision?' Claws asked.

'I think so, it seemed to be from one of their points of view,' Stalker replied.

'But was it literal? Is it something they've seen or is it symbolic?' Eyes asked, looking quickly from one pack mate to another.

'It felt like a combination,' Claws said. 'That last moment though, before we came out of it, that was symbolic.'

They all nodded in agreement. It was something to do with the Blue Moon. Again. Weaver stirred and Eyes' attention went straight to her. The crows took flight and disappeared into the black sky. Stalker rushed to Weaver's side and put a hand on her arm as she came out of her trance.

'That was so weird,' Weaver said, as Stalker helped her to her feet.

'What did we miss? At the end?' Stalker urged gently.

'Sparking Clank and Glimmering Wires are at war, it's their nature. Glimmering Wires is a fae from Alfheim, the realm of nature fae. He's been corrupted in Hepethia, influenced by his proximity to humanity. Sparking Clank is from Nidavellir, the Dwarven realm, he's a pure construct, innately at war with nature. The two of them were summoned here and told to share a throne. It was never going to end well. They have this strange relationship now, where they share the throne, each trying to grab power from it, along with Charge-of-Power, but their minions fight this nightly battle over smaller bits of territory.'

'It was the Blue Moon that summoned them.' Eyes stated blankly. He had no space inside for surprise at anything they learned about their old pack now.

'Yes,' Weaver replied.

'They must have had a good reason,' Stalker said. 'Probably to do with harnessing the grid and needing different aspects of power and electricity.'

Eyes smiled, he admired her optimism, though he didn't share it. He looked up at their ally, the shimmering dragon watching the scene with interested eyes.

'Can you add anything?' he asked, trying to keep the heat from his voice.

'Glimmering Wires is neglecting his duties. Something is drawing power from the web but he is ignoring it.'

'Can you fight him?' Eyes asked, suddenly struck by the obvious.

'Only if you weaken him first.' The fae bobbed his head

and flickered briefly, before taking wing and soaring away.

'How do we do that?' Eyes yelled after him, but he didn't respond.

'Well,' Claws said, rubbing his forehead with his fingers. 'If he can travel around the network, we might be able to isolate him somewhere, cut him off from the flow of power. That would weaken him.'

'Genius!' Stalker said, grinning.

'What about the others?' Eyes asked.

'We could try to recruit them, get them to fight against Glimmering Wires,' Claws suggested.

'What about after the fight though? Unchained Lightning won't want to share the throne,' Stalker said.

'We offer them their own thrones. Sparking Clank gets his factory in Northgate, Charge-of-Power gets somewhere else, or submits to Unchained Lightning.' Eyes spoke with authority. He caught Wind Talker's seething eye and sighed. 'Do you agree, Alpha?'

'Yes,' Wind Talker snapped. 'We'll go to Sparking Clank now.' He stormed to the door and flung it open. Eyes glanced at the others and they all exchanged furtive glances before following Wind Talker through the house and out into the street. They locked the house and set off at a brisk jog north towards the factories. The twisted streets were dark and quiet, the buildings seemed to breathe as the five shifters made their way quickly between them. Eyes thought of Holds-to-the-Light, the street lamp dragon that had nearly killed him, and wondered where he was, if he was prowling these streets somewhere. He briefly entertained the notion of a repeat encounter, this time with Wind Talker on the receiving end of an attack.

Guilt snapped him out of the vengeful image and he gave his head a shake as he picked up his pace to keep up with the others.

They reached the area that roughly corresponded with Northgate, past the maze of terraces and across an open crystal field, to where the factories worked tirelessly. At some point in time, shifters had made this a haven for constructs like Sparking Clank, they had created a habitat and allowed it to be populated. It had taken several months, but he was starting to see how little he had understood shifter life when the Blue Moon were alive. He had taken so much for granted, and it was taking some time to accept that things were very different from how they had appeared then. But he was sure that Fortune would have given him more lessons in how things worked in Hepethia had he been given the opportunity. Their time together was far too short, they had been denied the chance to get to know each other properly and Fortune had been taken from him just as he was beginning to be a father to him.

They came to the right place, it was instantly recognisable as exactly how it had appeared in Weaver's vision. A vast battlefield stood between the fence and the factory building, deep trenches ran the width of the car park and stationary guns were set up at intervals.

'It's probably mined,' Eyes said out loud, his train of thought leading him to that conclusion.

'Yeah,' Claws said softly. 'Well, Stalker and I can fly over it. What about you three?'

Eyes glanced at him, he had never known Claws to volunteer to shift before. Claws gave him a defiant glare, daring him to make a big point of his suggestion. Eyes smirked and shook his head.

'We'll have to be careful,' Wind Talker said gruffly. Stalker and Claws both shifted into owls and took flight, circling overhead. Eyes yanked at the chain-link fence and pulled it away from the post. He held it back for Weaver and Wind Talker and filed through behind them. They spread out and started to pick their way carefully across the battlefield. The tarmac had been ripped up and deep trenches gouged into the ground and spirals of barbed wire littered the field.

As Eyes took his first steps a machine gun spat bullets at the ground next to him. He leaped away from them and smoothly shifted into the Agrius, bounding on four giant paws right over a trench. He was aware on the edge of his senses of his pack mates doing likewise. The rapid fire of the machine gun dulled his hearing, echoing somewhere in the distance of his consciousness. He took another huge jump over another trench and landed hard on a wider space. As his back foot left the ground again he felt movement under it and heard a click. The explosion tossed him into the air, limbs flailing and he landed hard on his back twenty feet closer to his goal.

Eyes scrambled to his feet, mercifully unharmed by the mine, but for singed fur up his legs. He took a step before he felt the impact of a shot in his thigh, followed by a string of them up his right side. He stood stock still as the bullets pummelled his body. Then fell to his knees. Black spots appeared in his vision and a dull echo of gunfire filled his mind.

Suddenly there were hands grabbing at him and dragging him across the ground, they dropped him and he rolled over to look up at his rescuer. Weaver and Wind Talker both stood over him, looking gravely concerned. Weaver's face was pale and he noticed blood pouring from her shoulder.

Stalker and Claws appeared behind them, they must have reached the safe zone right in front of the factory, though he could hear the last echoes of gunfire dying on the battlefield. His pulse was deafening in his ears, but he could feel his body fighting to heal and forced himself to his knees.

'You've been shot, take it easy,' Weaver urged.

Eyes growled at her and looked down at his aching thigh. The bullet that was wedged into his muscle was moving, he felt it pushing against blood vessels. His body was healing from the inside out, pushing out the foreign body. The misshapen metal appeared at the entry site and fell to the floor with a clink. The other wounds up his side were minor and were healing just as rapidly. He shifted back into his human form, the pain intensified but he suppressed it and got to his feet.

'Any other casualties?' Wind Talker asked, looking around at the others. Weaver's shoulder had stopped bleeding and seemed to be almost healed, the others looked fine. Given the situation, they seemed to have done well.

'What do you want?' A voice snarled nearby, startling Eyes. They all turned to look at the doorway. Sparking Clank glared at them through yellow eyes as he separated himself from the metal of the door itself. 'I know you, I've seen you before.' His eyes settled on Claws and they narrowed to slits. 'Battery boy.'

'That's right,' Claws replied, taking the lead. 'We understand that all of this is to keep out Glimmering Wires and his army.' Claws nodded towards the trenches and machine guns. Sparking Clank nodded, the plates of his neck scraping against his body and showering the ground with sparks. 'What would you say if we told you that we could do something about him? Take him out of power?'

'An interesting proposition. You are different from your predecessors.'

'Yes, we are,' Eyes said firmly. The construct looked at him carefully, he shifted his weight.

'We wish to install our own ally on the throne at the substation,' Wind Talker said, irritation in his voice. 'Would you serve Unchained Lightning and accept this territory as your own?'

Sparking Clank growled, his tank-like body trembled and he lurched forwards a step. The Lightning Lords took a reflexive step back as one.

'I serve no one, not now, not ever.'

'I apologise,' Wind Talker said, instantly humbling and dipping his head. 'Would you ally with us in defeating Glimmering Wires?'

'You must do something for me, give me a reason to trust you. Come with me.' Sparking Clank turned around, every part of his body swivelling, his plates adjusting so that his body switched direction on top of his awkward legs without him actually turning in a circle. He stomped into the factory, the metal door grinding open to admit him. Wind Talker glanced at Eyes, a flicker of concern on his face.

'Can you walk?' His voice was almost tender. Eyes

was taken aback and nodded in reply, his side still ached, but he was well enough to walk. Wind Talker led the way inside and they followed the construct as he clanged his way through the vast building. The lighting was low, with no pesky humans to consider during the night shift in this Hepethian habitat. It was filled with machinery that rumbled, clanked and ground, constantly in motion. In the human world, the factory in roughly this position made windows and doors, but here in Hepethia it was purely symbolic of industry in general. They made their way carefully between machines and production lines, and followed Sparking Clank out through a set of corrugated iron doors. Eyes gasped when he saw that they had emerged onto a railway platform. It was lit with old fashioned gas lamps, and the tracks were overgrown and disused. The platform itself was dirty and deserted, the paint line along the platform edge was faded and completely worn away in places. On the far side of the twin tracks was a grassy wasteland, and in a partially hidden siding sat an ancient steam engine, with bits hanging off it and a thick layer of grime over every surface.

'This is where I was born,' Sparking Clank said, his voice a rumble. 'That engine was my sister. She was destroyed by a demon hybrid called Limb Chewer.' He spat the words like they tasted foul on his mechanical tongue. 'Destroy Limb Chewer for me, and I will consider allying with you.'

Eyes glanced carefully at Wind Talker. His face was often difficult to read, he had inherited Flames-First-Guardian's stoicism, although to the best of his knowledge there had been no biological connection between them. A muscle twitched in the Alpha's cheek.

'Where will we find Limb Chewer?' he asked.

'I don't know,' Sparking Clank replied. 'If I knew that I would take care of it myself.'

'Okay,' Wind Talker replied with resolve. 'We'll see what we can do. Thank you.'

The construct nodded his head and turned to gaze at his beloved sister's remains. The Lightning Lords quietly walked away, back through the factory and out onto the battlefield.

'I'm not crossing that again,' Eyes hissed.

'I think we'll be able to walk away,' Weaver said. 'It's a defence system against unknown intruders. We're leaving and we're known now.' Eyes raised an eyebrow at her. She winked at him and transformed into her cat form, then set off at a trot across the war-like terrain. Nothing happened, no gunfire, no exploding mines. Stalker glanced at him and shook her head. She wasn't going to risk it, and shifted into an owl to take flight. Claws watched her go, an apprehensive look on his face. He set his jaw in a determined expression and set off on foot. Wind Talker and Eyes exchanged glances before following, cautiously.

They all reached the other side intact, and Eyes looked at his watch; it was nearly 2am. He rubbed a weary hand over his brow. It had been a long day followed by a difficult night. His side still ached, he needed to sleep in order for it to finish healing properly.

'We'll call it a night,' Wind Talker said as they slid out through the gap in the fence. 'But in the morning we're going to find Charge-of-Power and secure his allegiance, then we find Limb Chewer.'

'Agreed,' Eyes said, his voice thick with fatigue. He was feeling it all now, the adrenaline from the fight with Chloe and the horrific crossing to get to the factory had left his system and the pain and exhaustion were taking hold. Weaver grabbed hold of him and supported him as he started to slump.

'Are you all right?' she asked quietly. He shook his head. 'Come back to Grove Street with us.' He grunted in reply and allowed her and Claws to half carry him back across St. Mark's. He didn't want to tell them that he had no choice but to go with them. That conversation would have to wait for another day. Stalker saw them all into the house from the air, then took off without a word. 'She'll be back,' Weaver said softly, a knowing smile on her lips. Why did she always know exactly what her pack mates were doing? Was it part of her special insight from Artemis? Or just female intuition? Eyes was dragged down the hall and deposited gently on the sofa. His form shifted reflexively into that of a wolf and he fell asleep, safe inside his animal mind, away from the chaotic misery of his human existence.

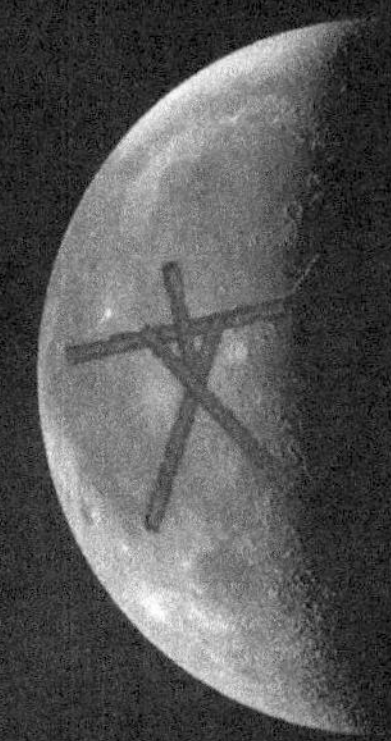

Chapter Twenty One

Stalker-of-Night's-Shadow

Stalker crossed the veil in flight and landed softly on her human feet in a dark alley at the back of Rhys's house. She approached the back door and tried it, it was locked. She checked carefully to make sure she was still safe to shift, and forced her body down into the form of a moth, gradually folding herself into the tiny creature. She had never tried to go smaller than this, flies and fleas seemed an impossible task, given how much effort it took to compress herself into an animal even this small. She flew up to Rhys's bedroom window, a skylight in the sloped roof of his terraced house. It was open just a crack, which was enough for her to crawl through.

He lay asleep in bed, under a crisp white sheet, his bare back gleaming in the cool light of the night. She shifted form and stood over him, watching him breathing softly. His tattoos snaked and weaved over his skin, impossible to ▓▓▓ in this light. She thought of the cloak that shrouded him, hiding his supernatural nature from everyone and everything. The only way anyone could ever glimpse the truth was if they looked right at him with a talisman like Wind Talker's, or some other way to see both the human world and Hepethia at the same time. In Hepethia, in Rhys's place would be the secrecy demon, alone, and here, like this, he looked like any other vulnerable human.

Stalker slowly lifted her dha over her head and placed them silently on the carpeted floor, she peeled off her boots and clothes and stood before him. He stirred, slid his arm out from under his pillow and turned his head in her direction. His eyes remained closed and Stalker tilted her head to match the angle of his. He looked so peaceful and his bed was so inviting. She slid, ever so gently into the bed, longing for the warmth of his arms and his breath on her face.

He jerked awake and his eyes locked with hers, full of alarm. A cry died on his lips as his conscious mind caught up with his senses and he frowned at her.

'Hi,' he whispered, his voice thick with sleep. 'How did you get in here?'

'Shhh,' she whispered, then placed her lips on his in a soft kiss. He wrapped her up in his arms and tugged the sheet over both of them. They made love, the rest of the world melting away into the distance, and afterwards, Stalker fell asleep in his arms, content for the first time in days.

As the pre-light of dawn sneaked in through the skylight, Stalker woke, glad that she had retained her human shape in Rhys's bed. She often reverted to her fox form with the pack. Although Claws was able to hold his human form when he slept, she didn't know how much effort it cost him. Rhys twitched beside her and she smiled, turning to watch him sleep. She wondered what he dreamt of, and suppressed an image of the demon enjoying being a passenger during sex. She shuddered and Rhys's eyes flickered open.

'Morning,' he croaked. He grabbed hold of her and pulled her close, kissing her softly. She gladly reciprocated and nuzzled against his warm body. 'What a lovely surprise last night,' he murmured.

'Yeah,' she replied, drinking in his scent. 'I like to surprise you.'

'How did you get in? Do I have a broken window to worry about?'

'No,' she said, burying her scarlet face against his chest. 'I didn't break in, don't worry.'

She had welcomed having one less person to lie to, but in truth she still didn't trust him enough to reveal how special she was. He stroked her hair and kissed the top of her head.

'It's Sunday,' he said, his voice uncharacteristically husky. 'We could stay in bed all day.' He lifted her chin and kissed her jaw, running little kisses all the way down her neck. Stalker groaned.

'I have to get back to St. Mark's soon, stuff to do today.' Rhys stopped and sighed. He propped himself up on his elbow and looked down at her, idly stroking her arm with his other hand.

'It'll always be like this, won't it? Fleeting rendezvous in between looming apocalypses.'

'I'm afraid so,' she said, attempting levity with a fake

sigh. 'But at least you can know about the apocalypses, at least if you wake up next to a fox you won't totally lose the plot. Or would you?'

'No, I think I could handle that, just,' he said with a smile. 'As long as the fox didn't nuzzle up to me, that would be weird.'

Stalker laughed, her first real laugh in what felt like an age. Rhys grinned back at her. 'I love your laugh, you should laugh more.'

'I'll try. There is way too much serious shit going on though.'

'Can you tell me about any of it?'

Stalker chewed the inside of her cheek and considered him carefully. It didn't feel like he was fishing for information, it felt like he was genuinely trying to help. But wouldn't that be true of a good spy?

'I don't know,' she said after an uncomfortable silence. 'Can I?'

'I completely understand your hesitation, really. If you don't want to tell me anything that's fine. I can live with that.' He kissed her, a passionate, dizzying kiss, and she felt herself melting into it. He drew back slowly, reluctantly.

Stalker let out a frustrated moan and rested her forehead against his chest.

'I had an encounter with an ancestor from the Underworld, who berated me for neglecting my duties and getting distracted. Here I am, distracted again.'

'I distract you?' Rhys asked. She looked up at him, an incredulous expression popping onto her face before she could stop it. He grinned and kissed her again. Why did he have to keep kissing her? She firmly pushed him back him and leaned away from him.

'Yes!' she snapped, smirking. 'Stop it.'

'Sorry,' he said, barely managing to hide a smile. 'But you were the one who showed up in my bed naked last night. What was I supposed to do with that situation?'

'Kick me out and tell me to go back to my pack.' She scowled at him, knowing he wouldn't take her seriously. 'I can't control myself, you will just have to do that for the both of us.'

He pounced on her, kissing her roughly and pushing her back down onto the bed. He straddled her and pinned her wrists down over her head as he ravaged her lips. She gave in to it, happily letting her mind go blank but for the pleasure of his actions. He broke off the kiss and grasped her head in both of his hands, staring at her with his intense, dark eyes.

'I can't control myself either, not with you.' He laid her head down gently and slid back down beside her. 'I've lived with this secret for ten years, never once even slightly tempted to re-join shifter life. Not just out of fear of what Caerton's shifters might do to me, but because I was content. I had found a way to exist that was relatively peaceful. I was always careful to preserve my secret, but was able to live a mostly human life. Then you came along. From the very first moment I saw you I knew what you were, or would become; I should have walked away from that competition last summer and never seen you again. But I didn't, I came over and made contact with you. I couldn't stop myself then and I can't now. I need you.'

Stalker listened and watched his earnest eyes. Every word seemed to pierce her soul and she felt a tear prickle at the corner of her eye. 'I love you. That must be it. This is what love feels like.' She swallowed hard and let his words sink in.

'I...' She wanted to say it back, she wanted to be a normal girl, with a normal boyfriend, declaring their mutual love for the first, uncomplicated time. But nothing about this situation was normal. 'I have to go.' She hurriedly climbed out of the bed and reached for her clothes. Rhys leaped up and grabbed hold of her, turning her to face him.

'Don't do that,' he pleaded. 'Don't.' He kissed her, holding her tight against his body. She kissed him back and grabbed at his back, digging her fingernails into his skin. She pushed him back to the bed and fell down on top of him, barely breaking the passionate kiss. She lost herself with him, let everything else fade away, and used the fire in the pit of her stomach fuel the passion. As she shuddered through the climax of their coupling an inner truth flowed through her, without her searching for it. She wasn't sure if it was his or hers, in that moment they were one, but it was love.

She collapsed down onto his chest and felt her ragged breathing begin to ease with the light caress of his fingers on her back.

'I love you too,' she whispered. His fingers rested for a moment and his breath caught in his throat. He didn't say anything, but she could feel him smiling and she allowed herself to smile too.

An hour later, Stalker stepped across the threshold of 32 Grove Street, a lovesick smile still on her giddy lips. She heard the others moving around the house and promptly wiped the expression off her face, wary of being insensitive to Eyes or giving Weaver cause to pass comment. It was bad enough that they would probably all smell Rhys all over her.

'Have you eaten?' Weaver called down the hall. Stalker walked slowly to the kitchen. Claws was the only one not there and she could hear him thumping about upstairs.

'Yes, thanks,' she replied. Her stomach was still full of the eggs Rhys had made for her.

'Good,' Wind Talker said, throwing a scowl her way. He was obviously unhappy with her staying out all night, but was going to just be passive aggressive about it. Stalker glared at him defiantly. 'We're going out in five minutes,' he snapped.

'Does anyone know where to find Charge-of-Power?' Stalker asked.

'Unchained Lightning thinks he can be found at the mobile phone mast in Crossway,' Weaver replied. Stalker's eyes flickered to Eyes, who sat hunched over the last pieces of bacon and sausages on his plate. He didn't react.

'Okay,' Stalker replied.

Claws came bounding down the stairs, looking fresh faced and cheerful.

'Morning,' he said, grinning. He gave her a warm hug and as he pulled back his expression had changed to curiosity. 'Everything okay?'

'Fine, thanks,' she said, with a knowing smile. 'Shall we go, then?'

'Yes,' Eyes said abruptly, standing and moving his empty plate to the sink. Wind Talker brushed past Stalker and led the way down the hall. They crossed the veil before leaving the house and set off at a jog through Hepethia towards Crossway. They would have to pass Eyes' house to get to the tower and Stalker kept a watchful eye on him as they made their way there quickly and quietly. She could sense his apprehension, but also his resolve. Something was different about him, she felt anguish but the old sense of internal division was absent. He had always been torn in two, as long as she had known him, but that was gone. She fell into step beside him, Wind Talker was up ahead and Claws and Weaver took up the rear guard, ever watchful for antagonistic demons.

'What's happened?' she whispered. He glared at her briefly, then returned to watching out for danger.

'Nothing,' he snapped.

'Don't try that on me,' she hissed back. 'Something has changed. It might help to tell someone.'

'Says the one with all the secrets,' he said sharply. It stung, but she shrugged it off, he was hurt and was lashing out at the nearest target.

'I'm dealing with my issues,' she replied calmly. 'Are you?'

'Chloe knows the truth,' he said, not looking at her. 'Her memories were restored when the madness was lifted. She remembered the Witch and Perfection-of-Flesh, and me, as the Agrius.'

'Ah.' Stalker flinched, sorry that she had pushed him for answers.

'She never wants to see me again, and I don't blame her.'

'Sorry,' Stalker muttered. She felt her cheeks burning and resolutely looked away from him to spare them both.

'Thanks,' he replied. He picked up his pace and left her

behind. She didn't speak to anyone else on the way.

Houses appeared out of the crystalline rocks, faded at the edges at first, like the edges of an old fashioned photo, then more solid. It was the street Eyes lived on, shaped here almost exactly as it appeared in the human world, imprinted here by familiarity. Eyes' house stood dark and deserted, still draped in police tape. Stalker glanced at him, he walked on at a brisk pace, not looking at the place.

As they neared the end of the street, Stalker looked up to where the tower stood in the human world. Against the pinkish sky was a glistening column, draped in haze. The pack walked briskly towards it and as they approached the haze gradually cleared, revealing a stunning tower of swirling mercury. The shimmering liquid metal wound its way up the tower in a spiral and then cascaded down the inside in a constantly flowing torrent.

'Wow.' Stalker gasped, her eyes wide with awe.

There was a sudden ripple in the flowing column and a bright white light shone out from the centre. Static filled the air and Charge-of-Power stepped out from the tower.

'What do you want?' a voice spat. The elemental was vaguely humanoid, but with dozens of limbs that thrashed about, its whole body was in a constant state of motion and flux, shimmering in and out of existence. It looked a little like an animated scribble, bright white and nauseating to look at.

Stalker heard a rushing sound above them and looked up to see Unchained Lightning soaring towards them. He landed with a heavy thud on the ground behind the Lightning Lords, and Charge-of-Power cowered back towards the mercury tower.

'You are a power elemental,' Wind Talker said, a smile playing on his lips. 'Like our friend here.'

'Yessssss,' the creature hissed. 'What of it?'

'Unchained Lightning needs a throne. We want the substation, and intend to take it. You can help us, and get to keep your current source of energy, or move on to new territory.'

The way Wind Talker spoke was compelling, he oozed confidence and authority. Stalker almost felt as though he deserved to be their Alpha in that moment. He was staking a claim to territory, just as they were meant to.

'Glimmering Wires is too powerful,' the elemental crackled. 'You can't defeat him.'

'That's why we've come to you,' Claws said, his voice soothing. 'We know you are powerful enough to help.'

'It would be to your advantage to only have to share the throne with one of your own, rather than with two other, hungrier constructs who don't really understand the flow of power.' Wind Talker's eyes glinted, and Stalker watched as Charge-of-Power stopped moving for just a fraction of a second while contemplating this compelling offer. The elemental was instantly back in motion and issuing a hiss of static.

'One of my charges has gone rogue. Return her to me and I will help you. She is in the human world, inhabiting one of those devices.'

Stalker felt her phone start to buzz in her pocket, and instantly tensed. The others all reacted similarly and ringtones began to sing and bleep from all of their pockets. They all looked at each other, then back at the elemental. Stalker glanced at the tower behind it and saw that the mercury was glowing faintly, feeding on the energy from their phones.

'She's in a phone?' Stalker asked. 'Do you know which one?' There would be millions of mobile phones in Caerton, she did not relish the prospect of having to find a specific one amongst them.

Claws pulled his phone from his pocket and looked at it, the others all suddenly stopped ringing, but his kept going.

'Is it this number?' he asked, holding the phone up. Charge-of-Power flared up more brightly in confirmation. Claws answered the call and the air was filled with hideous static and bleeping. He hastily ended the call and scowled at the elemental, who seemed to be chuckling.

'Find her and return her to me.' With that, Charge-of-Power turned and stepped back into the swirling column.

'How on earth do we do that?' Stalker hissed. The five of them moved closer together and Claws gave her a reassuring smile.

'I think I can probably do it,' he replied. 'Come on, let's go.'

They set off, Unchained Lightning bobbing along just above them.

Claws led them to the Watchtower, which was surrounded by snowdrops, and vines were creeping up the outside, signs of spring having arrived. They went inside and Stalker looked up the spiral staircase. Curiosity beckoned, and without realising what she was doing, her foot met the first step.

'We should see who's on the throne now,' she murmured softly, taking a few steps up. Weaver followed and they climbed the crooked stairs quickly and quietly. Last time Stalker had seen the throne room of the Watchtower it had been infested with brawling winter fae. Before that it had been carpeted in crunchy golden leaves. Each time, its occupant had been a powerful fae of the season. The vines that were growing up the outside of the tower were crawling in through little gaps in the stonework and a soft breeze met her face from the open sky above. Stalker stepped up into the room at the top and gasped. On the throne was a shimmering green and yellow fae made of grass and flowers. She had long golden hair that fell over her shoulder to the floor and on her head was a tall golden crown. Vines dotted with tiny white flowers wound their way up the throne from the floor and were wrapped around the fae.

She lifted her blue eyes to look at the two shifters and tilted her head to one side.

'Hello,' she said, her voice jingling softly.

Claws stepped onto the landing behind Weaver and Stalker heard a small noise issue from his throat. She smirked and glanced at his wide-eyed face.

'Hello,' he said, a slight squeak in his voice.

'You claim this space, you do human business here,' the fae said, her eyes locked onto Claws.

'That's right,' he replied.

'I feel you every time you come and go.'

Claws' cheeks burned red and Stalker pressed a hand to her lips to contain the giggle that threatened to spill out.

'I see,' Claws said, nodding and swallowing hard. 'I apologise for not coming to introduce myself. I'm Claws-of-Lead. These are two of my pack mates. We are the

Lightning Lords.'

'I know. I've not long been here,' she replied. 'I am Flute-of-the-Flowers. Pleased to meet you.' Her eyes never left Claws and Stalker felt suddenly as though she and Weaver were intruding on something that ought to be private. She glanced at Weaver, who was beaming unashamedly. Stalker's lips split into a grin and they hurriedly exchanged signals to make an exit. They stepped quietly back onto the stairs, leaving Claws and the queen of spring alone in the tower.

'What's going on up there?' Wind Talker snapped as they emerged.

'Claws has met a girl he likes,' Weaver said, still grinning.

'Don't be ridiculous,' the Alpha said, crossing his arms over his chest.

'There are actually legends of shifters and fae finding love. Human mythology is filled with variations of them, all those Greek gods taking human lovers,' Weaver said, her smile not faltering.

Claws appeared at the top of the stairs and came bouncing down them, a giddy grin on his face.

'Nice new tenant,' he said jovially. Stalker laughed and gave his shoulder a playful punch.

'We need to get on with things, come on.' Wind Talker uncrossed his arms and scowled at them, then checked across the veil to see that the coast was clear for them to cross.

'The building should be empty on a Sunday morning,' Claws said, 'but better safe than sorry.' The lobby was empty and the pack crossed the veil into the office building.

They followed Claws upstairs and into his office.

Stalker went to the window and looked out onto the street below. Cars rushed past every few seconds, but there were few pedestrians, it was fairly quiet. Claws fired up his computer and got to work.

'Is this like your bread and butter?' she asked, with a smile.

'Pretty much,' he replied, his eyes locked on the screen. A slightly distracted smile tugged at the corner of his lips.

Weaver watched over his shoulder and Wind Talker paced behind them. Eyes slumped into the chair opposite and closed his eyes. He looked like he hadn't slept in days, which was probably true.

'What are you doing?' Weaver asked, her voice low and curious. Stalker moved closer and peered at the screen.

'Trying to find out who owns the phone. It's hit and miss, but is a first port of call.'

Stalker took out her own phone and looked at it while she waited. The idea that something could be hiding in it, listening to her calls, seeing her texts or tracing her movements made her uncomfortable. Claws did this for a living, routinely tracking people down like this, and that was bad enough, but if a demon used that information to endanger lives it brought a whole new level of paranoia to mind.

She thought again of Rhys's demon and the fact that it must know everything about him, everywhere he goes, everyone he speaks to. Speaking to that demon could be the key to determining for certain who Rhys really was. But convincing it to part with its secrets might be impossible.

She shook her head, and put her phone away. She had

spent the night with him, been intimate with him and declared her love for him. She had decided to trust him, be that a wise decision or not, now she had to consciously act on it.

'Got it!' Claws exclaimed. 'It's a contract phone, I have a name and registered address, plus the network that it's connected to.'

'Can you track down where it is right now?' Wind Talker asked, halting his pacing and moving to look at the screen.

'Yep.' Claws hit a few keys and waited expectantly, Wind Talker and Weaver leaning over his shoulders. Stalker tried not to laugh at their eager faces. 'There,' Claws said, poking the screen. 'It's in St. Catherine's. Somewhere in that block.'

'What is that?' Weaver asked, peering carefully at the screen.

'It looks like a warehouse or something,' Claws replied.

Stalker grabbed Claws' car keys from the desk and jingled them.

'Come on then, let's go.'

They practically ran back to Grove Street, where Claws had parked his car. He drove, with Wind Talker up front, Stalker sandwiched between Eyes and Weaver.

'My car's bigger,' Eyes grumbled. Stalker hid a laugh behind her hand and turned to look at Weaver, whose lips were pressed firmly together, her eyes fixed on the window.

Claws sped to Red Bridge and crossed the river into neighbouring St. Catherine's. The area still carried negative connotations for Stalker, but she fought hard not to dwell on them. They steered north, avoiding the scenes of their past encounters with Knights and Witches, and into a more industrialised area. Claws pulled up opposite what looked like a disused warehouse. It was built from faded red bricks, had a corrugated iron roof, and a fire escape up one side. It was a rough neighbourhood, most of the buildings were in disrepair, and the pavement was strewn with litter.

Stalker heard dogs barking nearby and her hackles instantly went up.

'It's okay,' Weaver whispered, resting a hand on Stalker's tense arm. Claws set off again at a crawl, looking all around them as he drove carefully to the end of the street and pulled into a parking bay in front of one of the buildings.

'I'm going to check it out, Stalker, come with me. The rest of you stay here,' Claws said, his voice distant as his gaze roamed the street. Wind Talker's cheeks flushed and his eyes narrowed. Stalker glanced at Eyes and raised her eyebrows, he gave a discreet shake of his head to signal to her not to make a big issue of the situation. Claws looked at Wind Talker and flinched. 'Sorry, I went into business mode. I didn't mean to step on your toes, Alpha.'

Wind Talker nodded and waved a hand, dismissing him. Claws got out of the car and Stalker climbed out over Weaver. They hurried down the street, Claws constantly looking around, he was good though, discreet. The street was deserted, as best Stalker could tell.

'I dread to think how high tensions are running in the car right now,' she whispered. Claws ignored her and kept walking. 'It's dead here,' she said, trying to draw something out of him. He glanced at her and nodded.

'Yeah, pretty much. This way.' He pointed across the street to a side road and led her up it. They circled around to check out the other side of the warehouse. There was a small car park, a battered old estate car and a newer white van sat empty near the main door to the building. Claws kept walking and Stalker scurried along after him. As they passed the front of the building, she saw a light on inside the front door and heard voices. They walked right past and Claws led them around the block and back towards the rear of the building. 'Okay, so there is little or no security on the outside, but who knows what the inside is like. There was no signage on the building or van, so it doesn't look like a legitimate business operates there. I'll bring the car around and stake out the front. Can you get up the fire escape and see what you can check out from up there?'

'Sure,' she replied. She smiled, she liked this side of Claws: the confident expert. He was growing into his shifter skin more and more now, but still sometimes seemed like the new boy. But here, in his PI world, he knew exactly what he was doing.

'Be careful,' he cautioned her, then they went their separate ways.

Stalker snuck up the passage at the side of the building and thought about shifting form. The place seemed private enough, but it was broad daylight and she couldn't entirely rule out the possibility of onlookers. So she moved quickly and quietly to the fire escape and grasped the ladder. It was old and rusted and she made her way carefully up, with it creaking slightly as she climbed. She got to the platform and edged over to a long, narrow window high up on the wall. She could just see inside, but it was quite dark, no lights were on and not much natural light made it into the building from these small windows.

The sound of a car approaching drew her attention, and she looked to see Claws pulling up about twenty meters away. She turned her attention back to the window. She could tell that she was looking onto a large, open area that was the height of the entire building. It looked like there was an interior wall towards the front of the building, where they had seen a light on. She got right up on her toes for a better look and peered down inside.

She saw rows of tables but no sign of people. She looked along the fire escape to the fire door at the end, it must open onto a raised platform at this end of the warehouse, but wouldn't open from the outside. Stalker sighed and made her way back down the fire escape. As her feet touched the ground, a car swept past and she darted away from the building and back to the car. She climbed into the back, Weaver had slid into the middle to make room for her.

'I didn't really learn anything,' Stalker said with a frustrated sigh.

'What's the plan? Do we just barge in there?' Weaver asked.

'No,' Claws replied. 'We should watch the place. In fact, this car full of people looks particularly dodgy. Maybe I should stake it out on my own for a bit. You guys go off and get some food or something.'

Stalker noticed Wind Talker tense slightly, his fingers flexed and he tilted his neck with a click.

'Yes, good idea,' he said stiffly. He opened his door and climbed out without looking back.

'Call us if anything changes,' Stalker urged. Claws nodded.

'Do me a favour,' he said quietly to her, as Weaver and Eyes slid out of the car. 'Call Ragged Edge, or someone, and give them these names.' He slid a folded piece of paper into her hand, she hurriedly unfolded it and saw two names scrawled in Claws' messy script.

'What's this?' she asked, her hand shaking slightly.

'Your birth parents' names.'

'How did you find them?'

'It's what I do,' he replied with a shrug.

'Is that why you're sending all of us away? To corner me into acting on this stuff?'

He raised an eyebrow and shook his head in consternation. She gave him a gentle punch on the shoulder, then followed the others out of the car.

'Come on,' Wind Talker said under his breath. 'Let's get out of here.' He led them away, towards the heart of St. Catherine's.

'Is it wise for us to be here, out in the open?' Eyes asked, looking around anxiously.

'I doubt any of the Knights can identify us and there are no shifters claiming the area. We should be fine,' Wind Talker said, bristling with frustration. He was trying so hard to claim the authority of an Alpha, but clearly Stalker wasn't the only one making it hard for him. She almost felt sorry for him. Almost.

She got out her phone and found Ragged Edge's number.

'I need to make a call, go on, I'll catch you up.' Weaver gave her a sly grin and Stalker shook her head. 'Stop it,' she hissed. The others walked on ahead at a brisk pace and she slowed down to make the call.

It rang a few times before Ragged Edge's gruff voice answered.

'Ariana? Everything okay?'

'Hi. Sorry to bother you on a Sunday.' She cringed as she said it. As if the days of the week meant anything to their kind, it's not like he worked Monday to Friday and this was his family time. Or maybe it was, maybe he had a family that no one knew about. 'I had a visit from an old family member that has kind of rattled me a bit. I really hoped we could meet up and talk about it, and about finding my birth parents, maybe?'

'I see,' he said slowly. 'Of course. Is it desperately urgent?'

'Well,' she faltered. Was it? 'He did go through hell in order to see me, so I'd say he thought so.'

Ragged Edge cleared his throat.

'Okay, well I can meet you briefly this afternoon.'

'That would be perfect, thank you. I'm actually in St. Catherine's now, so I could head in the direction of Old Town, if that's okay with you?'

'Good God, what are you doing in that hell hole?'

'Just chasing something up.' She smiled and heard him grunt.

'Fair enough. Don't come here, it's not a good time. I'll meet you at the cenotaph in the city centre in an hour. How does that sound?'

'Fine. See you then. Bye.'

Ragged Edge hung up without saying goodbye and Stalker chuckled. He didn't have the best of manners, but was one of her favourite people, nonetheless.

She ran to catch up with the others and linked arms with Weaver.

'Do you have a date?' Weaver whispered conspiratorially.

'Not remotely!' Stalker laughed. 'Wind Talker? I need to meet Ragged Edge after lunch. You'll be able to reach me on my phone if Claws needs us.'

She wasn't going to give him the satisfaction of asking for his permission, she had never sought permission to act on personal business from her previous Alphas and wasn't about to start now. He gave a curt nod and she settled into her stride beside Weaver.

They found a greasy café and ate a quick and lively lunch. Stalker gave Weaver and Eyes brief hugs before leaving, not ashamed to exclude Wind Talker. Her brush with sympathy for him had repulsed her when she thought about what he had done. Maybe she was being childish, but she didn't care. She walked quickly down the street and joined a queue for a bus that went to the city centre. She would be cutting it fine, and really hoped that she wasn't called back to the pack.

The bus was crowded, and she had to stand near the front, pressed up against a student and a woman with bags of shopping. When the bus stopped near the central plaza, she hopped off and checked the time. She was a few minutes late and walked quickly past the fountain, fondly remembering the night they had filled it with washing up liquid and flowers. The cenotaph stood tall and proud in front of the museum, a pristine sandstone monument to Caerton's fallen soldiers.

Ragged Edge sat on the top step that surrounded the slender column, leaning heavily on his knees, his long, brown coat pooled around his feet. He looked up at her as she approached and got wearily to his feet. They grasped forearms in greeting and he pulled her into a warm embrace.

'How are you?' he asked as he released her.

'Not too bad, thank you. And yourself?'

'Still ticking, that's the main thing.'

'Why did you ask me to meet you here?' she asked, looking up at the immense column.

Ragged Edge chuckled and walked around the cenotaph, holding his palm an inch from the stone as he circled it. Stalker watched as his hand moved across the surface, and saw the faintest, shimmering shapes appear. She stepped closer and saw that they were shifter runes. She looked around in alarm at the people rushing past in all directions. A few cast furtive glances at her and Ragged Edge, but they all steered clear and no one spared the cenotaph a second glance. 'They can't see?'

'No, only we can.' He stopped beside her and indicated for her to take a closer look. She moved up onto the top step and peered at the tiny runes. There were hundreds, maybe thousands of markings, neatly inscribed in rows. There at the bottom, the last figures added, were the runes for "shadow" and "walk", Shadow's Step. She looked at Ragged Edge, a muscle in her cheek twitching.

'Why are you showing me this?'

'You're one of Odin's Warriors. One day your name

will be on there. It's important that you know about this. We are the soldiers that they will never recognise.' He jerked his head towards the humans passing them. 'We deserve a place of honour too. We protect them as much as any human soldier sent to war. This is no Scroll Archive, not a detailed record of every shifter's life and death, this is a simple memorial for Odin's Warriors.'

'How do you know about the Scroll Archive?' she asked, her curiosity piqued.

'I'm old, I've heard things over the years,' he replied with a smile. Stalker returned it and sat down on the step, her back to the depressingly long list of fallen Berserkers. He sat down beside her. 'This is a key part of our ethos, we honour the dead, we honour history and ancestry. Remember I asked you about that when we first met?'

'Yes,' she replied in a whisper. She had no idea then what she was really getting into. She was freshly changed and firmly under her guardian's wing. 'That's what my ancestor's ghost reminded me of. He accused me of forgetting where I came from and neglecting my duties.'

'I see. And this ghost crossed the veil to see you?'

'That's right.' She looked at him, his face was twisted into a severe frown. 'What?'

'That shouldn't be possible. Obviously ghosts do sometimes find their way here, or fail to find their way to the Underworld in the first place, but for one to deliberately open a door in the veil and cross into the world of the living is unheard of.'

'At the Danegeld we were told that the dead weren't moving on properly. Could this be connected? Maybe there's a weakness in the veil?'

'Possibly.'

'Could it be because of the King-of-Glass-and-Steel being missing?' she asked cautiously. Ragged Edge cleared his throat and shifted his weight.

'Possibly.'

'Sorry to bring that up,' Stalker said softly.

'Not at all, it's fine. Now then, do you know the names of your birth parents?'

'I do now,' she replied, passing him the paper. 'I was handed this paper right before I called you. It's the only information I have. Jane White and Malcolm Slater. My adoptive parents always told me that they never had any contact with my birth parents, never saw a birth certificate. I had been left in a care home, then bounced around a few foster homes before I was adopted.'

Ragged Edge looked at the names and ran a finger over them slowly.

'Do you know them?' Stalker asked.

'No, at least not by these names.'

'I was adopted and raised in another city, it's probable that they were never in Caerton.'

'Or maybe they were and took you away to leave you. There is a reason for you being here, there are no coincidences.' He stood and turned to the column. He placed a hand on it and leaned so close that his lips were almost touching it as he spoke. Stalker got up and moved close enough to hear him whispering the names she had given him. The runes flared bright white for a moment, then settled back to their pale, shimmering state. Ragged Edge looked over them carefully, then shook his head.

'Nothing?' Stalker asked.

He leaned close again and whispered something else that she couldn't make out. Again the runes flared up and died down again.

'It was worth a try, I wasn't sure how sophisticated these records were. It looks as though we need their shifter names, I tried the human name of a friend who I know to be recorded on here, and the cenotaph didn't recognise that one either.'

He examined the paper again and Stalker watched him carefully, curious to know what he was thinking.

'I'll ask Claws for more information, where these names came from for starters.'

'Where did your name come from?' the elder asked abruptly.

'Excuse me?'

'Did your adoptive parents give it to you? Or did you come with it?'

Stalker tried not to be offended by his flippant disregard for her humanity.

'It was the name on the adoption certificate. My adoptive parents didn't choose it.'

'Your birth parents gave you a completely new name, not one of theirs. They were trying to hide you. I would love to know why.' He regarded her carefully. Stalker swallowed against a hard lump in her throat.

'I don't know why.'

'Why are you lying to me, girl?'

Stalker blanched and stared at him.

'I'm not. I don't know why they wanted to hide me, I don't know anything about them. That's why I came to you, I need your help if I am to stand any hope of living up to the oaths I made.'

He grunted and relaxed a little.

'Can I keep this?' he asked, holding up the piece of paper.

'Sure.'

'I'll see what I can find out. There might be something in the Scroll Archive, so if you have access to it, I suggest you use it.'

'Thank you,' she said curtly, still feeling defensive from his sudden change in demeanour.

'If you think of anything I ought to know, you can tell me.' His voice was softer and his eyes crinkled kindly.

'Okay,' she replied, nodding. He pulled her into a tight embrace and she patted his back as her cheeks flushed.

'Take care, now,' he said, and he stomped away with a slight limp.

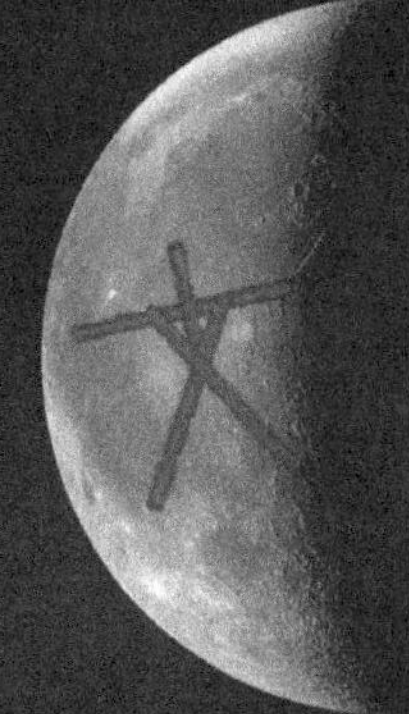

Chapter Twenty Two

It was sunset when Stalker arrived back in St. Catherine's and met up with the rest of the pack. Weaver greeted her with a hug.

'Everything okay?' she asked softly.

'Fine, just trying to find my parents. I need to get access to the Scroll Archive. What do you think the chances are of Scribe letting me in?'

'Slim to none,' Weaver said with a sad smile.

'I thought so. What's happening here, anyway? Are we meeting back up with Claws?'

'We're heading back to the warehouse now,' Wind Talker replied, suddenly right beside her. She recoiled from him and moved around Weaver to link arms with Eyes for the walk back. She felt Wind Talker's gaze on her as they hurried along the bustling, rush hour street. Fine drizzle began to fall and the orange street lights shone on the glistening street. Eyes placed a hand over hers on his arm and glanced cautiously at her.

'You need to give him a break, you know?'

'How can you say that to me?' she hissed under her breath.

'Of all people, Stalker, I have the most reason to be angry with him, but I'm finding peace with what has happened. He was right to challenge me, and win. You need to accept him as our Alpha. You need to forgive him.'

She glared at him. Their linked arms had become tense, but neither of them broke the link.

'I don't for a second believe that you've forgiven him, and I won't be doing so any time soon. It wasn't just the challenge, maybe that was called for, but what he did right before that, and the way he fought you on the beach in the wake of it. It was cold, Eyes, he is cold. I don't trust him.'

'I didn't say I had forgiven him,' Eyes whispered, with a small smile on his lips. 'But we both need to, or it'll tear this pack apart.'

'Well, that'll be on him, not us.'

Eyes released her arm and sighed. He shoved his hands into the deep pockets of his long, black coat and trudged ahead through the rain. Stalker watched his back with a scowl, as she puzzled over his words. How long could she stay angry? She wasn't sure. She had never exactly found it easy to let go of things, she clung to slights from other kids at school for a long time. Since she changed for the first time too many things had happened that had filled her with rage, they kept on stacking up and she had yet to let any of them go. It had been three months since the Blue Moon had been slaughtered, and it still hurt most days. The desire to avenge their deaths still motivated almost everything they did as a pack. War was brewing with the Witches, she knew it wouldn't be long now before it would come to open battle.

Everything they were doing now, to strengthen Unchained Lightning, was so that he would stay with them and help them fight. She thought of Shadow's Step's name on the cenotaph and wondered who had carved it there. It should have been her, or she should have been there at least. He was her mentor, her big brother, and he had left her virtually alone in this world, just weeks after discovering it. He had *left* her. A tear fell down her cheek, and she swatted it away angrily. She hadn't realised before that she was angry with him, and Fortune, and the others. She wasn't just angry with The Witches and The Phoenix Guard, she was angry with her own mentors for dying. A sob escaped her lips, and in an instant Weaver and Wind Talker were either side of her, linking their arms through hers. She felt them through their empathic bond, connecting with her, soothing her in the only way they could in this busy street. Eyes glanced over his shoulder and dropped back to walk beside Weaver. He cast a furtive glance at Stalker and caught her eye. She nodded at him, hoping to communicate that she wasn't upset or angry with him.

He nodded in reply and the four of them walked in silence, taking up the whole width of the pavement, causing passers-by to step out into the street to avoid them. They received frustrated scowls and fearful glances, but Stalker didn't care.

They soon left the busy street and headed into the unlit industrial estate, where Claws was waiting for them.

He had moved the car to the end of the street and was leaning back against the side of it. He pushed himself away from the car as they approached and locked eyes with her. Weaver and Wind Talker released her and she felt herself pulled into a hug by Claws.

'What's up?' he asked against her hair.

'Nothing, really, I'm fine.' He released her and glared at her with one eyebrow cocked. 'Those names were a dead end, so far, anyway. Where did you find them? Did you find my birth records?'

'We'll talk about it later,' he said, patting her shoulder. 'Wind Talker, there was activity about ten minutes ago, another car pulled up, two guys went inside. I have a feeling I know what's going on in there.'

'Drugs?' Wind Talker asked. Claws nodded. 'Okay, let's cut the lights in there, then drop in through the windows and call the phone, grab it and get out.'

Stalker had to admit it was a reasonable plan, given the situation. She couldn't think of any other way that wouldn't involve bloodshed, not that this plan was certain to avoid it. They moved into the shadows between two buildings and all shifted into their animal forms. Claws took off into the air, Weaver slunk out of the alley and rubbed her feline body against the corner of the building, Eyes trotted off in the opposite direction, Wind Talker shuffled after Weaver, and Stalker took to the sky after Claws in the form of a bat. It was the quickest way up to those high windows. The two of them landed on the roof of the warehouse, and waited for the others to get into position around the building.

There were lights on in the main warehouse now and Stalker could hear so much more in this form. It was among the strangest forms for her to take, the echolocation ability was so alien to her human mind. Instinct dominated any of her animal forms and helped to quiet her busy human mind, but it was still confusing. She kept quiet now, using her large ears to listen to what was happening in the building below. She could make out about half a dozen people moving around and talking, she could hear other sounds too, something that must have been a Bunsen burner, and liquids simmering. It was either some bizarre chemistry club, or they were manufacturing drugs in there. She took flight and started emitting the calls from her nose that instinctively issued for her to navigate with. She found Weaver on the fire escape that she had climbed earlier, Wind Talker was on the other side of the building, crouched under a window in his Agrius form. Eyes had found his way to the back of the building and was perched on the top of an adjoining wall, level with the window. Stalker took one last lap around the building, fluttering close to each of her pack mates to signal them, before landing on the roof next to a filthy skylight and shifting into her human form.

'Ready?' Claws whispered across the rooftop, as he crouched next to another skylight, his hand resting on a circuit box that fed cables down into the building. Stalker nodded. Claws pressed his hand flat against the box, his ring coming into contact with it. Stalker looked down through the skylight, the lights flickered out and she heard a window smash. She promptly drove her fist into the skylight and sent glass shattering down onto the warehouse floor below. She leapt down and landed softly on her feet. There were shouts and heavy footsteps thundering about in the dark. More windows came crashing in and her pack mates leapt into the building from all sides.

Wind Talker bounded across the room, his eyes catching what little light there was. With one hand, he overturned one of the long tables covered in test tubes and trays of powder. Stalker was spurred into action, she ran to the nearest table, where a row of Bunsen burners glowed and hissed under bubbling glass vials. She quickly ran along the row, switching the gas off, and yanked the burners from their taps. She swept her arm along the table, knocking everything to the floor with a cacophony of shattering glass. A phone started to ring somewhere behind her and she spun around to locate it.

It was madness, two men had bounded straight for Eyes, the others were clamouring at the door, trying to get out. Claws stood on a balcony at one end of the room, his phone in his hand and his eyes desperately searching for the source of the corresponding ringtone.

Weaver and Stalker ran towards the men trying to get out, the ringing was coming from there. Stalker grabbed the nearest dark and terrified figure and hurled him across the room, Weaver had her hand on the next one when he turned and threw a punch at her face. She dodged his fist, grasped it in her own surprisingly strong hand and yanked him to his knees. He had the ringing phone. Stalker let the last wannabe chemist get out through the door and run for it. She strode to the man on his knees and wrapped her arm around his neck. His hands went straight to her arm and he tried frantically to pull it away from his throat. But she was far too strong for him and held him firmly.

'Shhh, aren't you going to answer that?' she hissed in

his ear. He flinched and his hands fell still.

Wind Talker strode over, in his human form, Eyes hot on his heels. Stalker glanced across the warehouse and saw two men unconscious on the floor, Eyes had blood on his fists and was trembling slightly. Claws jumped down from the platform and ran across the floor to them. Wind Talker stooped over to fish the phone from the man's coat pocket. Its garish ringtone was some misogynistic hit song and the lit screen cast an eerie glow around the otherwise dark warehouse. Stalker kept a firm grip on him, and watched as Wind Talker answered the call and held the phone up to his ear.

'We good?' he asked.

'Yep.' Claws smiled and nodded.

Stalker released him and he dropped to the floor, coughing and clutching his sore neck.

'You can go now,' Wind Talker said. The wretch scrambled to his feet and charged out of the door.

Eyes strode over to the one remaining upright table and let out a whistle. Stalker and the others followed him and she gasped at the sight of piles and piles of money, it looked like someone had been busy counting it when they had broken in.

'I don't see any reason not to take this,' Wind Talker said, thumbing through a stack of fifties.

'We'd be doing Caerton a service, really,' Stalker added. 'Depriving its drug dealers of this much cash.'

Weaver scooped a large duffle bag from the floor and began sweeping the notes into it with Eyes.

When they had collected the bulk of the money, the Lightning Lords strode from the building and back to

Claws' car. The lights flickered back on in their wake and Stalker noticed that the van and cars had gone. She doubted the drug dealers would be calling the police over the incident. They climbed into the car and drove back to Grove Street, the others excitedly re-living the victorious raid. Stalker smiled and nodded as she lost herself in thought, their chatter a jumble of background noise. Somehow she didn't think this sort of activity was what her ancestor had in mind. But soon it would be time to take on Glimmering Wires, then The Witches. Then she would make him proud.

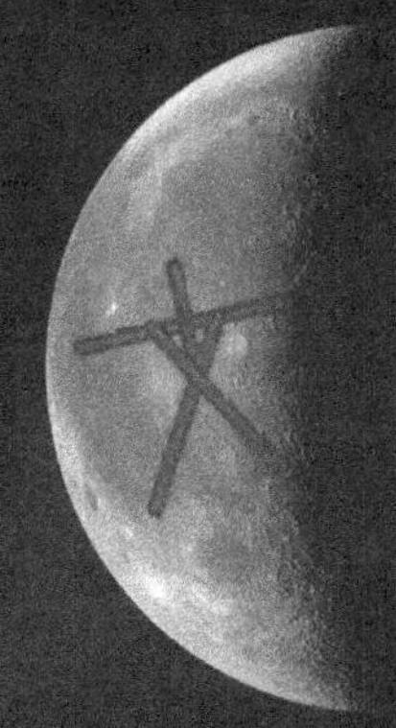

Chapter Twenty Three

Fights-Eyes-Open

'We'll take the phone to Charge-of-Power in the morning, it's late now and we all need a rest,' Wind Talker instructed as they piled into the house. 'I'll put this in the attic,' he said, hoisting the bag full of cash up in his hand. He strode up the stairs and the others filed into the kitchen. Claws set about making dinner, with Stalker lending a hand. Too many bodies trying to help at meal times had proven to be problematic, so Eyes and Weaver sat down at the table and kept out of the way.

'Are you all right?' Weaver asked him, indicating his bloody knuckles on the table. He drew his hands towards himself and nodded. Flashes of the fight came back to him, the rage that had erupted inside him as he dropped to the ground through that broken window was consuming. He hadn't shifted, he had just kept enough control to retain his human form, but he had thrown those men around like rag dolls and beaten their pasty faces to a pulp. The blood was mostly theirs, the cuts on his knuckles had healed in seconds, but the blood dried on them and remained. He slipped quietly out of the kitchen and up the stairs to the bathroom.

He locked the door and ran the hot water. Letting the water flow over his hands, he gently rubbed the blood off them, watching the red spiral down the drain. The mirror over the sink began to steam up, his distant eyes slowly disappearing into the fog. He felt like he himself was disappearing. The man he had known was gone, and he didn't know or understand the man who had taken his place.

He had lost his wife, as well as both of his fathers, and now he had lost the leadership that he had defined himself by. But it felt like something that had happened to someone else. He meant what he had said to Stalker, he had deserved to be challenged by Wind Talker. He had made a mess of leading them, been distracted by his human life, and failed to forge them into a single unit. Stalker was always off doing her own thing, still far too attached to her humanity too. Wind Talker was often lost in research and rituals, which he supposed was common. Flames-First-Guardian had been similar, and Wind Talker had learned closely at his side for two months before the attack. It was understandable that he had picked up his mentor's character traits. Were the Lightning Lords doomed to be cast in the roles of their mentors? Would they repeat the same mistakes?

He wiped his hand across the mirror, clearing away the condensation. His face was a state, he had dark circles under his eyes, his skin was pale and he had several days' growth of his beard. He took a deep breath and reached for a razor, not caring if it belonged to Wind Talker or Claws. Shaving was cathartic, it required a certain amount of focus, but it was rhythmic too, which was soothing. His bristles fell into the water, and clung to the wet surface of the rim of the sink.

When he had finished, he diligently cleaned the sink and surrounds and threw the wet towel into the laundry hamper. He had been fairly well domesticated by Chloe, or so he liked to think. He took one last look in the mirror.

'Better,' he muttered to himself. When he returned to the kitchen, steaks were being served on top of a colourful salad, that had to be Stalker's doing. He grinned as he took his plate from her. 'Thank you,' he said earnestly. She gave him a warm smile and they sat down together to eat.

As they all settled down to get some sleep, Eyes had to admit that he preferred being with the pack. When they were all together they seemed to accomplish more and it just felt right. Before he had been forever torn in two, and although he thought of his human family often, and longed to hold his precious daughter in his arms, and have the love and trust of his wife, he was relieved not to be living a double life.

Eyes woke as the room began to grow lighter with the first rays of the dawn, and he felt better rested than he had in days and was the first into the kitchen to make coffee and breakfast. The others woke soon after and joined him, in various states of fatigue.

An hour later they were heading out in Hepethia, straight for the mobile phone mast. Eyes kept his eyes on the road ahead as they passed his house and soon the swirling column of mercury came into view. Claws took out the phone and held it over his head.

'Charge-of-Power!' he called out, his voice echoing off the crystalline ground around them.

The mercury parted like a curtain and the elemental emerged, flickering and hissing like static.

'What is it?'

'We've brought you the phone.' Claws held the phone out towards the elemental, then bent down and slid it across the ground. Charge-of-Power seemed to look down at it with caution, then curled into a ball over it and discharged a surge of power down onto it. The phone screamed and jerked violently on the ground. Eyes took a reflexive step back, as did his pack mates.

A shimmering light emerged from it, spinning frantically and whistling loudly. Eyes flinched away from the sound and fought the urge to cover his ears. The phone burst, its pieces scattering across the ground, and the elemental above it fell silent.

Charge-of-Power suddenly expanded, and a dark maw opened wide in its front. It wrapped itself around the rogue elemental and swallowed her whole. The power fae glowed even more brightly and became still for a few seconds. Eyes watched, captivated by fae workings.

'Wonderful,' Charge-of-Power said, with a satisfied hum to its voice. 'Whole again. Now then, what are you still doing here? Be off with you.'

'We had a bargain,' Wind Talker said, an edge of a threat to his voice. 'Will you honour it and stand with us against Glimmering Wires?'

'Oh yesssss,' the elemental hissed. 'I look forwards to

it.'

'One last thing,' Claws said, raising his hand to halt the elemental from disappearing back into its tower. 'Do you know where we might find a construct by the name of Limb Chewer?'

'No,' the fae replied. 'Try the Shale Trading Post, there is a vault of secrets there, you can find out almost anything you wish to know about Hepethia. But be careful, the price can be high.' With that, it spun away and was absorbed back into the mercury.

Eyes raised his eyebrows and glanced around at the others.

'What do we have to trade for a secret? And why didn't we know about this place sooner?' he asked.

'I think I may have something,' Weaver replied. 'And I have an idea of where this trading post is.'

'Oh?' Eyes asked in surprise.

'Shale Trading Post? Shalebrook.'

'Ah,' Wind Talker said. 'Factory Boy turf. Do we know any of them to ask permission?'

There was a subdued chorus of "no"s and shaking of heads.

'It could be anywhere in Shalebrook,' Claws said softly.

'We can probably find a friendly fae to guide us,' Weaver replied. She was far too optimistic for Eyes' liking, but then, sometimes they needed that. 'Let's head south and see what the lay of the land is like.'

Eyes had to admit that he was curious to see the way another pack shaped Hepethia, but going there without permission could turn ugly.

'We should stop at the border and send a fae in to seek

permission,' he said firmly.

'Agreed,' Wind Talker replied with a nod. They set off at a run, with no idea how far they would have to travel. Hepethia didn't map precisely over the human world, it was a whole other plane of existence, there was no guarantee of even seeing a familiar landmark.

As they reached the southern border of their own territory, a stunning crystalline landscape stretched before them, a slight blueish haze hanging over it. They pressed on, looking cautiously around for signs of danger. Stunning natural formations of quartz in various hues filled the terrain. In places they couldn't run, they had to climb carefully over huge boulders of purple and blue crystal, and inch their way down steep cliffs. None of the formations were particularly high, perhaps there were vast mountains and valleys somewhere in Hepethia, but here, it was just about possible to traverse the formations without specialist equipment, or any particular need to shift form. Stalker did soar above them as an eagle, however, for security.

After an hour or so, she swooped down to the ground and landed in human form just ahead of the rest of the pack.

'We're nearly at the city centre,' she said, a little out of breath. 'Are we sure we want to do this? We've always been warned not to go there. I could see structures and movement, lots of movement.'

'I don't think we have much of a choice. Unless we cross the veil,' Weaver said, her eyes darting between pack mates.

'Is anyone else severely creeped out by this place?'

Claws asked, glancing around, his shoulders giving a shudder. 'Where are all the fae? We should have seen some signs of life, right?'

'There must be shifters, or *something* in China Town,' Wind Talker said softly. 'There must be, I mean just look at St. Catherine's and where we're about to go. That's what happens when there are no shifters to control things. No one has shaped Hepethia here, as far as we can tell, of course. They may have shaped it to look like we would expect it to look. But someone is routinely clearing fae and demons out of here, or has them tightly controlled to not show themselves.'

'We can't concern ourselves with that right now,' Eyes said. 'Are we going into the city centre?'

'We have to cross it to get to Shalebrook,' Weaver said with conviction.

'Well, no we don't,' Eyes said. 'We could skirt west and cross the river into Old Town, then cross again south of the centre. Or we could cross the veil right here.'

'Aren't you curious?' Weaver asked, her head cocked to one side as she eyed him carefully.

'Of course I am, insanely so, but I'm not sure this is the best time to allow curiosity to overrule our task.'

'If what we've been told about the centre is even half true, we may be lucky to get through it alive,' Stalker said, her voice low and dark.

'Let's get a bit closer and see with our own eyes,' Claws said, his voice slightly too bright. Eyes sensed the force behind it, but he looked at his pack brother with gratitude for his diplomacy.

'Agreed,' Wind Talker said, and he set off, leading the

way.

There was a jagged crop of bright green aventurine in their path, and Eyes climbed carefully, using his hands to grasp the rough surface. Stalker and Weaver practically skipped up the steep slope and he glanced at them enviously as he struggled to find a good grip. Claws climbed a few feet, then slid back to the ground. Eyes looked over his shoulder and saw Claws shaking his head. He sighed and grudgingly shifted form, flapping his wide wings to fly his way to the top of the slope. He landed in his human form, stumbling slightly and Stalker grabbed him and helped him to find his balance. Eyes looked at their serious faces, and scrambled past Wind Talker to the top. Claws helped him to his feet and he in turn helped Wind Talker up the last part.

He brushed the greenish dust from his hands before finally looking out at the view. The aventurine fell away from them in a steep slope down into a rocky valley, which gradually morphed into rough cobbles and then broken paving slabs. Huge towers of concrete, glass and metal erupted from the ground and stood at awkward angles, some propping others up, others seeming to have settled that way, like the Leaning Tower of Pisa. There was a loud moaning sound and Eyes caught movement at the corner of his eye. His gaze flickered towards it and settled on something vast and monstrous lurching between the buildings. It was like something from a horror film, some sort of apocalyptic kaiju story, where a giant creature from the deep had surfaced and rampaged through a metropolis, destroying everything in its wake.

To the east, not too far from where they stood, was a

huge barricade. A concrete wall stretched away into the distance, standing easily fifty feet tall. In front of it were huge wooden spikes, held together with vast coils of thick, barbed wire. The horrifying city centre was pressed up against the barricade, but it looked sturdy enough to keep anything out and as Eyes watched, he saw a shimmering against the rough urban landscape, like heat haze, and he wondered what magical protection might be repelling the inhabitants of the city centre from getting too close to Burnside.

'The Glass Wolves have got themselves covered,' Stalker said softly, clearly looking at the same thing as Eyes. He grunted in reply.

A hideous chorus of screeching voices echoed across the wasteland between the city and the Lightning Lords, and Eyes returned his gaze to the jumble of broken buildings and strutting crystals that erupted from the broken paving. A mass of small black shapes moved between the buildings, clambering over one another, and up the side of one of the half-fallen buildings. It was too hard to tell from this distance, but Eyes got the impression that these creatures were fighting, or eating something massive, swamping it with their sheer numbers.

'We can't go in there,' Eyes said firmly.

'No, we can't,' Wind Talker agreed.

A shudder went through Eyes as he thought about all of this being separated from humanity by just a thin, metaphysical veil. One tiny gap, one flaw in the skin of reality and it could all come flooding through. He swallowed hard and turned away. He couldn't look any more.

'Let's find another way,' Eyes whispered.

'Let's cross the veil,' Wind Talker ordered. He used his talisman to find them a safe location. It was a busy Monday morning in the city centre, so finding somewhere secluded was a challenge. When he guided them across, Eyes was surprised to find himself in a narrow alley at the edge of China Town, a row of huge waste bins blocking the end from the busy street beyond. A cat ran past him, its bell tinkling lightly and he watched it disappear around the corner.

Stalker shifted into the form of a collie dog, and sniffed at the ground. Wind Talker led them out of the alley and Eyes cast his gaze to the ground, looking for the cat, but it was gone. He caught a glimpse of a playing card under one of the bin wheels, a crushed and dirty two of hearts. He gave a derivative snort as he passed it, and turned his attention to navigating the bustling street.

The pavements were narrow and the road was filled with cars chugging slowly along. People rushed past in both directions and the Lightning Lords picked their way in single file through the throng, Stalker at Weaver's heel. They took a direct route across the city centre, making use of footpaths and back streets. Stalker seemed the most confident of the route and Eyes remembered a time when he would frequently visit this part of the city, before he knew anything about shifters, or territory, or Hepethia.

There was an excellent pub down a small street behind the city's gallery, a gnarled old Tudor building, reported to be the oldest tavern in Caerton. It had low beams, served real ales and housed a juke box full of classic rock music. He smiled at a memory of an afternoon spent in there with his friends from university, friends he had long since lost touch with. It seemed a lifetime ago.

He walked briskly behind Stalker and Wind Talker and tried to tune out the noise of the city. Soon they had passed the major landmarks and were entering unfamiliar territory. The disordered jumble of public buildings and offices gave way to neater rows of terraced houses, punctuated by shops.

Stalker led the way, sniffing the ground and walking slowly. She stopped abruptly and the others came to a halt behind her. Eyes could feel it, the tingle on the back of his neck that told him he could go no further, ahead lay claimed.

'Shall we follow the boundary to somewhere private?' Weaver asked. Wind Talker nodded and they set off back the way they had come, Stalker leading the way into the next street, carefully following the boundary markings. They found a small, fenced off park, surrounded by trees only a few meters from the territory border.

'I wonder what their defences in Hepethia are like,' Eyes mused. He couldn't imagine the Factory Boys having anything as grand as the Glass Wolves' wall, but maybe he underestimated them.

Wind Talker held out his talisman and Eyes took it, palming the copper eye. His vision distorted, like slipping on sunglasses, and he saw two layers of the world simultaneously. The park in Hepethia was an overgrown courtyard, surrounded by tumbledown sandstone walls. Cobblestones covered in moss and interspaced with growths of weeds and grass lined the ground. Beyond the park were derelict buildings, hanging over the edges of the courtyard like ancient watchmen. It looked deserted. 'Okay,' Eyes said softly. 'We can cross here.'

He stepped across the veil, still clutching the talisman and turned to see his pack mates crossing the veil behind him; the human world now a dark shadow behind the bright layer of Hepethia. The sun shone on the little courtyard, the surrounding buildings, casting long shadows across the cobbles. Stalker had shifted form as she crossed the veil, from the collie into a fox.

Eyes handed the talisman back to Wind Talker. He bent down next to Stalker and looked her in the eye. Her eyes were faintly amber, they reminded him of Shadow's Step for a moment, and he wondered if she chose to make them that colour on purpose. He wasn't sure how much control she had over the details of each form she took. 'Can you call out for us?' he asked her. She gave a gruff bark and he stood back.

Stalker lifted her snout and cried into the air, part howl, part bark. The intention was clear to him, even in his human form. It demanded attention, but not antagonism. There was a flicker of movement on the far side of the wall facing the pack boundary, but it was gone before Eyes could tell what had caused it. They waited for a few minutes, no one spoke and the air was filled with tension that lifted the hairs on his neck. Stalker resumed her human form and leaned against a wall with her arms crossed while they waited.

He felt their approach before any of his physical senses picked anything up. He just knew that the Factory Boys were on their way. A minute later two young men rounded a corner, scowls etched onto their hard faces. Eyes recognised them from the Danegeld, they were identical twins. They had closely-shaved heads and piercing eyes. One wore a cap backwards, the other had on a shiny, baggy jacket that reminded Eyes of something pop stars in his childhood wore.

'Who the fuck are you lot?' one of them snarled.

'We're the Lightning Lords of St. Mark's,' Wind Talker replied calmly.

Eyes understood their abruptness, it wasn't really the done thing to turn up on another pack's doorstep like this. 'I apologise for this unannounced arrival. We're on urgent pack business and are tracking information. We were told to go to the Shale Trading Post. We assumed it was on your territory. Is that correct? And would it be possible for us to enter?'

The two Factory Boys exchanged wary glances. One of them gave a small shrug and the other cocked an eyebrow. Eyes got the impression that a hurried telepathic dialogue was taking place.

'It is,' the twin in the backwards cap snapped. His name was Old Scar, Eyes felt it whispered to him, his ability unaffected by losing the Alphaship. 'Yeah, you can come onto our territory to visit the market. Other packs do sometimes. We'll escort you in and out, mind. No tricks, no trouble.'

'Of course,' Wind Talker replied at once.

The twins beckoned the Lightning Lords towards them, and Eyes led the way, climbing over the low wall of the courtyard. The old buildings leaned close, blotting out the sky, and the Factory Boy twins led them through tight, twisting passageways. Eyes felt as though he were a schoolboy exploring a ruined castle. A few minutes later they emerged suddenly onto a modern street, with a sheer wall of crystal lining the opposite side in both directions.

'Keeps trouble out,' the young shifter in the shiny jacket said abruptly, nodding first at the twisted old castle behind them and then at the wall before them.

'From the city centre, you mean?' Eyes asked. He shrugged in reply and set off along the street. Eyes glanced at Claws, who was hiding a smile. They followed their guides to a very thin gap in the wall, barely wide enough for Wind Talker, the biggest of their company, to fit through. On the other side of the high wall was raw Hepethia, untouched by shifters, as far as anyone could tell. Elementals moved freely among the jutting crystals, starting little fires, whipping up the wind and drenching the fires to put them out. A neat cycle that repeated itself over and over again across the landscape.

Eyes wondered whether it was laziness, or deliberate conservation on the part of this contradictory pack. To the west he could see the bank of the river, which wound its way through Hepethia in a perfect reflection of its human world existence.

To the south there were buildings, and the Factory Boys led them in that direction, skirting around the inhabited crystal plain.

'How did you get here?' asked the twin in the jacket. 'You never crossed the city did 'ya?'

'Not on this side, no,' Eyes replied. 'Have you ever tried it?'

'We go in sometimes, when we have to.'

'You've survived to tell the tale.'

'I don't recommend it for young'uns,' smirked the lad, who looked no older than twenty. Eyes raised an eyebrow, then remembered that he had only shifted for the first time less than five months previously. It was possible this boy had been a shifter for a decade or more.

They approached the little cluster of old buildings by the river. They looked like they had been shaped by shifters several generations ago, and were showing signs of age. Little patches of crystal peeked through the sandstone, where Hepethia was reclaiming the stone. There were half a dozen buildings of varying sizes and shapes. But one stood out; right at the heart of the cluster was a circular, three-storey building with a grand, domed roof and hundreds of windows. It had steps leading up to a huge set of double doors that were propped open and Eyes could hear the gentle murmuring of a crowd within.

'Here we are,' said Old Scar. 'We'll wait out here for 'ya.'

'Thank you,' Eyes replied, giving him a nod. He led his pack up the stone steps. Stalker fell into step beside him.

'That has to have been the strangest experience in Hepethia I have ever had,' she muttered.

Eyes sniggered as they walked in through the open doors. His mouth dropped open as he surveyed the scene. The interior of the building was wide open and circular. Light spilled down through the domed, glass ceiling, shining on all of the gold fixtures. The floor was wooden, and had a spring to it, and stairs led up from the centre to a gallery halfway up the high walls and all of the banisters shone gold. The noise echoed around the vast hall, cries, jeers and shouts rang out from sellers and buyers alike.

Small tables circled the hall, laid with wares of all kinds, from exotic-looking fruits, to stunning and intricate jewellery.

Eyes had never seen so much activity in Hepethia, not even at the Hundred Court, which had, he would hazard a guess, a hundred attendees. This was so much busier. The fae, demons and constructs here were bustling about, moving from one stall to the next, and each creature was so alien that it took a moment for Eyes to take in what he was seeing.

Stalker made a small noise in her throat beside him and he glanced at her. 'I take it back,' she whispered. 'This is the strangest experience in Hepethia I've ever had.'

Wind Talker brushed past Eyes and led them into the heart of the market, moving slowly through the crowd. They didn't seem to be drawing any particular attention by being there, Eyes wondered how common it was for shifters to visit the market.

'Can I help you?' a female voice asked in clipped tones. Eyes looked for the source, and found a slender, green fae, decorated in silks and beads. Her long red hair flowed around her head and shoulders, as if she were under water.

'I hope so,' Wind Talker replied. The pack came to a halt and drew close, pressed together by the crowd around them.

'Are you here to trade?' the fae asked, looking at each of them expectantly.

'Yes,' Wind Talker said curtly.

'We'd like to access some information in the vault. Can you tell us how we might go about that, please?' Eyes asked, putting on his most polite and professional air.

'Do you have an account?'

'No, we don't.'

'You need an account to trade,' she said, a soft smile on her thin lips. 'I will need to take a deposit.'

Eyes glanced around at the others.

'Do we have anything valuable?' he asked quietly.

Weaver put a hand into one of her many pockets and pulled out a large topaz ball. Eyes recognised it at once, it was the Sun that Weaver had stolen from The Witches when she had escaped captivity.

'I was going to suggest trading this for the information,' she said softly. 'But I think it will do better for this. I suspect we'll need something very different for the information.'

'Follow me, please,' the fae said, then turned and drifted away, the crowd parting for her. Eyes led the way after her, taking advantage of the gap before it closed behind them. She led them to the stairs, but rather than going up, she strode around them to another staircase leading down. Eyes gripped the gold bannister and ran down the steep stairs after the rapidly moving fae, his pack just behind him.

The lower floor of the trading post was lit by shimmering torches on the walls and shafts of sunlight down the stairs and through a gap in the ceiling to one side of the circular room above.

There was a wooden desk in the centre of the room, which was otherwise empty. Small doors lined the walls, however and Eyes could sense movement behind them, along with whispering voices. The fae lit a small lamp, and took out a metal box from a drawer in the desk. 'Do you have the deposit?'

'Here.' Weaver moved forwards with the stone in her open palm. The fae smiled, showing rows of sharp teeth. Eyes flinched in surprise. She took the topaz and put it gently in the box, then slid some parchment across the desk towards Eyes.

'I just need a signature from each of you.'

Eyes picked up the parchment and looked it over. It was a contract, but a simple one.

'It's okay,' he said, glancing around at the others. 'She's not asking for our souls or anything. It's just fairly standard stuff about agreeing to abide by the rules of the Trading Post, take up issues with the management and so on. The rules are here too, they should be simple enough to follow.'

'All right,' Wind Talker said, caution in his voice. Eyes passed him the contract to examine, and watched with a bemused smirk as Wind Talker hurriedly read through it. The Alpha put it back on the desk and bent to sign it first with a bright red quill that the fae had provided. The others each took their turn to sign it.

'Lovely,' the fae said, smiling again. She neatly folded the contract and slid it into the box. 'Now, you wanted to trade information?'

'That's right,' Wind Talker said, puffing up his chest. 'We need to find a missing construct.'

'I see. Is its location a secret? Or simply not known?'

'It seems to have deliberately hidden itself,' Claws replied.

Eyes felt Stalker go suddenly very tense beside him, worry clouded her mind. He tried to look at her discreetly, sure enough, her face had drained of colour. What was she so anxious about?

'I see,' the fae replied. 'Come with me.' She led them away from the desk, the box containing the topaz and contract clutched in one hand, a large key ring jingling in her other. She went to one of the doors and unlocked it. As she opened it, light spilled out and Eyes had to shield his eyes as he entered after her. The room was a brightly lit, high-tech vault. The walls were lined with small boxes set into them, each with a tiny keypad. The fae went to one of the boxes, tapped a few buttons and the little door popped open, a drawer slid out and a slight ripple flowed out of it around the room. Eyes watched as she placed the box into the drawer. She left it open and turned to face Wind Talker. 'Here is the code.' She passed him a small slip of paper. 'Memorise it and destroy the paper.'

Wind Talker looked at it and then passed it to Claws, who looked at it carefully for a moment, then screwed it up and swallowed it. Eyes resented not getting to see it, but trusted Claws far above Wind Talker, and was glad that he would now have it committed to his eidetic memory.

'Thank you,' Wind Talker said, softening to the fae a little.

'You're welcome. I'll leave you to it.' She swept from the room and closed the door. Eyes listened for it locking, but it didn't. He let out a long-held breath and glanced around at the others.

A shadow flickered in the corner and Eyes heard frantic whispering. The room was bright white, with no obvious source of light, this shadow shouldn't exist, yet here it was. It unfolded from the corner and moved into the centre of the room, flickering and shifting slightly as it moved.

'Ahhhhh,' the shadow sighed. There was something greedy about it as it shuffled forwards, its dark edges reaching out towards the shifters.

'Coveted Secrets?' Wind Talker addressed the demon.

'Yesssss?' The demon's voice dripped.

'We need to find Limb Chewer. Do you know where it is?'

'Hmmm, it's in here somewhere.' Shapes resembling hands unfolded from the shadowy creature and indicated the room around them. Eyes looked around in alarm, before realising that the demon meant the secret, not the construct itself. 'A secret for a secret,' the demon whispered.

Eyes looked carefully at Stalker, she was chewing a nail and her eyes darted from one pack mate to another. She wasn't parting with her secrets any time soon. Weaver and Claws exchanged concerned glances, before both settling their gaze on Wind Talker. Eyes knew what secret he would be willing to trade, and he suspected Wind Talker had come to the same conclusion. The Alpha lifted his chin and moved towards their deposit box. He locked eyes with the demon as he leaned close to the box and whispered.

'We found a Spiral Hand traitor, Hidden Voice, locked in a basement, and I killed him.'

Coveted Secrets released a disturbing moan, it was almost sexual and Eyes wrinkled his nose in revulsion.

'Perrrrrfect,' the demon sighed.

The deposit box whipped shut, almost catching Wind Talker's lip as the drawer sped past his face and into the wall. The door slammed shut and white light flared up around its edges for a second.

A box on the other side of the room slid slowly open and a whisper drifted up from it. Coveted Secrets reached out and caught the whisper in his shadowy fingers. 'Limb Chewer can be found in a factory in Northgate, Compton Limited.' The open drawer slid slowly back into the wall and locked itself.

'Thank you,' Wind Talker said, eyeing the demon carefully. 'Does the previous owner of that secret get to find out that someone came looking for it?'

'No,' the demon replied silkily. Eyes swallowed. It was unlikely, but remained possible that someone might trade something for the secret about Hidden Voice one day. Hopefully long after the Lightning Lords were gone. He was ready to put that event behind them, he had had his fill of repercussions, of echoes of the past.

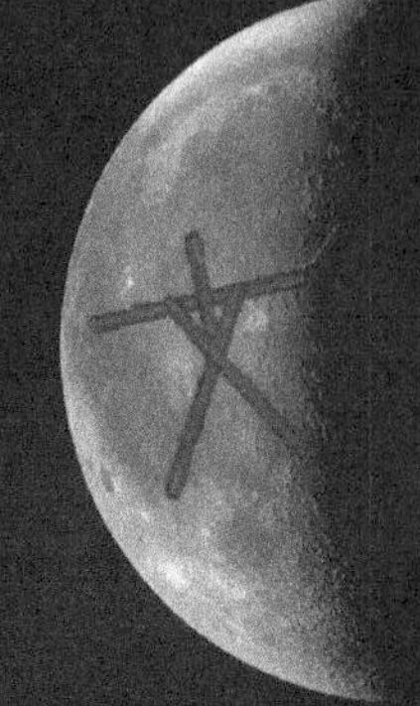

CHAPTER TWENTY FOUR

STALKER-OF-NIGHT'S-SHADOW

THE LIGHTNING LORDS LEFT THE BRIGHT LIGHTS of the vault, and crossed the dark basement to the sun-washed stairs. Stalker looked back over her shoulder as the vault door swung slowly closed and clicked shut. The green fae was gone, and the shifters made their way back to the main market.

'Can we stay and look around?' Weaver asked, her face lit up with curiosity.

'I don't see why not,' Wind Talker replied. Weaver dashed away, making a beeline through the crowd.

'I have to work,' Stalker muttered. Her hands were still shaking slightly, and she suspected that Eyes at least had picked up on her anxiety. She didn't want to draw questions from any of them. Claws placed a gentle hand on her shoulder and she looked at his kind smile.

'It's not as late as it feels,' he said at her ear. 'You've got time.'

She smiled back at him and drifted away from him, wandering over to a nearby table of trinkets. Her gaze settled on a wooden box about the size of a cigar box. It had tiny runes carved into the lid, and she ran her finger over the warm, smooth wood.

The creature behind the stall moved over to her. He was a short, gnarled man in a neat shirt and waistcoat. There was something goblin-like about his long nose and pointed ears, and when he smiled he showed sharp teeth like the green fae's.

'Do you like the pretty box?' he asked, his voice lower than she expected.

'I do. What do the runes say? I don't recognise them.'

'They belong to my people, rather than yours,' the goblin replied. 'A kiss hides me, a whisper opens me.'

'Excuse me?'

'That's what the runes say. Do you want it? Pretty box for pretty lady?'

'I don't think I have anything to trade for it,' she said with a reluctant sigh.

'What about those?' The goblin pointed a bony finger towards her neck. Her hand went reflexively to the two talismans hung on their black cords.

'No, they're not for sale.'

'Shame,' the goblin croaked. He tilted his head to one side and narrowed his eyes. 'I could take something else in exchange. Is there anything you want to part with? A burden you're tired of carrying, perhaps?'

Stalker regarded him carefully. Had he read her thoughts? Looked into her soul, the way she could? She didn't remotely trust this fellow, and suspected there could be a hidden clause to that sort of trade.

'I'm not sure,' she replied slowly.

'There's no catch, my dear,' the goblin said, with a wide grin. 'Give me a memory, or unhappy thought and the box is yours. I will only take what you freely offer.'

'Will it leave a hole? Or be filled by something else?'

'The memory is a curious thing, unpredictable. Some people experience a gap, they know they have forgotten something, but not what it is. Others find that their memory moulds itself around the missing item, making sense of it somehow, rationalising it.'

'And the box will hide itself? And its contents, I presume?'

The goblin simply inclined his head in reply. Stalker chewed her tongue, considering her options. There were plenty of things that she would like to forget, but she knew that those memories motivated her, and forgetting any of them might take some of the fight out of her. 'No,' she said with resolve. 'The price is too high, I don't want the box that much. Thank you.'

She turned and walked away from the stall. She heard the goblin chuntering about her as she went, but ignored him. Her eyes settled on Claws at another stall and she reached him just as he turned away, almost bumping right into her. They both laughed, and he held up a little paper bag.

'I bought something. You?'

'Not in the end, too expensive. What did you get?'

'It's crazy, I doubt I'll ever use it, but I couldn't resist.' His eyes shone and his grin lit up his rugged face. 'It's a bullet that is guaranteed to kill its mark!'

'What on earth?' Stalker said, stepping back from him in shock.

'No, don't look at me like that. It has one use, ever, right? It'd be destroyed on use. It has a price too, a really heavy one, using it would be a real last resort.' His face had sunk, like a shadow had fallen over it.

'What is it?'

'It'll kill its mark, but takes the one who fires it out too.'

'Right, so use it and take yourself down with your enemy?' She raised an eyebrow at him.

'Yeah. Like I said, I'll probably never use it, but it can't hurt to have something like that up my sleeve. You never know.'

'You'll have to load it into your gun first though. You'd have to know in advance that you were going to use it.'

'I know.' He looked resolutely away from her, and she shook her head.

'I'm going to have to head back to St. Mark's. I have to get to work for three. Where are the others?' She craned her neck, searching for the rest of the pack among the crowd.

'You go, I'll tell the others when I find them. See you back at the house later, yeah? We have to go find this factory tonight.' He looked into her eyes and she knew he was warning her not to go off to see Rhys instead of returning to the pack after work. She nodded in agreement and left the Trading Post through the main doors.

The twins were sitting on the steps, one of them was smoking a cigarette. Stalker cleared her throat and they turned to look up at her.

'You finished?' asked the one in the cap.

'I am, but my pack mates are still shopping.' It was a warm afternoon, the blue sky looked too tempting to resist. 'You don't need to escort me, I can fly north. You can watch me clear your territory easily enough from here. Is that okay?'

The twins looked at each other, then back at her. They both nodded.

'I suppose so,' replied the twin in the cap again.

'Thank you.' Stalker leaped into the air, shifting into a big barn owl and taking flight. She flew north over the perilous city centre. From overhead it looked just as terrifying as it had from the edge of China Town. She swooped east and skirted the boundary between the centre and the Glass Wolves' territory, following the line of their enormous wall. As she crossed into St. Mark's she felt more at ease and flew lower. She knew where to cross the veil like the back of her hand and emerged in human form in a wooded park just south of her dojo.

When she got to work, the dojo was buzzing with activity. Ron was chatting to some prospective students, and one of her colleagues was just finishing a class. She went into the staff changing room and hung her dha in her locker, along with her jacket. She didn't notice the extra weight in the jacket as it bumped against the back of the locker, and slammed the door without a second thought.

After her classes, Stalker left the dojo feeling reasonably light hearted.

'See you next week,' a student called to her as he got into his car and she raised a hand to wave.

Stalker walked quickly away from the dojo, and at the

corner broke into a run. She took a familiar route back to Grove Street, through a car park, over a fence, down off an overpass and along a high wall along the edge of the dual carriageway. The wind against her face was refreshing. It wasn't quite dark, the sun had dipped below the horizon, but the sky still glowed purple, and the street lights hadn't all come on yet.

She arrived at the house a little breathless, but feeling energised. The house was quiet, and she found the rest of the pack eating in tense silence in the kitchen.

'Everyone okay?' she asked, as she helped herself to the stew on the stove.

'Yeah,' Claws replied. 'Just anxious to get this done, I think.'

He got up and made space for Stalker to sit down. Wind Talker was chewing loudly beside her, wet, chomping sounds that grated on her nerves.

'Do we know where we're going?' she asked, hoping that conversation would distract her.

'It's right on the border of Redfield and Northgate, it's a printing press,' Eyes replied. Stalker saw something in his eyes, confidence that hadn't been there for days.

'We'll go there in the human world and take a look around,' Wind Talker said. He finished his food and took his plate to the sink. 'Sparking Clank wants Limb Chewer destroyed. So we find him and do just that.'

'Okay.' Stalker ate quickly, not wanting to delay them. Wind Talker left the room and stomped up the stairs. Stalker felt the familiar unease settle back in her gut, that resentment towards him for everything that had happened since finding Hidden Voice. She swallowed a particularly tough chunk of beef and scraped her bowl clean. She stood, the chair legs scraping loudly across the floor and everyone else got to their feet without a word.

'We're ready,' Weaver called up the stairs as she reached them. A moment later Wind Talker came jogging down, his bag across his shoulder and coat done up, ready to go. Stalker despised the way he had separated himself from the pack since taking control. He had criticised Eyes for doing that. She didn't want to admit that he was probably avoiding her and her hostility. He led the pack out and they walked north through the dark city.

Stalker noticed less of a chill in the air and realised that it was nearly March. The stars were just visible in the clear sky, despite the light pollution.

Weaver took her arm as they walked, and they exchanged small smiles.

'How are you doing?' Weaver asked quietly.

'Fine. You?'

'Adapting,' she replied, with another smile. Stalker griped her arm tighter.

'Yeah.'

They walked on in silence. The terraces of St. Mark's gave way to the factories of Northgate and Wind Talker led them to Compton Limited, checking a map on his phone periodically.

It was a stone block in the middle of a cluster of bigger factories, and had one long row of windows along the front wall, made up of small panes set into lead. The building was dark and quiet, the small car park in front was empty. The street was well lit, and the businesses surrounding Compton were just closing.

'Why do we keep finding ourselves at these places?' Stalker whispered. Weaver chuckled.

'This is North Caerton.' She gave Stalker a wink and Stalker couldn't help smiling.

'We need cover,' Wind Talker snapped. 'Claws?'

Claws approached a nearby street light, and pressed his hand against it. The light flickered out, along with several others nearby that evidently shared a circuit. Stalker ran towards the building, the others followed her. She found a side door and examined it. It was old and wooden, with a traditional Yale lock. She braced her shoulder against it and shoved hard. The wood splintered around the lock, and the door gave way. She swung it open and they filed inside.

The door opened into a narrow passage. Wind Talker led them quietly towards another door at the other end, which opened onto the factory floor. Rows of complicated machinery stood still and silent throughout the place. Stalker didn't know much about printing, but the machines all clearly had different roles in the process. Several resembled open mouths, with smooth surfaces inviting someone to risk placing their hands inside. She shuddered at the thought of losing a hand to one of them, and wondered in which one Limb Chewer had taken up residence.

'What's the plan?' Stalker whispered. They fanned out slightly, moving slowly between the machines.

'I think we'll have to wreck the right machine in order to drive the demon out, then we can destroy him.' Wind Talker didn't sound certain.

'How do we know which is the right one?' she asked.

Wind Talker glared at her then rolled his eyes. He tucked his talisman into his shirt so that it made contact with his skin, his eyes got that peculiar glazed expression as he looked across the veil.

Stalker felt something odd about the place. She looked around, but couldn't place what it was. She felt heavier here, as if gravity were stronger.

'This one,' Wind Talker said abruptly, pointing towards one of the mouth-like machines. It was huge, and shone silver in the glow from the re-lit street lights outside the windows. 'He's right here in the machine, I can see glowing eyes. It's so odd, like he occupies the same space as the machine.'

Stalker thought of Rhys's cloak and knew exactly what he meant. She strode to the machine and looked for a piece to tear off, and the others joined her. She soon found what she was looking for, a thick bar ran through the joint at the back of the mouth, and on one end was a metal lever. She shifted form, giving the Agrius a chance to do its thing. She wrenched the lever off with a grinding crunch of tearing metal and began striking the rest of the machine with it. The clanging echoed throughout the building.

Eyes and Weaver shifted form too, and added their strength to the job. Together they ripped the top jaw from the beast of a machine, and threw it across the floor. Stalker tugged the cables out of the back of the machine, and severely dented the lower plate with the lever. Weaver and Eyes took the legs out from under it and the whole thing fell to the floor with a deafening clunk.

Wind Talker held up his hand and they stopped to look at him. Stalker felt a change in the air; the veil had shifted, but it didn't ripple like it usually did. It felt more like the change in air pressure from a sealed door opening. Materialising in front of them was a grotesque, black and silver construct, all metal and joints, and enormous gnashing teeth. It had glowing red eyes, and as Stalker looked closely, she saw that bits of it were held together with flesh. Bile rose in her throat as she saw the stringy sinew and blood trickling down the side of the demonic construct.

Limb Chewer lurched towards them, crunching the pieces of its mundane host beneath his spider-like legs. Wind Talker roared and erupted in thick fur. He pounced onto the demon's back, punched furiously at it and tore frantically at any part that looked like it might come loose. Stalker was next into the fight, followed by Eyes and Weaver.

Stalker grasped one of the beast's four legs and wrestled to pull it out from its socket. Limb Chewer slashed at her with another leg, sending her flying across the factory and straight into another machine. She felt a rib crack on impact and snarled. She leapt up and bounded back to the fight. Ducking under the legs to get to the belly of the demon, Stalker pulled at cables and plates of metal, desperate to find something to rip off, but it was held together well. She heard a shot ring out and her entire body went rigid. She peered out from under Limb Chewer and saw Claws standing a few feet away, his gun aimed on the demon. He was alive, but so was Limb Chewer. He hadn't used his new bullet.

She scrambled out from underneath the demon and leaped onto his back alongside Wind Talker. Limb Chewer shrieked and thrashed about. Stalker grabbed hold of a ridge on his back but Wind Talker was thrown down his back, tumbling to the floor.

Another shot pierced the air and Stalker felt the impact into the metal somewhere below her. Limb Chewer reared up, Stalker held tight, and he lifted a leg to his eye socket, which was gushing black oil and red blood.

Weaver and Eyes got under its other front leg and Stalker felt the whole construct lurch towards the ground as they took it out. She dug her claws into a groove between thick, black metal plates and found her grip. She tugged hard and ripped the ridge-like plate up off the demon's back. She went flying, but a ripple effect pulled a sequence of the plates down with the one in her hands, like a spine peeling away one vertebra at a time.

Claws took another shot, and the demon crashed to the ground. Stalker scrambled backwards away from it, her breathing ragged and her pulse racing in her temples. There was a groan from Limb Chewer, and the clunking of gears slowing to a halt.

One by one, the Lightning Lords shifted back into their human forms.

'Shouldn't it go *poof* about now?' Claws asked, slowly lowering his gun.

'We have to get out of here, people will have heard that.' Eyes looked around anxiously.

'We can't leave this here,' Wind Talker said, shaking his head. 'We'll have to take it across the veil.'

'Why hasn't it done that itself?' Stalker asked. 'Aren't they supposed to sort of melt back into the realm they came from?'

'Something's very wrong here,' Weaver said, her voice trembling slightly.

'The veil doesn't feel right,' Stalker said in agreement. 'I noticed it when Limb Chewer crossed, it's too heavy.'

'Well, we do have to move it. We can't let humans see it.' Wind Talker strode over to it and picked up the torn-off leg. Claws and Eyes went to help gather up the disconnected pieces, they tossed them on top of the pile of wreckage. Stalker half-heartedly helped. A gnawing sensation at her gut stopped her from throwing herself into the task.

'Just like the car,' Wind Talker said, crouching beside Limb Chewer's remains. 'When we fought the Plague Doctor.'

'Just like the car,' Claws agreed with a nod.

Stalker went over and put her hands on the remains. She glanced at Weaver, whose face was frozen in fierce concentration.

'I'm telling you,' Wind Talker snapped, 'I can see across the veil and it's fine, there is no problem here. We need to move now!'

Stalker focused her attention on parting the veil. It was so heavy, she closed her eyes against the strain.

Muffled and far away, she heard Weaver's voice, a shout against the wind.

'It's a trap!'

Something brushed against Stalker's face, and she swatted at it with her hand. It clung to her fingers, and stuck to her hair. Everything was black, but slowly a light grew out of the darkness, and Stalker squinted to see where she was. She tried to turn her head, but more of the stringy substance clung to her face. It felt like when she had walked right into a spider's web in the garden as a child. Exactly like that.

Her eyes popped wide open with the realisation, and a cry rose in her throat. A scuttling noise behind her killed the scream before it left her mouth. The remains of Limb Chewer were just below her feet, she was suspended off the ground, caught in the sticky web.

'Stalker?' a voice nearby hissed. She made her head turn and cleared the thick web away to see Claws just behind her. Wind Talker was not far away and Eyes was there too. No Weaver. She was right, it was a trap and she hadn't tried to cross the veil with them.

'What the hell happened? Where are we?' she snapped, failing to keep her voice low.

There was a rattling sound and a rapid clicking, something was excited. Stalker didn't want to think about it, she didn't want to see it. Confronting giant spiders was not on her bucket list of things to do before she died.

'This isn't Hepethia,' Wind Talker said, his voice was steady and calm. 'We were drawn somewhere else, Svartalfheim, or maybe Niflheim.'

'This is why the veil was heavy,' Stalker said with a sigh. 'I knew it was wrong. I should have listened to my instincts.'

'Where's Weaver?' Claws asked.

'She stayed behind,' Eyes replied, his tone resigned. 'She knew.'

'You didn't see this, Wind Talker?' Claws asked, just a tiny hint of accusation to his voice.

'No, I told you, everything looked normal. This isn't

Hepethia, I couldn't have seen this.'

'What the fuck has trapped us?' Stalker snapped.

'Are you scared of spiders, Stalker?' Claws asked. She could hear his smirk, even though she couldn't quite see his face.

'Not normal ones,' she replied. 'But no normal spider did this.'

Soft laughter echoed around them and Stalker twisted around, trying to locate the source of it.

'Oh my goodness.' The voice was bell-like. 'What have we here? What has she caught this time?'

A dark figure emerged from the fog-like surroundings, moving easily through the intricate web. She was a beautiful young woman, with long, black hair as fine as silk, and a matching black, backless, silk gown exposing smooth, white skin. Beyond her the web began to grow clear, like it was taking form for the first time. White walls and floor appeared, just out of reach.

'Jorogumo,' Wind Talker said softly. 'She's a demon, don't be fooled.'

'Now then,' she said, gently scolding him. 'It's not polite to call people names. How do you know mine?'

'I always know the names of your kind. Artemis granted me the ability.'

Stalker watched carefully as Jorogumo moved towards Wind Talker. When the demon's back was turned, Stalker began carefully guiding the strands of web that held her, attaching them to one another instead of her. She moved slowly, carefully avoiding attracting the demon's attention.

'Did you build this web?' Claws asked. 'It's incredible.'

He had seen what Stalker was doing and was buying

her time.

'She built it,' the lilting voice of the beautiful demon replied. 'The other one.'

'Where is the other one?' Claws asked.

'Around.'

Stalker stopped working and looked around anxiously.

'So there's someone else here? Another demon entirely?' Claws asked.

'Yes,' she replied silkily.

'You're lying,' Claws said, a wry smile on his lips. 'You're the spider, Jorogumo.'

The demon let out a rattling breath, quite different from her musical voice. Stalker hurriedly went back to trying to free herself, she just needed to get enough of the web off her to be able to shift.

The demon began to change, black stalks protruded from her pale back and her skin grew darker. The stalks sprouted and lengthened, her body thickened and hair grew all over her lower body. Perched daintily in the thick web stood an enormous spider, with a bulbous lower body, but the torso and head of a woman. Stalker shoved her revulsion aside as she worked carefully and quietly to remove the web from her clothes and hair.

'Little flies, tasty treats. Not all for me, of course, got to save something for The Hunger.' The demon's voice scratched at the air like nails on a blackboard, and her web vibrated all around Stalker and the others. She moved around Wind Talker, looking him up and down. She moved easily on the web, barely causing it to tremble, despite her great bulk.

Stalker paused for a moment, watching the demon

nervously. Once satisfied that she was still going unnoticed, she resumed extracting herself.

'Did you expect us? Or did we stumble into your web by coincidence?' Claws asked.

'Stumble, stumble, stumble. Oh yes, quite by chance.'

'Were you expecting someone else?' Claws pressed on.

'Now that's a question. Curious little fly.'

'Well?'

The demon burst into laughter, her legs peddling frantically on the spot, causing the web to bounce. Stalker was flung loose and she reached out, desperate for something firm to grasp onto. But there was only web. Her reflexes kicked in and she shifted form rapidly before she fell into the web below and became even more tangled. She focused her energy on mimicking Jorogumo's form, and shuddered as extra legs erupted from her body. She couldn't take the form of the demon, but she managed a large spider, and scurried adeptly over the web and onto cold, hard ground behind the demon.

Jorogumo shrieked and scuttled after her, but Stalker was too quick. She shifted back into her human form, drew her dha and sliced easily through the web. Eyes fell down a few feet, before being caught in another layer.

'No!' yelled Jorogumo, and she darted back to try and retrieve Eyes.

Stalker stooped and ran under the vast web, running her dha through it as she went. Limb Chewer's remains crashed to the floor. A gap opened up and Eyes fell through it, landing heavily on top of Limb Chewer and rolling to the floor. Claws dropped too, but again got caught. Jorogumo went after him and sunk her fangs into his shoulder. He cried out and writhed around, entangling himself further in the thick web.

'Get Wind Talker,' Stalker ordered, and Eyes charged over to where the Alpha hung suspended above them. He began pulling at the web, slowly loosening the bindings. Stalker moved swiftly underneath the demon and thrust her dha up through the web. She caught the back end of Jorogumo's enormous body, and the demon screamed in pain and lurched higher into the web to get away from Stalker.

'Pointy, stabby! Bad fly!'

Claws jerked down in the web, upset by the sudden movement. Stalker reached up and grabbed hold of him. She pulled him down and scraped as much of the web off him as she could. She held onto his arm and tried to cross the veil. Nothing happened. The veil was thoroughly coated in the demon's silken trap.

'Let us go,' she demanded, staring up at the vile creature, as it hurriedly spun more web to replace what had been cut away. Eyes had got Wind Talker mostly free, both of them were furiously scraping the clingy white silk from their clothes. Claws lay limp on the floor, his hand clutching his bleeding shoulder. His face was pale and clammy. Something wasn't right, he should be healing from what was a relatively minor wound.

'No,' snapped Jorogumo. 'Shan't let you go. You're mine; breakfast, lunch, dinner and supper.' She jabbed one of her eight legs at each of them in turn, saving Stalker for last.

Stalker lifted one of her dha, and sneered at the spider.

'Let us go, or I will kill you.'

The demon flinched and hissed.

'I will let three of you go. You must leave a sacrifice, for The Hunger.'

Stalker instantly raised her free hand and pointed a finger right at Wind Talker, with no trace of hesitation.

'You can have him.' Stalker's voice was as calm as still water. There was an instant of total silence in which Stalker lowered her arm, her gaze never leaving the demon.

'What?' Wind Talker snapped. Stalker felt his eyes on her.

Jorogumo cocked her head to one side and regarded Stalker carefully.

'Excellent,' she clicked. She leaped down from her web and landed in front of Eyes and Wind Talker, snatching the Alpha in two of her legs and biting into his neck in one fluid movement. He went limp in her grasp, his eyes glazed over and he fell unconscious. She began bundling him up in more fresh web. As she did so, the demon raised another leg and parted the web overhead.

Stalker felt the veil ripple, just as it was meant to. Just as she was about to take a step through it, a whistling sound reached her on the breeze through the veil. It grew louder and louder, like a rocket zooming towards them. She leaped to one side, throwing herself over Claws to shield him. Eyes dropped to the floor beside them and a pair of shoes materialised in front of Stalker's face. Weaver's shoes.

Stalker looked up just as a blinding flash filled the white room. Unchained Lightning landed with a thud that made the floor shake. Web fell away in the power fae's wake, hanging limply from the ceiling and walls. Static filled the air and the demon let out a piercing scream. She gathered Wind Talker close to her body and tried to climb up into what remained of her web. Unchained Lightning whipped his tail towards her with a crack of thunder, and she dropped the Alpha. He landed with a *thunk* underneath her, and Eyes dashed over to him.

'We'll be going now,' Weaver said, her voice ringing with authority. She stooped and hooked her arm under one of Claws' arms, Stalker did the same with his other arm. He winced as they hoisted him up, and gingerly put his weight on his own feet. Eyes had hold of Wind Talker and they all stepped across the veil. They ended up in Hepethia, Unchained Lightning arrived a moment later, and Stalker felt the veil fall closed, shutting them off from the demon realm that they had stumbled into.

The factories of Northgate were alarming monstrosities in Hepethia. Living, lumbering and tireless machines, chugging out smoke, and belching chemicals. They stood on a bumpy track between two such monsters, too small to be noticed by them.

'You came for us,' Claws croaked. Stalker looked at him, he was gazing at Weaver, a soppy smile on his face.

'Let's get back to the house,' she replied coldly.

Unchained Lightning crackled and took flight, soaring overhead, brighter than the full moon in the sky.

'I can't carry him,' Eyes said, letting Wind Talker's unconscious body slide to the ground. Stalker stiffened, part of her resented that he hadn't been left behind. How had it been so easy for her to make that sacrifice? It had to be the coldest thing she had ever done. She had been feeling extremely angry towards Wind Talker, but she was just as surprised by her willingness to sacrifice him as he had been.

Weaver placed her fingers in her mouth and let out a shrill whistle. There was a sudden rumbling sound and a rush of air, as a huge black taxi roared into view and hurtled to a stop beside them. The door popped open and Stalker was surprised to see Tar Peter in the driver's seat.

'Get in, hurry,' he snapped. Weaver helped Stalker ease Claws into the back, then helped Eyes with Wind Talker. Weaver slammed the door and got into the front beside Tar Peter.

'You called the cavalry?' Stalker asked Weaver through the little window, as the car started moving. Weaver ignored her. Stalker felt a frown crease her brow and she settled back into the seat, Claws slumped sideways against her. 'Are you okay?'

'Yeah, shoulder's killing me though.' He tried to laugh but a wretched cough hacked out of his throat instead.

'Do you think she was poisonous?' Stalker asked, suddenly very worried for her brother. Somehow, she couldn't feel the same concern for Wind Talker, who lay unconscious and partially wrapped in thick web on the cab floor.

'Yeah, I think she was,' Eyes replied, his eyes cast down. He was perched awkwardly on the little folding seat behind the driver and he clung to the seat tightly with both hands as he stared at the unconscious Wind Talker. Stalker felt anger pulsing out from him, but she couldn't tell who it was directed towards. In that moment she would have given anything for their old telepathy.

Tar Peter drove extremely fast, taking the corners at

such a speed that the car tilted and Stalker had to grab hold of the large, yellow handle on the door.

'I don't blame you,' Claws said softly, barely audible over the roar of the engine and squeals of the tyres.

'Sorry?' Stalker said, dipping her head closer to his.

'For what you did back there. You were trying to get most of us out of there alive. I understand.'

'Thanks,' she muttered, her cheeks flushing.

'But he might not,' he said, jerking his foot slightly towards Wind Talker.

'If he survives,' Stalker whispered. She didn't think it was loud enough for anyone to hear, but Claws lifted his head and looked her in the eye. He didn't say a word, he didn't need to. He sat up and inched away from her, repulsed by her callousness.

The taxi skidded to a halt and Stalker looked out of the window to see 32 Grove Street right next to her door. Weaver was the first one out, followed by their driver, who came to open Stalker's door and help Claws out.

'Thanks,' she muttered, not quite wanting to look at their demonic ally. 'How do you have a taxi in Hepethia, anyway?'

Tar Peter grinned and winked at her. That was all she was getting out of him. Weaver approached him and gave him a hug. Stalker couldn't hide the surprise from her face, so she hurriedly looked away and helped Claws to the house door. She heard the car doors slamming shut and the wheels spin as Tar Peter drove away.

Once they were all inside and assembled in the living room, an icy chill filled the air. Weaver stood in the doorway, her arms crossed. Eyes diligently cleared the strands of web off Wind Talker, and the Alpha started to come around, groaning at first, then turning his head and lifting his arm to his face.

Weaver disappeared and came back a moment later with a glass of water.

'We'll need to treat the poison in both of them,' Eyes said, taking the water and sitting Wind Talker up to feed it to him.

There was a crackle of static throughout the room, Unchained Lightning was present, even if he couldn't fit into the house. The charge seemed to shock Wind Talker into full consciousness and his eyes popped open. They darted around the room, taking in his surroundings and finally settled on Stalker. She felt her cheeks redden and looked resolutely at a worn patch on the sofa.

Before Wind Talker could open his lips to berate her, Weaver strode across the room and slapped him hard across the face. The sound was like a whip cracking.

Everyone gawked at her in stunned silence.

'How dare you!' she yelled. 'How dare you risk the lives of everyone in this pack. You reckless, arrogant son of a bitch. I told you! Stalker warned you! We knew something was wrong and you totally disregarded our concerns. You led them into a trap that very nearly killed you all.'

Stalker had never seen Weaver like this. She swallowed a hard lump in her throat and tried to keep a satisfied smirk from appearing on her face by pressing her tongue to the roof of her mouth.

Claws lifted a hand to object, but Weaver's piercing eyes stopped him and he let his hand drop back into his lap.

'We had no choice,' Wind Talker replied. His face was bright red, his eyes narrowed and as hard as steel. 'The police would have been on their way, there were gunshots and the most horrific noises imaginable to humanity. They would have found Limb Chewer and our world would have been exposed.'

'They would have found a load of broken machinery!' Weaver snapped. Her eyes flashed dangerously. 'They would never have made sense of it, yes it would have looked suspicious, especially with the flesh parts, but never in a million years would they have realised that it had been alive, nor would our kind or Hepethia have been exposed. We could have found a way out of there without crossing the veil. You thought you could see everything with your toy around your neck. You thought you were oh so clever. Your cocky attitude nearly got you killed.'

'No,' he shouted, lurching to his feet. He pointed a thick finger at Stalker, but kept his eyes fixed on Weaver. 'She did.'

Weaver blinked hard and looked between him and Stalker. Stalker released a slow breath, suddenly realising she had been holding it.

'It's true,' Eyes said quietly. Weaver glared at him. 'Right before you arrived, Jorogumo agreed to let the rest of us go if one of us stayed as a sacrifice. Stalker nominated Wind Talker.'

Silence filled the air, though Stalker was acutely aware of her own heart thumping wildly.

Light filled the room and Unchained Lightning's voice crackled around them.

'I ate her, no sacrifice necessary now.'

'Well, that's a relief,' Claws whispered, a small smile just about making it onto his pale and sickly face.

'This pack is a joke,' Weaver said. Her voice was low and threatening. 'I won't have any more part in it.'

She swept from the room, crossed the veil into the human world and disappeared. Stalker felt a wrench in her gut. Weaver was gone from her mind, disconnected from her soul. Weaver was no longer a Lightning Lord.

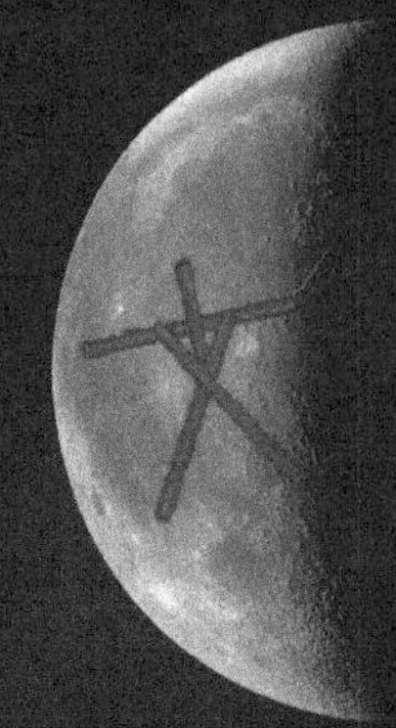

Chapter Twenty Five

Stalker stared at the empty doorway, suspended in shock. The entire room seemed to be on pause, the tension was palpable.

'Did Weaver just... Did she just leave the pack?' Claws asked, getting shakily to his feet.

'I think so,' Stalker whispered.

'Can she do that?'

Stalker turned to look at Claws, his face was a sickly shade of grey, deep shadows under his bloodshot eyes aged him by a decade.

'Apparently.' Stalker ran after Weaver, Claws limped behind her. They crossed the veil and quickly checked the house, but Weaver was gone. Stalker tore out through the front door and looked both ways along the street. 'There!' She pointed and set off at a sprint towards Weaver's rapidly retreating back, she was almost at the end of the street. 'Wait!' Stalker shouted.

Weaver stopped and turned to look at her, tears streaked down her face. Stalker stopped in front of her and reached out for her shoulder, but Weaver pulled away. She looked over Stalker's shoulder and a look of concern swept the severity from her face. Stalker looked back to see Claws limping down the street, clutching his shoulder.

'What are you doing?' Weaver called. When Claws reached them he was gasping for breath.

'You can't leave,' he panted.

'He's right,' Stalker said, grasping Weaver's arm. 'We can fix this. Come back to the house, we'll talk it over.'

'There's no point. I can't be in a room with him right now, or you for that matter. I'm too angry.'

'Me?' Stalker blurted. 'Why are you angry with me?'

'You were willing to leave him behind. No matter what he's done, no matter how bad of an Alpha he is, we never leave a pack mate behind.'

'Oh really?' Stalker snapped, crossing her arms over her chest. 'Even if they betray the rest of us? And it's perfectly okay to stand back while they walk into a trap?'

'I went for help, in case you didn't notice.'

Weaver turned and marched away. Stalker clucked her tongue and glanced awkwardly at Claws. He rolled his eyes at her and set off after Weaver.

'Wait!' he called. Stalker followed them, lurking just behind as the other two walked in uncomfortable silence. Dawn was breaking, the sky just beginning to glow pale blue. Caerton was starting to come to life. She heard cars on the nearby main road and the muffled sounds of televisions inside the houses they passed.

'Where will you go?' Claws asked at last.

'I have friends,' Weaver said softly. She wiped the tears from her face and came to a halt. 'What happened today was unacceptable.'

'I know,' Claws replied.

Stalker stood behind them feeling isolated. She chewed the inside of her mouth, and fought back the image of Wind Talker's astonished face when she offered him up to the demon.

'I'll agree to come back and talk things over once the dust settles. And only if that maniac is no longer Alpha.' Weaver lifted her chin defiantly.

Stalker felt relief wash over her. She had thought that Weaver had warmed to Wind Talker as Alpha. To hear her speaking out so defiantly against him gave her hope that they could mend their relationship.

'We'll sort it,' she said, a grin splitting her face. Weaver looked at her and managed a small smile.

'Look, I'm going now, storming out and all that. Call me in a day or so.'

'Okay,' Stalker said, suppressing a grin. Weaver turned and swept away, her long skirt brushing the pavement. Stalker glanced at Claws, he looked like he was about to collapse. She grabbed hold of him and draped his good arm over her shoulder. 'Come on, let's get you back. I hope Eyes and Wind Talker haven't killed each other.'

Claws coughed and slumped heavily against her. They walked slowly back to the house.

Eyes and Wind Talker sat in silence in the living room, resolutely not looking at one another. Eyes jumped to his feet as they entered and helped get Claws into a chair.

'Where is she?' he asked anxiously.

'Gone,' Stalker replied. 'We caught up to her but couldn't convince her to come back. She's too angry to talk.'

Eyes' cheek twitched, fury flashed in his eyes. He wheeled around and marched over to Wind Talker. He grabbed hold of the Alpha's shirt and pulled him to his feet.

'You did this. You shattered our pack.'

Stalker flinched, taken aback by Eyes' anger. Claws put a gentle hand on her arm, holding her back without the need for force or words.

'I... I...' Wind Talker spluttered.

'I admit that I made mistakes as Alpha. Fortune made it look so easy, but it isn't. I appreciate that. But I never led us into such danger, I never disregarded the knowledge, skills or advice of my pack. I would never assume that I knew everything important about a situation, and I would NEVER betray my pack mates.' His volume mounted, his face grew red and Stalker could see the veins throbbing in his temple as he shouted in Wind Talker's face.

Wind Talker roughly knocked Eyes' hand from his clothes and stepped back. He too had turned scarlet, a combination of anger and embarrassment, Stalker supposed. She watched open mouthed, her own pulse racing. She didn't think their little house would remain standing if these two lost control and let their Agrius beasts take advantage of the situation.

'Are you challenging me?' Wind Talker spat.

'I am,' Eyes replied, squaring up to him.

Wind Talker smirked and took another step back, his shoulders instantly relaxing.

'Shall we cross the veil?' he asked. Eyes nodded and the two of them disappeared. Stalker grabbed Claws and they crossed after them. Eyes was following Wind Talker through the kitchen and Stalker moved quickly after them, still supporting Claws. 'I'm in no shape for a fight,' Wind Talker stated, as he opened the back door and led them into the garden. His skin was even more grey than Claws', and covered in the same dirty layer of sweat that soaked his clothes. Where Jorogumo had bitten him his clothes were torn and Stalker could see an oozing open wound.

Unchained Lightning was perched on the roof of the house, looking down on them with a glint in his eye. The air was charged with static, and Stalker felt her hair start to lift.

Wind Talker looked up at their allied fae and held his hands out in front of him in supplication. He was shaking slightly. He seemed to be generally faring better than Claws, despite having been rendered unconscious by Jorogumo. But in this moment, he looked on the brink of collapse. It wouldn't be right for Eyes to fight him now, even she could concede that.

'I don't want to fight you,' Eyes said, his voice quiet and sympathetic.

'You don't need to,' Wind Talker replied, pulling himself up to his full height. 'I relinquish my claim on the Alphaship. The position is rightfully yours.'

Stalker and Claws exchanged nervous glances. Eyes blinked in surprise.

'Right,' he said slowly.

'You were making mistakes, you admit as much yourself. I had to do something. I had to shake you up and make you see that. I had to remind you why you were our Alpha in the first place, and point you in the direction of good leadership.'

Stalker slumped, she felt her gut lurch sideways, and leaned heavily on Claws so that they were propping each other up. All of this had been to teach Eyes a lesson. Betraying her, killing Hidden Voice, challenging Eyes, it was all to make Eyes a better Alpha. A spark ignited and pulled her from her stupor. She lurched forwards, a snarl rising in her throat.

'You bastard!' she yelled. She strode across the garden, drawing a sword from her back. Eyes caught hold of her and spun her away from Wind Talker. She resisted, pulling hard away from him. The rage was overwhelming and she felt the Agrius roaring to life within her.

'Oh no you don't,' Eyes whispered in her ear. Claws was there in an instant too, stroking her hair.

'Calm down, Stalker.'

She tried to shake them off, but they had a tight hold of her. She caught sight of Wind Talker standing against the garden wall, looking genuinely petrified. That seemed to satisfy part of her and she began to calm down. Claws gently sheathed her sword for her, but Eyes only relaxed his hold on her once she had taken a deep breath.

'I'm all right,' she said, a bite in her voice. 'I'm not going to gut him. Thank you for stopping me.' She glared at Wind Talker, and accepted Claws' arm around her shoulders.

'I accept the role of Alpha of the Lightning Lords,' Eyes said, looking hard at Wind Talker, then up at Unchained Lightning. The fae crackled, nodded his head, then took flight, soaring away into the pale blue sky overhead. 'He always does that,' Eyes mused, watching the fae fly away.

Stalker shrugged off Claws' arm and stomped into the house. She stopped and looked back at the others, every eye was on her.

'I'm glad you're back, Alpha,' she said pointedly to Eyes. 'But order isn't restored until we get Weaver back. I need a day myself to calm down, then I'll talk to Weaver and we'll finish sorting this mess out.'

She turned and left them gawking after her, crossed the veil and set off to find Rhys.

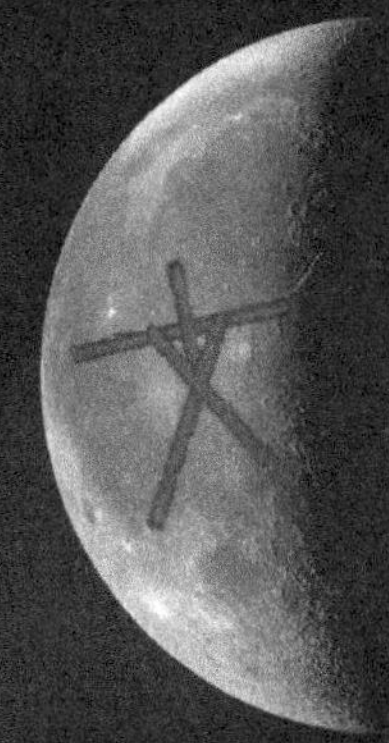

Chapter Twenty Six

Fights-Eyes-Open

'Right,' Eyes said in a business-like tone, deciding to switch off his frustration with Stalker. She hadn't left the pack, like Weaver had, she'd be back. She just needed to cool off, probably with her human lover. He hoped with all his might that she wasn't walking into a situation like his. 'First things first, we need to get you two back to full strength. I need to know if this poison will work itself out, like the last lot, or if we need to treat it. Wind Talker, that's your area of expertise.'

'Right on it,' Wind Talker said, wiping a shaking hand across his brow.

'For now, both of you get some rest. We'll reconvene in a few hours.'

He marched into the house and went to gather up his things. He had been staying here since walking out on Chloe, but the little house was really too small for all of them, and was beginning to smell terrible. He left the house and went to sit in his car. He needed to decide what he was going to do. He looked longingly at his phone. There were no missed calls or messages. He checked his emails and saw an agenda for a meeting at Free River Tower that afternoon. He hit the "attending" button with a heavy sigh, then started the engine.

He drove to his house first, the work had begun on replacing the windows and cleaning it all up, and it was starting to look normal. It was still early enough that no workmen were there yet. He went inside and leaned heavily on the inside of the front door. Life was never going to go back to how it was before, but he had a small glimmer of hope that whatever new life was taking shape was going to be simpler.

He went slowly to the kitchen and peeked cautiously inside. The blood had been cleaned up, and some of the kitchen units had been replaced. It smelled of fresh paint and sanded wood. The living room was clear of debris, new windows filled the bay, but the furniture was still covered in dust sheets and the new carpet was yet to be laid.

Upstairs everything looked perfectly normal. He went to his and Chloe's bedroom and picked out a clean suit. He filled a bag with other clothes. Images of the attack on his family kept trying to intrude, but he forced them out of his mind, and left the house as quickly as possible. He knew he would never be able to live there again, and doubted his family would either.

With a shaking breath, he set off for his mother's house. He parked outside and approached the front door with caution. He had no expectations of being well received, or of reconciliation with Chloe, but he couldn't leave things the way they were. It had been three nights since he had left, with no contact whatsoever from any of his family. He had to know if they were all okay.

He put his key in the lock, half expecting the locks to have been changed. But it turned and the door opened easily. The house was still and silent. He closed the door behind him and walked quietly through the rooms on the ground floor. When he reached the kitchen he found a note pinned to the fridge door with one of Amy's colourful magnets.

> *Martin,*
>
> *I assume you will find this eventually. Amy and I have gone to stay with my parents in London. I went back to the house on Sunday, I see the work is coming along, but we can't go back there. I'll be sending for more of our things in due course, once we get settled.*
>
> *Your mum has decided to stay with her brother in Canada for a while. She's not coping well at all. Please contact her, she says you have his address and phone number. She says you can house sit if you need to, she wants to make sure her house is secure.*
>
> *Please don't try to contact me. We'll sort out something with regards to you seeing Amy, of course, but only if you can reassure me of her safety.*
>
> *I'll be in touch once the dust settles.*
>
> *Chloe*

'Right,' Eyes said quietly to himself. For a moment it seemed the world had stopped spinning. Time itself was suspended. He heard his own heartbeat drowning out all other sound, and the saliva dried instantly from his mouth. 'Well yes, it's probably for the best. They're all safely out of Caerton, The Witches can't touch them, or me now.'

He shook his head, suddenly aware that he was talking to himself. He made his way upstairs to the room he had been staying in, and collapsed on the bed.

When he woke, the early afternoon sun was struggling to break through the grey clouds. He'd slept longer than he intended, and rushed to shower and dress for the meeting.

Free River Tower was bustling with activity when he arrived. Theodore was in an agitated state, issuing orders in a loud voice, and clearly alarming the human workers scurrying around him.

'Martin,' he called out as soon as he laid eyes on the new arrival. Eyes nodded in greeting and moved into the meeting room. People were dashing to and fro, stacks of papers littered the huge conference table. The meeting was mostly attended by legal types, staff of Harris Intermediaries, but two men from the council sat along from where Theodore stood, both looking petrified. Eyes recognised one of the men from previous meetings, the other looked like a junior assistant, and sat scribbling notes. 'Take a seat,' Theodore ordered. His normally genial tone was absent.

'Apologies for being late,' Eyes muttered, keeping his eyes down as he took a seat next to the note-taking youngster. 'I had other business.'

'Of course, of course,' Theodore replied distractedly.

The meeting proceeded with Theodore generally arguing with people about how quickly work on the underground railway could be completed. Eyes had always thought of Theodore as someone with it all together. Seeing him this flustered was equal parts disappointment and relief. It was reassuring that even a powerful elder had bad days and didn't always get his own way, it put Eyes' own struggles into perspective. But at the same time, he had aspired to be like Theodore. It was unsettling to know that even after decades of power and influence he might still have trouble controlling his plans.

The scribbler persisted throughout the meeting, noting every task issued, every deadline. Eyes concealed a smile, amused at the young man's eagerness. As the meeting drew to a close, Eyes helped him gather his notes and gave him what he hoped was a reassuring smile.

'Thanks,' the young man said, shovelling the papers into his briefcase. He stood up and smoothed down his suit, and Eyes caught a glimpse of his security identity badge, clipped to his jacket. A jolt of recognition ran up his spine and he drew a sudden breath.

'No problem, Ben, is it?' Eyes said, indicating the badge.

'That's right,' the young man said with a nervous smile. 'First meeting here.'

'I could tell,' Eyes smiled. 'It isn't always like this. Hopefully those notes will be useful.'

'Yeah,' Ben replied. His superior was engaged with Theodore, and Eyes watched carefully over Ben's shoulder.

'I made myself clear,' Theodore was saying. 'Your department will have to keep up. I'll see you for an update in two weeks.'

The council official turned away, his cheeks blazing. He marched back to Ben and gave Eyes a look of sheer exasperation.

'Deluded,' he muttered. 'You'd think the world revolved around him. We can't dig up that much of the city at once, it's just not possible. But he won't listen.'

'I suggest politely nodding and agreeing with him in the short term,' Eyes said conspiratorially.

'It's been like this all year,' he hissed. 'Come on Ben, back to the office.'

Ben and Eyes exchanged troubled glances and half-hearted smiles. Eyes looked down at the table as they walked away. He caught sight of a map of the electricity supply network for the whole city. Theodore was busy fending off another complaint from someone, so Eyes hurriedly rolled up the map and slipped it into his case. He glanced nervously around, and let out a slow breath. It seemed no one had seen him take it.

As everyone left the conference room Eyes got out his phone and typed a text message to Stalker.

> Just met your friend, Ben. You might want to make sure he's ok. Theodore's not having the best day. Hope you're ok. See you soon x

'Martin,' Theodore called, just as Eyes reached the door. He stiffened slightly, slapped on a polite smile and turned to face his boss.

'Theodore.'

'Close the door, would you?'

Eyes did as he was asked and walked back to the table.

'Everything all right at your end?'

'Fine, thank you,' Eyes replied stiffly.

'I gather there was an upset among your group. Seems to have righted itself now.'

Eyes felt the question of how Theodore knew anything about that die on his lips. He knew the names of every shifter he met, Wind Talker that of every other supernatural, Claws knew a lie when he heard one, and Stalker could dig deep to find someone's inner truth. There was no telling how much more information an old shifter like Theodore could tell from a single glance.

'That's right,' he said. 'Everyone is back where they belong.'

'Well, almost,' Theodore said softly.

'Okay, I can't let that one go. How?' Eyes snapped impatiently.

'Teri came to me early this morning.'

'Oh.' Eyes blinked in surprise. 'I see.'

'Don't worry, she hasn't told me anything. She was obviously upset, and wanted somewhere to stay, but I didn't pry.'

'I didn't even know you two knew each other.' Eyes couldn't hide the chagrin from his voice.

'Speaks-With-Stone introduced us. The science department of the university is just up the hill, so it was appropriate that we be introduced. And it was decided once her talent became evident that she would need a mentor for that.'

'Oh,' Eyes said, fighting back even more surprise. This was the first he had heard of Theodore being gifted with visions. He couldn't help but feel a stab of jealousy that

Weaver had never mentioned any of this to him. 'Is all of this because of a message from above?' He swept his hand over the table, still littered with blueprints, schematics, and plans.

'Yes,' the elder replied.

'I wish I'd known,' Eyes snapped. 'Is she all right?' he added more softly.

'She will be, she feels betrayed. Wounds like that take time to heal. But I believe she'll be back with you once she knows you're back in charge. Shall I tell her?'

'No, let us do that. Just look after her until she's ready to come home. Please.'

'Of course,' Theodore replied, inclining his head.

'Well, I'd better be going,' Eyes said. He held out a hand and Theodore shook it.

Eyes drove back to Grove Street, his mind churning over recent events. He was just parking outside the house when a message came through on his phone. It was a reply from Stalker.

> Ok, I'll call him. You ok?

> Yeah, fine thanks. I need you back with the pack tomorrow. We need to finish what we started.

He went inside, rather than waiting for her reply. Wind Talker and Claws were talking quietly in the living room.

'How are you both feeling?' he asked as he joined them.

'Better, thanks,' Claws replied, looking up. They did both look improved, but Claws' wound was still not healed, and Wind Talker looked drained.

'We have anti-venom,' Wind Talker said stiffly, not making eye contact with Eyes. 'The poison's not as bad as it would be if we were human, but it wasn't getting better on its own.'

'We went to the hospital,' Claws said reluctantly. 'We said something crawled out of our bananas.'

'And bit both of you?' Eyes asked, raising an eyebrow.

'We couldn't ask for any more supernatural healing,' Wind Talker said, shaking his head. 'That has hardly worked well for us in the past.'

Eyes' jaw twitched. It didn't seem like a dig at him, so he let it go, but he felt responsible nonetheless.

'It's fine, there are two hospitals in Caerton, we went to one each. Sorted,' Claws said.

'Have either of you slept?'

'Not yet,' Wind Talker replied.

'It became problematic when my joints totally seized up after you left this morning,' Claws said, rubbing the back of his neck.

'Ah, sorry.' Eyes sat down next to him. There was an uncomfortable silence, broken after a minute by a message coming through on his phone.

Fine. Have you spoken to Weaver?

'It's from Stalker. She'll be back tomorrow. I picked this up at Theodore's office today.' He got the electricity map out of his briefcase and passed it to Wind Talker. 'We can study it to find a good place to cut the power and trap Glimmering Wires.'

'Excellent,' Wind Talker said, his face lighting up with

a smile.

'I just want to get one thing done this evening, then we should all get some sleep.' Eyes stood up and led them out to his car. 'We're going to visit Sparking Clank,' he explained, as the three of them climbed into the car.

'Are we taking your car across the veil again?' Claws asked, a wry smile on his lips.

'Yes,' Eyes replied. 'It ought to get his attention and bring him to us, instead of us having to get across that minefield again.'

'Good plan,' Wind Talker said with a grin.

They drove north towards Northgate and on an empty street with poor lighting, the three of them willed the car across the veil. The car rumbled, then emerged in Hepethia, where there was no road. The four-wheel drive came into its element, traversing the rocky terrain easily. Eyes drove to where the huge factories worked tirelessly, and found a rough road up to the gates of Sparking Clank's domain. They all climbed out, and looked expectantly towards the factory doors. They were flung wide and Sparking Clank came lumbering towards them with remarkable speed. The construct jumped over the high fence that surrounded his territory and landed heavily before them, nose to nose with Eyes' car.

'What do you want?' he snarled.

'We destroyed Limb Chewer, like you asked,' Eyes replied. The construct looked at him with narrowed eyes. 'Will you ally with us against Glimmering Wires?'

'Hmmmm. You have my gratitude. I will assist you.'

'Thank you,' Eyes said, bowing his head. 'We will move against him as soon as possible.'

'I will know when you do,' Sparking Clank replied.

The three shifters dipped their heads and climbed back into the car.

'Wind Talker, can you get us safely back across the veil without being seen?' Eyes asked, glancing sideways at his pack mate, a smile tugging at the corner of his mouth. Claws stifled a laugh behind his hand.

'I believe I can manage that,' Wind Talker replied stiffly. And he did.

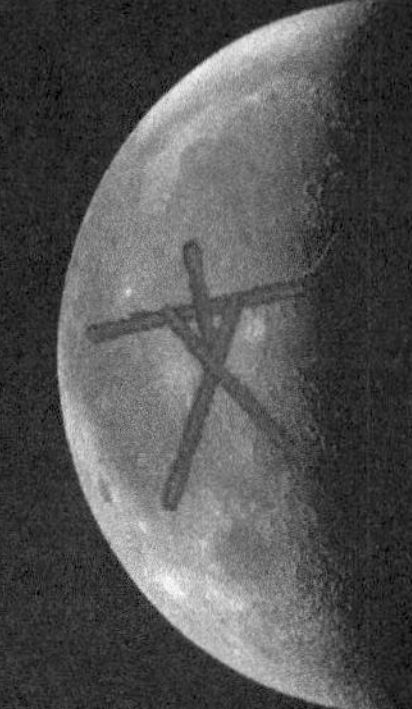

CHAPTER TWENTY SEVEN

STALKER-OF-NIGHT'S-SHADOW

THE RING TONE WENT ON AND ON, with still no answer. Stalker hung up and tossed her phone onto the pile of her clothes on the floor. Rhys stirred next to her and flung his arm across her middle. She rolled over to face him, and kissed his lips softly.

'Morning,' he murmured sleepily.

'Morning. You have to get up, you'll be late for work.'

'What day is it?'

'Wednesday.'

Rhys groaned and buried his face in his pillow. 'It's understandable how I lose track,' Stalker teased, 'but I don't see how you can. You have your whole routine thing going on.'

'It gets muddled up when you show up at all hours.' His voice was muffled against his pillow. Stalker gently shoved his shoulder and he turned to look at her. 'Did you sleep okay?'

'So-so. It's still weird for me to sleep in a bed with someone else.' She was used to sharing a floor with her pack, but sharing sleep with assorted animals was a very different experience to sleeping in bed with Rhys.

'Stuff on your mind too, though.' Rhys stroked her hair. He understood her so well, even though she hardly told him anything. She kept her pack's secrets, mostly.

'Yeah.'

Her phone started buzzing with an incoming call, and she lurched across the floor to get to it. Weaver's name showed on the display, and Stalker answered breathlessly. 'Hi. Thanks for calling back. Are you okay?'

Rhys looked at her carefully for a moment, then discreetly eased out of bed and into the bathroom.

'I'm fine. How are you?' Weaver asked.

'Not bad. Eyes took control back. Wind Talker backed down as soon as Eyes challenged him. He said he had done it all to make Eyes a better Alpha, if you can believe it.'

'I don't, but hey, that's a pretty good way to keep the peace going forwards.'

'Sort of. It upset me a lot.'

'Where are you?' Weaver asked, a sudden edge of caution to her voice. Weaver knew Stalker well too, well enough to know that she typically bailed when she was upset.

'With a friend. Where are you?'

'With a friend.'

'Oh?' Stalker felt a rush of intense curiosity.

'*Just* a friend,' Weaver said, a smile in her voice. 'Not your sort of friend.'

'I don't know what you mean!' Stalker laughed. Relief

washed over her, it was wonderful to be chatting to her sister like this. 'Please come home.'

'I can't, I'm still too angry.'

'Come and talk to us, let's try and work this out.'

'I don't know.'

'We need you back. Remember what you said when Claws came to us? Remember how we all just knew that we were special, that Artemis had brought us together for a reason? We're not complete without you.'

There was a heavy silence on the other end of the phone. Stalker was vaguely aware of the shower running in the next room. The seconds ticked by.

'Okay,' Weaver said softly, barely audible.

'Really?' Stalker sat bolt upright, a grin spread across her face.

'Yes, I'll meet you back at Grove Street before lunch. Promise you'll be there.'

'Of course! Oh thank you, Weaver. I can't wait to see you.'

'Yeah, well, it's just to talk. No promises of reconciliation.'

'Okay, okay.' Stalker bounced up and down, giddy with excitement. 'See you soon.'

'Yeah. See you.'

Stalker hung up and grinned at her phone. She heard Rhys singing in the shower and jumped out of bed to go and join him.

Later that morning, Stalker walked into 32 Grove Street to find her pack brothers laughing together in the kitchen. She paused, surprised to hear such happy noises, then went on through to join them.

'Morning,' she called out, certain that they hadn't heard her enter. Wind Talker stood at the cooker frying bacon. He looked well, and free from the heavy weight that had been hanging off his shoulders for the last week. He paused in his laughter, his smile lingering on his face, but clearly nervous to see her.

Their awkward eye contact was broken by Claws virtually tackling her from the side. He threw his arms around her and they stumbled sideways slightly. Stalker laughed and patted him on the back.

'Welcome back,' Eyes said softly from the table. Claws released her and looked embarrassed.

'Sorry about that,' he muttered.

'No problem. You seem to be recovered.'

'Yeah, we got sorted out yesterday.'

'Oh?' Stalker raised an eyebrow. 'Do we owe anyone anything?'

'No,' Wind Talker replied gently, turning his attention back to the bacon. 'We went to the hospital.'

'Oh, okay. Sorry.' Stalker didn't know where to look.

'It's okay,' he replied, not quite looking at her. 'Totally understand why you would ask.'

'Weaver's coming to talk,' Stalker said, promptly changing the subject.

'Oh, that's great.' His eyes lit up.

'She said no promises.'

'Fair enough,' Eyes said soberly.

'Do you have any idea where she's been?' Claws asked, pouring coffee for Stalker.

'She just told me she was with a friend. I've never known who her shifter friends are.' Stalker caught a glimpse of Eyes as he drained his coffee mug. There was something in his eyes, a glimmer of knowing. 'What?' she asked him, catching hold of his arm as he moved past her to the sink. 'What do you know?'

'She's with the Glass Wolves.'

'Really?' Stalker blurted, shock gushing forth.

'That's a surprise,' Claws said, frowning.

'Apparently she's on friendly terms with Theodore.'

Stalker took the coffee held out to her by Claws, and struggled with the fact that she didn't know Weaver half as well as she ought to. She felt guilty, she realised she had spent so much time wrapped up in her own concerns that she had neglected to form the sort of bond with pack mates that she ought to have. She glanced at Wind Talker, and wondered if they could ever move on from what had happened between them. At least she wasn't alone in finding this news about Weaver and Theodore surprising. Evidently, Weaver had kept this close to her chest. That lessened Stalker's guilt somewhat.

'She hasn't joined the Glass Wolves though, has she?' Stalker asked nervously.

'No, she'll be back with us,' Eyes stated firmly.

Right on cue, the front door opened and Weaver walked in.

'Hi!' Stalker called out, a little too enthusiastically.

'So, you were just taking about me, then?' Weaver asked, a wry smile on her lips as she entered the kitchen.

'Yeah, guilty,' Claws said. He drew Weaver into a gentle hug, which she returned. Claws was the warm glue of the pack, he had a connection with every one of them.

'How are you?' Eyes asked, his face and voice soft with

concern.

'Better, calmer. Thanks,' she replied. The tension in the kitchen was palpable. Stalker looked from one pack mate to another, trying to judge how this was going to play out. Wind Talker stood by the sizzling pan, his gaze fixed on the food. Stalker saw a muscle twitch in his cheek. 'I thought about what you said to me this morning, Stalker.'

She looked immediately at Weaver, who stood fiddling nervously with her sleeves.

'Oh?'

'I might have been wrong about Artemis bringing us together.'

'Oh.' Stalker felt a stab of pain in her chest. She had been sure that would bring Weaver back. She hadn't meant to make her sister question it.

'I *might* have been, but I've seen what we can do when we work together properly. It's incredible. When we fought the Plague Doctor, we shouldn't have won that fight. That was crazy!'

Stalker broke out in a grin, remembering that victory, and seeing how happy it made Weaver was something to cherish.

'We were certainly outmatched on paper,' Eyes said, a smile tugging at his lips too.

'There are no coincidences in this life,' Wind Talker said softly. All eyes turned to him. 'I truly believe that we were brought together to achieve great things. All I've ever wanted is for this pack to reach its potential. How is it that the four of us survived the attack on the Blue Moon? What are the odds of that happening? Four newly changed shifters surviving a coordinated and meticulously planned attack by experienced warriors, when their elder pack mates are all obliterated? It shouldn't have happened. Artemis stepped in and protected us, I am sure of it. And then she brought Claws to us, just when we needed strengthening.'

They all glanced around at each other. Stalker felt faintly inspired by what he was saying, and a lightness filled her chest. 'It's sort of a taboo to use special abilities on a pack mate, but I welcome anyone who wants to try and validate the truth of what I'm saying.' He looked pointedly at Claws and Stalker in turn.

She glanced awkwardly at Claws, he returned her apprehensive expression.

'I don't know, mate. Like you said, it's taboo.' Claws took a sip of coffee and gazed into his cup.

Stalker cleared her throat and fixed her gaze on Wind Talker. She didn't share Claws' reservations. She focused on his eyes, searching them for the entry point. He looked right back at her, totally open to her ability. She probed into his soul, and saw flashes of his life. Childhood memories of lessons poring over ancient runes, battle tactics, myths and learning the songs of his kin. She swept them aside, looking for his inner truth.

She saw her face in his heart, and the rest of the pack. She saw him embracing each of them and felt his love for them all. Her consciousness rushed out of him, like travelling backwards at light speed with images of memories flashing past her. Her breath caught in her throat and she staggered slightly. Weaver caught hold of her and looked at her expectantly.

'He loves us, all of us.'

'You really want us to thrive together? All five of us?'
Weaver asked. Wind Talker looked her right in the eye and
nodded.

'Yes, I want us to be together and to become a strong
and powerful pack, with Eyes as Alpha.' He glanced at
Claws, his expression soft and almost yearning. Claws
shifted his weight and nodded slowly.

'He's telling the truth.'

'Okay,' Weaver said softly. Stalker snaked her arm
around Weaver's waist and rested her head on her
shoulder. 'I'll re-join the pack.'

The air crackled with approval from Unchained
Lightning across the veil. Eyes rushed forwards and pulled
Weaver into a warm embrace, dragging Stalker with her.
Stalker felt Weaver's consciousness re-join the rest of the
pack in her mind, stronger than before. Claws and Wind
Talker piled into the group hug and a sudden breeze
swirled around them.

Thank Artemis.

Yes!

It's good to be home.

They broke apart and stared at each other.

'What was that?' Claws asked, looking unnerved.

'Telepathy,' Wind Talker said with a grin.

'I had stopped missing it,' Stalker said. A laugh
burst up out of her chest. They had shared a telepathic
connection with the Blue Moon, but never before as the
Lightning Lords, only empathy. 'Oh my god! Think of the
battle strategies we'll be able to pull off with non-verbal
communication!'

Eyes laughed and shook his head.

'Speaking of which, we have plans to make right now.'

The next two days were filled with heavy research, planning and preparing. They had their allies lined up to act on cue, but now they needed a thorough strategy. They examined the electrical plans carefully, and found a dead end in which to trap Glimmering Wires, cutting him off from his supply of power. Stalker spent several hours with the pack going over ways in which they could maximise their physical advantages, and they practised sparring with each other in the street in Hepethia, where they had the space.

It was fitting that they were ready on the first of March, there a warm breeze in the air and a few crocuses pushing up through the soil in the garden. Spring was well and truly stirring. They were going to take Unchained Lightning's throne for him. For once they were not racing against the clock, and would be able to strike at the time of their choosing.

The others were out of the house, taking care of any remaining business. Stalker had an hour to herself to clear her mind and prepare her body. A deep breath filled her lungs and she slowly released it into the still, warm air of the attic. She opened her eyes and looked around at the dust floating in the shaft of light from the open door. She gave her head a shake.

'What was I doing?' she muttered out loud to herself. She looked around at the empty room and shrugged. She left the attic and locked the door, then went downstairs to the kitchen and started preparing dinner for the pack. The plan was to eat and go out after dark. Her phone rang and she wiped her hands on a towel before answering.

'Hello?'

'We're on our way back now, everything's in place.' It was Eyes. He was with Claws out at the docks in the very north of Caerton, beyond Northgate.

'Okay, I'm just getting dinner ready. See you soon.' She hung up the phone and went back to chopping vegetables.

A few minutes later Weaver and Wind Talker arrived in a flurry of excited chatter. Stalker smiled, happy to see the two of them getting along so well. Stalker hadn't forgiven Wind Talker yet, it was going to be a long road, but for now she was able to ride on the reassurances he had given them all. The three of them finished the dinner amid friendly banter and soon the Alpha and Claws arrived. Wind Talker passed Claws his gold ring the moment they saw one another.

'It'll turn the power back on as well now,' he said with a smile. Claws nodded and slid the ring back onto his finger.

They sat down to eat a roast gammon joint and trimmings together, a nervous excitement in the air. Eyes poured wine and raised his glass in a toast.

'To the Lightning Lords, and the future.'

'Hear hear,' Wind Talker said. They all clinked glasses and sipped their wine.

'Here's to a smooth execution of our plan,' Claws said, tilting his glass in a second toast. Stalker nodded, butterflies squirming in her stomach.

They ate quickly and quietly, nervous tension gradually increasing as the time approached. As the last mouthful went down, Eyes got to his feet and cleared his throat. They all looked up at him expectantly.

'Let's go,' he said. He swept from the room and

grabbed his jacket from the hall. The others filed out after him, and paused a moment in the street. 'Good luck guys. See you soon, one way or another. Stick to the plan as best as possible.'

Eyes grabbed Stalker and gave her a tight hug. Wind Talker and Claws bumped fists, then Claws grabbed Weaver and pulled her into his arms. She patted him on the back, and he released her. Stalker exchanged nervous farewells with Weaver and Wind Talker. 'Look after each other. See you soon,' Eyes said softly.

Weaver, Wind Talker and Eyes climbed into the Alpha's four-wheel drive, and set off north. Claws and Stalker got into his battered old estate car and set off for the substation. Stalker gazed out of the window at the city passing by. It was sunset, the sky was filled with pinks and blues, and a bright orange glow on the horizon. People rushed past on their way home from a hard day's work.

Claws parked his car at the end of Legion Way and the pair of them stepped out into the cool evening air.

'Ready?' he asked. She nodded in reply and they walked briskly down the street towards the substation. She glanced sideways at him and saw him anxiously spinning the ring on his finger with his thumb.

'Don't worry, one way or another we're taking him down tonight.'

Claws nodded back.

They got to the substation, it was dark and empty, but the hum in the air from the power lines overhead was surprisingly loud. The sun dipped below the horizon and a long shadow fell across the street. The sky above was turning hazy grey. Cars streaked past, their occupants apparently ignoring the two shifters lingering on the street corner next to the substation that provided power to most of St. Mark's.

The pair of them went into the alley between the high brick wall of the complex and the end of the terrace of houses that led away from it. Claws slid his ring off his finger and passed it to Stalker. The gold was warm from the heat of his body. They checked that the coast was clear, then Claws shifted form and landed heavily on Stalker's shoulder. She grinned at him and held up the ring. He bobbed his head and hooted softly, then snapped the ring up in his small beak and flew up over the wall.

Stalker glanced around, then leaped into the air, shifting form mid-leap and flew after him in the form of a barn owl. Claws made straight for the wall-mounted security camera and landed on top of it. He dipped his head, pressing the ring to the casing. Stalker saw the blinking red light under the lens go out. She swooped down and landed in human form at the foot of one of the metal pylons. Claws leaped down, shifting form and stumbling slightly as his feet hit the ground.

'We have less than a minute. Where's the circuit breaker?' Claws whispered.

Stalker kept low and scurried into the heart of the complex. They had studied the station plans, but on the ground it was a whole different world.

'Here.' She spotted the encased, grey box and darted over to it. Claws was right beside her. Stalker ripped the casing open and Claws plunged his hand into the box of switches. He pressed his palm against the console and there was a series of loud clunks around them. The humming of flowing power slowed and finally stopped. The nearby street light flickered and went out, followed by the next one down the street and the lights in the houses followed. A wave of darkness rolled out from the substation.

Thick grey clouds swelled overhead and lightning flashed behind the clouds. 'He's coming,' Stalker whispered, her eyes on the sky.

'Go, now!' Claws hissed. They performed the same trick with transferring the ring to Claws' beak, then took off high into the darkening sky. The two owls circled, looking out for trouble. Lightning flashed again. Stalker knew that Glimmering Wires, wherever he was in the network, now knew that he was under attack.

Stalker searched the city for a sign. The blackout extended for a mile radius around the substation. Charge-of-Power would be in there now, supposedly guarding the throne, while Glimmering Wires was out roaming the network. He would be anxiously testing routes for a way back to his throne now. Would he suspect that he had been betrayed? The power would be coming back on any moment now, at which point they had mere seconds to act.

Below the substation began to clunk and hum, life returning to it. A buzz filled the air and Stalker felt changes to the air currents as static charge built up. Thunder rumbled across the stormy clouds from the telecoms tower and lightning flickered ominously. Unchained Lightning would time it just right, she trusted him totally. She hooted to Claws, and he returned her call. She flew across the veil, hidden against the darkening sky.

Darkness had flooded Hepethia in response to the blackout, and she knew that it was about to get worse.

She swooped low, catching sight of dozens of demons clamouring over one another like a macabre sea. The substation was glowing, a roar echoed out from beneath the web of cables and Stalker watched as blue light spilled into them. This was it. Glimmering Wires had returned and was about to flood the network in search of the breach.

Unchained Lightning tore from between the black clouds overhead with a furious hiss of static and struck the station. Sparks flew out from the throne and the glowing blue cables went momentarily black.

Now! Stalker screamed in her head. She crossed the veil into the black city, the lightning strike having caused a second blackout. She nearly crashed into Claws as he circled the nearest street light. He landed clumsily on top of it and touched his newly upgraded ring to it. It flickered to life, drawing Glimmering Wires out of his useless throne. He would be compelled to go to the only source of power. Claws took flight and made for the next lamp post, he ignited it and flew on to the third. Stalker crossed the veil again and watched from the sky as the cables glowed blue with Glimmering Wires' presence. He was taking the bait, following Claws' trail.

She flew north, watching the light moving along the cable, pausing at each lamp post to wait for the next one to flicker to life. Claws led the crazed construct north, through Northgate and beyond. Stalker crossed back into the human world and found Claws easily, as he swooped towards their final destination.

They flew lower in unison, connected to each other through their new telepathic bond. In this form their thoughts were loose and primal, but the connection was still there. They searched the ground below with their incredible eyesight, for a glimpse of Eyes' car.

Stalker saw it first and flew to the ground. They landed in the blackened and empty street beside the Alpha's car. The dockyard's power was served from two substations: the one in St. Mark's powered this section on the east of the river; and another in St. Catherine's served the docks on the west of the river. The two halves were totally isolated, with power being directed into each one by its respective station, both dead ends. Claws had created one route into the dock, and Glimmering Wires was being funnelled along it, perfectly according to plan.

Stalker found Wind Talker, standing outside one of the vast dock buildings. She ran to him, gasping for breath. His eyes had that glazed expression that indicated that his talisman was in use.

'What do you see?' she asked.

'He's coming.'

Claws gave a nod and took flight again, soaring into the purple sky and over to the last street light on the route. Wind Talker grabbed Stalker's hand and a shudder went down his arm and into hers. Her sight shifted, and she gasped when she realised she was looking into Hepethia.

She could see a light rushing towards the dark factories down the hill, superimposed over the human world. The wires of the pylons glowed bright blue as the construct tore along them. No human would be able to see it, this was Wind Talker's toy giving her the ability to see both worlds at once.

The moment Glimmering Wires had passed the pylon upon which Claws was precariously perched, both Stalker and Wind Talker cried out with their minds.

Now!

Claws activated his ring, and the power all around the station went out yet again. He remained where he was, ready to hit the pylon again if they ran out of time.

Stalker and Wind Talker crossed the veil and sprinted under a huge crystalline arch right where the building had been. A deep crater spread out from the arch, down to the coast, where crystal clear water gently lapped at the sparkling white shore. The waning gibbous moon hung in the sky above, casting its silver light over the scene.

Glimmering Wires was tethered to the ground, limp and writhing against the smooth crystal. He thrashed about, his long cables lashing out at Weaver and Eyes, who stood just out of his reach. He had dimmed, cut off from the grid, slowly burning his own power.

Stalker and Wind Talker reached the others, satisfied smiles playing on all of their lips.

'Now then,' Eyes said, stepping forwards, still just out of the reach of the construct. 'Our friend, Unchained Lightning, requires a throne. He wants yours.' He leaned forwards, taunting Glimmering Wires. The construct snarled, sparks skidding off him along the ground.

Unchained Lightning circled overhead, his huge wings beating the still air.

'Well, he can't have it,' Glimmering Wires hissed. He lurched suddenly and lifted himself up to his full height, towering over the Lightning Lords. He flared up bright white for an instant, blinding Stalker and she shielded her eyes.

She felt a sudden jolt go through her.

'Claws!' He had disappeared from her mind. Wind Talker's face went slack, he turned and sprinted back up to the archway. 'What did you do?' Stalker shrieked at the construct.

He glowed brightly, flooding with power. His laugh echoed off the crystal and he flew into the air, rocketing south, back towards his throne.

'Come on!' Eyes shouted. They ran after Wind Talker and crossed the veil at the warehouse doorway. Stalker was by far the fastest, she sprinted past Wind Talker along the street towards the pylon. There was a dark figure lying crumpled on the ground. Stalker skidded to a halt over him and dropped to her knees. She bent over him to feel for breath from his nose or mouth. Her heart stopped dead.

'He's not breathing!' she screamed.

Wind Talker reached her and landed heavily beside her. He rolled Claws onto his back and tried to find a pulse. Claws' hair was all puffed out around his head like a halo. Stalker's heart was pounding in her ears, drowning out all other sound. White spots popped at the corners of her vision. She was only vaguely aware of Wind Talker bending over Claws, or of Weaver and Eyes at her back. Someone had hold of her shoulders.

'One, two, three, four, five.'

Who was speaking?

'One, two, three, four, five.'

It was Wind Talker, his voice soft but urgent. Stalker blinked back the tears that threatened to spill, something was happening. Wind Talker bent low to breathe into Claws' mouth, then sat up to resume pumping his chest.

Breathe. Breathe. Breathe.

Who was thinking that?

'One, two, three, four, five,' Wind Talker chanted, then stooped to breathe into Claws' mouth again.

Please breathe! Stalker looked at her pack mates. The voice didn't belong to any of them. It was Claws' voice inside Stalker's head.

There was an enormous gasp, and Stalker's senses snapped back into focus. Claws coughed and gulped for air. Stalker looked up to see a handful of onlookers. Humans.

'Is he all right?' they murmured.

'We'd better get him to hospital,' Eyes said loudly. He helped Wind Talker lift Claws to his feet and they dragged him to Eyes' car.

'Someone call an ambulance,' a voice in the small gathering said urgently.

'It's okay,' Eyes called out. 'We'll take him, it'll be quicker than waiting.'

Weaver and Stalker scurried behind them and they all climbed into the car. Stalker sat beside Claws on the back seat, stroking down his frazzled hair.

'You're okay,' she whispered. She needed to convince both of them of that. Claws smiled weakly.

'Where are we going?' Weaver asked, looking out of the window. Stalker looked out too. They were driving south, almost certainly above the speed limit. The nearest hospital was east, out towards Fenwick.

'The substation,' Eyes replied.

'But the hospital,' Stalker baulked.

'I'm fine,' Claws replied. 'Or I will be in a few minutes. We need to finish what we started.'

Eyes drove through the underpass under the dual

carriageway and when they emerged on the other side they were in Hepethia.

'Eyes!' Weaver gasped. 'What if someone saw?'

'Not now,' he snapped at her. 'The road was quiet and still blacked out, don't worry.'

Eyes pulled to a sudden stop at the substation gates, sending everyone in the car lurching forwards. He was the first out of the car, the others scrambled after him, even Claws.

'I'm fine,' he said, brushing Weaver's concerned hands from his chest and arm. He strode after Eyes to the huge gates, topped with coils of barbed wire.

Unchained Lightning landed behind them and dipped his head low.

'I am glad you are alive,' he crackled. Claws turned to look at him over his shoulder.

'Hey, what's a little electric shock between friends? Eyes took a lightning bolt to the chest not so long ago.'

Stalker let out a slightly hysterical laugh and everyone looked at her.

'Sorry, I'm fine.' She held up a hand and wiped the smile from her face.

Claws reached out and pressed his palm to the metal gate. Stalker watched in confusion. There was no power running through the gate. As far as she could tell, there was no connection between the gate and the terminals inside. She didn't even know if his ring would do anything in Hepethia. Something was happening though. The struts of the gate began to shudder, the tops curled over their heads. Weaver reached out and grabbed hold of the gate as well, as did the others. Stalker realised what was happening a moment later, not using Claws' ring, but shaping their territory.

The gate curled up and fell in two pieces to the ground on either side of the pack. They strode inside, to find Glimmering Wires alone on his throne. There were no minions scurrying around him with contributions now, and no support from the other Sparkbloods. His light was dimmed, his head hung down against his chest.

'Yield,' Eyes commanded.

'Not a chance,' the construct said, standing from his throne.

Stalker leaped forwards, drawing her dha. She slid across the floor, and right between his long legs. Her swords sliced through some of his cables, spilling sparks down all over her. They were white hot and stung for a second, but did no real harm. She had dealt the first blow, however, and there was a moment of stillness as everyone present absorbed what had happened.

Glimmering Wires flew into the air, hissing. Claws took a running jump and grabbed hold of a swinging cable. He held tight, swinging back and forth underneath the flying construct. His weight seemed to drag Glimmering Wires down, and prevent him soaring off again.

Unchained Lightning flew in circles around the substation. The clouds above grew thicker and darker, hiding the moon from sight. Stalker sensed static in the air. She jumped up and grabbed hold of one of the metal supports around the throne. She sheathed her dha and climbed up the slanted pole, using the rings around it like rungs on a ladder. If the power had been running through it, no doubt she would have been electrocuted. She got to the top and climbed awkwardly onto the beam that connected two of the poles. She was level with Glimmering Wires, and got carefully to her feet. She drew her dha again and inched along to the corner. She leaped and thrust both of her swords into the mess of cables that formed the construct's body. He howled and spun around, trying to reach the monkey on his back. She clung to her swords, which were buried to their hilts in his back.

Down below, there was a sudden sound of scraping metal on metal. She looked down and saw Sparking Clank unfolding himself from the rusted metal plates of the throne. Thunder cracked overhead and Unchained Lightning swished past her so fast that he was little more than a white blur.

'Claws!' she shouted. There was no way he would hear over the din. She reached out with her mind instead. *We have to let go!*

Are you crazy? he replied.

Probably, still right though.

She pulled with all her might, yanking her right dha out of the construct first. She dropped a few inches as her other dha dropped down between loosening cables. Glimmering Wires continued to thrash around wildly. The other shifters on the ground looked on helplessly.

Her legs swung uselessly beneath her, but Stalker heaved her hips up and found purchase for her feet. She used them to push out and slide her remaining dha out of his body. She flipped over and went into free-fall, plummeting towards the ground head first. Her talisman kicked in and slowed her down to a gradual float, and she held her dha out to her sides as she glided gently to the ground. She looked up to see Claws shift form and fly away from the construct.

Unchained Lightning struck, lashing out with his long tail and striking Glimmering Wires in the face. The two of them fell to the ground and landed in front of the throne so hard that the concrete floor cracked. Stalker and the others scrambled back out of the way, just as Sparking Clank ambled over and opened his enormous jaws. Unchained Lightning whipped around and rammed into Glimmering Wires with his large head, shoving the construct backwards, right into the waiting mouth of Sparking Clank.

There was a shriek, a hiss, and then a bright light flared up inside Sparking Clank, peeking out between all of the plates on his body. Steam billowed out through the narrow gaps and the light faded.

'Thank you,' the metal construct said slowly. 'I could never have done that alone.' He bowed his head to Unchained Lightning and backed away from the throne. There was a sudden bleeping noise nearby and Stalker spun around to see Charge-of-Power slinking in through the destroyed gateway.

Unchained Lightning flared up, filling the courtyard with bright light. Lightning flashed overhead and a fork darted down to strike the fae, charging him up with infinitely more power. He expanded, then settled back to his former size. He stepped back and the throne behind him shifted form, from a chair for the humanoid figure of Glimmering Wires, to a vast platform a few feet off the ground for the huge dragon. Unchained Lightning sat down and wrapped his tail around his body. He seemed to purr, and the substation flickered to life. The poles around him started to pulse with light and little elementals crept in along the incoming wires. They left their first, very small offerings and backed away slowly, bowing.

'Are you satisfied, Unchained Lightning?' Eyes asked, his voice carrying on the light wind.

'Very,' their ally replied.

Sparking Clank bowed his enormous head and folded away into the metal of the substation, disappearing from sight. Charge-of-Power let out a flurry of beeps, and Unchained Lightning zapped him with a few volts by way of a thank you for his assistance. The peculiar creature disappeared out of the gate.

Stalker drew a shaking breath and turned to her pack mates.

'We did it,' she whispered.

'We did,' Eyes replied. But his expression remained serious. 'Now we just need to take care of those Witches.'

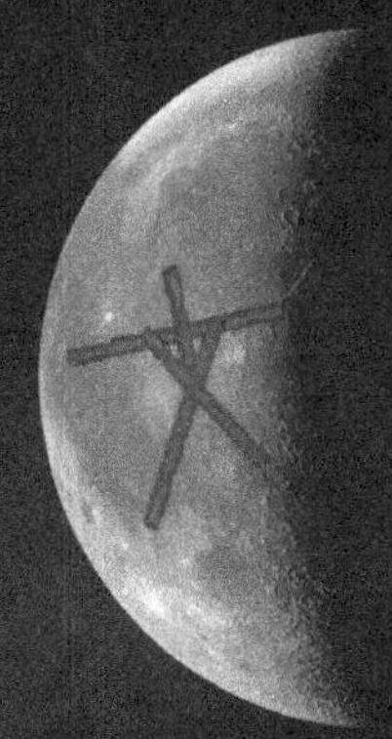

Chapter Twenty Eight

The sun was high in the sky, soaking the city in the first truly warm day of the spring. The flower beds that decorated much of the city centre were beginning to bloom, after being cold and bare all winter.

The city was buzzing with anticipation and frustration, as major roads were closed and routes diverted for the construction of the new underground railway. Commuters complained about their extended travel times, and grudgingly muttered about the benefits of extra jobs and taking traffic off the streets once work was complete.

Stalker listened to one such conversation on the bus, idly playing with a penny that she had found on her seat. She got off at her usual stop, avoiding Burnside. Pocketing the penny, she made her way to the cenotaph, where Ragged Edge was already waiting for her.

He greeted her stiffly, his brow even more deeply furrowed than usual.

'Hi,' she said, looking at him with concern. 'People are starting to warm to the underground, slowly. What's wrong?'

'We have a name to engrave.'

'Who?' Stalker's heart started racing. Her thoughts whisked through all of Odin's Warriors, many of whom she considered siblings. First Strike was foremost in her mind, a guilty knot forming in her chest.

'Fire Talon,' Ragged Edge replied gruffly.

Every passing pedestrian, every car on the nearby street, every plane in the sky, everything stopped. The world was suspended around Stalker, the wind knocked out of her as she stood mute, staring at him. There had to be a mistake. Slowly, she swallowed and took a breath. The ignorant world began to turn again.

'You have to be joking,' she whispered. 'It's not funny, it's sick. You can't do that to people.'

'I'm not joking. All of the Storm Riders are gone.'

'Gone? Just like that? A whole pack?' Even as she said the words she realised how they sounded. That had been the plan for the Blue Moon, obliterated in one go. 'What happened?'

'No one knows, but they're not there anymore. A raven brought Red Scythe the news of Fire Talon. They always do, when one of our own is lost. All we know is that they were seen fighting on the beach. Now they're all dead. Well, except for Lost, but she's . . . lost.'

'Lost?' Stalker's head was spinning, she didn't understand.

'A member of the Storm Riders. I didn't know her well, no one has known any of that pack well for decades.

But a few years ago she disappeared. She didn't die, Fire Talon told me she hadn't even left their pack, he was still connected to her, but no one knew where she was. As far as I'm aware, she wasn't attacked, she's still out there somewhere.'

'When did it happen?'

'Yesterday. So, we're here to do the honours.' He held out his hand and she walked slowly up the steps of the cenotaph and placed her hand on the smooth sandstone. Shimmering runes slowly began to appear on the surface, above the brass plaque dedicated to the humans who had given their lives in human wars. Ragged Edge discreetly pulled out a small blade and began inscribing the runes "Fire" and "Talon" at the bottom of the list.

'Did you find anything about those names I gave you?' Stalker asked.

'No. You?'

'Claws is working on it, he has a list of people who shared the names, we just need to narrow it down. I'm going to the Scroll Archive straight from here.'

'Good luck,' he said, his voice devoid of any genuine feeling. He finished the inscription and stepped back. They stood in silence for a minute that stretched into the warm afternoon. Stalker had lost a friend, someone she had shared poignant moments with. He had left a daughter in the world. One day she might turn and wonder who her family was. She might stand in this very spot, staring at his name, and all the names after it. Maybe Stalker's name would be there.

'I'll let you know if I find anything that could bring me closer to finding them,' she said softly.

'I was meaning to ask,' he said, his voice tilting unnaturally high. Stalker looked at him warily. 'What form did Odin grant you? When you were initiated? You've never said.'

Stalker let out an audible whimper. She hadn't been prepared for this question, she should have been. A battle raged inside her mind, whether to lie to her mentor, or tell the truth.

'He didn't,' she said after too long a pause.

'Sorry?'

'He didn't grant me an extra form.' She was being honest. It was easy, so easy that the full truth rushed up into her mouth. 'I could already take any animal form I chose.'

Ragged Edge blinked hard at her for a moment, absorbing her words.

'Really?'

'Yes, Shadow's Step didn't want me to tell anyone. Only my pack knows.'

'I've heard of such things in legends, but never anything verifiable as real.' His head was cocked to one side as he studied Stalker through his shrewd eyes. 'I understand why you would keep this secret, but I wish you had trusted me sooner.'

'I'm sorry.' She felt like she had disappointed him, and cast her gaze to the ground.

'It's all right. We'll keep looking for your parents, it seems even more important now. But I suspect that the gods are the only ones who truly know where you came from.'

'What are you saying?'

'Well, we all come from Artemis, of course, but you're special. Maybe you were chosen for something else, something other than protecting the veil.'

'My surname, you asked about it last time. It means gate keeper.' Ragged Edge's question last time they met had prompted her to search the internet for a clue.

'Interesting,' he said carefully. 'And your first name?'

'Holy one,' Stalker said, blood rushing to her cheeks.

'Let me know if you find anything in the Scroll Archive,' he said, sweeping her embarrassment away decisively.

'I will.'

He pulled her into a fatherly embrace. When he released her he cleared his throat and stalked away, leaning heavily on his staff. Stalker watched him go. She gave one last look to Fire Talon's name on the cenotaph, and watched as all of the runes faded away, hidden until the next time a shifter revealed them.

Stalker decided to walk to the river and follow it north to the Scroll Archive. She walked slowly, gazing at the floor. Was it possible that she had been chosen for something special and that her parents knew about it?

As she walked along the river bank through China Town, street traffic picked up. It was always busier here than in St. Mark's, where most people drove or took the bus, more people seemed to be trying to get out of St. Mark's. The street markets in China Town gave it a different atmosphere to the rest of Caerton. Along the river were dozens of stalls, which attracted a lot of tourists.

Stalker passed a row of benches facing the river, which was less polluted here than further north, where debris collected before being spewed out into the estuary. She caught sight of a playing card wedged into the back of a bench between the wooden slats and metal frame. She tugged it loose and kept walking, thumbing the soft edges of the browning card. She hummed a melody and folded the card neatly twice.

The path clung to the river bank as the stalls gave way to office buildings, and foot traffic all but disappeared. Stalker followed it into St. Marks, past the place where she and Eyes had first met Claws, and all the way past Red Bridge, to the other bridge in Northgate.

A familiar figure sat on the stone wall that ran along the bank, her long black skirt catching in the breeze and blowing about her feet. Last-Breath-Echoes slid gracefully from the wall, and greeted Stalker with a soft smile.

'Hi,' she said as Stalker drew level with her.

'How are you?' Stalker asked, glancing around them for onlookers. A couple of men in suits walked briskly by, and cars swept past; it was fairly quiet.

'Fine, thanks.'

'Did you hear about the Storm Riders?'

'I did,' Echoes replied softly, the corner of her mouth twitching. 'I always hear when...' Her voice tailed off.

'Will there be a funeral?' Stalker asked, looking resolutely at her feet and trying not to recall the funeral they had held for the Blue Moon.

'Not really. That's normally a pack matter and there were no bodies to recover. We think they were either washed out to sea, or taken by whoever did it. But Scribe and I will light black candles for them and raise a howl. You would be free to do something similar.'

'Okay,' Stalker replied, her voice barely audible over

the sound of the river and traffic on the busy main road crossing the bridge.

They set off walking together, a slightly awkward silence between them. Stalker led the way down onto the clay bank under the bridge. She trudged through the sticky substance, up to the hidden door into the Scroll Archive. Last-Breath-Echoes stepped forwards, seeming to almost float across the clay. She unlocked the door and shoved it open. A torch flickered to life inside and Stalker peered in over Last-Breath-Echoes' shoulder, drawn towards the warm glow. It was a doorway through the veil, she felt it clearly this time.

'If Scribe ever finds out about this...' Echoes murmured. She moved inside and held a hand out to Stalker. Stalker took it and stepped across the threshold into a little pocket of Hepethia. Echoes closed the door, shielding them from the human world. Stalker looked around in awe. The door opened into a small chamber with pale, stone walls. Every inch of the stone was covered in tiny runes and engraved drawings that reminded her of cave paintings. Echoes led Stalker along the narrow passage and into a larger cave. Wall-mounted torches flickered to life as they entered, throwing deep shadows into crevices, and illuminating more of the intricate markings. There was a large desk in the centre of the cave, piled high with curled up scrolls and several enormous ledgers.

Along one wall of the cave was a vast wooden shelving unit with dozens of square compartments, each one stacked with scrolls.

'I didn't expect actual scrolls,' Stalker muttered.

'We ran out of wall space a few centuries ago. I guess

we haven't moved into the twenty first century yet, we might get a computer at some point,' Echoes said absently, as she moved over to the desk and heaved the ledgers around. 'Scribe has been working on finding information on the King-of-Glass-and-Steel.'

Stalker moved over to the wall and looked at the little drawings. They depicted battles, small groups of humanoid figures armed with spears and bows and arrows fought off fae and demons of all shapes and sizes. The cave smelled a lot like a library, a musky scent clung to the dust in the air.

Echoes leafed quickly through a ledger, running her finger down the pages. Stalker moved closer to see what she was looking at. Each page of the hefty tome was divided into tightly packed columns.

'What is that?' she asked.

'A birth registry. I'm looking for your name. When were you born?'

'I don't even know if either of them were born in Caerton. Hey, does this go up to today?'

'Yes,' Echoes replied, her voice soft and far away, her attention fixed on the tiny writing. Stalker noticed many different styles of handwriting on each page, some neat, some barely legible.

'Do you record the births of every child born to every shifter? How do you know you've got them all?'

'We fill in what we can, when we can.'

'You know Eyes has a daughter?' She decided not to mention Claws' son, she didn't know anything about him or where he was born, and Claws kept his existence very close to his chest. She wasn't going to betray that confidence.

'Yes, she's in here.'

'Oh.' Stalker noticed that the information on each page was quite thorough, though there were plenty of gaps. Each entry noted a birth date, human name, parents' human and shifter names; and a change date, shifter name, and pack for each offspring that had undergone the transformation. Those that hadn't had empty spaces in those columns. 'There, that's the year I was born.' She jabbed the page with her finger and Echoes slowly trailed a finger down the second column.

'Here you are.' Echoes slid the book over to Stalker. Her pulse suddenly soared and she just stared at Last-Breath-Echoes, her breathing heavy as apprehension rocketed through her body. 'What's wrong?'

'I don't know if I dare look.'

'You asked me to find this,' Echoes said with a frown on her usually unworried brow.

'I know. I need to know, but it's a big step for me.'

'I see,' Echoes replied, confusion evident on her face. Stalker suspected she had no idea what Stalker was feeling.

Slowly, Stalker lowered her eyes to the faded parchment. She found her birth date and human name, Ariana Yates. She was born here. Mother: Jane White. Father: Malcolm Slater. Also known as Symphony and Heart's Blood respectively. Stalker's heart felt like it was going to leap right out of her throat. Her own first change and shifter name were recorded in the untidy scrawl of Flames-First-Guardian.

'Can we look for my parents' births in here?' she asked, her voice shaking.

'Of course,' Echoes replied, slowly taking the ledger

back. 'We can look for siblings too, if you like.'

It had never occurred to Stalker that she might have siblings. That was a door she didn't want to open right now.

'Just my parents, thanks.'

Echoes flipped back a chunk of pages and began hunting. They had no idea when Stalker's parents had been born, they could have been teenagers when they had her, or relatively seasoned shifters. She thought of the shifters that she knew of who had children, and the course of their lives. These brutal lives, filled with violence. Parents forced to abandon children in order to protect them. How many other babies were shipped off to other cities? How many names in that book were missing further information because they had simply disappeared into obscurity? She thought of Father Ash, up on the hill in his white house, with his framed photographs of the young woman now poring over lists of names. 'Were you raised by your parents?' Stalker asked, trying and failing to keep her voice casual.

'My mother died when I was a baby, my father raised me and my brother.' Echoes glanced up at her, her eyes shrewd. 'You met him, I believe.'

'Father Ash?'

Echoes nodded, then went back to her search. 'He asked after you,' Stalker said softly. Echoes didn't respond. 'When did you last see him?'

'Before he was exiled. I was thirteen.'

'Oh.' Stalker thought she should probably drop the subject. But Last-Breath-Echoes was opening up, she was thirsty for more. 'Did your brother take you in, then?'

'No.' Echoes sighed and looked up. 'Father Ash killed him.'

'Oh, I'm sorry.' Stalker blushed, suddenly filled with remorse for probing.

'It's okay, my brother had gone astray. Father did the right thing. I changed right after all that, my pack looked after me from then on.' Her voice was as steady as a rock, passive and detached. Stalker supposed that she had had a decade to live with these events in her life, this was how she coped.

'I see.' Yes, perhaps it was best that Eyes' family had left. She moved away from the desk and looked over the shelves of scrolls. Each section had a label with what looked like names on. She squinted in the flickering torchlight and read a few. She stopped still as her eyes settled on a label reading *The Watch*, next to it was *The Hand of God*. Pack names. She glanced at Echoes, who was busily scanning through the birth records. She looked back at the shelves and quickly scanned the labels. Some were badly faded, others popped out as shiny and new, relatively speaking, such as *Wrecking Crew*. There, she found the two she was looking for side by side, *Blue Moon* and *Lightning Lords*. The latter was virtually empty, one scroll sitting alone. Stalker longed to take it down, but she had a nagging sensation that such action would be unforgivable. It was about her own pack though. Surely she had a right to see what it said? The Blue Moon's slot was packed tight with scrolls and her eyes lingered on them longingly.

'Found something!' Echoes called out. Stalker swept swiftly to her side, though she was torn between the two sources of information. 'I found your mother, here.'

She pointed and Stalker bent low to read the record. Symphony, her mother, had changed around the same age as Stalker and had been a member of the Wrecking Crew. Stalker blinked several times as she read along the line. Numbness filled her senses. They were just words on an old page, she had no connection to the woman they referred to.

'And my dad?'

'I'll keep looking,' Echoes said softly. Stalker nodded and stared at the pages as Echoes scanned them carefully. 'Here,' she said after a few minutes.

Stalker leant over the ledger to read the entry for Heart's Blood. He had been quite young when she was born, early twenties. He'd changed in puberty, like Echoes. Stalker's eyes lingered on his pack name. Her thoughts stalled, hung up on that one detail, two words, intimately familiar to her. Blue Moon.

'Small world,' she whispered. She felt Last-Breath-Echoes' eyes on her.

'In other circumstances that wouldn't be a surprise, my father was Hand of God, too. But I was raised around my kin, never moved. How did you end up living and changing in St. Mark's?'

'It was where I could afford a place when I moved to Caerton,' she replied. She felt numb, and slow. Was she guided here? Did some subconscious signal reach her and direct her to house hunt in the area her father had lived? Then the thought struck her like a lorry, that Fortune and the others would have known her father. Flames had noted her change in the records, he would have seen her parents' names, he would have known her father and realised who she was. They knew, they all knew, and never told her.

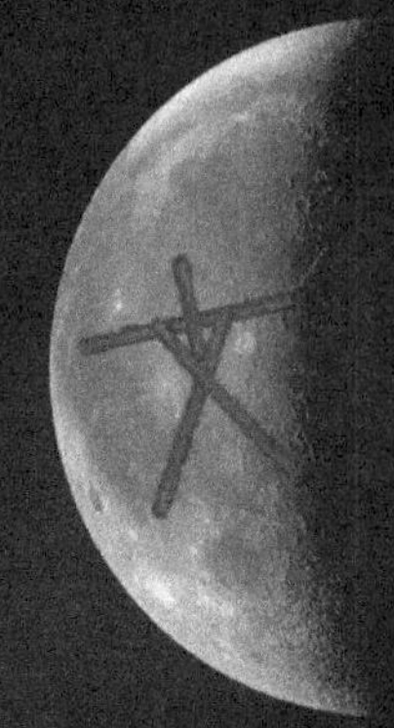

Chapter Twenty Nine

 with a twisting sensation turning her insides in knots. Last-Breath-Echoes locked the door behind them.

'Will you be all right?' she asked, a slight crease to her brow. Stalker nodded in reply. 'I'll be going then,' Echoes said softly and gave Stalker an awkward smile in parting. Stalker felt the cool breeze on her skin, after the stifling warmth of the underground archive. She stared out over the river, her mind running over the revelations of the day. She had had enough, finding out what had become of her parents would have to wait.

She set off at a run for Grove Street, covering the territory swiftly. Running often helped her to get her thoughts in order, but as she burst in through the door she still had no idea what to start with.

'The Storm Riders are gone!' she blurted out as she swept into the kitchen. Wind Talker and Weaver were the only ones there, and they both looked at her in alarm.

'Gone?' Wind Talker said, his eyes wide. 'What do you mean gone?'

'They're dead. Attacked. Ragged Edge told me this morning.'

'Who attacked them?' Weaver asked, getting to her feet.

'He didn't know, but at a guess, the thing from the sea that they've been trying to warn us all about.'

'Oh my god.' Weaver sat back down again, her eyes filling with tears.

Wind Talker strode from the room and grabbed his coat from a peg in the hall. The front door slammed. Stalker stared down the hall after him. He had known the Storm Riders a little, he shared some of their affinities and had been to them for information before. Maybe he had to see for himself before he could believe that they were gone.

'Should we go after him?' she asked, a slight crack in her voice.

'I think he probably needs to work it out for himself. We should tell the others.' Weaver started tapping out a message on her phone and Stalker paced the kitchen anxiously. 'What is it?' Weaver asked, not looking up from her phone. 'The other thing?'

'The other thing?' Stalker stopped pacing and stared at Weaver.

'Oh, your parents?' Weaver looked up, her eyes wide and curious. Stalker sighed. Telepathy made it hard to keep anything private.

'I found out who they are. Last-Breath-Echoes let me

into the Scroll Archive.'

'What was it like?' Weaver asked eagerly, suddenly distracted.

'Like your idea of paradise. Maybe you should consider becoming a Scroll Keeper.'

'I am, actually.'

'Oh, well, good.' Stalker smiled. 'My mum was in the Wrecking Crew and my dad was a member of the Blue Moon.' The truth just tumbled out of her mouth against her will and she stood in shocked silence as Weaver glared at her for a moment that seemed to stretch into eternity.

'That's a surprise.' Weaver finally broke the silence with stating the obvious. Stalker let out a slightly hysterical laugh and slumped into a chair at the table.

'You could say that. What I wouldn't give for a vision from Artemis about now, showing me what on earth I am supposed to do with this knowledge.'

'I'll let you know if she sends me one.' Weaver tried for a sympathetic smile, and placed a hand on Stalker's.

'Thanks,' Stalker replied, looking at their hands. 'I have to go, I have work.'

'You won't be able to keep juggling it all, you know.' Weaver withdrew her hand and Stalker stopped still for a moment, trying to read her pack sister.

'What do you mean?'

'Your human life and this one. It's not right, it's not how we're meant to live. You're cracking under the strain, like Eyes did.'

'I'm managing just fine,' Stalker snapped. She shoved her chair back and stalked to the door.

No you're not.

She wasn't sure whose voice it was in her head, hers or Weaver's. It caused her the briefest pause at the front door, before she shrugged it off and left the house.

She ran to work, her vial of cool waters bouncing on her chest. She drew on its energy but stepped into her judo class with frustration still gnawing at her. Her younger students were pre-teen and straight from school. They were always difficult to rein in at the start of a class, and Stalker fought her impulse to shout at them and struggled to keep her cool. It got easier as the class went on, but as the kids filed out she ran for some privacy in the staff locker room.

She snacked on the fruit that she kept in her locker but longed for a giant steak. It seemed like she hardly ever had time for a proper meal. Her head spun with everything that she was juggling, Weaver's words echoing constantly. She absent-mindedly pocketed her apple seeds and went back to her next class.

Her students bustled in, chatting loudly.

'Quiet!' Stalker snapped at them. 'Drills, now.'

Her teenage students glanced at her warily, but she had too much spinning in her mind to care. She *could* have a normal life, she had to. Her mind was still attached to her job. She had to have an income and a cover. She needed a place in human society, a foot in that world. Shadow's Step had cautioned her about needing to cling to her humanity, otherwise she risked losing herself to the Agrius and the darkness in which she was born. Had he known about her parents when he said that?

Weaver had it all wrong, she couldn't just give in to the beast inside. She couldn't forsake her humanity, or what would she be left with?

Her attention came back to the room, everyone was staring at her. She had one student in an arm lock. Caught by surprise, she let the girl go and looked around in alarm. The faces around her swam in and out of focus. They looked at her with mild surprise. The girl she had been grappling stepped away and frowned.

'Is everything all right?' she asked.

'Yes. I think so. Where was I?'

'You were going to show us a new technique to break out of an arm lock,' the girl replied, concern evident in her voice.

Stalker sighed with relief, she had been teaching on auto pilot, not attacking her students.

'Of course I was.' She ushered the girl back into her grip and continued with the lesson, focused this time, Weaver's words shoved firmly into the back of her mind.

As the last student left, muttering quietly to his friend about Stalker's odd behaviour, Stalker went to the window and looked out over the dark city. Work had been more stressful ever since Fury had turned up and nearly broken her arm in front of her class. The fear demons were rife in St. Mark's, apparently. They had done nothing to act on Fury's warning. She could be back any day to do worse than intimidate her in front of the innocent humans in the dojo. Fury, from the Wrecking Crew. Her mother's old pack. Did the current crop of shifters in that pack know her? Did they know what happened to her?

Stalker pressed her forehead against the cool glass and stared at the carpet of lights that stretched away from the building. The human world hurried past, full of its own dangers and troubles, but blissfully unaware of the monsters in its midst. Monsters like The-Knight-of-Shadowed-Fear, the leader of the fear demons that were causing problems for the Wrecking Crew.

Buzz.

Monsters like the Witches and the Spiral Hand.

Buzz.

Monsters like Stalker.

Buzz.

Stalker looked around the room, confused for a moment. It was her phone ringing on silent. She dashed to her bag at the back of the room and fished in it for the phone. Eyes' name lit up the screen, and she answered in a fluster.

'Hi.'

'Are you all right?' the Alpha asked, his voice heavy with concern.

'I'm okay, thanks. Just finishing work.'

'Weaver told me about the Storm Riders.'

'Is Wind Talker back yet? Where did he go?'

'He's back, he went to confirm it. The territory's empty, their allies have dispersed. He said something about the Dreadnought having been sunk, but I don't know what he meant and he won't elaborate.'

'Right.' Something hard settled in the pit of Stalker's stomach. That was it then, short of actual bodies, that was as good a proof as any. Not that she had doubted Ragged Edge.

'I know you had a friend among them. Are you all right?' Eyes asked.

'Sort of, I will be.' A sad silence lingered. 'I have some

personal business to take care of. Is that okay?'

'Of course. Take some time. We have plans to make, but no urgent business.'

'Okay, thanks. I'll see you over the weekend.' Eyes ended the call and Stalker slowly lowered her phone. Fire Talon was really gone. She never really knew the others, but he had been her friend. A single tear slid down her cheek. She needed to feel supportive arms around her, she needed strength before tackling the problems that lay ahead.

Stalker grabbed her bag and cast her eyes over the studio. She stooped to pick up a discarded sweet wrapper and shoved it into her pocket as she left the dojo.

'See you tomorrow!' Ron called to her retreating back as she jogged down the stairs.

'Bye!' she called back absently. As she emerged onto the dark street she caught sight of a bus heading for the city centre trundling down the road. She sprinted for the nearby stop and thrust her hand out to signal the driver. The bus was full of people on their way into town for the evening and she took a cramped seat next to an old man who smelled of fish. She was glad to jump off the bus in China Town and walk the rest of the way to Rhys's dojo, away from loud voices and jostling people overwhelming her senses.

Weaver thought that Stalker's not-so-secret boyfriend was an innocent human, whose life she was putting at risk. How long could she keep the secret of what he was? It was bound to slip into her thoughts and be picked up by one of them at some point. If not from her mind, then from Claws', who also knew the truth.

She arrived at the Central School of Martial Arts just as the upstairs lights flickered off. She went inside and lingered in the empty reception, anxious to see him and feel his warm arms around her. She heard the slight sound of movement upstairs and then felt his presence on the stairs, he moved almost silently out of the shadows and into the light of the lobby. A surprised smile lit his face as he approached and she rushed into his arms.

'This is a nice surprise,' he said, as he pulled her into a tight embrace. 'Everything all right?'

'No,' she muttered against his firm chest. 'Can we go to your place?'

'Of course,' he replied, gently pulling her away from him. He looked down at her with concern, then kissed her forehead softly. He released her and moved swiftly around the desk, as lithe as a leopard. Stalker waited impatiently while he moved about in the office, out of sight. Lights went out in the back and Rhys returned, locking the office door behind him.

He led her to the big glass doors and ushered her out into the night. Once the lights were out, doors locked and shutters drawn, Rhys took her hand and led her swiftly to his house. They didn't say a word, it was as if he could understand what she was thinking. She hated that she always seemed to go to him at times like this. Just once, she would like to see him under happy circumstances.

Once safely in the privacy of his house, Stalker felt her shoulders relax and a sigh escape her lips.

'Your companion,' she said softly, pointing vaguely over his shoulder. Rhys's eyes reflexively twitched in the direction she was pointing. 'It must know everything about your life. It knows a lot of secrets, including some of mine.'

'I suppose so. It's not like we converse. I didn't deliberately summon it. I got the tattoos, understanding enough about the symbolism of shifter magic to know that they might protect me. Over time I became aware of the shroud.' He perched on the back of the sofa and looked at her earnestly. 'Why?'

'Well, it's a worry, you know. What if someone gets to it and gets the information?' She thought of Scourging Agony, so easily bought out of the Witches' service. 'Just because you attracted it with your secrets doesn't mean it will be happy to live off you forever. What if a bigger secret comes along?'

'I don't know, I've never given it too much thought.' He glanced at her, worry etched onto his face. 'I've never had someone else's secrets to protect as well as my own. I take it your pack doesn't know about me?'

'Not really,' she replied. 'I haven't betrayed your secret. Most of them think you're human, none of them know your name. One of them knows you're not what you appear, but that's all. Though he is a private investigator, so who knows.' She tried to smile and he returned it with a reluctant smile of his own.

'Okay, so am I your big secret? Because my demon friend already knows that one.' He smiled more warmly and Stalker let out a nervous laugh. Had the demon seen how she entered Rhys's room through the skylight? 'Oh, right.' His smile vanished and he looked at her cautiously. She had given herself away. She swallowed a hard lump in her throat and twisted her fingers together.

'I'm not what I appear either.'

'Oh?' Rhys shifted his weight and watched her carefully. Stalker took a deep breath. She had shared her secret with Ragged Edge already, it was starting to come out now, and there may be no stopping it. The words wouldn't come, even if they would, there was no substitute for showing Rhys the truth. She dropped her bag and shook out her arms, shifting them seamlessly into small wings that fluttered briefly while her body caught up. She shrank into the smooth, white form of a dove and took flight around the room. She landed in front of Rhys and forced her body into the form of a sleek panther, her black coat glistening in the lamplight.

Rhys lurched backwards away from her and she circled behind him and jumped onto the sofa. She rubbed her head against him and purred, before jumping back down and shifting again into a long, thick python. She slithered across the floor and lifted her head up to the same level as his. He stared at her, open mouthed. Stalker returned to her human form and stood waiting for his reaction. The silence was heavy as they looked at each other.

'You should shut your skylight properly at night,' Stalker said at last. 'Or any old moth could get in.'

'You...? That's how you got in that night?' Rhys spluttered. He wiped a hand across his forehead and let out a shaking breath.

'Yeah.'

'That's quite some gift you have. How do you do it? Can you turn into anything?' His face lit up eagerly and he rushed over to her. He grabbed her shoulders and looked into her eyes, his own alive with excitement.

'I don't know, I just can, ever since my first change.

And yes, pretty much. I haven't gone smaller than a moth though. I think fleas and microscopic organisms might be beyond my capabilities.'

'What about bigger?' Rhys seemed to be daring her. She laughed.

'I've shifted into a lion before. You know, it's never really occurred to me to try and go much bigger than that. I suppose I could try for a giraffe some time, or an elephant. We should go out to sea and try for a whale. I prefer the stealthy creatures though.' Her smile slipped from her face as she thought about the sea, and Fire Talon.

'So this is your big secret?' Rhys cupped her face in his warm hands. She nodded and looked into his dark eyes. 'It's a great one, you're really special. You know that, right?'

'Yeah, I do. Only a few people have ever known about this. I want to keep it that way.'

'Who would I tell?' he asked, incredulous.

She kissed him, desperately needing to feel connected. She felt the relief flooding her senses when he kissed her back. She hadn't lost him.

The evening rushed past in a dizzying blur. Stalker lost her worries in Rhys's warmth, and she let her passion for him drown everything else out. If work was her foot in the human world, Rhys was her solace away from every obligation. Maybe one day, he would be the source of her honouring her ancestors with the ultimate offering, a child. But for now, he was her escape.

They fell asleep in each other's arms, the waning crescent moon just visible through the skylight in Rhys's bedroom. In three days it would be a new moon, Stalker's birth moon, and a mere four months since her first change. How had she come so far in so short a time?

She drifted in and out of sleep, something clawing at her subconscious and flitting in and out of her dreams. Suddenly yanked from her sleep, Stalker sat bolt upright in bed and glanced around the room, her breathing ragged, as if she had been running. Her last dream came back to her, she had been running. She had been chasing Pursuit-of-Midnight-Solitude. A shadow twitched in the corner of the room, the shadowy demon inviting her out to play. Rhys slept soundly at her side, his breathing soft and untroubled.

Stalker slipped from the bed and gathered her clothes. It was nearly 4am, she had time to fit in a run before sunrise. She dressed and left the house silently. Taking fox form, Stalker darted off into the quiet, empty city streets. Her guide led her through Burnside, and she followed without hesitation.

I will protect you, a voice whispered in her mind. She trusted it.

The Glass Wolves' territory was neat and orderly, with no trace of activity at this hour. The chase took her out into Fenstoke, territory of The Hand of God. First Strike flitted into her vague and inhuman thoughts, barely a memory. Pursuit-of-Midnight-Solitude led her north, and disappeared over the border into Fenwick. Stalker skidded to a halt, her paws sliding on the tarmac in the middle of the road.

A car appeared around the corner, its lights blinding her. She stood motionless for a moment, dazzled by them, then came to her senses and darted across the road and into the shadows at the edge of the Witches' territory. Her guide teased her, urging her on, deeper into the enemy's turf. She followed cautiously, sniffing her way forwards. The boundary was heavily scented by multiple shifters, all female, of course. One was familiar. The one who had bitten Weaver before she was abducted. That scent was forever etched in Stalker's memory.

Stalker crept through gardens and along alleys. Her guide wasn't leading her any more, though she was still there, protecting her from discovery. She was familiarising herself with the streets and landmarks, building a mental map of the place, so that she could easily flee if necessary.

The first rays of sunlight touched the horizon and Stalker looked up at the purple sky. She let out a small bark and turned tail, running swiftly out of danger.

She entered the house the same way she had that night, through the skylight. Rhys had rolled over in his sleep and was across the middle of the bed. Stalker shed her clothes and eased back in beside him, lifting his arm to settle underneath. He stirred and pulled her tightly against him, and she smiled, content at last.

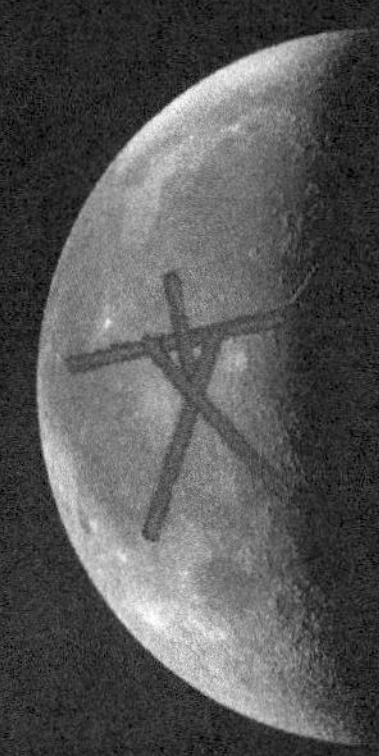

Chapter Thirty

Fights-Eyes-Open

Eyes scoured every inch of the local newspaper. He didn't really know what he was looking for, but assumed he would know it if he saw it. Accidents, deaths, disappearances, mentions of familiar names, anything like that would be a red flag. There were, of course, many incidents that could get his attention in a big city like Caerton, but nothing leaped out at him as being of interest to the shifter community. He closed the paper and neatly folded it, then added it to the pile of daily papers he had been collecting. The box by the back door was getting full. Chloe had trained him to recycle, it was habit now. He felt grief threaten to bubble to the surface and firmly pushed it back under.

Wind Talker and Claws were asleep in the living room, he could just hear their gentle snores. Weaver was out patrolling. Artemis only knew where Stalker was. He sighed. He didn't know how other packs conducted themselves, but had always thought that the Lightning Lords seemed different. They were a collective of individuals, far more so than a unified force. They seemed to be putting their differences behind them now, which gave him hope, and he suspected that the way he would get the best out of Stalker was to continue to give her a relatively loose rein. He wondered if it was her birth moon's influence, or whatever it was that made her unique among shifters. Perhaps it was having been adopted. Something gave her that fierce independence, or was it defiance? He thought about the night that they had snuck out of the betting shop to go and keep watch over his family. Stalker had taken the most convincing. Had he corrupted her?

The front door opened softly, and he leaned back in his chair, expecting to see Weaver, but Stalker entered and closed the door almost silently behind her. She looked up and saw him. He smiled and she tiptoed past the living room to join him.

'Hi,' he whispered. 'It's barely still the weekend.' He glanced at his watch, it was gone midnight. 'Scratch that, it's now Monday morning. Where've you been?'

'Scouting,' she replied softly. She sat down and pulled a folded piece of paper out of her pocket. She unfolded it and pressed it flat onto the table in front of him. He looked down at the hand-drawn map.

'Is this Fenwick?' he asked in alarm, his gaze darting to her eyes.

'Yes,' she replied. She reached into her pocket again and pulled out a cereal bar.

'What are you doing going into Witch territory without telling me first? What if something had happened to you?

We wouldn't have known where you were.' He kept his voice low so as not to wake the others, but his anger hissed out in his hushed voice.

'I'm sure the Witches would have let you know one way or another, sent you bits of my body or something.' She spoke through a mouthful of the cereal bar.

'I'm serious,' he snapped, not bothering to keep his voice down. 'Don't do it again. I give you a lot of leeway, and I am perfectly happy for you to scout Fenwick, but tell me you're going beforehand. Understood?'

'Yeah,' she replied, looking suitably chastised. Eyes felt a small swell of guilt, but shrugged it off. He was right. He shouldn't have to treat her like a child.

He turned his full attention to the map, it was quite well detailed.

'How long have you been working on this?'

'Just three nights. I came in early tonight, caught fresh scents and didn't want to take too big of a risk staying out there with them active.'

'Good, thank you.' Eyes glanced at her and gave her an appreciative smile. 'This is valuable work.'

'They're not based at the shop,' she said, slowly chewing her food. 'We thought they were, remember? But they're hardly there. Maybe they ran out of pack mates to staff the place.' A dark expression crossed her face and Eyes nodded solemnly. 'I haven't found their base yet.'

'It's a big territory,' Eyes said softly. 'You'll find it.'

'Thanks.'

'This isn't all you've been doing. But I don't suppose you're going to tell me what else you've been up to.'

'I had work yesterday,' she replied, a little defensively.

Eyes smirked and patted her shoulder.

'I know, I'm teasing. What you do with your time is your business, mostly. But look, if it's something dangerous, or that could cause a conflict of interests I do need to know. It would take a hell of a lot to prompt me to stop you, but a heads up would be appreciated. Like the scouting.'

'I'm absolutely certain I'm not endangering the pack, or anyone else. It's just personal, that's all.'

Eyes looked at her carefully, he wasn't sure if he could believe her or not. His family matters were personal, but look at the trouble that had brought on everyone. Maybe Stalker believed what she was saying, or maybe she was covering herself. He didn't have Claws' gift. He had to trust her, and when it came to it, there was no one he trusted more.

'Get some rest, especially if you haven't been getting much sleep with all of this scouting and working, and whatever.' He left the implication of her having a sex life hanging unspoken.

'I will. You too.' Stalker didn't rise to the bait, and she stood and drifted away upstairs. Eyes sat in the quiet and listened to her moving around upstairs. He thought he heard her go up to the attic, but couldn't be sure. He studied the map and tried to picture the bits of Fenwick that he knew, until Stalker came back downstairs and went into the living room to settle down.

Eyes rubbed his hands over his weary face. He had intended to wait up for Weaver, but exhaustion was setting in, and he followed Stalker to the living room to sleep.

Dawn broke and the pack gradually woke up. Weaver was the last to rise, and Eyes took her to one side as the others went about getting ready.

'Any news?' he asked.

'All quiet. The border is marked more strongly, but no incursions.'

'What about our northern border?'

'With the Wrecking Crew?' Weaver asked, a frown creasing her brow.

'Yes.'

'Quiet. Why?'

'I want to meet with them. I've had an idea and need their assistance.'

'Okay. Sounds intriguing.'

'What do you know about pack alliances? Besides that they're really rare?'

'They're usually short lived and difficult arrangements, forged out of necessity. You saw what happened at the Danegeld. That's typical of shifter society; someone calls others to arms and someone else shoots it down. Small scale alliances work better. Crimson Dawn's Blood and The Hand of God have been cooperative for a long time, decades I think. They've stayed close throughout changes in Alphas and all sorts of turmoil. They can usually be counted on to take similar views on things.'

'Being on good terms isn't the same as going into battle together though,' Eyes said.

'They've done that too. There was a big fight with some Furies about fifty years ago. There are songs about it. The pack that used to claim Shalebrook was wiped out in the battle, the Factory Boys rose out of the ashes a few years later. The Hand of God and Crimson Dawn's Blood defended the city against the incursion and took out a whole pack of Furies in retribution.'

'We have a lot of ground to make up with the Wrecking Crew. The Blue Moon were on hostile terms with them for a long time, and now they're angry with us for the fear demons. But we need to cooperate if we're going to stand a hope against the Witches.'

'Did Stalker talk to you about her parents?' Weaver asked, her voice low. Eyes glanced past her to the others eating breakfast and chatting loudly.

'No. What about them?'

'I should probably keep her confidence,' Weaver said, looking warily at Stalker. 'But it might go some way to explaining the animosity between the Wrecking Crew and Blue Moon, maybe. I don't know.'

Eyes narrowed his eyes. He was sick and tired of secrets.

'I'll ask her about it.'

'Okay. You'll need to find what Rust needs and sell it to him, he's motivated by greed, pure and simple.'

'Okay, good. Thank you. I'm glad you're back.' Eyes drew Weaver into a brotherly embrace. She had the most level head of any of them, and she knew how to get the best out of people. She might make a formidable Alpha one day. But for now, she was his most valuable advisor.

They re-joined the others in the kitchen for breakfast, and Eyes rushed his food. He had a meeting to get to.

He arrived at Free River Tower early, before many of the human workers. Theodore was waiting in his office, the door wide open. His assistant hadn't arrived yet and the whole floor was quiet.

'Martin, come on in,' Theodore said, rising from his

wide chair. Eyes closed the door behind him and took an uneasy seat on the opposite side of the desk. 'How can I help?'

'I wanted to thank you for looking after Weaver.'

'Not at all,' Theodore said with a wave of his hand. 'But that's not all.'

'No,' Eyes said, a wry smile tugging at the corner of his mouth. 'I understand your position on uniting against the Furies, I understand your scepticism. However, we do have a situation with the Witches. As you share a border with them, I would have thought you would share at least some of my concern.'

'I do, Martin, believe me.' Theodore steepled his fingers in front of his face and narrowed his eyes through his rimless glasses. 'They seem quiet for the moment though. What makes you think there is anything significant to worry about at this time?'

'That's just it, they are quiet. Too quiet. Ever since I changed they have been pushing boundaries, snatching members of my pack, breeching our border, attacking us. But since the attack on my family, there has been nothing.'

'Perhaps their losses in that attack warded them off?'

'They lost one. No. I think they're preparing for something big.'

'They surely weren't anticipating your alliance with the Wrecking Crew. Facing far greater numbers than they expected must have given them pause for thought.'

'Yes, I believe so. But I believe they are preparing for a full assault and are working on bolstering their numbers.'

Theodore drew a long breath and watched Eyes calmly. Eyes held his gaze steady, careful not to betray his measured demeanour, though inside his chest his heart was racing. The rage he felt about the Witches wouldn't be placated by words and politics. Whether the Witches really were coming back for them or not, he would have his revenge for his family. He needed the firepower of the Glass Wolves on his side if he was going to succeed.

'You're going to attack them anyway, whatever happens,' Theodore stated bluntly, his face unreadable.

'Yes,' Eyes admitted. 'We need to end this.'

'You realise that this could incite the very thing that Red Scythe is worried about? Full scale war with the Furies?'

'Possibly. I agree with him that it's coming anyway. Taking out the Witches now will help our side in the long run.' All of his cards were on the table now. Theodore would either laugh him out of his office, or agree. He waited with baited breath for a response.

'But if you're wrong, if the Furies aren't preparing for war, and you do this,' he paused and shook his head slowly. 'You could provoke an attack that was never coming otherwise. We have a strong border and have had no trouble with the Witches in years. It would be suicide for me to agree to participate.'

'Think of it this way, my pack will be taking them on, whether you agree to help or not. If we fail, the Witches may well start looking to their southern border for another toy to play with. If we succeed, the Furies will come sooner rather than later. Either way, you will be first in the firing line. Isn't it in your best interests to help us ensure we succeed and weaken the Furies?'

Theodore let out a rough bark of laughter. He tilted his

head to one side and smirked.

'You cocky son of a bitch. Are you certain I can't persuade you out of this rash action?'

'I'm afraid so.' Eyes waited, his breath held.

'Fine,' Theodore said, pushing his chair back away from the desk and raising his hands in defeat. 'Fine. We'll help you. I'll have my people prepare. Spark will be in touch with Wind Talker to discuss joint ritual aid. Vengeance can speak to Claws about gearing up. I'll have Terrance and Word Spider do reconnaissance and research.'

'Let me be clear,' said Eyes, getting to his feet. 'This is my mission, I'm asking for support, not for you to lead.' His pulse pounded in his veins, but his voice held true and no hint of apprehension showed. Theodore narrowed his eyes and pursed his lips.

'Very well, let me know when you're ready to go.'

'I will. Thank you for your cooperation.' Eyes thrust his hand out and Theodore slowly got to his feet and shook it firmly.

Eyes swept from the office with the upper hand. He allowed himself a satisfied grin as he rode in the lift back down to the lobby. Now he just needed to work similar magic on Rust.

Back at Grove Street, the rest of the pack was busy making plans. Eyes swept through the house checking on each of them and nearly bumped into Claws on the landing.

'Sorry,' he said, stepping out of the way. Claws was clutching a roll of paper and had a glint in his eyes that Eyes couldn't ignore. 'What is it?'

'I've been working on something that I think you

might like.'

'Oh?'

'Well, you know how we've taken your car across the veil? How about trying to take something a little bigger?'

'Okay.' Eyes was intrigued, and raised an eyebrow as he waited for Claws to continue.

'When the Wrecking Crew turned up at your house in their van I was kind of inspired. What if we got a van like that and tooled it up with weaponry? We could take it across the veil to attack in Hepethia.' He unrolled the paper and held it out to Eyes. On it was a sketch of a van kitted out with spikes on the front, a machine gun mounted on the roof and protective bars along the sides.

'A battle van?' Eyes asked, glancing at Claws' eager face. 'Nice. But where on earth would we get a machine gun?'

'Wind Talker says he knows a guy.'

'Of course he does. Okay, go for it. The Wrecking Crew can probably help with this. In fact, it might just be the thing to inspire them to ally with us.'

'Great,' Claws said with a grin. He ran off down the stairs. Eyes hadn't seen Stalker yet, and heard scraping noises in the attic, so he climbed the narrow staircase to find her. She was hunched over, examining the map that they had pinned to a cork board. The attic was almost bare these days, the Witches having stolen the boxes of notes that were up here. Dust had gathered on the wooden floorboards, and just a few folders of recreated notes now sat in a pile to one side. It didn't bear thinking about, what the Witches now knew about the Blue Moon.

'Hi,' Eyes said softly, not wanting to startle her. She

glanced up at him and nodded. 'We're going over to meet the Wrecking Crew at sunset. Are you up for a thorough scout after that?'

'Yeah of course.'

'What are you doing?' He moved over to her and crouched down to examine the map. It was rapidly filling up with tiny markings, resembling Flames' old one.

'Looking at the boundary. I know it so well now, like the back of my hand. But it's different out there on the ground, you know. I wanted to get a more academic feel for it.'

There was a thick red line marking the edge of Lightning Lord territory. It followed some of the main streets and the edge of Redfield Park. But over in Crossway there were no neat and tidy lines in the landscape to follow. It was a sprawl of curved roads and big houses, and they had drawn their territory boundary right through the middle, cutting across roads and through gardens. This was not a boundary that had been negotiated, either diplomatically, or through years of border skirmishes. This was a rough and ready line in the sand that said "Do not cross". Eyes wondered where the Wrecking Crew drew their boundary with the Witches, and how they had come to it. Tensions with their neighbours had always been so fraught, Eyes really didn't know much about them or their struggle with the Witches. He would change that.

'Weaver suggested I talk to you about your birth parents.' He cast a sideways glance at her. She stiffened but kept her gaze resolutely fixed on the map.

'Right, yeah. Sorry, I should have told you as soon as I found out. My dad was Blue Moon. Flames-First-Guardian had noted my change in the Scroll Archive and had to have seen my parentage. So he knew who my dad was, knew he was a lost pack mate. He never said.'

'I see.' Eyes nodded. Stalker's voice was too casual, too unconcerned. She was faking disinterest. She had to be immeasurably hurt. He placed a gentle hand on her shoulder and she closed her eyes for a moment.

'My mum was Wrecking Crew though. I wondered if their relationship might be the cause of the animosity between the two packs, somehow.'

'Maybe, or maybe it pre-dates them. Rust might know.'

'Yeah, I thought that too. I don't know if I'm ready to probe further though. It was a shock to find out and I need time to process it before I go further. Does that make sense?' She looked at him, her eyes wide and glistening. Eyes nodded solemnly.

He turned his attention back to the map. It extended over most of Runmead and Fenwick, and Eyes looked over those areas now. The shop that the Witches claimed was marked in Stalker's handwriting. She had noted other details about their territory, but there was a large gap in the north. Eyes tapped it.

'You haven't scouted this yet?'

'No, not yet. I want to ask the Wrecking Crew if they're scouting that area. I didn't want to accidentally run into Fury on Witch turf and end up having a fight.' She rolled her eyes and Eyes held back a chuckle.

'Well you can do that later.'

'Sure.'

Stalker was really engrossed in the map, though her thoughts were tumbling over her parents, so Eyes left her to it.

As the sun set, the Lightning Lords set off for Redfield Park, on foot. The air was warm, with a cool breeze that lifted Weaver's long hair and made Eyes' knee-length coat billow out behind him. It was a new moon, and Eyes could feel Stalker buzzing with energy, itching to shift and run through the night.

The park was quiet. The last of winter's dead leaves blew across the grass with each gust of wind. Eyes led the pack out into the centre of the wide, grassy space and came to a stop under the dark purple sky. He felt prickles all over his skin when the Wrecking Crew entered the park, before he could even see them. They approached, emerging out of the darkness with Rust leading them.

'Eyes,' he said, with a curt nod.

'Rust, thanks for coming,' Eyes replied. 'First of all, I wanted to apologise for any trouble caused on your territory by the fear demons that were drawn here recently. We discovered a new occupant at my house, The-Knight-of-Shadowed-Fear. He appears to be raising an army.'

'I see.' Rust crossed his arms over his chest and scowled in Eyes' direction. 'And what are you doing about it?'

'We'll deal with him in due course. For now we have a more pressing issue. The Witches.'

Sky Runner leaned close to Rust and whispered something. Eyes watched the two of them carefully, but Rust was a difficult man to read. He gave a nod and she stepped back, her gaze cast out to the tree line.

'The attack on your house seems to have changed their behaviour,' Rust said, choosing his words carefully. 'We've had no skirmishes with them since and the border has been far too quiet. I take it the same is true for you guys?'

'That's right,' Eyes replied. 'I'm convinced they're preparing for a major offensive. I want to beat them to it.'

'Have you been scouting Fenwick?' Stalker asked Sky Runner.

'Only the border. Have you?' Sky Runner cocked an eyebrow.

'Yeah. I didn't want to head too far north and risk bumping into any of your people.'

Eyes thought he caught a glimpse of something dangerous in Fury's eye as she glared at Stalker. He was wary of their enmity, it could cause a serious problem for the alliance of their packs.

'You've been going right into their territory?' Rust snapped, gaping at Stalker. Eyes held up a hand to settle the tension.

'We're preparing for war, Rust. Scouting is essential.'

'Are you mad? What if they catch her?' Rust turned his anger on Eyes.

'That's extremely unlikely, with Stalker's unique skill set.' He allowed himself a small smirk, but quickly reined his amusement back in. 'I trust her, and if anything were to happen to her we would deal with it. I would like you to be able to trust me.'

'Hmm,' Rust huffed. 'We'll see. Stop being reckless and give me a reason to trust you.'

'Well, if we're going to take on the Witches together you will have to trust me.'

'I haven't agreed to that,' Rust said warily.

'You will,' Eyes said with a small smile. 'How would you like to help build a special vehicle?'

'A special vehicle?' Rust raised an eyebrow and leaned a little closer. Eyes had his curiosity. Now to exploit his greed.

'Claws, do you have the sketch?'

Claws stepped forwards and slid the rolled up paper from his jacket pocket. He passed it to Eyes, who unrolled it and handed it to Rust. 'If you can acquire a van, and fit the parts, we'll share it with you. We can pay you very well for the parts and the work.'

Rust shifted his weight and glanced at his pack mates. Eyes watched as Rust considered the offer. His eyes feasted hungrily on the sketch.

'How much are you willing to pay?' Rust's gaze darted up from the sketch and fixed on Eyes.

Eyes glanced at Wind Talker, who gave a discreet nod. They still had most of the money left that they had taken from the meth lab, and Wind Talker had been keeping it safe at the house.

'A hundred grand.' Almost all of it. A neat, round number. There were almost certainly other uses for that money, but Eyes needed the Wrecking Crew. If this is what it cost, then so be it. Wind Talker let the black bag slide off his shoulder and tossed it into the gap between their packs. It landed heavily on the grass and Rust regarded Eyes carefully, before stooping to peer inside. He drew a sharp breath through his teeth. Other members of the Wrecking Crew exchanged gleeful glances.

'We have a deal,' Rust said. He extended his hand and Eyes took it with a silent sigh of relief.

'Excellent.'

'Do you have a plan yet?' Rust asked, folding the sketch

roughly and tucking it into his jacket pocket.

'It's coming. I have the Glass Wolves on board too, so I'll be in touch to coordinate our efforts.'

'You managed to get Theodore Harris in on this?' Rust asked, the surprise evident in his voice.

'I did.' Eyes lifted his chin, satisfied with Rust's reaction.

'Wow. Okay then. I look forwards to hearing more from you. You have my number. We'll get to work on acquiring this.' He tapped his chest where the sketch was secured. 'You,' he jerked his head towards Stalker. 'Be careful, okay?'

'I will,' she said, with a trace of humility in her eyes. 'Thanks.'

Sky Runner cleared her throat and looked imploringly at her Alpha. Eyes smiled and looked away discreetly.

'I could probably help with the scouting.'

'Probably,' Rust said slowly. 'But I think we'll leave it to the foolish, for now.'

Eyes felt a flash of anger, partly from himself, but mostly from Stalker. He grasped her wrist to hold her back. Rust chuckled. He picked up the bag and slung it over his shoulder. He turned on his heel and the others followed him across the park, Sky Runner taking up the rear with an awkward backward glance at Stalker.

Stalker held up her free hand in the shape of a phone and held it to her cheek. "Call me" she mouthed. Sky Runner stifled a laugh and nodded slightly, before turning and jogging after the rest of her pack.

'Don't,' Eyes hissed in Stalker's ear. 'Don't encourage her to disobey her Alpha. Rust isn't like me.'

'I know,' she replied, tugging her arm free of his grip. 'I won't. We're friendly, that's all. It can't hurt to talk to her more about what she's seen from her border.'

'Okay,' Eyes replied, reluctant to believe her. 'Be careful out there tonight. I'll see you in the morning.' He gave her a brief hug, which she grudgingly returned.

'Yes, *Dad.*'

He let the jibe go and led the others back the way they had come, while Stalker shifted into her fox form and scampered away towards Fenwick. It had been a good day's work. Now he just needed to come up with a watertight battle plan that would have made Fortune proud.

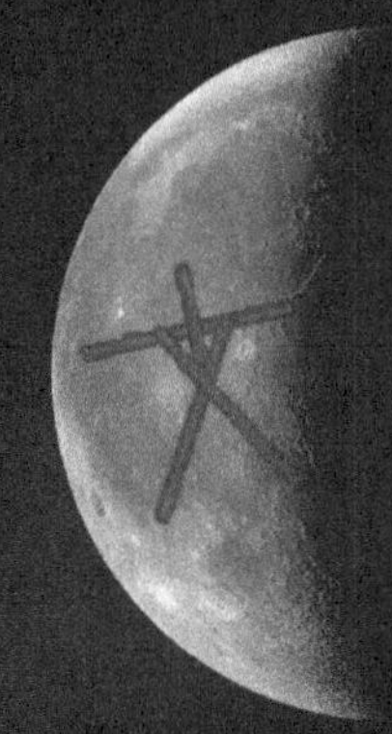

Chapter Thirty One

Stalker-of-Night's-Shadow

Her paws padded softly on the tarmac. The night folded around her, hiding her. The northern part of Fenwick was unfamiliar to her, the streets were wide and lined with small trees. Houses stood back from the road and short parades of high-end shops interrupted the residences periodically.

She sniffed the ground and the walls as she jogged. Stalker rounded a corner and caught the faintest scent of a Witch on the wind. She hesitated, one paw hanging in mid-air. The scent was hours old.

Stalker walked forwards, sniffing even more carefully. Perhaps she could follow the scent and find the headquarters that they so needed to locate. She glanced up and saw a strange bundle of sticks hanging from the lamp post beside her. They formed the rough shape of a person and were tied together with black ribbon. The lamp post stank of the Witch. This was their sign, their warning to go no further. Stalker felt the magic of it prickling at her senses. But she had to go on, she had to follow the trail.

The warning subsided as Stalker walked past the lamp post, and she gave her head a short shake to get rid of the remaining doubt. She pressed on, carefully following the scent. It grew stronger, and she passed another macabre stick man. This one was tied to a hanging shop sign, too high to catch the eye of the average passer-by.

Stalker ignored the nagging voice that told her to turn back. She pursued the strengthening trail, occasionally ducking out of sight of passing car headlights. The scent began to get clearer, and it was naggingly familiar. She kept her nose to the ground, moving slowly on. The scent made her think of family, it reminded her of someone close to her, yet it was slightly different.

The next stick marker that she came to was hanging by the neck from a small tree by the roadside. Twisted around the twigs was a thick lock of dark blond hair. It smelled of the Witch she was tracking, but also someone else, the source of the familiarity. It smelled of Weaver. Stalker stared up at it, unblinking. She could only see the hanged man, everything beyond it was out of focus.

The warning was clear: go no further, or Weaver dies. Did they know she had been on their territory? Or was it a general warning just in case someone from the Lightning Lords should be doing precisely what Stalker was doing? It was all the more reason to press on. She would not be intimidated by this. She was clearly on the brink of discovering something important about them and their territory.

The ominous stick man swung slightly in the breeze.

Stalker forced herself to look away from it. She was at the end of a wide street, with an even wider road crossing it just a few yards away. The orange street lights cast their eerie glow on the young trees that lined the two streets. Houses stood behind high walls and hedges. At the end of the street were large green stretches on both sides of the road, distancing the grand houses from the adjoining road and the factory opposite. Her eyes focused on the building properly for the first time, finally free of the spell that kept her from seeing it.

It was an old factory, set back from the road behind a tall chain link fence. The once grey stone was now dirty and partially covered in a layer of moss. It had been abandoned for years and nature was reclaiming it. Yet Stalker caught the sound of voices on the wind, and the unmistakable stench of a pack of female shifters.

She darted away from the road, clinging to the shadows of the wall of the end house. She ran swiftly to a spot just opposite the gates into the compound, and crouched down in the shadows to watch.

There were flickering lights inside some of the glassless windows. Stalker couldn't make out the conversation, but it sounded as though someone was issuing orders, presumably the Alpha. After a while, two shadowy figures emerged from the side of the building and moved towards the gate. They were talking animatedly and one of them laughed at something the other had said. Stalker hunkered down, willing the night to mask her. As the two young women passed under the street light, their faces bright and smiling, Stalker's breath caught in her fox throat. Their faces were forever etched in her memory, their likeness to one another unmistakably making them twins. The same twins that she and Eyes had killed.

When the coast was clear, Stalker turned tail and sprinted for home. She leaped over fences, bounded down alleys, and traversed rooftops on a direct line for Grove Street. She shifted form in the alley at the end of the road and ran into the house gasping for breath. It was late, but Eyes was sitting in the kitchen talking quietly with Weaver. They both looked at her in alarm as she charged into the kitchen, not even trying to keep quiet.

'The Witches we killed are alive.' She strode to the sink and poured a glass of water. She turned to look at their stunned faces, and gulped down the cold liquid.

'Excuse me?' Eyes whispered.

'I found their base, at least I think I did. An old, overgrown factory in the north of Fenwick. There are some serious wards around the place, but I got through them. I saw the two supposedly dead Witches coming out. The one from St. Catherine's, and the one from your house.' She looked at Eyes. She avoided looking at Weaver as she shared the other news. 'They're threatening you, Weaver. I found a stick person hanging by the neck, with your hair wrapped around it.'

'What?' Weaver snapped, her eyes wide. Her hand went immediately to her hair and stroked it protectively. 'They cut some of it off when they captured me. I guess they kept it. That's gross.'

'There's something else.' Stalker paused, unsure if it was wise to go on or not. 'Weaver, do you have a sister or a female cousin?'

'A sister, yes. Why?'

'I think she's with them. I picked up a scent that was familiar, but I only managed to identify it when I found your hair. She had probably been the one to put the signs up. I'm so sorry.'

'It's not entirely unexpected,' Weaver said, her voice distant. 'I prayed to Artemis not to let it happen, but I knew it was possible.'

'Hang on,' Eyes said, a frown creasing his brow. 'What do you mean, the dead girls aren't dead? How can that be?'

'I don't know. But I bet Last-Breath-Echoes does.'

Stalker slept badly that night, plagued by dreams of the dead rising from their graves. The face of the girl she had killed haunted her, as fresh as the night she had committed the act. Three months of recovery undone in an instant. She sensed Eyes sharing similar nightmares, and saw the other dead girl through his eyes in the moment that he had slaughtered her on the landing in his house. When she woke, her feelings of guilt and regret were mingled with his rage and thirst for vengeance. She found that she couldn't quite meet his eye as they moved around the house. He seemed to be having the same problem. On reflection, she hadn't really missed the telepathy much.

Once the pack was refreshed and gathered together for the morning briefing, Eyes made the call they had to make, and put his phone on speaker in the middle of the kitchen table. Stalker watched the lit screen with Last-Breath-Echoes' name on it, hardly daring to breathe. Finally the ring tone ended and a sleepy voice responded.

'Hello? Eyes?'

'Hi. Sorry to trouble you so early.'

'I was on the night shift, so was just getting to sleep.

Don't worry about it. Is there a problem?'

'Not exactly. I need to know what happened to the girl who was killed in St. Catherine's last December, after she left your care.' Eyes glanced warily at Stalker, but she ignored him and focused on the phone. Flashes of the fight troubled her mind and she dug her nails into the underside of the table to keep the tension from her jaw.

'Oh, well, her body will have been sent to the crematorium in Fenwick.'

'Are you certain? Do you remember or would you need to check paperwork?' Eyes asked anxiously.

'I remember, I always remember what happens to those cases. I make a mental note.' Echoes yawned loudly, and Stalker could just make out the quiet squelching noise of her rubbing her eye. Her voice was distant, but that was no different to when she was wide awake.

'I see. And what about the other girl from that family? The one that was removed from the scene last month by Theodore's associates?' Eyes was being deliberately vague. Stalker understood why. They couldn't be sure who might be listening to the call.

'That one never passed through my hands. You'd have to ask Theodore. What is this about?'

'I saw something that I would have thought impossible last night,' Stalker said softly. 'Those two girls, walking, talking and laughing.'

'Really?' There was a hard edge to Echoes' voice that Stalker had never heard before. It was as if she had been yanked out of her dream land into the real world for a rare glimpse of its true horrors.

'Yes, I'm confident that they had just been with their

mother. They looked in good health.'

'There are a number of possible explanations,' Echoes mused, her voice back to its dreamy tone. 'I'll talk to Scribe and do some research for you.'

'Thank you,' Eyes said. 'Let me know when you have something. We'll let you get some sleep now.'

Eyes ended the call. Stalker took a deep breath.

'So what now?' she asked.

'Patrols, research, building the battle van, preparing weapons. Wind Talker, can you prepare some talismans?'

'Yes, of course. I was going to ask Spark from the Glass Wolves to help. She is a very experienced ritualist, I'm sure I can learn from her.'

Stalker stared at him, she had never known such humility from him. Perhaps he had grown from his experience as Alpha, or her decision to sacrifice him. She picked up a pen from the table and rolled it idly between her fingers, before stuffing it into the back pocket of her jeans without thinking.

'Great, I want as much collaboration with the Glass Wolves and Wrecking Crew as possible. We need a firm alliance if this has a hope of succeeding. Stalker, talk to Sky Runner and coordinate patrols with her. Just make sure Rust's okay with it.'

'Will do.'

'Claws, touch base with Rust today and go over plans for the vehicle. Where are we on the weaponry?'

'I have a meeting today with a friend of Wind Talker's. I'll keep you up to date.'

'Okay. Great. I'm going to go and see Theodore about the dead girl. We'll reconvene here tonight. I want to go to

Redfield Park and speak to Crimson Thorns.'

'What?' Stalker snapped. Weaver didn't seem surprised, but Wind Talker and Claws both exchanged troubled glances. 'She's mad. We've been warned a dozen times not to go near her.'

'Exactly.' Eyes wore a grim but determined expression. 'That's exactly why we should talk to her. We need to see for ourselves what the situation is there in Hepethia. We've always taken the word of the Blue Moon for granted, and look where that's got us. If nothing else, we might be able to gather intelligence on the Witches from her.'

'Alpha,' Wind Talker said quietly, but firmly. 'She is their ally. We could be putting ourselves in danger going to see her.'

'I know, but I won't budge on this. Speaking of Witch allies, someone should check in with Scourging Agony.'

'I can do that,' Claws volunteered. 'I suggested his feeding ground to him, I think he trusts me.'

'Okay, thank you. Weaver, I want you to come with me to Theodore now. Use whatever influence you have on him.'

Weaver simply nodded in reply. Stalker liked seeing Eyes like this, all business and professional. This was the Alpha they needed, firm, decisive and in charge.

The pack dispersed for the day. Eyes and Weaver got into his car, Wind Talker retreated to the attic, Claws set off to see Scourging Agony first. Stalker paused in the doorway of the house and watched the others leaving. Her mind ran over everything they had to do and she frantically tried to decide how she could best be useful. Her decision clicked into place, and she ran after Claws as he set off down the street.

'Wait, I'll come with you,' she called. He slowed down as she caught up. 'He might be more talkative if someone's inflicting pain on themselves.'

Claws nodded and the two of them walked briskly towards Red Drop of Ink. The tattooist was just opening the shop when they arrived. Red greeted them with a warm smile and held the door open for them.

'This is nice, customers on my doorstep so early.' He glanced at Claws, a slight frown on his brow. Stalker stifled a laugh. Claws really didn't look much like he was in the market for a tattoo, he looked exactly like a private investigator. 'I remember you,' Red said to Stalker, a curious smile on his lips. 'Ariana, right?'

'That's right,' she said, smiling back.

'I did the eclipse over your heart. I hope it healed okay.'

Stalker nodded. They both knew he wasn't talking about the ink, she had been close to tears when she had sat in his chair.

'How's business?' Stalker asked.

'Pretty good, thanks. I've had a lot more people interested in the extreme stuff in the last few months though, weird. Not that I'm complaining, it pays well.'

Red had a side-line, the thing that made this place perfect for a demon who thrived on masochism. Red performed scarification and extreme piercings on willing and paying customers.

'Nice,' she replied, a hint of sarcasm in her voice.

'How can I help you today?' Red asked her, though he cast a furtive glance at Claws as he moved around the room, looking at the posters on the walls and peering into the back room.

'I know I haven't booked a slot, but I hoped you'd be free to do another tat for me now.'

'Sure, my diary's clear for the next hour or so. What do you want?'

Stalker suddenly realised that this wasn't planned. She had no idea what she wanted. She glanced at Claws, her brother. She had ink for her fallen pack, but nothing for her living one.

'Lightning,' she replied. She remembered the shifter from the Hellsclaws with the lighting all down her arm. That must have taken a lot longer than an hour. She would have to go for something simpler, but she found herself smiling at the thought.

'Nice. Okay, come on through. Is your friend okay out here?' Red glanced at Claws again.

'Yeah, I'm fine thanks. I'll wait here for you, Ariana.' Claws looked pointedly at her. *Feed him, then we'll cross and see him,* his voice echoed inside her head. She nodded and followed Red into the back room. She sat in the chair and Red passed her a book full of stock images. She began flicking through it, her eyes lingering on the more simple, tribal images that were scattered throughout the more realistic flashes of lightning. She caught sight of one that made her stop flipping the pages. It was lightning, with a wolf and large bird of prey emerging from the heavy lines.

'This, this is great. I don't suppose you can make the bird look more like an owl, and work in a cat and a badger too?'

Red looked at the image and then gave her a curious glance.

'I'd have to plan it first, but yeah, I could probably do that.'

'Okay, just do the lightning and wolf now and can I book another time to come in for you to finish it?'

'Sure, no problem.' Red got his equipment ready and then looked at her expectantly. 'Where are we doing this?'

'Oh.' She shrugged off her jacket and lifted her top. She tapped her right side, just above her hip. She settled into the chair on her side and watched Red work over her shoulder. The chill in the room didn't bother her, nor did baring so much flesh. A shifter wasn't the best creature to invoke a pain demon, as it took a lot more than a scratching electronic needle to cause Stalker pain. But Scourging Agony appeared to appreciate the gesture, nonetheless. Stalker caught a glimpse of the demon peeking at her across the veil behind Red's back, just as he had done the last time she was in this chair.

When Red finished he held up a mirror for Stalker to admire the work. She grinned at the sight of a wolf just like Eyes leaping across a streak of lightning. It was perfect.

'What do you think?'

'It's great. Thanks. I look forwards to getting the rest added.'

Red wiped the blood from her back and side, and he smiled at her as she continued to grin at the new ink.

'I'm glad you like it. This is the reaction I like to get from my clients, rather than tears.'

'Yeah, it's good to be looking forwards, not back.' She wasn't going to open up to this relative stranger about the meaning behind her tattoo choices. She put her clothes back on, handed the cash over to Red and went out into the front to meet Claws.

'What did you get?' he asked, as he stood from his seat in the window.

'I'll show you later.' Red hadn't followed her out, and she glanced back to see him tidying up. 'Thanks, Red! See you later!' she called out.

'No problem. Bye,' he called back. Claws went to the door, opened it, then closed it again without leaving. The two of them crossed the veil, neatly folding out of sight of Red and the bustling high street outside. Stalker looked around at their new surroundings.

In Hepethia, the shop was part of the tangled maze built by the Blue Moon. The interior was bare, like the back of a stage set, with Hepethia's raw crystals poking through the brickwork where the job hadn't been finished off neatly. It was surprisingly dark, the light from outside seeming to not reach into the shell of a building, but Stalker could smell blood. Tiny trickles of the sticky substance ran down the walls in places, and small pools formed on the ground in the grooves of the crystal and stone.

'What is this?' Claws whispered.

'Our influence,' she replied softy. She led him away from the large front window, towards the narrow doorway through the wall at the back. The sound of a rattling breath stopped them in their tracks. The chink of metal on metal came from the other side of the wall, and a sensual sigh made Stalker's stomach turn. She stepped through the doorway, Claws by her side.

Scourging Agony was hovering a foot off the ground, suspended in mid-air, with his bladed arms and fingers outstretched and his head tipped back. Slowly he turned to look down at them, a sickening smile on his pallid face.

'Why thank you for that. Though I do prefer it when they at least groan a bit, screams are better.'

Stalker suppressed a shudder.

'No problem. How is this place working out for you? I gather the business has changed slightly for you.'

'Yesssss. The pretty young things do seem to want to experience more pain here these days.' The demon grinned at her.

'We need to talk to you about your old mistress,' Claws said, tension in his voice. Not much rattled him, but this demon seemed to get under his skin. 'When did you last see her?'

'A few days ago,' the demon replied, his face eager for a reaction.

'What business did you have with her?'

'Oh, nothing terribly important. She summoned me, I went, we talked.'

'What reassurance can you give us that you're loyal to us and not her?' Stalker asked, her patience growing thin.

'Well, I doubt you would believe anything I told you, so you'll just have to decide to trust me.'

'What has she had you doing?' Claws asked, rubbing his temples.

'Oh, the usual; retrieving bodies, sending messages. That sort of thing.'

'Have you sabotaged any of those jobs?' Claws asked, raising a curious eyebrow.

'No, there was nothing to be gained in doing so. But I can assure you, if the need arises I shall do my best to protect you and not her.' His voice dripped as he attempted to ingratiate himself upon them. It was almost impossible for Stalker to tell how much of his demeanour was faked, but Claws had his special skill and she looked to him for a clue. Claws nodded solemnly.

'I see. You mentioned retrieving bodies? Care to elaborate?'

'Yes, actually. One of them would concern you a great deal. I was responsible for finding her dead daughter and returning her home.' The demon grinned wickedly. Stalker flinched and shook her head. This was just the information they were looking for, it all felt too convenient to be falling into their laps now.

'Why didn't you inform us of this before?' Claws asked.

'That was never our arrangement,' the demon stated plainly. 'I don't volunteer anything, but will answer when asked.'

Stalker searched her memory. Could that be what they had agreed? Demons were slippery creatures, but agonisingly literal at times. Perhaps he was right, perhaps that is precisely what they had agreed at the time.

'Fine,' Claws snapped, his patience wearing thin. 'Have you told The Witches, or their Alpha, anything that would compromise us?' He glared at the demon.

'No, I have not.' Scourging Agony leaned forwards and enunciated clearly, daring Claws to find him a liar.

'What did you do with the girl's body?' Stalker asked, getting them back on point.

'Took it to the crematorium, where all dead bodies go to die.' His black lips twisted into a sneer.

'Well, she isn't dead now. What do you know about that? About dead girls up and about, living their lives?'

Stalker spat the words.

'Very little. I don't know how they did it, it's none of my concern. If it's any consolation, the first one that you killed can't show her face in public, as the authorities believe her to be dead. She's hardly living her life. Living her death might be more accurate.'

Stalker twitched. Why did this have to haunt her? Why couldn't the girl have stayed dead and buried in Stalker's past?

'I see,' Claws replied softly. 'Well, thank you for your cooperation.' He turned to leave and Stalker moved with him, her mind still on the Witches who should be dead.

'You're planning to attack them, aren't you?' There was something urgent in his voice, and the two shifters stopped and turned back to look up at him. 'You're going to kill them all. Again.'

'And?' Claws asked, lifting his chin in defiance.

'It's not my usual flavour, but can I be there?' His black eyes glared at them hungrily.

'I don't know,' Claws said slowly, caution written on his face. 'I'll have to check with our Alpha.'

'Of course,' Scourging Agony said, slowly bowing his head. His fingers clicked together. Stalker and Claws left and stepped out through the door into the street. They paused and exchanged troubled glances.

'What do we do with this?' Stalker asked, feeling lost and confused.

'Take it back to Eyes. It's his call.'

'We need to end this relationship, don't we?'

'I think so. We can't trust him. He didn't lie once in there, but he's clever. There could so easily be ways for him to slip around the lies and give me nothing but truth, while still betraying us relentlessly.'

Stalker nodded.

'I'm heading back to Grove Street. I have to call Sky Runner.'

'Okay, I have to see a man about a very big gun. Take care. I'll see you tonight.' Claws drew her into a one-armed hug. She patted him on the back, and he released her. They went their separate ways.

Back at the house, Stalker made her way up to the attic, hardly aware of what she was doing. The house was still and empty. She hummed some tune that sometimes got stuck in her head, and went to the corner where there was a mysterious hole in the fabric of reality. She reached inside and pulled out a small wooden box.

'Open,' she whispered softly, her lips almost caressing the rune-inscribed lid. The box slid open, and Stalker took out the pen from her back pocket. She placed it gently in the box alongside assorted small objects, including two folded playing cards, a penny, some apple seeds, a crumpled packet from a cereal bar, and a small key for a padlock. She lifted out the tooth on a black leather cord, and ran her fingers over it. She tied it around her neck, closed the lid and kissed it. The box vanished in her hands, invisible to every part of her mind. She slid it back into its hiding place and walked away. Halfway down the stairs she paused, shook her head and looked around at where she was. She'd been getting this strange feeling a lot lately, walking into a room and forgetting why she was there. She had always thought it was a phenomenon that crept up on the elderly, but apparently not. With a sigh she continued down the stairs and went about her day, blissfully unaware of the box hidden in the attic.

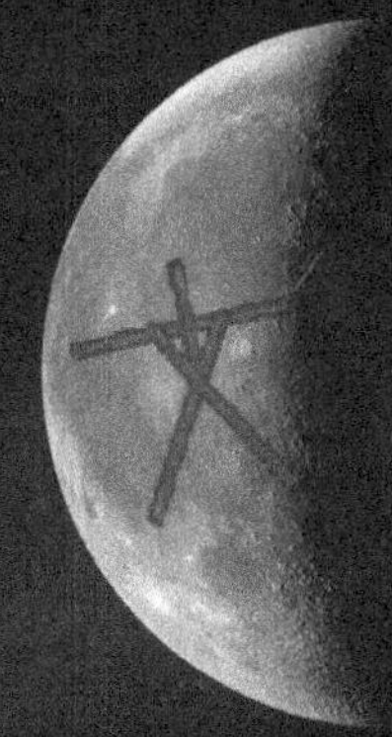

Chapter Thirty Two

Fights-Eyes-Open

Eyes slammed his door shut and pounded his palms on the steering wheel. Weaver sat quietly at his side, waiting for his anger to abate.

'How could he lose the body and not tell us?'

'It would have shown weakness. He's all about strength.' Weaver's voice was quiet and calm. Eyes glared at her.

'Why aren't you angry? Why are you so calm?'

'What's to be angry about? This wasn't a personal insult, he didn't do anything to deliberately hurt us, he was simply looking after his own interests. Do you go broadcasting every upset that we encounter to other packs?'

'No, I suppose not.' Eyes sighed and rested his head on the seat back. Weaver was usually right. 'Okay, let's get back.' He started the car and swept from the car park under Free River Tower.

'I disagree with him, by the way,' Weaver said, a small smile on her lips. 'He should have told us. The repercussions of the body going missing could well affect us, therefore it is our business.'

Eyes glanced at her and let out a short bark of laughter. He shook his head and gripped the wheel tighter.

'I'm glad to hear you say that. I was worried about where your loyalties lie for a moment there.'

'No you weren't,' she replied with a smile.

'I wish you didn't always know what I was thinking.'

'It's a burden.' She shrugged and settled back in her seat. Eyes didn't entirely mean it, he was thankful for their telepathy. He knew that they would be a stronger pack in combat for it, as they had been against Glimmering Wires. It wouldn't be long now. Everything was clicking into place.

They arrived back in St. Mark's and pulled up outside the house. Weaver got out of the car and looked expectantly at Eyes. 'You coming in?'

'No, I need to do a few things. I'll see you and the others at Redfield Park after sunset.'

'Okay. Be careful.'

'You too.'

Weaver shut the door and Eyes drove away. He went to his mother's house first, picked up post and checked the house over carefully. He changed his clothes, and put some washing on. Then he drove across St. Mark's to Crossway and pulled up at his own house. He was going to have to sell it. He needed to sort through their things, ship Chloe and Amy's belongings to them, and dispose of the rest. He could never live here again.

He moved through the house, ghosts lurking in every corner. The kitchen sparkled and smelled of fresh varnish, but Eyes could still see his father's body slumped against the cupboards and blood pooling on the floor. Up on the landing there was no visible trace of what had occurred, but Eyes stood where he had crushed the Witch. Uncovering how and why the twins had been resurrected was the single most important thing to him, and Stalker likely felt the same. But he mustn't allow it to side-track them from the main objective. It was irrelevant really, if they were going to eliminate the entire pack then what were two more youngsters? But they had to know if killing them would do any good, or if the whole lot of them would spring back from the hell they were sent to.

He peeled his gaze from the carpet and moved through the rest of the house, checking that it was secure. He paused at his daughter's bedroom doorway on his way out again and placed a hand on the door frame.

'Thank you, Perfection-of-Flesh, for your sacrifice, thank you for protecting my family.'

Eyes strode down the stairs and crossed the veil. The house had been fixed up on this side too, but a shadow hung over it, and demons lurked in the corners. He went to the kitchen and slammed his fist into the pristine worktop, cracking the marble. He roared and shifted into his Agrius form, goading the Knight-of-Shadowed-Fear. He didn't know any other way to draw the demon here.

'Do you honestly think I have nothing better to do?' The Knight's deep, dark voice echoed around the room and Eyes spun around to locate him. The demon peeled out of the shadows between the kitchen and the hallway, his enormous sword clasped in both hands and pointing to the ground. Eyes shifted back into his human form and straightened his tie.

'You're here, aren't you?'

'What do you want?' the demon snapped.

'I want to persuade you to keep your army in St. Mark's. They're spilling into Runmead and upsetting the neighbours. I need them to not be upset with us right now.'

The Knight let out a low rumble from inside his helmet.

'Why?'

'Because I intend to finish the fight that was started in this house.'

'You are raising an army too, then?'

'In a manner of speaking.'

'Will the battle strike fear into the hearts of innocents?'

'Maybe.' Eyes hoped to scare the living daylights out of the other Furies, but he couldn't consider them innocent. It was likely that residents of Fenwick would be aware of the attack, and become fearful of whatever creatures caused the noises and possible destruction of property that were bound to issue from the battle. He didn't want the Knight to grow stronger, he wanted to be able to take him down at some point, but right now he needed to bargain with the demon.

'Good. In that case, I will order my soldiers to confine themselves to your territory.'

'Do you mind me asking who your war is with?'

'The-Baron-of-Blooded-Shards.' The Knight spat the name, his voice thick with venom. Eyes blinked a few times, caught off guard. He knew that name. The pack had seen the Baron on their territory once, right after the Blue

Moon were killed, but hadn't heard anything of him since.

'I see.'

'What do you know of him?' The Knight leaned closer to Eyes. Cold poured off him and seeped under Eyes' skin.

'Nothing really, just the name.' Eyes shuddered and averted his gaze from the black, empty helmet.

'Hmm, puny whelp of Artemis, why should you know of these things?' The Knight lifted himself up to his full height, his head almost touching the ceiling. Even in broad daylight, the demon sucked the light right out of the room. 'I will keep my army contained, and eagerly await the bloodshed you will inflict.'

The Knight shimmered out of sight, and Eyes slumped back against the nearest kitchen cabinet in relief. That should appease the Wrecking Crew, but the effect it might have on St. Mark's was not a comforting thought.

He crossed the veil and sighed as he looked around the un-lived-in kitchen. He took out his phone and tapped a message to Rust.

> May my pack have permission to enter Redfield Park on the other side this evening?

He put his phone on the worktop and stared at it, locked in limbo between productivity and frustration.

> Ok. But it's your funeral

Eyes rolled his eyes, then hastily thanked Rust.

He spent the rest of the day in the unpleasant task of sorting through everyone's belongings, and as the sun dipped below the horizon he set off for Redfield Park.

The rest of the pack were just arriving when he got there.

'Updates for the day, please.'

'Stalker and I got some useful information out of Scourging Agony,' Claws reported. 'He was responsible for stealing the body from Theodore's people and returning it to the Witches.'

Eyes groaned and ran his hands through his hair.

'Okay, well at least we know. What else?'

'He claims to remain loyal to us, but I have a bad feeling about him. I think we may need to terminate the agreement.'

Eyes nodded. He had never trusted the tricky demon, nor did he care for the perversity it exhibited. He had no problem whatsoever in ending the foul creature. 'He wants to be at the battle,' Claws added.

'I see, well that might provide an opportunity for him to get caught in the crossfire.' Eyes noted the nods of agreement from the rest of the pack.

'I spent the afternoon with Spark,' Wind Talker said. 'We have some ideas for things that might help. She suggested some enhancements to the battle van as well, which I think could prove very interesting. I'd like to discuss them with Tar Peter.'

'What sort of enhancements?' Claws asked. Eyes hid a smile of bemusement as Claws looked at Wind Talker with a mix of curiosity and offence.

'Well, it's possible to get constructs to inhabit things, like that phone we found. They can use their influence to enhance machinery. A demolition construct, for example, might ensure that the front of a van has the strength and durability of a wrecking ball.'

Claws' eyes lit up, and Eyes cleared his throat to bring their attention back to the moment.

'Excellent,' he said with a wry smile.

'Sky Runner and I are coordinating patrols for the borders,' Stalker said. 'She's had no luck convincing Rust to let her join me on incursions, but she'll gather what intelligence she can through her networks and border patrols. I shared what we knew about the factory. Do you want to let the Wrecking Crew know about the walking dead?'

'Not right now, I want a little more information first. We need to focus on the task in hand. Wind Talker, what do you see?'

Wind Talker grasped the pendant around his neck, clasping the copper eye in his bare hand. His eyes drifted out of focus and he turned towards the park. A muscle in his cheek twitched, and he released the talisman.

'A wall of thorns, at least eight feet high. There's no way through. The thorns are covered in blood.' His demeanour didn't falter, he was as composed as ever, but Eyes sensed his apprehension.

'Well then, we'll have to enter the park here and take another look at the inside from there.' He led them under the trees that lined the roadside, away from the reach of the street lamps. He nodded to Wind Talker, who once again looked across the veil. The colour drained from his face and he quickly released the talisman. 'What's wrong?' Eyes asked anxiously.

'It's, well, it's not looking good. Are you sure you want to do this?' Wind Talker spluttered.

'Yes. Tell me more.'

'Here.' Wind Talker lifted the cord over his head and passed the talisman to Eyes. He took hold of the copper eye and his vision instantly blurred. The dark park around them faded, and imposed over it was a jungle of twisted, bloody thorns. Eerie red light cast deep shadows that were filled with glowing eyes and tiny, scuttling movements. Eyes refused to be perturbed. He walked slowly forwards, searching for a clearing. He felt his pack following close behind as he edged towards the little boating lake. In Hepethia there was no lake, but there was a dip in the ground and the slopes into it were bare. In the very centre, where in the human world there was an island with a copse of trees on it, was a similar island. On it was an enormous rose bush, with hundreds of thorny tendrils reaching out from it. It wasn't in bloom, early March was too soon, but it was very much alive and writhing around. It almost seemed to be conducting the orchestra of fae and demons around it.

'I'll bet that's Crimson Thorns,' Eyes whispered, as he passed the talisman back to Wind Talker. His pack mate looked for himself and nodded in agreement.

Weaver suddenly gasped and clapped a hand to her mouth.

'What is it?' Eyes asked, turning to her and glancing around them for signs of something she might have seen.

'Don't you remember? It was about five years ago now, they found bodies on the island.' She raised a hand and pointed towards the little island. 'A dozen girls had been raped and sliced up. My mum rang me daily for weeks and wouldn't let my sister out of the house. I was at university at the time and there were warnings up all around the halls of residence and university buildings, urging the female students to avoid going anywhere alone. I don't think they ever caught the person who did it.'

'There's a very good chance that's how this place was created. It would take a horrific act to shape Hepethia like this.' Wind Talker stared towards the island, half transfixed in horror and half in wonder.

Eyes remembered the case, he had been keeping an eye on it, eager to prosecute the perpetrator once caught. It had been just before he and Chloe decided to start a family. Could the Witches have done this? Crimson Thorns was reportedly allied with them. Had they made this home for her? Perhaps they had influenced a human to do the deed, rather than dirty their hands directly. That was perhaps more their style.

'We cross here and confront Crimson Thorns.' Eyes gave a firm nod. He glanced around at the others, hesitation hung on all of their faces.

'What are you hoping to achieve?' Weaver asked.

'Don't you remember what The Orchard told us? She said that Crimson Thorns would block our path to defeat our greatest foe. I want to remove that block. Maybe we can get her to ally with us, or maybe we'll have to kill her. Either way, I want her out of the way.' He saw their reluctant expressions and heard their thoughts inside his head, urging him not to blunder. 'Hey, guys, we can do this. I understand your reservation, really, but I feel strongly that The Orchard was giving us a clue, she was trying to help us. We can't ignore Crimson Thorns, or she could seriously jeopardise our plans. Trust me.'

Stalker nodded and took a step towards him.

'I trust you.'

'Thanks,' he said with a smile. He looked expectantly at the others. One by one they softened and agreed to follow him. He led them across the veil, stepping towards the lake. His foot landed on dry land in Hepethia. The gentle slope down towards the island was soft, the loose soil shifted under his shoe, but he didn't lose his footing. He stepped carefully down the slope, his pack close behind him.

The thorn bushes behind them rustled and a squawk rent the air. He stopped and looked anxiously over his shoulder. A huge black bird took flight from one of the bushes. It flew low over their heads, straight for the island. Eyes kept his gaze fixed on it as it soared right into the tangle of thorns on the island. The whole island shuddered. There was movement all around the edge of the dip. Small creatures darted out of the shadows, their red eyes glowing and casting an unsettling light into the empty space. Many of the creatures were like oversized stick insects, their limbs twitching and jerking as they hung eagerly at the edge of the slope.

Eyes took a step forwards, the earth moved under his feet again, but he pressed on carefully.

'Who dares enter here?' A voice rustled up from the island.

'Eyes,' Wind Talker hissed at his ear. 'That is Crimson Thorns, but there are dual personalities. There's a fae and a demon in her.'

'So we might be able to kill the demon and save the fae?' Eyes whispered back, not taking his eyes off the squirming island.

'Yes,' Wind Talker replied. 'But we'll have to separate them first.'

Draw out the demon, Weaver's voice whispered in Eyes' mind. *Tempt it.*

Eyes picked his way carefully on down the slope.

'Lightning Lords,' he called out as they got nearer. 'We come to parley.'

'Why should I parley with abominations of Artemis?' The voice was layered, like multiple voices speaking at once. Eyes could sense now what Wind Talker had gleaned with his special ability.

The demon is Slice-of-Flesh, Wind Talker thought.

'Can we speak to Slice-of-Flesh alone, please?' Eyes asked. He came to a halt just out of reach of her thorny tendrils. The whole island was writhing, and the air was filled with the scent of damp soil and the metallic tang of blood.

Wind Talker was fishing in his bag for something, Claws and Stalker moved in front of him to conceal him from the demonic plant before them.

'We are never apart,' the rustling voice replied. 'We are one. What do you want?'

'Are you allied with the Witches?' Claws called out.

'Ahh, if only life were so simple,' Crimson Thorns replied. 'Simple creatures with your clear divides. One side fights another side, one wins, one loses.'

'We don't see the world that way,' Claws said, a small smile tugging on his lips.

'It's infinitely more complex than that. People are complicated, conflicted. They do bad things in the name of a good cause, they make mistakes, they redeem themselves. Perhaps we have more in common than you would like to think?'

'Perhaps,' the creature said with a hiss. Eyes looked down at the roots bursting out of the ground. Snakes were slithering up out of the soil. The imps around the edge of the pit were growing agitated, eager for a fight.

Hurry, he urged the others.

Wind Talker and Weaver moved behind him, hurriedly working together.

'My pets are so very hungry,' Crimson Thorns whispered, the threat clear in her voice.

'Did the Witches have a hand in creating this place? And you?' Claws asked, a hint of desperation creeping into his voice.

'Agents of Megaira were here, I believe you call them Witches, yes. They brought a sacrifice for The Hunger. That was ever such a long time ago.' There was pain in her voice. Eyes saw a trickle of moisture running down one of the tall stems at the heart of the mass of tangled thorns. He sensed Stalker moving closer to Crimson Thorns, swift and silent in the dark, shielded by her shadow allies.

'Did they hurt you?' Eyes asked.

'They made me stronger.' The demonic fae seemed to double in size, as its hundreds of whip-like tendrils uncurled. Eyes held his ground, his heart hammering in his chest. Out of the corner of his eye, he saw Stalker duck under a sweeping vine and dive for Crimson Thorns' tangled roots. She thrust something from her hands into the mass, then rolled out of the way of the vine as it slashed the air.

Eyes took a few steps back to where Wind Talker and Weaver stood, just out of reach of the vines. Claws followed, not taking his eyes off the plant creature on the island.

'What was that?' Eyes asked, raising his voice over the mounting cacophony of the screeching demons all around them.

'A charcoal poultice, to draw out the infection,' Wind Talker bellowed over the din.

Stalker sprinted up the slope towards them. She was covered in dirt and had a cut on her cheek.

Crimson Thorns lashed out and writhed frantically, a sickening scream issued from her. The snakes were fleeing the area, slithering up the slope and heading for the cover of the bushes at the top. The red-eyed imps were in disarray, some of them scurrying away, others lurking nearby, waiting for orders. A vine whipped out of the darkness and struck Stalker on the back. Her eyes widened in the instant that she was suspended mid-stride, then she fell flat on her face. The vine coiled around her waist and tugged her back down the slope.

'No!' Eyes shouted, taking a reflexive step towards Crimson Thorns. Stalker was dragged along the dirt and then hoisted up into the air. *Shift*, he urged. A moment later, Stalker disappeared suddenly and the vine dropped back to the bush. Eyes searched the black sky for a sign of his pack mate, but she was either too small to be seen, or something had gone wrong. His chest felt tight as he forced himself to breathe.

There was a soft thud right behind him and he wheeled around to see Stalker standing there, casually brushing dirt off her clothes and face.

'Moth?' Weaver asked, totally un-phased.

'Moth,' Stalker said with a nod.

Eyes turned his attention back to the writhing, screeching mass of plant life. The demon flailed around as the poultice worked its magic. Shadows seemed to rip themselves from each vine, doubling the number of thrashing tendrils. It was impossible to tell where the shrieking was coming from, it echoed all around them. Finally, with an ear-splitting cry, Slice-of-Flesh was separated from Crimson Thorns. A dark, dripping shadow lurched sideways and stumbled on the slope. The imps that were gathered around the top swarmed down and covered it, their evil eyes glinting red in the dark.

On the island, Crimson Thorns shrank back to the size of a normal rose bush. Her stalks strong and green, her thorns no longer dripping blood. She seemed to sigh, and a ripple flowed out from her, up the slopes and into the bushes around the park. A faint light radiated from her, and the scent of freshly-cut grass overpowered the lingering trace of death.

Eyes led the pack cautiously towards Slice-of-Flesh and his swarm. The imps chattered quietly in a language he couldn't understand. Wind Talker held his knife out and slashed at the air. He tossed a handful of herbs over the demon and it squealed underneath its hoard of imps.

'We cast you out, Slice-of-Flesh. We draw you out of this world, and send you back to the realm from which you came.' Wind Talker slashed at the air again and a tear appeared in the veil. Eyes caught a glimpse of shadows moving beyond the rip and a horrifying shriek filled the air as the heap of demons were sucked through it into their own realm. Wind Talker quickly repaired the veil, sewing it back together with arm gestures and a whispered chant.

Eyes turned back to Crimson Thorns and made his way carefully towards her.

'Thank you,' the fae sighed.

'You lived with that demon for a long time. How do you feel?' Claws asked.

'Tainted, but I will heal with time.' Her voice rustled like dry leaves, but it was one lone voice now. 'Why did you come here? Why did you free me?'

'We were warned that you were in trouble,' Eyes replied, twisting the truth a little. 'We wanted to help.'

'You are not like the others.'

'The others? The Witches?' Claws asked.

'I don't know, I don't remember.'

'What can you tell us about the Witches?' Claws pressed on gently.

'Beware the Green Man!' Crimson Thorns suddenly stretched up and out, a shudder going right through every stalk and thorny vine. Eyes stepped back reflexively, but the fae settled back down and gave a smaller shake, as if clearing her head.

'The Green Man?' Wind Talker asked.

'He walks with the Witches. They will invoke him at the equinox and he will be at full strength, master of life and death, lord of rebirth.'

'I see,' Eyes said softly. 'How long is it until the equinox?' he asked, turning to Weaver.

'Eight days,' she replied solemnly.

'Can you tell us anything else about him or them?'

Claws urged.

'They corrupt all, they serve the Envious Anger of Megaira.'

'Is that the Hunger?' Stalker asked. Eyes thought of the murdered girls, saw flashes of the images from the news coverage of the island surrounded in crime scene tape and the police cars parked on the grass by the lake. Another memory bothered him, too vague and distant to recall properly.

'No,' Crimson Thorns said, her voice jingling softly like distant bells. 'Megaira is a Fury, one of three. The others are Alecto, the Never Ending, and Tisiphone, Voice of Revenge. The Green Man is bound to Megaira, just as the Witches are.'

'Then what is the Hunger?' Claws asked. Eyes glanced quickly between his confused face and the faceless fae.

Where have I heard this before?

From Jorogumo, Stalker replied. He shot a sideways look at her and saw her chewing the inside of her cheek.

'I don't know. I just know that it's coming, and feasting.' Crimson Thorns gave another shudder, dropping a few leaves. 'They made a sacrifice to it here, urging its arrival.'

'Years ago? And it's only coming now?' Eyes asked, frowning.

'I cannot explain it,' the fae whispered. 'It is not a demon I understand, and I have never understood your kind.'

'Thank you,' Claws said, bowing his head.

'Yes, thank you for answering our questions,' Eyes added with a resigned sigh.

'Not at all,' the fae replied. 'Thank you for freeing me

from that evil being. Good luck.'

Eyes led the Lightning Lords back up the slope. The wall of thorns remained, but the demons were gone and nothing but small fae remained to serve their mistress. The Lightning Lords crossed the veil back into the human world. The park was pitch black and deserted. He cast a wary glance at Stalker, then Wind Talker. The tension between them kept them from meeting each others' eyes.

'Sorry,' Stalker muttered. Eyes frowned, he still hadn't connected all of the dots, but clearly the others had.

'You were angry,' Wind Talker replied. 'You didn't know that the Hunger was something separate from the spider. The main thing is that you rescued me, you got me out of there before it could sacrifice me.'

The final cog clunked into place and Eyes let out a huge sigh.

'Of course,' he said, a little too pleased with himself. The others glowered at him. 'So the spider demon was serving the Hunger, and so are the Witches?'

'It looks that way,' Claws replied. 'Or at least, they were five years ago when they made this mess. Maybe they aren't anymore, maybe they turned over a new leaf?'

'Guided by the Green Man?' Eyes suggested. 'Well, either way, we have a week to intervene before they bring him up to full strength. I would hazard a guess he's pretty powerful, and responsible for the walking dead girls, given his association with rebirth. We don't want to risk waiting too long and having a demigod to deal with as well as a pack of Furies. Let's get to work.'

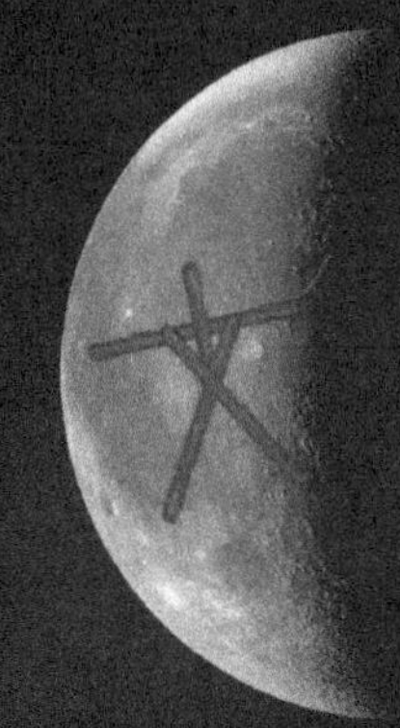

Chapter Thirty Three

Stalker-of-Night's-Shadow

The noise was maddening. Constant, inane chatter that crowded Stalker's mind. She closed her eyes and took slow, deep breaths. The vial around her neck seemed to be having no effect. A vein in her temple throbbed ominously. It had been two days since she retrieved the tooth talisman and almost every moment since had been like this. Even when it wasn't against her skin, but in a pocket or bag on her person, it seemed to heighten her adrenaline levels. She lifted the cord from around her neck and shoved the necklace into her bag at the side of the room.

Instantly, the noise in her head subsided and she could think again. Right now she needed to focus on teaching her class and not injuring any youngsters. But she needed to figure out how to use the talisman safely. It could be vital in a fight, and she had to admit that she was looking forwards to confronting the Witch that had once owned it.

The class fell silent as Stalker moved to the front. It

wasn't yet dark outside, and the dull grey sky filled the huge windows behind the group of teenagers. Stalker slapped a smile onto her face and began the class.

After they had warmed up, Stalker had them practising some blocking moves and she moved among the students to check their form. The calming talisman against her chest had nothing blocking it now, and she was able to hold back her strength in the way in which she was now well accustomed. Teaching was almost easy these days. Stalker smiled and laughed with her students, they felt comfortable enough to tease her from time to time, the way they used to before she ever changed. It had been a struggle to get here, but she felt some satisfaction at having achieved a balance that she was happy with.

She got through three classes that evening, and as the last group filed out to enthusiastic analysis of the class, she went back to her bag to retrieve the tooth. She ran her fingers over it and turned it over in her hands, examining every tiny groove in the yellowing surface. She felt her pulse picking up the longer she studied it.

A presence in the doorway dragged her from her reverie, and she looked up to see Wind Talker standing there uncomfortably.

'Hi, come on in,' she said, waving him into the studio.

'What did you want to see me for?' he asked, moving over to her.

'I need your help figuring out how to use this safely.' She passed the talisman to him. He looked at it closely and lifted it up to let it spin on the cord.

'Its name is Savaging Fury. I'm guessing it increases your adrenaline levels?'

'Yeah, just a bit,' she replied sarcastically. She heard Ron locking his office door at the end of the hall and dashed out of the studio to see him. 'Hey Ron, I'm still here but I can lock up for you when I'm done.'

'That would be great, Ariana, thank you.' He tossed a thick bunch of keys to her, which she caught easily, then he set off down the stairs to the exit. She went back to her pack mate and dumped the keys with her things.

'Show me,' Wind Talker said, passing the talisman back to her. She took it and put it around her neck.

'Okay,' she said, nerves causing a shiver to go through her. This was a training dojo, she rationalised, she was simply training in a new discipline. The strip lights on the ceiling felt brighter under the influence of the talisman, the traffic in the street was louder. Wind Talker smelled as though he hadn't showered in weeks. 'It amplifies all my senses,' she explained. 'It's like the Agrius is closer to the surface.'

'That's interesting.'

'No, no it's more like someone else's Agrius. I don't feel connected to it.'

'Like someone's controlling you?' Wind Talker asked, concern flickering into his voice.

'No, there's no one in control.' She started pacing the room. Why didn't he understand? He was getting it all wrong! 'No, it's like the first time I changed, before I understood my beast. It feels alien.'

'I see. I think that probably means that it needs attuning to you, it's still attuned to its previous owner at the moment, or perhaps to no one. We'll need a demon to help, fear I think. I'd say the purpose of the talisman is to make the wearer more fearsome. We can get it focused to you so you won't feel like this, and you should be able to use it then without feeling less in control.'

'Okay,' Stalker agreed, nodding.

She switched off the lights, and rubbed her throbbing temples. Wind Talker got some supplies out of his bag. He lit a black candle and passed it to Stalker. The flame sent eerie shadows dancing across the room as the candle shook in her unsteady hands.

'You okay?' Wind Talker asked, as he lit a smudge stick.

'Fine,' she snapped. Wind Talker eyed her warily, which only frustrated her more. He walked in a circle around her, wafting the smudge stick around. Its sickly fumes made Stalker gag.

'Fear and darkness, we call on your assistance,' Wind Talker uttered into the still room.

The shadows at Stalker's feet seemed to darken, the flickering candle went out and a tendril of smoke rose from the wick. There was the faint clink of metal, and Stalker's hackles immediately went up. Her head whipped one way then the other, her eyes desperately searching the dark for the presence she felt.

'Well, well, well. What have we here?' The voice was deep and dangerous, and agonisingly familiar.

'Knight-of-Shadowed-Fear,' Wind Talker said, his voice trembling slightly. 'I didn't expect you to answer.'

'Really? It felt as though you were addressing me directly.'

He was right behind Stalker, she felt his breath on the back of her neck. A sudden shiver ran down her back and she dropped the candle with a clatter to the floor. 'A fine young spine you have there,' the demon sighed.

Oh God, Stalker's inner voice cried. Her heart pounded violently and she felt bile rise in her throat.

'You asked for assistance,' the Knight said. His voice sent a tremor through Stalker's veins, but she stood paralysed, unable to turn to look at him, or move away from him.

'Stalker has a talisman that needs a fear demon to attune to her. It will allow her to strike fear into her opponents with her impressive might. Can you help?' Wind Talker's voice was barely above a whisper and his breath left a little mist in the cold air.

Wind Talker! she snapped. *What is he doing to me?*

Her body began to convulse. She felt the Knight's heavy, plated hand on her shoulder. Each finger digging into her flesh. He inhaled deeply at her neck, his empty helmet mere millimetres from her ear.

The tooth felt white hot against her skin, compared to the ice cold air that the Knight had brought with him. The Agrius inside that didn't belong to her began to howl.

'Stalker! No!' Wind Talker cried out.

But it was too late. Her body wrenched away from the Knight's clutches, and she fell onto all fours. It was crawling up inside her, the Beast was tearing its way out. Her whole body shook and she could hear nothing but the pounding of her pulse. Fur erupted all over her body, and her limbs cracked as they doubled in length. 'What did you do?' a faraway voice screamed.

Stalker leaped away from the demon, lost to the Agrius. She bounded across the floor, splintering the wooden boards with each thunderous pound of her huge paws. She reached the fire exit and ripped the door from its hinges as easily as if it were paper.

The cool air of the night rushed over her fur as she leaped down onto the street below. She landed with a crunch and cracked the tarmac. Without a backward glance, Stalker galloped through the city, consumed by the mindless Agrius. Behind her, a flickering light rose behind the windows of the dojo, and smoke slithered out of the open fire exit.

She ran for a few miles before skidding to a halt in the middle of a large park. The Agrius released her and she fell to the ground, shrinking slowly back into her human form. She pressed her cheek to the cool grass and closed her eyes. She felt sick and dizzy. Eventually her eyes peeled open and she risked lifting her head to look around.

The dark sky overhead was cloudy and the glow from the city's lights coloured the clouds. The park was vast, with woods along the edge up a shallow slope from where she lay. She knew this park. She groaned and rubbed her face with her hands. She was right in the heart of Fenwick; the wood that she could see was where the Witches had held Weaver.

It was very likely that her scent was far from suppressed when she stormed the border in the form of the alien Agrius. She took a few moments to draw in the power of the night around her, masking her scent from other shifters and hiding her in the shadows. She shifted silently into her fox form and trotted swiftly for the cover of the trees.

She made her way towards civilisation, running over

the events of the evening in her mind as she jogged. The Knight had had a very powerful effect on her. Had he been able to trigger the talisman? Or did she simply react strongly to his fear-inducing presence? The most troubling thing was that she felt drawn to him. Her alliance with the dark was perhaps exerting some influence. Maybe he was drawn to her too?

Stalker glanced around, suddenly aware that she wasn't concentrating on where she was going. There was the scent of a Witch on the air, then another. Startled, she ran for cover in a garden. Voices reached her from nearby, and a van door slid shut. Carefully, she picked her way to the garden gate and peeked out between the wrought iron struts. She was almost directly opposite the crematorium, and a large van idled at the kerb.

The Alpha of the Witches, Gaze-of-Purity, stood by the van and a gormless-looking driver sat behind the wheel staring at the road. Stalker could just make out two other figures moving in the shadows on the other side of the perimeter wall of the grounds of the crematorium. Two Witches that she didn't know by sight emerged from the dark, carrying heavy bags that weighed them down.

'We move the rest tomorrow,' the Alpha barked. 'Patrol the south-western border tonight, both of you. I want that breach found.'

Stalker swallowed, that's where she would have entered Fenwick on her trek from the dojo. The burdened Witches set off walking towards the park, while the Alpha climbed into the van beside the glazed-over driver. Stalker suspected he was not in complete control of his faculties, a puppet of the Witches.

The van was about to set off somewhere. Stalker snarled in frustration, she had to confirm what they were moving, though dead bodies would be a very good guess. She shifted into the form of a moth and fluttered swiftly across the road and crawled into the back of the van through the small gap in the doors. She landed and shifted silently back into her human form.

A stack of lumpy shapes in thick plastic body bags was piled against the wall of the van. Stalker covered her mouth and looked around. There was no window between her and the cab, no sign of a camera either. She breathed a silent sigh of relief and crept to the pile of bags. She poked one carefully, inside was something heavy and as hard as she would expect a dead body to be. She kept her nose and mouth covered with the sleeve of her jacket as she very carefully and slowly unzipped the top bag.

The smell of death greeted her and she gagged. The van lurched into motion and she lost her balance, staggering slightly. Grabbing the side of the van, Stalker steadied herself and peered into the partially unzipped bag. There was indeed a body inside, recently deceased, or well preserved at a guess. She hastily zipped the bag back up and shifted back into moth form to wait out the ride to wherever they were going.

When the van pulled to a halt a short while later, Stalker clung to the ceiling, her wings twitching slightly. She heard gates creaking open and the van rolled slowly forwards and down a slope. They were at the factory! Stalker flew to the doors and squeezed out through them. She didn't want to end up trapped inside the Witches' headquarters. The night air was cool and there was a strong breeze. Stalker pushed off from the back of the van and soared into the sky over the factory. Once she was high enough to not be seen against the cloudy sky, she shifted into owl form and flew swiftly back to St. Mark's.

Why were the Witches moving bodies from the crematorium to the factory? A pillar of smoke caught her eye and she flew towards it. A heavy feeling sunk in her stomach as she flew over the burning dojo and the memories from earlier in the evening came flooding back to her.

Wind Talker! She flew lower over the burning building. The fire engines were already there working on the fire. There were people in the street, pointing and looking worried. Ron was there, his hands clutching his balding head. There was no sign of Wind Talker, and she felt her connection with him was intact. She flew higher and soared to Grove Street, landing in the dark alley that they usually used to change form. She shifted and ran to the house, bursting in through the door to hear the raised voices of her pack mates.

'I'm here! I'm all right!' she called out as she ran down the hall. Wind Talker grabbed her and hugged her so tightly that he was in danger of suffocating her. She patted his back and he released her.

'I'm so glad you're okay,' he said breathlessly.

'Likewise,' she replied. 'I saw the fire. Was that you?'

'I had to cover the damage you'd done to the place. I'm so sorry.' He really seemed to mean it. His cool demeanour was quite abandoned and he chewed his lip anxiously. She nodded and tried to give him a smile. She looked around the room and noted the absence of Weaver and Claws.

'They went looking for you,' Eyes explained, seeing her confusion. 'Wind Talker told us what happened and which direction you ran, so they went to see if they could track you. I'll call Claws now.'

He drifted into the living room, his phone to his ear. Stalker and Wind Talker exchanged awkward glances.

'Do you know what happened?' Stalker asked, her voice trembling slightly. 'Why I lost it like that?'

'I don't know exactly,' he replied, sitting heavily at the table. He clutched a glass of whiskey. Stalker joined him and poured herself one. She felt her heart begin to settle as she drank the warming liquid. Her hand went quickly to the talismans around her neck and she tugged off the tooth and slid it across the table. 'That's probably wise. I don't think the Knight unleashed any powers on you. I think the talisman just had you really fired up already and the Agrius took over when we introduced fear. I'm so sorry.'

He picked up the necklace and examined it carefully. He poked it and it swung back and forth, spinning on the cord.

'Does it have a demon inside it?' Stalker asked, unable to wrench her eyes off the tooth.

'Yes.'

'I want to be able to use it like the Witch did. I want control over it.'

'We were on the right track. I think we could try again, just not anywhere in the human world.' He cast her a wry smile and she let out a nervous laugh.

'What happened after I... left?' Stalker asked.

'The Knight laughed and disappeared. I ran to the

fire exit and saw which way you were heading. The room was pretty badly torn up, big sections of the floor were smashed, and the door, obviously. So I collected your things and started a fire.' He dropped his eyes to the table. 'I'm sorry.'

Stalker felt a strange surge of anger and gratitude at the same time. Her place of work had burned down, she would be out of a job. Ron, who she thought of fondly, had had his business destroyed. But the shifter population would be concealed. There weren't many plausible explanations for a little dojo in St. Mark's being ripped apart like that.

Eyes returned from the living room and sat down next to Stalker, drawing his hands together on the table.

'So, what happened? Where did you end up? Claws says they tracked you very easily to Fenwick. Seems you left a few bent lamp posts in your wake.'

'Oh shit,' Stalker whispered, closing her eyes. 'I lost consciousness, I had no idea. I woke up near the woods. I was going to come straight back, but I saw the Witches and followed them. Eyes, they're doing something very wrong. They're taking bodies from the crematorium and moving them to the factory I told you about.'

'What?' Wind Talker snapped. 'That's... that's just... no.' He stood up suddenly, his chair scraping back across the floor and he strode from the room and stomped up the stairs.

'Okay,' Eyes said slowly. 'I wonder if Last-Breath-Echoes can help us puzzle this out. If they can resurrect their own from the dead, maybe they can raise others. Maybe they're raising an undead army.'

Stalker nodded solemnly. She hadn't wanted to face

that possibility.

'If they are, then they're very quiet soldiers. I didn't hear or smell a crowd of people, dead or alive. Although I didn't go inside, I couldn't risk getting caught.'

'Quite right,' he said, nodding firmly. He reached out and took her hand. 'Are you okay?'

'A bit shaken and confused, but yeah.'

Wind Talker came clomping back down the stairs and returned to the kitchen with an open notebook in his hands. He flicked through the pages, searching for something. He paused and ran his finger over the crinkled paper. He passed the book to Eyes and dropped back into his chair. Stalker watched the whole exchange with a bemused smile.

'There are stories of shifters who've messed about with the dead,' Wind Talker explained, as Eyes scanned the tiny scrawling writing in the book. 'Flames mentioned them in his notes. That book escaped the theft, it was in my bag at the time. It's strictly against the code of the Furies to meddle with death. We don't know much about them, sure, but things have been figured out over the centuries. They're not allowed to disrupt the dead because it interferes with their transition to the underworld, which would piss off Hades.'

Stalker knew she needed to talk to Rhys about this if they were ever going to understand any of it fully. As his name and face flickered through her thoughts, she noticed Eyes glance at her with an expression of curiosity and confusion. She shoved Rhys out of her mind and cleared her throat.

'So they could be going against the other Furies, then?'

she asked.

'Could be,' Wind Talker replied. 'Or the Furies could be changing their beliefs.'

Stalker yawned and rubbed her eyes. Academia had never been her strength.

'Go get some rest,' Eyes ordered. 'You can catch up with the others in the morning.'

Stalker left the table and wandered into the living room to curl up on her pile of cushions. She dreamed of Nyx, the goddess of the night, giving birth to the Furies under a cloak of darkness.

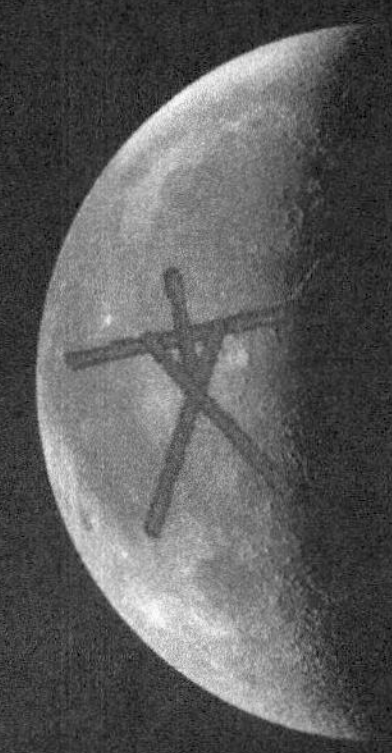

Chapter Thirty Four

'They're doing what?' Last-Breath-Echoes narrowed her eyes, her voice uncharacteristically high and tight.

'They're taking bodies from the crematorium,' Stalker repeated.

'What are they giving the families instead of the ashes then?' Echoes asked shrewdly.

'We have no idea,' Eyes replied. They were all sitting in the tiny living room of 32 Grove Street, still fairly early in the morning. Last-Breath-Echoes fiddled with the rings on her slender fingers and stared at each of the Lightning Lords in turn.

'We were hoping you would have some way of tracking a body through the crematorium and seeing what happens to it,' Weaver said softly. 'I've heard of such things happening before, with magic.'

'Yes, it can be done. I've never done it though. I can try.' Echoes sighed. Her eyes returned to their usual wideness.

'I have a body in the morgue now. I can recommend Fenwick to the family.'

'Can you think of any reason why they might be stealing human bodies?' Stalker urged.

'It's just not the done thing. I know some of us study death very carefully, and get closer to it than others, but we don't disrespect the dead. Shifters, despite our nature, find it hard to change traditions. We managed to adapt to the human custom of cremation from burial, because in Caerton we're influenced a lot by the Norse burial rituals, as well as the Greek and Egyptian ones. But the Furies aren't, so I would imagine it was a lot harder for them. I assumed that the Witches were just using the crematorium in Fenwick to get their own home for their traditional burial. But it sounds as if they have a more controlling interest in the business of disposing of the dead.'

'Maybe they see themselves as rescuing those destined for cremation and burying them according to Greek tradition?' Weaver said, hope in her eyes.

'I wouldn't expect them to care about the human dead,' Wind Talker said, shaking his head. 'They want to rule humanity, not hide from them. They see humans as cattle.'

'I know.' Weaver sighed.

'I'd better get to work,' Echoes said, standing up. She swept from the room, catching her thumbnail on the door frame on her way out, Stalker noticed, adding another little mark alongside the others from her previous visits. Stalker wondered whether she left a tally everywhere she went.

'Thank you,' Eyes said as he saw their guest out. He returned to the others, his expression business-like. 'I want patrols along the border all day. Double up as much as possible. The Witches may come looking for trouble after Stalker's incident last night.'

Stalker's phone started ringing and everyone looked at her.

'I don't recognise the number,' she said, looking at her phone. 'Hello?'

'Is this Ms Yates?' a cool voice enquired.

'Speaking.'

'This is PC Hutchins from St. Mark's Police Station. Are you aware of an incident at your place of work last night?'

Stalker swallowed hard and looked up at the others, her eyes wide. They had clearly heard and returned her gaze with mixed expressions of apprehension.

'No,' Stalker lied. 'What sort of incident?'

'A fire. We'd like you to come in and answer a few questions. We understand you were the last person to leave the premises.'

'Of course. Now?'

'Yes please,' the constable replied. His voice firm.

'I'll be right there.'

'Thank you.'

Stalker hung up the phone and stared at Eyes.

'I'll come with you,' he said without hesitation. He grabbed his jacket from the hall and she followed him out, not daring to look at the others. Wind Talker caught hold of her arm as she passed him.

'I hope they can't pin it on you. I really do. I'm sorry.'

She shook her head.

'It's okay. You did what you had to do to protect our

secret.'

She followed Eyes to his car and climbed in. He drove carefully, keeping to the speed limit and observing every traffic signal, clearly on his best driving behaviour. Stalker tried to smile but found the muscles in her cheeks frozen. 'What do I say?' she asked quietly.

'Stay as close to the truth as possible. I'll make sure you don't answer anything incriminating.' Eyes didn't look at her the whole drive to the little police station near the telecoms tower.

They parked in the small car park at the back of the big old house that now served the community as an outpost of Caerton's constabulary. 'Ready?' Eyes asked, finally looking at her.

'Yeah. I'm glad you're with me.'

'No worries, it's what I'm here for.'

They climbed out of his four-wheel drive and he led her into the station. Her palms were sweating and she felt a cold, wet sensation in her throat that usually signalled her to reach for a bucket.

The hallway they entered was painted a vile green, which matched the extremely dated linoleum floor. The décor did nothing to settle Stalker's churning stomach. Eyes strode over to a desk, behind which sat a dopey eyed and portly police officer.

'Can I help you?' the mild-mannered man asked.

'I'm Martin Davison. I have Ms Yates here, to see PC Hutchins.' Eyes was putting on his best barrister persona.

The officer behind the desk nodded and got up from his seat. He ambled into the room beyond. Stalker clucked her tongue impatiently. His lack of urgency clashed with her wriggling desire to get this interview over with as quickly as possible. Eyes placed a steady hand on her shoulder and she felt a wave of calm flow through her. She took a deep breath.

'Ms Yates?' The cool voice from the phone rang out across the reception.

'That's me,' Stalker said, looking straight at the tall, young police officer. He had neat, blond hair and a soft face. He approached, a file in his hand, and looked warily at Eyes. 'This is my friend, Martin Davison.'

'I'm a barrister,' Eyes said, extending his hand. PC Hutchins shook it firmly. 'I'm just here to support my friend. I'm sure we don't have an issue. Do we?'

'Not at all. Shall we go in here?' He held out a hand towards an interview room and Eyes led the way inside. Stalker's insides squirmed as she took a seat next to Eyes. The police officer sat opposite them and opened the file on the table in front of him. He clicked a ballpoint pen and wrote the date at the top of a blank sheet of paper. 'Your employer, Ron Hammell, informed us that you were the last person to leave the premises last night. Is that correct?'

'Yes,' Stalker said. She discreetly wiped her hands on her jeans under the table.

'Is that a normal occurrence?'

'Not really, no. I stayed after my last class to practice some moves, so I offered to lock up.' She glanced at Eyes, who was totally impassive, his eyes fixed on the police officer.

'Isn't it difficult to practice martial arts on one's own?' The officer raised a glossy eyebrow.

'I practice Banshay,' she replied coolly. 'Sword art. It's a sort of solo dance. I can show you a clip if you like?' She started to get her phone out, but he raised a hand to stop her.

'That won't be necessary. Do your swords require a license?'

'We are not here to discuss Ariana's personal possessions,' Eyes interjected.

Hutchins narrowed his eyes slightly, but nodded his head. Stalker bristled. She had been happy to answer the question, as her swords were perfectly legal. But she knew Eyes was just trying to protect her, so she let it go.

'So, Mr Hammell left you alone on the premises at approximately ten past eight. Is that correct?'

'Yes, I think so. My last class finished at eight.'

'And what time did you remain there until?' He scribbled down her answers in the file as he asked the next question.

'I'm not sure. I didn't check the time. I didn't stay long, though.' She tried to keep her voice cool and steady, but her hands clenched the sides of her plastic chair.

'And how did you leave?'

'Through the door,' she replied, a slight hint of sarcasm in her voice. The officer raised his eyes from the file. 'I locked up and went home.'

'I see. Did you see anything of concern before or as you left?'

'No, everything seemed totally normal.'

'The initial report suggests that the fire started in the studio that you were teaching in.'

'Oh really?' Stalker said casually. 'I don't know how it

could have happened.'

'We'll know more once the full report comes through. Are you sure you didn't see anyone suspicious in the vicinity of the dojo?' The word "dojo" flopped awkwardly out of his mouth, as if he had never used it before. Stalker tried to stifle a smile.

'No, no one,' she replied.

'I see. Well, I think that's everything for now. We'll contact you if we have any further questions.' Hutchins stood up and closed the file. Eyes got to his feet and Stalker glanced at each of them, surprised that the interview was really over so quickly. She rose from her chair and followed Eyes silently out of the station. Once they were buckled into the car she was finally able to breathe a sigh of relief.

'That wasn't so bad,' she said softly.

'It was just information gathering, I don't think he really suspected you of anything. That might change if the report indicates arson though. We should be prepared for that.'

'Okay,' Stalker replied solemnly.

They arrived back at the house to find Wind Talker and Claws out patrolling. Weaver greeted them as they entered.

'How did it go?'

'Fine. For now.' Stalker dropped onto the sofa and laid her head back on the soft cushion. She closed her eyes and felt the others leave the room. It had been a thoroughly exhausting twenty-four hours and she slipped easily into a shallow sleep.

'Weaver,' Claws snapped, his voice raised. 'Calm down.'

Stalker was yanked from a dreamless sleep; she leapt from the sofa and ran to the doorway. Weaver stood in the kitchen door next to Stalker, her hands on her hips and her nostrils flaring. Stalker felt the intruder before she saw her. Her head swivelled towards the front door, where Claws stood next to the Witch, his hand gripping her shoulder tightly. She had long blond hair, just like Weaver's. Her eyes danced and she wore an arrogant sneer on her red lips. Eyes stood halfway down the hall, his hands raised as if to keep Weaver and the Witch apart.

'What is she doing here?' Weaver snarled.

'She was waiting on the border for me as I was patrolling,' Claws replied, still holding her tightly.

'Oh nice,' the Witch hissed, rolling her blue eyes. 'Talking about me as if I weren't here. I've come to take you home, Teri.'

Weaver's sister, Stalker realised.

'This is my home,' Weaver said, her voice dangerous.

Her sister glanced around the shabby hall in disdain.

'Don't be ridiculous. Come back with me where you belong.'

'You don't understand,' Weaver said with a sigh. Her hands dropped from her hips and her face softened. 'The Witches have poisoned you, Maria. I was lucky to change here and be taken in by these shifters. This is why I begged you to move into Caerton. I didn't want them to get to you.'

'Do you have any idea who our family were?' The Witch scowled. 'The power and prestige we are entitled to is just incredible. The Witches haven't poisoned me. They've shown me who I really am.'

'You *do* know that they abducted Weaver a few months

ago?' Stalker said, glaring at the Witch.

'I know they brought her home and that you kidnapped her back to induct her deeper into your cult.' The Witch spat the last word with such venom that Stalker was momentarily stunned. How could this Witch stand there in their hallway accusing *them* of being the cult?

'They didn't bring me home! They snatched me in the street, they attacked me and then herded me into Fenwick!' Weaver shrieked. She took a threatening step down the hall and Stalker thrust an arm out to stop her going any closer. Weaver snarled at Stalker, but backed down with a calming breath. Her sister shot a filthy look at the pair of them down the hall.

'You're the one who came stomping onto our territory last night,' she said, looking pointedly at Stalker. 'What was that all about?'

'I think you'd better leave,' Eyes said, his voice low and threatening. He took a step towards the Witch and she threw her head back and laughed. 'Claws, escort her back to the border.'

Claws opened the door, without taking his hand off her shoulder.

'We want you back with us, Teri. We should talk alone some time.'

'That's never going to happen,' Eyes said menacingly. Stalker fixed her gaze on Weaver. Her bottom lip trembled slightly, but she remained resolutely silent. Claws steered the Witch out into the street and Eyes walked swiftly to the door to close it.

'Are you okay?' Stalker asked. She took hold of Weaver's shoulders and tried to catch her lowered gaze.

Weaver's body gave a shudder and she burst into tears. Stalker pulled her into a hug and just held her for several minutes. Slowly, Stalker loosened her grip on her pack sister.

'I'm okay, really, I'll be fine,' Weaver said, her voice husky and distant.

'So that was your sister?' Eyes said softly, following the women into the living room.

'The one and only.'

'What did she mean about your family?'

'Our grandparents were in the inner circle of the heir to the throne of Caerton. I knew nothing about what I was before I changed. Our parents raised us away from all of that. There was some big dispute in the family, I think. When the Witches took me I picked up some of what they believed. They really wanted me back within the fold because of my family.'

Stalker felt a long held breath escape her lips with a slight whistle.

'I expect they're treating her like royalty, no wonder she's been convinced by them, and it's understandable she'd want you there too.' Eyes patted Weaver gently on the shoulder. Weaver snorted in reply.

'Don't be fooled. She was here on behalf of them, not for herself.' There was such bitterness in Weaver's voice that it startled Stalker.

'Well, she's gone now.' Stalker tried to reassure Weaver.

'Yes, for now,' Weaver replied. She stood and moved towards the door. She paused and lowered her head. 'But we'll have to kill her.' Weaver swept out of the room, leaving Stalker and Eyes gawking in her wake.

That evening, Stalker met Rhys from work. He greeted her warmly and they walked hand in hand to his house through the narrow residential streets in the heart of the city. Stalker felt awkward and uncomfortable. A nagging sensation of being followed tugged at her, and she kept checking over her shoulder.

'Is something wrong?' he asked as they approached his front door.

'I don't know,' she replied quietly. 'Let's get inside.'

Rhys unlocked the door and held it open for her. She looked back up the street. It was empty. Cars rushed past the end of the road and pedestrians bustled past, but no one had followed them up Rhys's road. She went inside, still not entirely satisfied. Could one of the Witches be tailing her? The problem of the city centre being unclaimed was that anyone could come and go unchecked. But if a Witch was on her tail, they would have had to pass through someone's territory to get this far into the city. It was known to happen, of course, but she tried to reassure herself that at this time of extra vigilance it was more unlikely.

If it wasn't a Witch, why did she feel as though they were being watched? She took a nervous seat on the sofa as Rhys fetched them drinks from the kitchen.

'Were we followed?' he asked, sitting down next to her and passing her a cup of coffee.

'I don't know. I thought I sensed something. But I might just be on edge. Did you feel anything strange?'

'No, nothing.'

'What about your, friend? Can it sense when your

secret is at risk of discovery? Would it warn you?' She sipped her scalding hot drink and eyed Rhys warily. She always felt uncomfortable to mention the demon on his back.

'In theory, yes. He's there to protect me, and part of that is alerting me to a possible problem. But I've never received a warning. Given that I know at least one person has found me out, I'm not sure whether that particular tool works.' He gave her a wry smile.

'It tried to hush me, you know? When I looked across the veil and saw it on you, it raised a finger to his... your lips.' She fumbled over the words, unsure which was correct. 'I think it wanted me to not let on that I had seen it.'

'Maybe, or maybe it just wanted you to keep it secret from others. Maybe it trusted you and that's why it didn't warn me.' He leaned over and kissed her lips softly. He pulled back and Stalker smiled serenely at him, momentarily forgetting her worries. 'Why are you on edge, anyway?'

'A few incidents on top of each other, same old same old really.' She filled him in on her clash with the Agrius, her incursion into Fenwick, the dead bodies and the visit from Weaver's sister. Rhys let out a whistle as she finished.

'So, I guess you want to know more about the Furies?' He raised an eyebrow and stroked her shoulder, teasing and reassuring her at the same time.

'Yeah, I do.'

'Well, I don't know anything about the Witches specifically. But in general, Furies don't care about the human dead. They have no respect for their remains. So it's not really against their code to be meddling with them. But it's fucking gross. I wonder what they're doing.'

'It honestly doesn't bear thinking about,' Stalker replied, shaking her head. 'War's coming.' She glanced at him, unsure how he would react. He nodded solemnly.

'I know, it has been brewing for a long time. It has to come to a head sometime soon.'

'How do you feel about it? I mean, my people fighting your people?'

'They're not my people. They haven't been since they slaughtered my family and I ran from them.' There was a hint of bitterness in his voice, his jaw clenched.

'Do you know why they did it?'

'Not really. You sometimes talk about the Furies as if they're this united force. In some ways they are, they're united under the banner of the heir, but it's a feudal system and there's a lot of fighting between sects. My kin were dedicated to Alecto. I think the pack that slaughtered them were loyal to Megaira. They wore silver jewellery. That's their thing, they hurt themselves for their patron.'

'Like the Witches,' Stalker whispered, not meaning to say anything out loud.

'Oh?' He looked at her sharply, a twitch flickered across his face.

'Could the Witches have been responsible for killing your pack too?' Stalker asked, her mouth hung open at the end of her question. They stared at each other with wide eyes.

'Maybe. I'd need proof.' He shook his head, as if to dismiss the urge for revenge that had surely flared up inside him. Stalker knew the sensation well.

'You still feel like you want to avenge their deaths, then?'

'Sort of. I didn't think so, but just now…. I don't know. They lied to me, they brought me up with some really fucked up ideas. But they were my family. It's really confusing.' He ran his hands through his hair and flopped back against the arm of the sofa.

Stalker thought of the Blue Moon. A hard lump formed in her throat. They had learned things about the Blue Moon that made her skin crawl. This desire to avenge them by killing the Witches had consumed the Lightning Lords for months. Stalker didn't want to face the possibility that the Blue Moon didn't deserve such fierce loyalty.

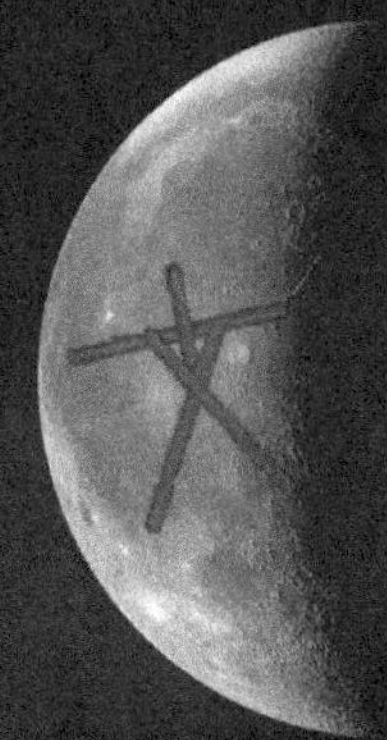

Chapter Thirty Five

Fights-Eyes-Open

'What do you think?' Eyes asked, a hopeful glint in his eye. The demon sucked a breath through his yellow teeth.

'It's almost as if you know exactly how to tempt me.' Tar Peter's voice dripped like honey.

'Can it be done?' Eyes was growing impatient, but he tried to tread carefully, not wishing to push the demon away.

'Oh yes, of course. It's a bold plan. I should have seen it coming the moment you took your car across the veil.' A wry smile pulled at his thin lips. 'I'll find the right construct for your van.' Eyes' heart leaped into his throat but a raised finger from the demon sent it plummeting back down. 'If you and your kin will help the flow of traffic in St. Mark's.'

'How can we do that?' Eyes asked, forcing a polite smile onto his face.

'Well this ridiculous underground network has been the bane of my existence for months now. There are significant roadworks and delays in three locations.'

'I can't stop the railway,' Eyes said with a heavy sigh.

'No, I'm sure you can't. But there must be something you can do to ease the congestion.'

'I'll see what I can do,' Eyes replied. He would have to bring it up with Theodore. 'I'm sure you're right. But this matter with the Witches is somewhat pressing. Can I have some assurance of your help in the meantime?'

The demon tilted his head and narrowed his eyes, which were half hidden in shadow from the brim of his black trilby hat. He gave a curt nod.

'Very well. If nothing else, it'll be interesting to see if you can pull this off.'

Eyes smiled and clapped his hands together.

'Great. Are you able to liaise with the Wrecking Crew? They're putting together the van now.'

'Very well,' the demon replied in his lazy drawl. He sank into the crystal ground and disappeared, leaving behind a small pool of tar.

Eyes ran his fingers through his hair and released an exasperated sigh. One down, one more to go. He shifted into his wolf form and set off through the rocky, crystalline landscape of Hepethia. He skirted the edge of the twisted maze of red brick houses that the Blue Moon had built and sprinted north. The wind blew his long fur back and his paws skimmed over the ground. He felt free and wild running like this. He could relate to Stalker so much more when he shifted form. His thoughts became more primal and his instincts took over. He was liberated from the worries of his human life and the stresses he had been under.

Eyes reached the enormous factories of Northgate, monstrous animated versions of their human world counterparts, with gigantic metal limbs and cogs. It was a haven for the constructs and demon hybrids from the realm of Nidavellir, a home away from home. Eyes picked his way carefully through the battlefield that lay in front of Sparking Clank's territory, his light grey paws treading lightly and avoiding all of the traps. He came to a halt in front of the huge metal doors and shifted into his human form, his neat suit restored. He raised a hand and rapped firmly on the door, the clanging echoed through the vast chamber beyond.

'No offering this time?' A creaking, groaning voice rumbled out of nowhere. The doors slid open, scraping on the concrete. Sparking Clank stood just inside, his vast body of machinery in constant motion. 'Last time you wanted my attention you did something quite radical with your vehicle.'

'That's right,' Eyes replied, with a fond smile. 'Not today, I'm afraid.'

'Well? What do you want?' The construct snapped, his metal-plated body clanging ominously. Eyes always had the impression that something was about to drop off.

'I'm afraid I come to ask your help in defeating another foe.'

Sparking Clank grunted with laughter, his body shaking.

'Is that right?'

'The Witches of Fenwick are enemies of progress and technology. They seek to dominate Hepethia and rule humanity. We intend to destroy them before they can do any more harm.'

'That may be true, but it's not the real reason you want to wipe them out. I know.' The construct rumbled, almost like a purr. 'It's far more personal than that.'

'Yes, it is.' Eyes admitted, not letting go of his conviction. He stared up at the construct, his own blue eyes piercing the lamp-like eyes of the living machine before him.

'Don't tell me what you think I want to hear. Tell me why you want to end them. I have little patience for shifter politicians. Authenticity is more endearing.'

'Forgive me.' He immediately regretted not bringing Claws with him for this. 'The Witches participated in slaughtering my old pack, the Blue Moon, and they destroyed my human family. This is indeed, very personal.'

'And do you think that by obliterating them some sort of balance will be restored?' The construct sounded sceptical.

'I do. It's how society works. Checks and balances. Justice.'

'You don't seek justice, you seek vengeance.'

'Perhaps.' Eyes shrugged, but wouldn't allow his resolve to crumble. 'I consider you an ally to the Lightning Lords. Will you help us?'

He felt the hair on the back of his neck prickle and glanced around, certain that someone was watching. The pale blue sky was turning grey as clouds formed in the south. There was a glint against the thickening clouds and Eyes recognised Unchained Lightning making circles beneath the clouds. He turned back to Sparking Clank and smiled knowingly. Unchained Lightning was now the authority over the former Sparkblood, granting him a share of the power in the region. Sparking Clank would have to bow to his master. The construct seemed to have realised that too, and he dipped his large head.

'Of course.'

'Thank you. There is a factory in Fenwick that the Witches operate out of. I will see to it that it is of benefit to you.'

'That would be appreciated. How can I help you?'

'Join us when we attack on the equinox. We will need to neutralise their nature fae allies. Can I count on you to take the lead on that?'

'It would be my pleasure.' Sparking Clank bowed his head again. There was just a hint of resentment at being threatened in his voice, but Eyes wasn't worried. It was the natural order of things in Hepethia. The beings that came to call it home were hierarchical at heart.

'Thank you. I will see you in battle.' Eyes graciously bowed his head and turned to go.

'Be careful,' Sparking Clank said softly. Eyes glanced back over his shoulder as the metal doors scraped shut. He shifted form and picked his way cautiously back across the battlefield.

Once he was safely back at 32 Grove Street, Eyes found Claws sitting in the living room, a broad smile on his face as he admired his new acquisition.

'I can't believe you actually got it,' Eyes said as he stepped into the room. A huge machine gun took up most of the floor.

'There are a lot of decommissioned weapons like this around, if you know where to look. With a little T.L.C., it'll be in full working order.' He stroked the long barrel tenderly. Eyes rolled his eyes and left him to it. He would never understand a shifter who chose bullets over talons. They were walking weapons in their Agrius form. But Claws was still cautious of his alternate forms, and Eyes had to admit that his ability with firearms had served them well on occasion. He thought of Stalker's swords, and the fierce weaponry that had been on display at the Danegeld. Fortune himself had carried a huge war hammer. A weapon like that would certainly strike fear into his opponents. Perhaps some weaponry and the addition of a machine gun to their van may just give them an advantage. With only a few days until the equinox they needed every advantage they could gather.

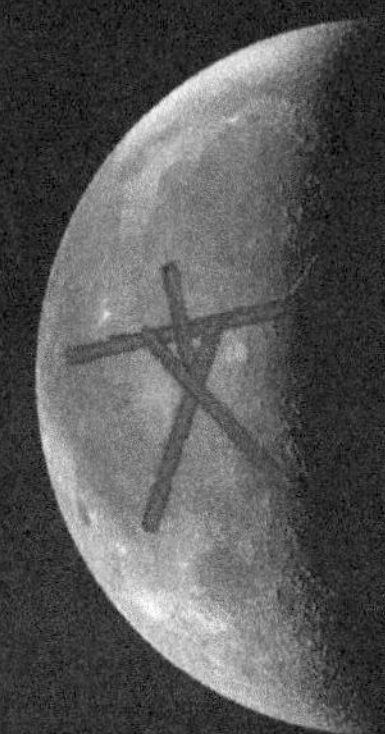

Chapter Thirty Six

Stalker-of-Night's-Shadow

Late on Sunday evening, Stalker set out to patrol and scout. It had so quickly become routine, and yet on this occasion she felt emotional and fragile. Still shaken from her encounter with the Knight, and subsequent loss of control, she went cautiously and was distracted. She hadn't been able to return to see the Witches move the remaining bodies from the crematorium the following day.

Her interview with the police flashed through her mind and caused a ripple of discomfort to radiate from her gut. Ron had not answered her calls when she had tried to contact him over the weekend. She had a terrible feeling that the dojo would be closed for a long time and even if it did reopen she might not be welcomed back. She had just been getting into the swing of balancing her new nature with her human life and now it felt as though it had been torn in two.

Weaver had been telling her for months now that it

wasn't possible to have a foot in both worlds, not really. A cover was necessary for survival, but it was folly to try too hard to keep up the pretence of a human life. Had she been right? Would disaster always follow her through the human world? She thought of Eyes and his family and felt a tear prickle at the corner of her eye.

As she rounded an unfamiliar corner on the southern border of Fenwick, Stalker felt a creeping sensation along her spine. She looked around, suddenly realising that she wasn't where she had intended to be. She had been so lost in thought that she had wandered off course.

Little stick figures hung from every lamp post along the street and the stale stink of Witches clung to the air. She wasn't far from the Glass Wolves' territory, if she needed to bolt, she would be safe there. Next to her was a green door with faded and peeling paint. It stood alone on a brick wall. The building had no windows and stretched out in both directions with no other doors in sight. She sniffed at it carefully, but there was no particularly strong scent on it; it wasn't claimed any more so than any other random building in Fenwick.

But something about it drew her to it. A familiarity clawed at her consciousness. It was a gap in the veil, not just a gap, a door. A deliberately created entry to another world. If the Witches had made this, surely they would have staked a claim. She looked around again. Cars passed by behind her and across the road was a group of teenagers chatting loudly as they walked along, some stepping into the road to walk alongside the others. They didn't seem to see her. Foxes were a common enough sight in Caerton that perhaps they thought nothing of seeing one in the street. But something told Stalker that wasn't true. They may be a common sight but most humans still seemed fascinated whenever they caught a glimpse of one. They were walking towards her.

Overcome by boldness, Stalker shifted form, not taking her eyes off the group. They were distracted and occupied with each other, but there were a dozen of them and at least a few had been looking vaguely in her direction. They showed no reaction whatsoever to her transformation. They continued past as if she wasn't even there.

Stalker looked back at the green door. It must be shielded with some powerful magic, something even stronger than the cloak of night that mostly concealed her. Pursuit-of-Midnight-Solitude didn't make her invisible, just easy to overlook. Were she to shift form in front of a human under normal circumstances, she would send that human insane.

She pressed a hand against the door. It was warm to the touch and smelled of home. Though what that really meant she wasn't sure. As she removed her hand, a shimmer passed over the spot where her hand had been. A faint rainbow appeared.

'What the..?' She stepped back and craned her neck to look up at the building. Aside from the lack of windows and doors, it looked like an ordinary terrace of houses, not unlike Grove Street. Her gaze dropped back to the patch of shimmering rainbow on the door. It was still there and had taken on a translucent quality. Something seemed to move behind the spectrum of colour and she peered closer to look.

She felt a sudden tug behind her navel and was dragged

through the closed door, as if passing through a waterfall. A cry died in her throat as she was propelled forwards through a dark tunnel, with bright colours flashing past her like lights on the walls and floor. Wind whipped at her hair and shook her cheeks. She squinted against the stinging pressure on her eyes, and fought the fear that was trying to rise inside.

Suddenly her feet made contact with a hard surface and she was surrounded by blindingly white light. She stumbled and fell forwards, her hands slapping against a cool, white quartz floor. She retched, but nothing came up. Her head spun and she could see black spots floating in front of her.

'Well, this is a surprise.' A cool, deep voice said nearby.

Stalker staggered to her feet and swayed. It was so bright. She could hardly see. She raised a hand to shield her eyes, and searched for the source of the voice. Slowly her eyes adjusted to the brightness and the world began to come into focus. Immediately around her was a courtyard of clear quartz. The walls were only a few feet high and beyond them was the most astonishing landscape. A turquoise lake that sparkled in the sunlight lay all around the small island courtyard. A long bridge of quartz crossed it, leading to steep cliffs and an enormous palace that towered overhead, seeming to reach almost to the dazzling sky. It gleamed bright white, with touches of every colour of the rainbow flecked here and there on the smooth, curved walls.

She spun on the spot and came face to face with a tall man in furs and armour. He had pale skin, and wild, red hair, and he carried a golden staff.

'Where am I?'

'You are not human.' He walked slowly around her, examining her carefully. 'You are one of the chosen.'

'I'm a shapeshifter,' she said defiantly. 'One of the Chosen of Artemis.'

'Hmm.' He stood still and stroked his chiselled jaw as he regarded her through narrowed eyes. 'How do you come to be here?'

'I don't know. I don't even know where I am.'

'This is Asgard.'

Stalker swayed slightly and blinked at him in surprise.

'Really?' She couldn't hide the shock from her trembling voice.

'How did you get here? What were you doing before being transported?'

'I was examining a strange door in the veil, in the human world. I got dragged through it. I'm a Berserker, one of Odin's Warriors.' She raised a hand to the back of her neck and lifted her hair out of the way, so that he could see her tattoo.

'I see. That explains why the door opened for you. Your people have created such doors to allow passage between our worlds. But we have not actually had a visitor in some time. I believe you would say decades. I am Heimdall. I guard the bridge between our worlds.' He held his hand out to her and she grasped it just below the elbow, the way she would greet one of her fellow Berserkers. He returned the gesture and his entire demeanour softened.

'So why am I here?' Stalker asked, growing uncomfortable under his clear blue-eyed gaze.

'A very good question,' Heimdall replied. He cocked

his head and gazed at her.

A soft rumble in the distance caught Stalker's attention. She looked towards the bridge and saw a dark shape thundering across it towards them. Every muscle in her body tensed, though a voice in her head tried to reassure her that she was safe here. The snow-capped mountains in the distance were hazy in the bright sunlight, and the vast lake shone, effervescent and calming.

Heimdall turned his head slightly to see who was approaching and nodded sagely. The approaching figure became more clear. Stalker saw that it was someone on horseback, with long flowing hair and cloak billowing out behind them. The thundering grew louder and more distinct, as the horse's hooves pounded on the crystal bridge.

As the rider galloped into the courtyard, Stalker saw that the grey horse was mounted by a beautiful young woman with hair the colour of the sun. She was dressed in fine armour that was trimmed with dark fur with feathers protruding from it, and wore a helm of shining steel. She dismounted her horse, who was enormous and almost silver, and also wore armour. She removed her helm and shook out her long hair, which rippled like water. Stalker's breath caught in her throat.

'Stalker-of-Night's-Shadow?' The woman asked, wedging the helm under her arm.

'Yes,' Stalker croaked.

'I am Gudra. You're early.'

'Gudra is a Valkyrie, Stalker,' Heimdall explained, with a kind smile.

'Oh!' Stalker looked at the tall, muscular warrior before

her with new appreciation. She bowed her head slightly, unsure how she was supposed to greet such a legendary being. Gudra reached out and took Stalker's arm in the manner of her fellow Berserkers.

'You have many great battles to come before we will invite you into Valhalla, Stalker. Why are you here?'

'I don't know.'

'I brought her.' A light, shimmering voice rang out across the courtyard. The three of them turned to face the source. A glowing figure rose out of the water, shimmering blue and silver. It floated over the white wall of the courtyard and landed silently in front of them. The shimmering light that emanated from the creature faded a little and Stalker could just about make out a humanoid shape inside the watery aura.

'Fylgia?' Gudra said, mild surprise in her voice. 'What is the meaning of this?'

'Stalker-of-Night's-Shadow is my charge. She has been lost for some time, so I brought her home.'

'You're not supposed to show yourself to your charges,' Heimdall said, an edge of anger to his deep voice. He stepped in front of Stalker protectively. Stalker peered around him. 'Not until the moment of death.'

Stalker looked up at him in alarm. Was she dying? But Gudra had said she had many battles yet to face. She didn't know who had the final say. Odin, she supposed. Would he have to come out here to settle this? Was she going to meet the Allfather himself? Panic began to rise in her chest and she found it hard to breathe or think straight.

'I sent an envoy from the past to speak to her, but he didn't seem to help her.' Fylgia's form was becoming more firm, and Stalker watched in awe as the aura faded to reveal a beautiful woman. She had long dark hair that seemed to float around her, as if she were under water. Her blue eyes looked just like Stalker's and Stalker felt as though she were looking at a long lost sister.

'You sent Hands-and-Face?' Stalker asked, still peering out from behind Heimdall.

'I did. I have always belonged to your family, he was my charge once.'

'I'm sorry,' Stalker said. 'I don't understand what that means.'

'Fylgia are family guardians,' Heimdall said. Still resolutely separating Stalker from the watery spirit. 'Inviting their charge home is what you would call death.'

'Oh,' Stalker said with a frown. They were getting nowhere.

'I don't mean for Stalker to enter Valhalla,' Fylgia said, her voice tinkling like rain drops on glass. 'I mean for her to find herself.'

'Can any of you tell me what I am?' Stalker asked. She stepped out from behind Heimdall and looked into each of their faces. 'I'm not like other shifters.'

'No, you're special,' Fylgia replied with a smile. 'Only Artemis can truly answer your question. She rarely leaves her realm and none can enter it. Your special connection with Odin allows you to come here. This was the best I could do to get you closer to the answers you seek.'

'I see. You mean Olympus, right? That's her realm?'

Heimdall raised a hand and pointed to the mountain that stood on the opposite side of the vast lake to the magnificent kingdom of Asgard. It was the tallest mountain, the highest peak was invisible, lost in the hazy sky. 'Oh,' Stalker said, swallowing hard. 'Could I not fly there?'

Gudra laughed and Fylgia looked affronted.

'No one goes to Olympus. It is forbidden.'

'But in Greek myths people did go there sometimes. Didn't they?'

'And usually suffered the consequences,' Heimdall replied. He smiled at her like he was observing a cute puppy. Stalker drew herself up to her full height.

'Fine. How do you expect me to find answers if Artemis is the only one who can provide them?'

'You are as much of Asgard as of Artemis,' Fylgia replied. 'This is where you will one day come, when you come home for good. You draw much of your power from this place. Your heart beats for Odin. I know, because I am in your heart too, I am always with you.'

Stalker felt something stirring at her words, and a tear prickled at the corner of her eye.

'You're always with me?'

'I am.' Fylgia nodded.

'Then you know what I've been through. You know the loss I've felt, the betrayal, the rage.' Stalker's cheeks trembled and her voice cracked.

'And the love,' Fylgia said softly, taking a step towards her. 'I know the love you have felt for others and that they have felt for you.'

'Don't ever forget about that,' Gudra urged, placing a hand on Stalker's shoulder. 'You are a powerful warrior, with so much yet to accomplish. I am honoured to be connected to you and look forwards to the day we share a toast in the Great Hall. But you have much to live for yet, and I don't just mean the battlefield. You are a woman too.'

Stalker had never been one for planning for the future. She lived in the moment and had never considered the possibility of growing old. Since she had found out what she truly was she had assumed she would live a short and brutal life, and she was mostly fine with that. She wasn't ready to die yet, though, she had the Witches to finish off.

'And Rhys,' Fylgia said, smiling knowingly. 'Don't forget the love.'

'You can read my thoughts?' Stalker asked.

'I am within you, always. I experience your thoughts with you.'

'Will I ever find out why Artemis made me different?' She looked around at each of them, but was met with the steely resolve of people who could not answer.

'I expect she will find a way to communicate with you when the time is right,' Fylgia replied.

'When I was newly changed, someone told me not to let go of my humanity, that I would need it. But it has brought me so much trouble. I've seen what it can cost, to cling to that life. I don't know what to do.'

'Shadow's Step's words were wise, and you do well to heed them,' Fylgia replied. 'You could so easily disappear into the black if you allow yourself to forget everything that you were. But you are not human, you are something else. I think they key is to remember and learn from your humanity, but not try to pretend that you never changed. Does that make sense?'

'Yes, actually it does.' Stalker took a deep breath and

turned her face to the bright sky, her eyes closed. There was a caw overhead and Stalker chanced a glance through squinted eyelids. A raven circled them a few times, then swept away towards Asgard.

'It is time for you to return to Midgard,' Heimdall said, his eyes on the raven as it disappeared into the distance.

'Wait!' Stalker turned to Gudra. 'I need to learn so much. How do I make the most of my abilities in the forthcoming battle? Can you help me?'

'You are so skilled, I don't believe there is anything I could teach you. Use your eyes and your wits, know your enemy, be bold but wise. You will prevail if you can remember that.' Gudra placed both hands on Stalker's shoulders and looked into her eyes. 'Above all, be honourable. That is what Odin prizes. Show mercy where possible and fight with a clear head.'

As Gudra lifted her hands from Stalker's shoulders, she felt her swords on her back grow heavier. She peered over her shoulder to look at the hilt of one of them. A rune flared up on the pommel, shining orange for a moment, before fading away. *Snake.*

'What was that?' she asked, staring at Gudra.

'A gift from the Allfather, something to help you in battle.'

'You must go. When you return, go quickly to your pack,' Heimdall urged, taking her by the elbow and leading her to the edge of the little island.

'Is something wrong?'

'You may be in danger of discovery by the Witches. Go quickly, conceal yourself. I wish you good fortune, Stalker-of-Night's-Shadow. I hope that it is many years until we meet again.' He smiled and she returned the gesture.

'Until the next time,' Gudra said, bowing her head.

'Will it be you that comes for me?' Stalker asked, unable to stop the question that burned inside.

'Almost certainly,' Gudra said softly.

Fylgia smiled and shimmered out of sight. Stalker looked out across the water. The surface shimmered with many colours. She felt dizzy for a moment, and then as if a large hook had grabbed her around the middle, she was yanked forwards. She left Asgard behind as she tumbled through the dark tunnel with a rainbow of light flashing past below her.

She closed her eyes to stop her head from spinning. Suddenly she was still, though she didn't recall stopping. She was sitting and leaning against something. When she opened her eyes she was in the street where she had left, sitting against the green door. She felt tired and her eyes were crusted with sleep. She stood up hurriedly and looked around the deserted street. Could she have dreamt it all? The door looked perfectly ordinary, the sensation of there being a gap in the veil had gone.

Looking cautiously around one last time, Stalker caught the scent of a Witch. Her human form had the weakest senses, so if she could smell her enemy now she must be close. Stalker shifted into her fox form and sprinted as fast as she could for the nearby Glass Wolves' territory. She leapt over fences and darted through gardens, making a direct line for safety.

When she reached it she skidded to a halt and looked back. There was no sign of anyone following, and she allowed herself a moment to catch her breath. Theodore would probably not take kindly to her lingering, so she set off at a jog back to St. Mark's. Her mind raced over the events of the evening, unable to decide how real they had been.

When she was back in the safety of the house and back in human form, Stalker unstrapped her dha and examined the hilts. Very finely engraved on both pommels was the rune for "snake". It was no dream. Her face lit up with a grin as she swiftly unsheathed one of the Burmese swords. *Try it,* a voice inside urged, and she knew that it was Fylgia.

Her pack mates were sleeping, the house was dark and still. She felt the blade humming in her grasp. She closed her eyes and focused her breathing. There was energy emanating from the sword. Something alive was now inside it. Flames-First-Guardian had once suggested doing something to her swords to make them more powerful. Was this what he had meant? She opened her eyes and looked up and down the sleek blade. Faint light from the kitchen window glinted on the steel in the dark room. Stalker swished the blade across her body and felt the hum run up her arm. The serpent inside seemed to respond to the movement, the vibration increased in frequency. She shivered, unnerved by the sensation.

There was no real way to tell what her dha could now do without getting into an actual fight. But she sheathed it with a grin, longing to test them both properly, preferably on the neck of a Witch. Her story would have to wait until the morning, however. Exhaustion overwhelmed her, and she went to curl up next to Weaver. She dreamed of Asgard, and Fylgia, and Hands-and-Face proudly clapping his hands as she slaughtered her enemies.

The following morning the pack was just stirring when a loud rap at the door dragged them from their nest-like living room. Stalker was the first to the door, rubbing her eyes wearily as she opened it. Last-Breath-Echoes stood on the pavement outside, her eyes even wider than usual, with the distinct look of someone who had not slept.

'Come in,' Stalker said, perking up instantly. She stood aside and Echoes strode in, giving the wooden door frame a flick with her thumb nail as she crossed the threshold. Stalker closed the door and followed her to the living room, where the others were straightening the place up and making space for their guest. Claws was out patrolling, but the rest of them gathered around as Echoes paced the floor, refusing the offered seat. She wrung her hands and chewed her lip. Stalker had never seen her so anxious.

'What is it?' Eyes asked. Echoes stopped pacing and glared at him.

'The body that I tracked, it's not at the crematorium anymore, and it hasn't been cremated.'

'As we suspected,' Eyes said with a heavy sigh.

'The body was moved yesterday to the crematorium in Fenwick. Last night it was moved again, to a disused factory. I was able to create a strong enough connection with the deceased that I could catch glimpses of the surroundings. I saw the dead twins, walking about. I also saw a significant number of corpses. They were laid in rows, no longer in body bags, and had been dressed in leather armour. I think, I don't want to, but I think they are planning to raise an army of undead.'

'Oh,' Eyes said, his face paralysed.

'Great Artemis,' Weaver whispered.

'It certainly sounds plausible,' Wind Talker said, stroking his chin. Stalker looked from face to face, trying to wrap her head around the idea.

'But they haven't done it yet?' she asked, looking to Echoes for confirmation.

'No.'

'What about the dead twins? They've been reanimated already. They obviously have the power to do it. What are they waiting for?' Stalker looked around, searching for an answer.

'Remember what Crimson Thorns told us?' Weaver said softly. 'About the Green Man coming to full power on the equinox? I'd bet my visions from Artemis that they're waiting for that. He is the one with the power to resurrect the dead. While he's weak he can't handle more than one or two reanimations, but once they restore him to full health he'll be able to raise an army.'

'Yes,' Wind Talker said, standing abruptly. 'That makes sense. They couldn't wait for him to bring back the girls. Assuming that the bodies need to be reasonably fresh. And they would want their pack members back as soon as possible. So he used what power he does have in winter to restore them.'

'We have to stop them!' Stalker said, panic rising in her chest.

'Yes we do,' Eyes said, his voice low and dangerous. 'We can't just destroy the Witches, we have to stop the Green Man too. We have to take him down before he comes to full strength.'

'They'll be at their most vulnerable during the ritual,' Wind Talker said. 'They'll be distracted. Until then they may be expecting an attack, but they'll need as many of them present for the ritual as possible, meaning fewer patrolling. Spinner-of-Crystal will most likely be in a trance, so she'll be weaker too. I think we have to do it then, we have to time it just right, so that we disrupt the ritual and prevent the Green Man being restored.'

'I want to come,' Last-Breath-Echoes said firmly, her face full of determination. 'I want to be part of this fight. I have to see what they are doing to the dead and be there to ensure it doesn't happen. Someone has to advocate for the dead in this. I'll do it.'

'What about your pack?' Eyes asked, a glint in his eye.

'I'll speak to them. They've defended the city from Furies before, they may want to get involved.' She gave Stalker a determined nod, then spun and marched back towards the front door. Eyes followed her out and Stalker was left looking at her pack mates in shocked silence. When Eyes returned he leaned heavily in the living room doorway and crossed his arms over his chest.

'It'll be really great if The Hand of God join the fight,' Stalker said, breaking the silence.

'Yes, it would be very helpful,' Eyes replied, though a frown marred his brow.

'Don't you think they will?'

'You know Crimson better than I do,' he replied. 'What do you think?'

'I think there are a few people in her pack, herself included, who thirst for the fight, and who support Red Scythe in his wish to see the packs of Caerton unite. But she is cautious. I don't know.' Stalker shook her head. Suddenly the thought of standing shoulder to shoulder with First Strike made her very uncomfortable. She hadn't seen or heard from him since breaking things off with him. She wondered if he was okay, and how he would react to her next time they saw each other.

'Well, we'll soon find out.' Eyes turned and headed for the kitchen. Stalker heard the unmistakable sounds of the coffee maker being turned on and a frying pan being slapped onto the hob. Her stomach suddenly gave an almighty rumble.

The front door opened and Claws stomped in.

'They're twitchy!' he called out from the hall, as he hung his coat up. Stalker rushed into the hall, Weaver and Wind Talker close behind her. 'They've increased their patrols. I would hazard a guess that's in reaction to your jaunt the other night.' He winked at Stalker.

'We should make sure we don't leave the border undefended for too long,' Eyes said from behind them.

'The Wrecking Crew are out there this morning. I saw Speaker-of-Steel and Sky Runner. I also ran into Terrance Platt from the Glass Wolves. Stalker? Did something happen last night?' Claws fixed his steely eyes on her.

'Yes. I haven't had chance yet to tell anyone.' She returned Eyes' irritated glare with defiance. 'Nothing with the Witches. I stumbled through a door in the veil and ended up in Asgard.'

'What?' Wind Talker snapped, fixing his penetrating gaze on her.

'Oh for goodness' sake,' Stalker said with a huff. She bustled everyone out of the hall and into the kitchen.

'Seriously? You went to Asgard? Why didn't you wake us to tell us as soon as you got back?' Weaver looked truly hurt by Stalker's lack of urgency.

'I wanted to tell you all at once. Claws wasn't here. I didn't go right into Asgard itself. The bridge between worlds deposited me on an island on a lake between Asgard and Olympus.' She took a deep breath and recounted what had happened. When she finished she looked at her pack mates expectantly. They all just stared at her in awe.

'Wow,' Weaver breathed, her fingers pressed against her lips. 'Did they tell you what was going to happen?'

Stalker hesitated, unsure how much detail she wanted to share.

'That we can win this fight if we go in knowing our enemy.'

'Good advice,' Eyes said, a small smile tugging at his lips. 'I had a thought on that subject. We tried before to get information on the Plague Doctor from the constructs at the telecoms tower. We could try again.'

'Good idea,' Wind Talker said, nodding.

'I need to get the machine gun to the Wrecking Crew today,' Claws said.

'Okay, we'll all go to the tower together, then Weaver, I want you patrolling.'

'Is it wise to let Weaver patrol alone?' Wind Talker asked, a little hesitantly. Weaver snarled at him across the kitchen table. Stalker felt affronted on her behalf. 'Nothing at all about your abilities,' Wind Talker said hastily. 'But they're obviously still interested in getting you on their side. What if they try to snatch you again?'

'I'm confident that Weaver can handle herself,' Eyes said firmly. 'Let's eat, then get over to the tower.'

They followed the Alpha's instructions, eating a hasty

breakfast. Weaver wanted to know more about Stalker's trip to the realm of the gods, and Stalker answered her eager questions as best she could. Though she held on to some of what happened. She didn't want to admit to Weaver that she had been right all along about not trying to be human. She also didn't want to mention Rhys and the fact that Fylgia had talked to her about being in love. She knew that Weaver was likely to catch some of her private thoughts, but hoped they would be vague.

Eyes hurried them along, but before heading out, Stalker ran upstairs to freshen up. She hummed to herself as she washed and brushed her teeth. She quietly made her way up to the attic and went to the hidden corner. She pulled out her secret box and deposited a feather from Gudra's fur-trimmed armour inside. Halfway down from the attic she shook her head, unsure what she had just been doing. She was having that feeling more and more often.

The Lightning Lords crossed the veil and ran together across their territory for the border with the Witches. They inspected it carefully for any signs of an incursion. The coast was clear and they made their way back into the heart of what was theirs, to the huge metal tower. In Hepethia it was more foreboding than in the human world. It dominated the landscape, its steel struts looked as though they had erupted from the ground, rather than been buried in it.

Stalker craned her neck to look up the tower. Right at the top sat The-Lord-of-Storms-and-Rain, though it appeared he was resting as the sky above blazed blue and cloudless.

'Are you going to try calling the tower again?' Claws asked. Eyes shook his head.

'Wind Talker? Could I have your knife please?'

Wind Talker retrieved his ritual knife from his shoulder bag and passed it to the Alpha. Eyes sliced his palm and passed the knife to Claws. 'You too, all of you.' He pressed his bleeding palm to the nearest part of the tower. Claws copied him and passed the knife to Stalker. She pressed the blade into her palm and sliced neatly and virtually painlessly through her skin, drawing blood. She handed the knife to Weaver, then joined the others at the base of the tower. Once Weaver and Wind Talker were also connected to the tower by their bloody hands, Eyes looked up the tower.

'We call upon the construct of the tower itself,' Wind Talker said, calmly taking the lead. 'We offer our blood and our service in exchange for information. Please come before us.'

Stalker felt the cool metal vibrating beneath her palm. She looked up but could see nothing unusual yet. The vibration grew stronger and the metal began to feel hot. She winced through the pain shooting from her open wound and glanced at the others. They were reacting to the heat too. Claws was the first to yank his hand away. Stalker started to see spots, and finally leapt back from the tower, cradling her burned hand close to her chest. The skin was raw and blistered. Weaver was nursing her own hand next to her. Eyes and Wind Talker were still clinging to the metal, determined expressions on their faces. Stalker watched them both, transfixed. They kept stealing glances at one another, and resolutely gripped the metal more tightly each time they caught each other's eye. They were competing, Stalker realised. She rolled her eyes at their foolish macho attitudes. Though if it got the pack what it needed, maybe it didn't matter too much how they got there.

Eyes' hand began to smoke and he yanked it away with a snarl. Wind Talker tried to hide a smile, but Stalker saw it before he turned his head away. He still didn't let go. The air around them prickled with static and when Stalker looked up she saw the Lord flying around his throne in a frenzy.

'Wind Talker?' Stalker urged, not taking her eyes off the soaring Lord above.

Her pack mate snarled, low and threatening. She turned to look at him. His hand was smoking, but he steadfastly kept hold of the tower. He grasped hold of it with his other hand and his shoulders shook with pain. His snarl turned into a roar and Stalker readied herself to pounce if his Agrius took control.

'Enough.' A voice hissed like static. Stalker looked around for a source, but it seemed like it had come from Wind Talker himself. He released his hands and stepped back. As he turned to face the others, Stalker saw that his eyes had glazed over and were completely white.

'What is this?' Stalker whispered. 'Is something controlling him?'

'Yes,' Weaver replied, looking worried.

'What do you young whelps want of me?' Wind Talker's lips moved, but it wasn't his voice that came out.

'We need information,' Claws said calmly, though Stalker noticed his hand resting inside his jacket where his gun was holstered. 'Is there anything you can tell us about the Witches of Fenwick, or their ally, The Green Man?'

'I am The Uplink. I am connected to every communication in this city, and beyond. I hear and see everything. Every scrap of data, every word exchanged digitally or wirelessly. I am Knowledge,' the voice that wasn't Wind Talker's boasted.

'And Knowledge is Power,' Claws said with a wry smile.

'I know things that would cripple you. Why should I help you?'

'Because we allow you to remain on our territory at present,' Claws said. 'That could change.'

Stalker raised an eyebrow and glanced at her pack mate with renewed respect.

'And because it's in your best interests to keep the information flowing,' Weaver added. 'We could offer you information in exchange.'

'There is one sort of information that eludes me,' The Uplink hissed.

'Oh?' Claws cocked his head to one side and observed Wind Talker shrewdly.

'Memories, thoughts. Unless they are expressed and transmitted I cannot grasp them. They intrigue me.'

Wind Talker began convulsing suddenly, he coughed and retched and doubled over. Stalker ran forwards, as did Claws. Before they reached him, Wind Talker stood up and held up his hands to keep them back. His eyes were still white, but he had clearly regained some control of his body.

'You can take mine,' he croaked. It was definitely his voice, as hoarse as it was. 'Take my childhood.'

'All of it?' The Uplink's voice came out of Wind Talker's mouth again.

'Yes!' Wind Talker replied.

'No!' Weaver cried out and lurched forwards. Eyes caught hold of her and held her back. 'Wind Talker, no! You can't do that. He means to remove them from your head, not copy them.'

'I know,' he said, looking towards Weaver, his eyes still eerily white. 'They're yours. As long as you give us information that will help us defeat the Witches and their allies.'

Stalker closed her eyes, she couldn't watch. He was so often the only one of them that knew something about shifter mythology or history. He was the only one of them to grow up with shifters, and he was offering it all up in exchange for whatever scrap of information this construct decided to part with.

'You seek to defeat the Green Man?' The Uplink enquired.

'We do,' Eyes replied, still holding onto Weaver.

'He is anathema to me. I do not understand what he is. But I do know something that the Witches do not wish you to know. He can't be killed, nor can he be banished, for he is life itself. However, he can be bound by cold iron. He is rendered virtually powerless by it, for it represents industry and the domination of nature. Bind him in cold iron and he will bend to your will.'

Stalker looked at Eyes. He was beaming, and had released Weaver.

'Thank you,' Eyes said.

'That's very useful, thank you,' Claws added.

'You're welcome. I will take my payment now.'

Before they could react, Wind Talker started shaking violently. Claws was the first to reach him, though he seemed clueless what to do to help. They gathered around him, watching helplessly as he collapsed and writhed on the ground. Stalker could feel his memories being ransacked, she saw flashes of his childhood before they disappeared from his memory. Tears welled up and began to fall silently down her cheeks.

Finally Wind Talker lay still, bent over on his side, his arms over his face.

'Wind Talker?' Claws whispered, crouching beside him.

He slowly lowered his arms. His eyes were back to normal and he looked up at them with a sort of innocence that Stalker had never seen before. Claws helped him to sit up. 'Are you all right?'

'I think so,' Wind Talker said softly. He looked around anxiously. 'The Uplink was in my head.'

'That's right,' Weaver said, stooping to look him in the eye.

'He was powerful. I've only ever encountered a handful of beings like that before. Not even that many. The Lord-of-Storms-and-Rain, Dreadnought...' His voice trailed away. He blinked several times and rubbed his eyes.

'Do you know what he took?' Weaver asked, placing a hand on his shoulder. His eyes dropped to her hand, then he looked back up at the rest of them.

'My childhood. It's all gone. But I know it was there, I know I had one. I didn't just spring into being a fully-formed adult.' He frowned. 'There are things that I know, that I don't remember learning, like what we all are and where we are. It's strange.'

'I expect it will be strange for quite some time,' Eyes said. 'You did something very brave for us. Thank you.'

'Not at all, it was worth it. Now we know how to defeat the Green Man, right?'

'Right,' Eyes said. He held out his hand and helped Wind Talker to his feet. 'So we'd better round up as much iron as Caerton has to offer.'

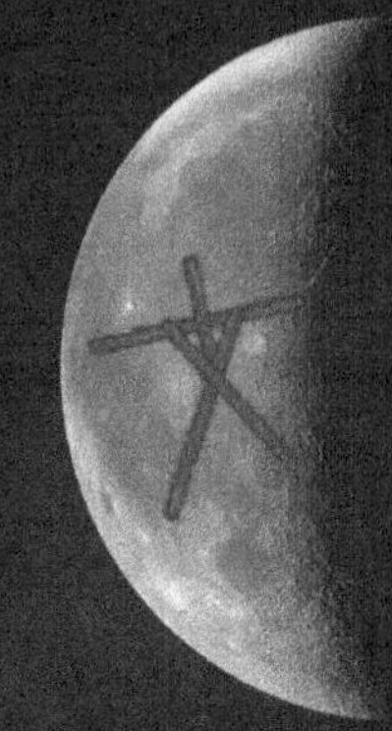

Chapter Thirty Seven

Fights-Eyes-Open

The Lightning Lords returned to the human world. Weaver separated from the others to patrol the border, jogging away from them in cat form. Eyes watched her go with slight trepidation. Despite sticking up for her earlier, he did have reservations about her getting close to Fenwick alone. But he couldn't spare any more of the pack, they had too much to do.

'I have supplies to gather and a meeting with Spark to finish off a few talismans,' Wind Talker explained. Eyes nodded and let him go.

As they arrived at Grove Street, Eyes called Rust.

'Eyes,' Rust answered sleepily.

'We have the item for the top of the van. Can we bring it to you this morning?'

'Sure, great. Bring it to Plenty o' Scrap in Runmead. I'll meet you there. Everything okay?'

'Yeah, we got some great intel just now. I'll fill you in

when I see you. Have you got bodies on the border?'

'I've just sent Fury out. You?'

'Weaver's out there. We'll see you soon.'

'Sure.' Rust ended the call abruptly and Eyes stowed his phone back in the inside pocket of his jacket.

'Where is the best place to find iron these days?' he asked, looking at Claws and Stalker.

'Cemetery fences,' Claws replied swiftly. 'That's about the only place they didn't swipe it from during the war, because they thought it kept the ghosts in.'

Eyes hesitated.

'Well, they might have been right. Is that a risk we can afford to take?'

'More to the point,' Stalker said, frowning, 'can we really get away with stealing cemetery fences in broad daylight? It's not going to be a quick and easy job, is it?'

'Let's not remove any cemetery fences,' Eyes said hastily. 'Let's get over to Runmead. I bet the Wrecking Crew can help with this.'

Claws covered the machine gun with an old blanket and Eyes helped him carry it out to his car. Stalker locked the door and ran out to the car after them. Eyes drove across St. Mark's, ever conscious of the fully functioning heavy artillery in the boot. 'Do you have ammunition for the gun?' he asked, glancing at Claws beside him.

'Of course,' Claws replied with a grin.

'I take it you want to man it?'

'Well, yeah,' Claws said, stating the obvious. Stalker sniggered in the back seat. Eyes ignored her. They crossed into Runmead, something they had never done before. Eyes felt the significance of it. He had done something that

Fortune had claimed impossible: forged a relationship with the Wrecking Crew. He wondered whether his father and former Alpha would be proud of him now. He hoped so.

Claws checked a map on his phone and directed Eyes to the scrap yard that Rust had mentioned. It was right in the heart of Runmead, near Caerton's football stadium. They drove down a quiet street in the industrial area; office blocks squatted to either side, hidden behind tall red brick walls. A fence of corrugated iron hid the yard from view, but the gates stood open and Eyes drove inside. Huge piles of dented and rusting cars were piled on either side of a narrow driveway. Eyes navigated carefully between them. The narrow lane opened up to a large, circular courtyard at the centre of the site. There was a Portakabin to one side, surrounded on three sides by stacks of rusted appliances. Eyes parked next to it and turned off the engine.

'So, this is Wrecking Crew turf?' he said softly. He opened his door and climbed out of the car, his shiny shoes landing softly on the dirt. The others followed his lead. The Portakabin door opened and Rust stepped out, blinking in the bright sunshine.

'Eyes,' he said in greeting. Eyes strode over to him and extended a hand, which Rust took and shook briefly.

'Rust. Thanks for having us.'

'No problem,' the other Alpha said stiffly. 'What's the word, then?'

'We were told that the Green Man can be bound by iron. We need chains, lots of chains.'

'That shouldn't be a problem,' Rust said with a smirk, glancing around them.

'No, I guess not,' Eyes replied. Relief washed over him and he allowed himself a small smile.

'The van is round here.' Rust indicated another passage through the piled up cars. Eyes popped his boot and he and Claws lifted the covered machine gun carefully out. They followed Rust through the yard, past some equipment that looked as though it was for crushing cars, past two huge skips full of small parts. The narrow lane twisted and turned between the piled up wreckage, and the gun was growing heavy in Eyes' sweating hands.

Buried deep in the heart of the maze, was a big, black van. It had been fitted with thick bars down the sides and a spiked battering ram on the front.

'Brilliant,' Claws said breathlessly.

'This can never be seen on human roads,' Rust cautioned.

'No, we know. We plan to take it across the veil,' Eyes said, still gazing at the van.

'I heard something about you guys doing stuff like that,' Rust said, a wry smile on his lips. 'Nice one.' Eyes looked at him, Rust was nodding appreciatively, his arms crossed over his chest. Eyes returned his smile. Yes, relations were definitely warmer between their packs these days.

'Will we be able to get it out of here on the other side?' Eyes asked, looking around at the towering cars.

'Not a problem,' Rust replied. 'So, you need chains of iron? Speaker-of-Steel can sort that out for you. What's the attack plan?'

'We're going to attack during their equinox ritual. We think that's when their defences will be lowest, they'll be busy and distracted. We'll need a contingent in the van to hit the factory in Hepethia to subdue the Green Man, at the same time as another group in the human world to interrupt the ritual and take down the Witches.'

'Which group are you leading?'

'The van group. Stalker will take the lead against the Witches in the human world.' He glanced at her, catching her look of surprise.

'I see,' Rust said, indignation colouring his freckled cheeks. 'I understand that you want your own people at the head of this; but if you'll take a little advice, you don't want to put the other Alphas' noses out of joint. Where do you picture myself and Theodore?'

Eyes thought quickly, seeing the battle playing out in his head, like he had a hundred times before, now with the addition of the chains.

'You and yours at the factory. I'll head the assault on the building itself, we'll need to break in to it, which is what the van is all about. You'll be responsible for leading the attack on the Green Man. I take it Speaker-of-Steel has expertise with metal-crafting?'

'That's right. He has a special skill set.' Rust grinned.

'I saw, at my house.' Eyes' voice wavered slightly at the memory of the Witches' attack on his family. Through the smoke he had seen a member of the Wrecking Crew peel the bonnet off a car like it was a banana.

'That's right,' Rust said stiffly.

'So wrapping the chains around the Green Man quickly shouldn't be a problem.'

'With any luck. What about the Glass Wolves?'

'I want them covering the Witches and the perimeter. I need to go over the details with Theodore still. Have you ever seen them in a fight?'

'Oh yes,' Rust chuckled. 'They're like a well-oiled machine.'

'I somehow have trouble picturing Theodore getting his hands dirty,' Eyes mused.

'He won't if he can help it, but you can tell by the size of him that he's capable enough.'

'Well look at you two, all friendly.' The slick voice interrupted them and all of the shifters span to face Tar Peter as he sidled out from behind the van.

'I told you never to set foot on my yard again!' Rust snapped, his chest puffing up.

'I see you two know each other,' Eyes said, bemused by the exchange.

'Oh, we go way back, Tar Peter and me.' Rust strode over to the demon and swung his fist towards his face. Tar Peter was ready, however, and his entire head turned into liquid tar before Rust's fist could make impact. His knuckles flew straight through the tar and came out the other side coated in the sticky substance. Tar Peter's face reformed, a smarmy smile fixed to it.

'You missed me, you missed me, now you have to kiss me,' the demon mocked.

'Okay, that's enough,' Eyes said, stepping in between them. Rust flicked tar onto the ground and pulled a rag from his back pocket to wipe the rest off his hand. He scowled all the while at the demon. 'Tar Peter is our ally, he's going to help us. Aren't you?' Eyes looked pointedly at him and the demon's smile slid from his face.

'Yes. I found the perfect construct for your special van, here.' He looked up at the van beside them with a look of derision. 'I still think it's a ridiculous plan.'

'What construct?' Rust snapped.

'An old friend of mine who has spent the last five years living in a wrecking ball, due to his intense desire to smash things. He says he quite fancies a change of scenery, so is willing to move into your battering ram.' Tar Peter managed to amble his way through his words without looking directly at Rust. Eyes wondered what the history was between them, and fought between amusement and irritation at their animosity.

'Excellent,' Eyes said, forcing a smile. 'That should help us get through the factory wall.'

'I'll tell my friend he can move in then, shall I?' Tar Peter drawled.

'Yes please,' Eyes replied. Rust nodded in agreement, and Tar Peter sank into the ground, leaving a small pool of liquid tar behind.

'Do you need any help attaching this to the roof?' Claws asked, indicating the gun. 'There should probably be some sort of strap to buckle the gunner in up there.' His eyes gleamed and Rust seemed to cotton on to Claws' desire to be that gunner.

'We can handle it, thanks,' Rust said in amusement. 'I look forwards to seeing you in action up there though.'

'Thanks.' Claws grinned.

'Great. Well, we'll leave you to it. I'll be in touch as soon as we have a time for Wednesday.'

Rust escorted them back to Eyes' car and waved them off. Claws sat beside Eyes, twitching nervously. 'I'm sure your precious new toy will be just fine in their care,' Eyes reassured him.

'Yeah, you're probably right,' Claws said with a sigh. Eyes tried not to laugh.

'Why didn't you tell me you wanted me to lead the attack on the Witches?' Stalker asked. Their eyes met in the rear-view mirror.

'I didn't want to make it sound like a really big deal, because it's not. You're my deputy, as far as I'm concerned, and it's only natural that my most capable fighter would lead the attack.'

'What about Theodore and the Glass Wolves though? They're all more experienced than me. And Rust is right, there's bound to be bad feeling about being made to fall in line behind me.' She spoke hurriedly, but didn't take her eyes off his in the mirror.

'You can do this. You've faced a lot in the last few months.'

'Where will Wind Talker and Weaver be?' Claws asked, glancing sideways at Eyes.

'Wind Talker in the van with us, Weaver with Stalker. They are by far the stealthiest, so can get closest without detection. We need to surprise the Witches.' He looked back up to the mirror. Stalker was nodding, her cheeks ablaze.

'That makes sense.'

'The Glass Wolves will have your back,' Eyes reassured her. 'The primary aim is to disrupt the ritual, take out Spinner-of-Crystal, don't take on the whole pack. Okay?'

'Yeah, I think we can handle that. Do you think Weaver's okay with it?'

'Why wouldn't she be?'

'Well, what if her sister's there?'

'She made her feelings about her sister very clear,' Eyes said firmly. He couldn't spend time second guessing what his pack may or may not be capable of. He had to trust them to get the job done, and by and large, he did.

They got back to Grove Street, and Stalker set off to relieve Weaver from patrol duty.

'I know the timing could be better,' Claws said tentatively. 'But I have an open case that I need to just dip into this afternoon. It won't take more than a couple of hours. I just need to keep my business ticking over.'

'Of course, I understand. Now that Stalker's employment situation looks... uncertain, we need to make sure we have enough money coming in to keep us fed and what not. Take care of your business. I want a really thorough scout of the factory tonight, on both sides of the veil, and I want to build a weapon for myself.'

'Oh really?' Claws raised an eyebrow. 'You want something more than your teeth and claws?'

'Yes,' Eyes replied defiantly. 'I know, I know. Look, I'm joining the weapons club, let's just accept it and move on without further comment.'

Claws grinned, then set off for work. Eyes went over all of the plans several times, pacing the kitchen and running things over in his mind. This was going to work, it had to work. Everything ached and eventually he had to give in and get some rest. He was going to need it.

It was nearly dark when he woke up. There were voices in the kitchen and Eyes dragged himself from the sofa and rolled up his shirt sleeves as he stumbled through to the other room. Weaver, Wind Talker and Claws were sitting around the table, a selection of strange little ornaments in front of them.

'Evening,' Wind Talker said, smiling.

'Looks like you had a productive day with Spark,' Eyes said, nodding at the trinkets on the table.

'Very,' Wind Talker replied. He picked up a small coil of electrical wiring coated in blue rubber and handed it to Eyes.

'What's this?'

'Well, I know about your weapon plans,' Wind Talker said, a small smile tugging at the corner of his lips. 'This is for the grip. It's wire from the substation. It won't be missed, don't worry. Unchained Lightning gave his blessing before I took it.'

'Thanks.' Eyes smiled. Wind Talker stood and hoisted up something heavy from behind the table. It was a charred war hammer. Eyes glared at it, disbelief numbing him. 'Is that what I think it is?'

'Yes,' Wind Talker said, passing the maul to the Alpha. 'I dug it out of the wreckage the day after the attack on the Blue Moon. I've been saving it for when you were ready.'

'I was going to make my own,' Eyes said absently, turning the weapon over in his hands. The grip had been destroyed in the fire, a few bedraggled remnants of leather remained stuck to the metal core. The once smooth wooden handle was splintered and black, but it seemed structurally sound. The huge iron head had small dents in it from a lifetime of use. Eyes remembered Fortune wielding the impressive weapon against demons. The mere sight of it had been enough to turn the Wrecking Crew back that night in the street when Weaver escaped the Witches. 'Thank you.' He looked up at Wind Talker, who was watching him with reverence.

'You're welcome. We need to make it battle-worthy though. I didn't want to press on with that, I thought you would want to craft it yourself.'

'Yeah, thanks. I was thinking about getting it imbued with extra powers. Do you have any thoughts on that?'

'I do. Unchained Lightning isn't at the top of the food chain of power fae in Caerton. There's something bigger, it lives in the nuclear power plant.'

Eyes glanced at Claws and Weaver, who didn't seem surprised or alarmed by this revelation. Had Wind Talker already talked to them about all of this?

'Are you suggesting what I think you're suggesting?' Eyes asked, his eyes wide.

'I am. But I don't think you need to worry, I don't think she would turn your hammer into a nuclear weapon,' Wind Talker added hastily. 'She's a power fae and was drawn to the place in Caerton that generates the most power, that's all. She might up and move if they ever build that offshore wind farm that they've been talking about forever.'

'Okay, let's pay her a visit then.' He took the wire and spent a minute winding it tightly around the hilt of the maul. It was a symbolic gesture, using wiring that had fed their power ally in the construction of a powerful weapon. The shamanistic magic of their kind had a power that Eyes didn't pretend to understand. But it worked. Eyes didn't know what exact effect it would have, but he was excited to see.

The four of them set off in Eyes' car. The power station was across the river and out to the west of the city, on what had been the territory of the Storm Riders. They no longer needed permission to enter, as that pack had perished. Eyes wondered what would happen to the area. If no one rose up in place of them to claim it, it would end up like neighbouring St. Catherine's. That could cause a whole heap of trouble for themselves and the other shifters of Caerton. Would the Furies use it as ammunition against them? As a way to justify their intervention? If Caerton's shifters couldn't control the city sufficiently then there might be a case in their own laws for the Furies riding into town to take over. His hands twisted nervously on the wheel.

The power station had a sprawling car park that was nearly empty, and Eyes parked in a space at the perimeter. The vast, grey cooling towers dominated the skyline, white steam billowing into the dark blue sky.

'Claws, can you take out any security cameras and these floodlights, please?' Eyes asked. Claws nodded and strode to the fence that separated the car park from a line of trees. He placed his hand on the nearest lamp post and the rear half of the car park was immediately plunged into darkness. They crossed the veil unseen and Eyes stopped in his tracks at the sight that greeted them.

Where the towers and domes and blinking red and yellow lights stood in the human world, an enormous structure of crystal jutting out of a flat plain stood in Hepethia. Vast towers of clear, orange and red quartz erupted from the ground at odd angles, forming a stunning palace, taller than the cooling towers of the power station, that glinted in the pale light of the waxing crescent moon. Somehow the crystals shone with a light of their own, casting eerie coloured light across the plain.

Eyes wished Stalker was with them, but they couldn't risk leaving their territory unguarded during their excursion. He would have to recommend that she visit this place another time.

Movement behind the first layer of crystals caught his attention, and Eyes led the pack across the plain towards the structure. As they drew closer, Eyes saw that there were ripples of energy flowing up the crystal struts. Occasionally little sparks would be emitted, and when two fluctuations leapt from neighbouring struts at the same time there was a discharge of static that caused lightning to leap from one strut to another. It was breathtaking.

Something else moved inside the structure, however, something disconnected from the crystals. At first Eyes just caught glimpses of a rippling body through the narrow gaps. But the fae was working its way closer to them and undulating between crystals.

Unchained Lightning soared overhead and landed heavily next to the Lightning Lords, stretching his leathery wings with a flourish.

'Thank you for the wire,' Eyes said softly. Their ally nodded his huge head slowly. 'And thank you for coming here. Do you have many dealings with this fae?'

'Not directly,' the dragon beside him said with a throaty hum. 'But all power in and out of the city flows through her, we are connected on the vast web and are aware of each other.'

'I see.'

'You are going to ask her to add power to your weapon.'

'Yes. Do you think she'll agree?'

'I do not know.' Unchained Lightning launched himself

into the air and circled above them. Eyes took another few steps towards the magnificent crystal formation and cleared his throat. He glanced at his pack mates, who all bore expressions of awe and wonder as they gazed up.

Wind Talker caught the Alpha's eye and they exchanged nods. He took his knife out of his bag and cut his thumb. He rubbed the blood onto a small, white bag stuffed with ritual herbs and set light to it. The air filled with pungent smoke, and the movement inside the crystalline palace became frenzied. Static discharges filled the air with thunder and flashes of lightning. The ground trembled. From out of the structure soared a vast, bright white bird, which lit up the plain as if by the most powerful floodlights.

She lost substance in the almost black sky, becoming shimmering smoke that slowly settled over the palace like a cloak.

'Do you think we upset her?' Weaver asked softly.

'No, she's fine,' Wind Talker replied. 'She wasn't expecting me to do that, but she's not hostile towards us.' Eyes noticed a shining copper bangle around Wind Talker's wrist, etched with tiny runes. A new toy from his day with Spark. Claws was wearing one too and he nodded in agreement. 'Forgive us for startling you, Furnace-of-Sol. Would you please grant us an audience?' Wind Talker's voice echoed off the grand crystalline structure and rebounded back at the shifters in a hundred tiny shards.

The smoke slowly dissipated, as if being sucked back inside the palace. As the last tendrils disappeared, a great fire suddenly burst to life, sending ripples of light up the smooth crystals. Eyes took a step back, his skin prickling against the sudden, blazing heat. The others stepped back as well and Weaver raised a hand to shield her eyes from the bright flames.

The bird rose again from the flames and soared overhead. Eyes watched her in awe. Music was just audible inside the palace, beyond the roaring of the fire, and he realised they were in the presence of a phoenix, not a bird. The phoenix flew down to the ground and landed gently in front of them. She flickered, as if alight from the inside, glowing like the embers of a fire. She was as tall as any of them, and her wings were tipped with gold. Her long tail shimmered deep turquoise, like that of a peacock and little sparks showered off it onto the sandy ground as she swept it from side to side.

'Who are you?' Her voice was melodic and curious.

'We are the Lightning Lords,' Eyes said, lifting his chin. 'Thank you for agreeing to see us.'

'You gave me little choice. Few have ever come before me so brazenly. I see you have one of my own in your party.' She inclined her head towards Unchained Lightning, who still circled overhead.

'We do,' Eyes replied.

'That pleases me,' Furnace-of-Sol said, a smile to her voice.

'We had hoped to speak to you about imbuing this weapon with power.' Eyes held out the war hammer across his palms. It looked sad and broken in the flickering firelight, and Eyes wished he'd had time to repair it before approaching this magnificent fae queen.

The phoenix stepped forwards and looked carefully at the maul.

'Why would I do such a thing?'

'Because The Lightning Lords are powerful,' Claws said, his voice deep and dangerous. 'When our Alpha wields that weapon in battle, and destroys our enemies, it will be a mighty display of that power. It will make people quake. You could have your stamp on that display of power.'

The phoenix bobbed her head slowly and looked first at Claws, then to Eyes, appraising them both. Eyes felt her probing his mind and heart; he put up no resistance. He wanted her to see his intentions, that was the only way she might grant him some of her power.

At his core, if he was totally honest with himself, he wanted to be more powerful, to make people tremble in awe of him. He wanted to be the big hero, who united the packs of Caerton against the Furies. He needed a weapon to inspire others. Furnace-of-Sol bobbed her head, and a pearlescent tear appeared at the corner of one eye.

'Don't let arrogance override your guiding motivation,' she said softly, so that only he could hear. 'But don't carry the weight of the dead either. Honour them and release them. Will you do that for yourself?'

'Yes, of course,' he replied, dipping his head and swallowing a hard lump that had formed in his throat.

'Very well,' Furnace-of-Sol said sharply. Without warning, she burst into flames, engulfing Eyes and the hammer. A scream rose in his throat, but died before it reached the air. Energy roared through him, and plenty of heat, but he wasn't burning. The flames surrounded them and a fierce wind blew up around them, swirling and dragging the flames into a blazing spiral. He could hear his pack mates shouting and screaming on the other side of the fire, though they sounded muffled.

'I'm okay!' he tried to cry out, but his throat was dry and closed tight, and nothing but a strangled whimper escaped. *I'm fine*, he impressed with his mental voice instead, hoping it would get through to them amidst the chaos.

The phoenix was floating just above the ground, her head turned to the dark sky, and he realised that her wings surrounded him. She had drawn him into herself, it was her fire that surrounded him. The hammer in his hands grew hot and heavy and he gazed down at it. Little chips of wood and iron seemed to be sucked out of the surrounding flames and attached themselves to the maul. Gradually it was rebuilding itself, layer upon layer.

The weapon became sturdy and new once more. The wire that he had wrapped around the hilt sealed itself firmly in place, forming a strong grip. The dented iron head was restored to a smooth, gleaming surface, and the wooden handle was no longer charred and splintered, but smooth and polished.

The fire died down and Furnace-of-Sol stepped back, unwrapping her wings from around him. Weaver was at his side first, checking him over. He brushed her back. 'I'm fine,' he muttered. He could feel the hammer vibrating, it hummed slightly and he stepped back from Weaver to swing it through the air. There was a rush of wind as it sped past his body and for the briefest second a ripple of light ran down the handle and flickered out at the head. He stopped still and grasped it in both hands, staring at it. 'What was that?'

'Power,' replied the phoenix.

Unchained Lightning crackled overhead and Eyes looked up at him. Dark clouds were swirling above the flickering dragon and Eyes felt static in the air. His gaze still fixed on their fae ally, Eyes began to swing the hammer in a huge arc by his side. He felt the energy soaring through his arm and into the weapon. He could hear it humming, and felt the warm glow gathering in the head.

'Bring the lightning!' Eyes roared, and at the zenith of the circle that his arm was making the hammer suddenly stuck, as if caught in a trap. Lightning erupted from the head and streaked up into the sky.

Weaver gasped and clapped her hands to her mouth, Claws and Wind Talker stared, awestruck. Eyes felt his arm shaking violently with the weight of the mighty weapon. He let it drop to his side and let his gaze settle on Furnace-of-Sol. 'Thank you,' he croaked.

'My pleasure,' she replied, the music back in her voice. 'Use it well.'

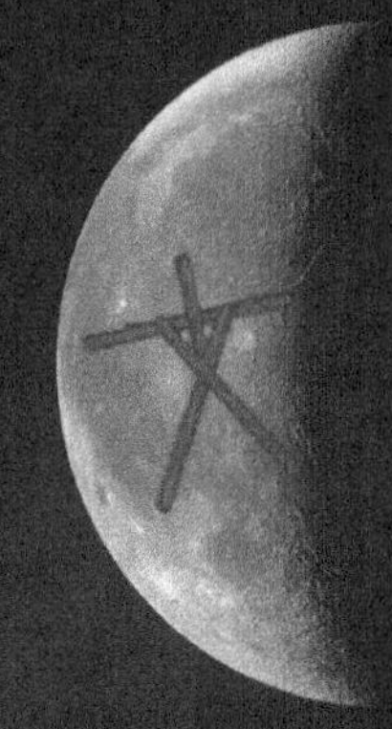

Chapter Thirty Eight

Stalker-of-Night's-Shadow

There was tension in every muscle in Stalker's body. She was aching with the adrenaline coursing through her veins. Tonight was the night. The sun was just dipping below the horizon and there was a palpable prickle in the air. Maybe it was her sensitivity to celestial events, rather than anything to do with the fight that was coming. The spring equinox was upon them, with just an hour to go until the exact moment that the sun was due to pass over the celestial equator.

Stalker and Weaver waited cautiously on the very edge of their territory. The Glass Wolves were positioned at strategic points along Fenwick's south-western border and Stalker could just about make out the scent of one of their number, Terrance Platt, on the wind. Stalker's phone buzzed in her hand and she stared at the message on the screen.

> The Hand of God aren't coming. But Echoes is with
> us.

'Damn,' she hissed.

'What's wrong?' Weaver muttered, not taking her eyes off the street. Her fingers absently spun a new ring on her finger, a gift from Wind Talker.

'No Hand of God,' Stalker hissed.

'Well, we thought it might go that way. Let's just carry on with the plan.'

Stalker nodded and stowed her phone in her pocket.

'Okay. Let's do this.' She shifted silently into a tawny owl and flew out from the cover of the bushes. Weaver ran out after her as a slinky black cat. As Stalker flew into Witch territory she felt a ripple run through her; every instinct in her body told her to turn back. This was enemy territory, claimed, possessed. They reserved the right to execute intruders on sight. Stalker pushed the urge to flee aside and checked the ground to make sure Weaver was still there. Her dark shadow weaved between trees that lined the avenue. The pair of them moved swiftly and silently through leafy Fenwick, through a small park and north towards the factory. It was an overcast night and the clouds reflected the orange street lights that lined the road that swept past the old factory. There was a fine drizzle in the air and Stalker felt droplets rolling off her silken feathers.

She landed on the branch of a tree opposite the factory. Weaver kept running, jogging across the empty street. Stalker watched the fence, there was a lone Witch patrolling the perimeter of the factory about fifty yards away from the gate. Stalker took flight and soared straight towards the Witch. In the shadows near the gate, Weaver hunkered down to wait. Stalker was coming up fast behind the guard, her heart hammering in her feathered chest. She recognised the scent now, one of many that she had detected on her scouting missions.

If this worked, she would never even need to see the woman's face.

She swooped down over the tall fence and shifted form silently right behind the guard and levitated a foot from the ground for a second, before her hands darted through the darkness and grasped the Witch around the throat and across her face. She landed and yanked the struggling woman against her chest. Hands with long nails clawed at Stalker's hand and arm, the guard's slender neck was tucked neatly into the crook of Stalker's elbow. She closed her eyes and pinned the Witch against her body, waiting for the struggling to stop. Her legs thrashed at the ground erratically for a few seconds. Gradually her movements slowed, her hands dropped to her sides and her feet fell still. She was unconscious.

Stalker laid her softly on the grass and sprinted back to the gate. She caught sight of Weaver in the shadows, just two bright eyes catching the light above. The moment Weaver saw Stalker she squeezed through the small gap under the gate and pressed herself against the concrete wall to shift form.

With no need for words, the two of them ran down the ramp towards the garage. As they reached the closed door, Weaver placed her ringed hand on the control panel and the door began to roll slowly up, clattering loudly. They exchanged glances, relieved that the talisman worked, but anxious at the racket the door created.

Wasting no time, the moment the door was a foot from the floor they both dropped to their bellies and squeezed underneath. Weaver darted to the inside control panel and pressed her ring to it. The door shuddered to a halt and then began its noisy descent to the ground. Stalker watched the door opposite, ware that at any moment Witches might come pouring through it. The door thumped to the floor and Weaver shifted her slender hand into a huge Agrius fist and punched the panel, which crunched and disintegrated.

Stalker pointed to the nearest truck and the two of them sprinted for it and threw themselves to the ground, crawling quickly underneath. Weaver shifted form and hid behind a wheel. Stalker's gaze was fixed to the door as it swung open, spilling soft candlelight across the concrete floor and two pairs of feet scurried into the garage. There were voices chanting in the room beyond and Stalker prayed that they weren't too late.

'What the hell?' a familiar voice snapped. Its owner's feet were by the door. She stooped to pick up a piece of the broken plastic casing for the control panel, her long blond hair falling like a silk scarf over her shoulder. Weaver's sister.

Stalker felt Weaver tense up, but she didn't freeze. She followed the plan and darted silently for the next truck over. Stalker shifted into a grey tabby cat and followed.

'Check over there,' ordered the other Witch, sending Maria towards the first truck, while she appeared to check around the door. Stalker and Weaver slunk silently through the shadows, darting from one vehicle to the next until they were tantalisingly close to the open door. The air was heavy with incense and the chanting continued.

They haven't stopped, came Weaver's anxious inner voice. Stalker hadn't expected them to. This ritual was too important, timing was critical. They would keep going through an air raid if they had to. But only as long as Spinner-of-Crystal was still conscious.

I know. Cover the door. Stalker willed her body to shrink, squeezing her feline shape right down into that of a moth. She fluttered out from under the car and flew, unseen, through the open door.

The room was bathed in flickering light from a hundred candles. There was a huge circle of petals on the floor and inside it four figures sat, each holding a candle and chanting. Painted on the concrete floor was a detailed mural of the Green Man. Beyond the circle the floor was cracked and broken, with long grass growing up through the cracks. The walls all around the room were thick with greenery and sections of the roof were missing and open to the dull sky above. Lying on the overgrown floor, were dozens of bodies. They were laid out in neat rows. Each one had been awkwardly dressed in mismatched armour. A fine sheen of rainwater glistened on their pale faces.

There was a deafening crash and Stalker twisted in mid-air to see the door swing closed and a car scrape across the floor, blocking the door. She heard Weaver's Agrius roar and knew that she had to act fast.

The Alpha, Gaze-of-Purity glanced at the door, and twitched as if to leap up. But she was rooted to the spot and a frustrated snarl crept into her chanting. The two supposedly dead girls were on opposite sides of the circle, their eyes serenely closed, their lips softly chanting the words over and over.

'Invocato a viridis vir, ostensor vitae.'

Spinner-of-Crystal sat opposite her Alpha. She was wearing robes of green and brown and her long, thick greying hair fell wild and tangled over her broad shoulders. Her hands were raised over her head and she swayed slightly as she chanted. Her fingers were smudged green, evidently she was responsible for the artwork on the floor.

There was another crash next door, and Gaze-of-Purity flinched again. Spinner-of-Crystal got slowly to her feet, her hands still raised over her head. Stalker felt the room shudder. Something was happening. There was another loud crash from the garage and the doors trembled.

A crack like a whip rent the air and all eyes around the circle opened. The Green Man on the ground looked crooked. Stalker fluttered directly over it, unable to pick out the details with these dull, moth eyes. All she could tell was that the image had suddenly moved.

Then there was another terrible crack and the concrete floor shifted. The mural split in two and a green tentacle slithered up through the gap that had appeared. Stalker was out of time.

She flew down and straight into Spinner-of-Crystal's face.

The rite-mistress reeled backwards, stumbling out of the circle. The chanting stopped and Stalker was vaguely aware of rapid movement and shouting. She beat her tiny wings against the woman's leathery face, as her thick fingers swatted wildly at her. The Witch's hand made contact and sent Stalker spinning across the room. Every millimetre of her fragile body ached and she felt herself shaking, losing control of the form. Her wings wouldn't beat and she fell towards the ground as her body erupted and shifted out of her control.

Stalker stopped, her nose inches from the concrete floor, her human hands either side of her face to break her fall. But her levitation charm had stopped her from making impact, and only now did she float softly to the floor.

The room was silent and she felt eyes on her prone body. Every muscle and bone throbbed and she didn't dare look up. Where were the others? They should have arrived by now. Why could she no longer hear Weaver rampaging in the garage? She felt her connection to each pack mate, so knew that they were all alive, but they needed to be here. Now.

'Huh.' The bemused utterance was right overhead. Finally Stalker forced her body to roll over. She found herself staring up at Gaze-of-Purity. 'Well I never saw anything like that before. What are you?'

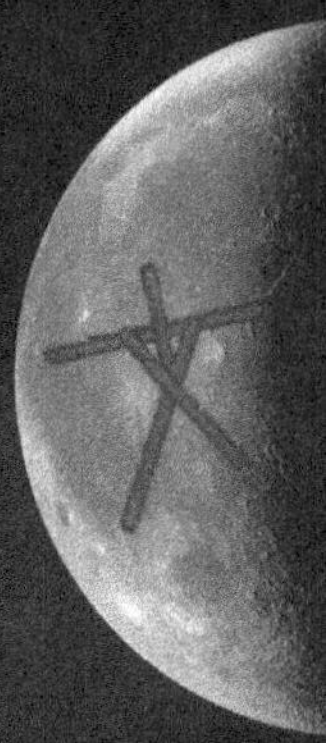

Chapter Thirty Nine

Fights-Eyes-Open

The side door of the black van slid shut and slammed into place. Claws grasped the ladder on the back and swung himself onto the top. Eyes watched as Claws carefully secured himself with the harness that had been tethered to the top next to the machine gun. Eyes wiped his clammy hands on his black jeans. He had abandoned the suit tonight.

Rust and the Wrecking Crew were climbing into their white van on the opposite side of the small circle at the heart of the scrap yard. Eyes crossed the yard quickly and caught Rust by the shoulder before he could heave himself up into the cab. Rust glared at Eyes' hand and Eyes hastily removed it.

'Sorry. Look, thanks for all this. I want you to know that whatever happens tonight you have my gratitude.'

'All right,' Rust said shortly. 'It's in all our interests, isn't it? I wouldn't be doing this if the Witches didn't pose a threat to my crew.'

'I know,' Eyes sighed. 'But I'm grateful all the same.'

'Sure.' Rust hung there in the door of the van, one foot still in the foot well. He wiped a greasy hand across his brow, smearing it black. 'Look, don't be crazy out there. I know this is personal and shit, but don't take unnecessary risks. Right?'

Eyes nodded, somehow touched by this surprising sign of concern. He patted Rust firmly on the shoulder and turned to head back to his own pack. He heard Rust's door slam shut.

'Are we ready?' Wind Talker asked, as Eyes climbed into the driver's seat.

'We are.' He glanced across at his pack mate, who sat with his arm hanging out of the open window. Between them sat the slight figure of Last-Breath-Echoes. She stared out of the wind screen, idly twirling her hair.

Eyes felt his phone vibrate. He tugged it from the tight pocket of his jeans and saw Theodore's name on the screen. He answered and put it on speaker. 'Theodore.'

'The girls have crossed the border.'

'Good, we're on our way. We don't have Crimson.'

'No, I suspected we might not. We'll manage. I'll see you there.' Theodore hung up. Eyes tossed his phone into a small nook in the dashboard and turned the key in the ignition. Wind Talker smacked the side of the van twice, and Claws returned the ready signal from the roof.

'Hold tight,' Eyes cautioned Echoes. She looked at him vacantly. Eyes pushed his foot down on the gas pedal and released the handbrake, and the van lurched forwards. He focused on the veil and set his sights on Hepethia beyond it. The van shot forwards, straight for a precariously balanced tower of wrecked cars. Rather than crashing into them, however, the van sped through the veil and the landscape opened up before them.

The Wrecking Crew had fashioned Hepethia like a massive fort. All around them were huge, steel walls and straight ahead was an open portcullis. Eyes drove straight through it and checked in his wing mirrors to see the Wrecking Crew's van following. Rust was leaning out of the window and pumping his fist in the air. Eyes laughed and patted the steering wheel.

'You're even crazier than me,' Last-Breath-Echoes called over the roar of the engine. Eyes flashed her a grin.

Beyond the fort, there were mounds of earth and a roughly-paved road wound between them. The road led due south, toward the Witches' territory. Constructs were busily digging and building on either side of the road. Rough buildings were going up, brick by brick, giving purpose to these beings from another realm.

The van sped past older sites, where completed brick buildings lined the road and spread away into the distance. The area was heavily populated with constructs and fae. Fascinating creatures scurried out of sight as the two vans rolled through the neighbourhood. A crowd of small, red brick, dog-like creatures trotted along the side of the road, looking warily at the shifters as they raced by.

'Wrecking Crew appears to be a misnomer!' Wind Talker shouted. 'I've never seen so much construction in Hepethia. They're building their own city.'

'Very clever!' Eyes replied. 'Who would ever think that a pack who smashes stuff for a living would be doing this as well? I must ask Rust about it later.' He missed off the words that formed in his head at the end of that sentence. *If we survive.* But Wind Talker caught them and nodded solemnly at Eyes over Echoes' head.

As they neared the edge of Wrecking Crew territory, the row of bright white street lights that lined the road stopped abruptly and plunged Hepethia into darkness. Eyes hit the van's lights and they shone on the road ahead. The mounds of earth gave way to rough crystal.

There was a honk from the van behind and Eyes glanced in his wing mirror. Rust was flashing his lights. Eyes looked back at the road just in time to see the road ending and a hill of rose quartz jutting up right ahead. He slammed on the brakes and the van stopped a few feet from the edge of the tarmac. He heard Claws clatter forwards on the roof, and cursing loudly. Eyes pulled himself up through his open window and saw Claws clinging to his harness, his face white.

'Fucking hell, mate!' Claws yelled.

'Sorry, so sorry. It snuck up on me sooner than I expected.' Eyes' heart was pounding and he reached out across the roof towards his brother. Claws made a fist and gently bumped it with Eyes' own, a slightly hysterical laugh bubbling up out of his throat.

Rust came striding from his van with Fury at his heels.

'I couldn't make a gap before now, for security,' Rust explained, pointing at the jagged crystal.

'Of course,' Eyes said, climbing awkwardly out of the van.

There was a strange noise on the wind and the shifters all seemed to hear it at once. They began searching the darkness for the source of the clanking, clattering sound. A dull, yellow light appeared beside the road and the clanging grew louder.

'What is that?' Rust whispered.

'One of our allies,' Eyes said, his shoulders relaxing as he realised who it was. 'I told him he would know when it was time.'

Sparking Clank came rushing towards them with remarkable speed, his short legs working hard and every inch of his metal body clanging and crashing with every movement of his ancient joints.

'It's a good job we're not going for stealth,' snorted Fury.

'No, that's Stalker's job,' Eyes hissed, shooting a filthy look at her. She glared back at him, the whites of her eyes standing out in her dark face.

'Now now,' Rust said softly.

Wind Talker and Last-Breath-Echoes climbed out of the van to join them, and Eyes felt his pack mate's firm hand on his shoulder, cautioning him to cool his temper.

Sparking Clank came to a halt next to the black van, wheezing and bobbing his huge head. He dwarfed the vans, being the size of a lorry himself. To Eyes' surprise, a figure slithered down off the construct's back. Tar Peter lifted his hat and dipped his head.

'You didn't think I'd miss this, did you?' he said dryly, his gaze fixed on Eyes.

'It never even occurred to me you would want to come. I didn't think you would want to dirty your hands.'

'Oh no, I don't, but I do love to watch.' Tar Peter grinned. Wind Talker tensed beside Eyes, and it was the

Alpha's turn to urge caution. He knew Wind Talker had not forgotten Tar Peter's appearance at the ruins of the betting shop. 'Besides, you'll need my help to get these vehicles through their territory.'

Eyes had to admit that the demon was correct.

'Yeah, but will you do the honourable thing and actually finish the job properly this time? Or is there a hidden fee for every hundred yards like there was for this road?' There was venom in Rust's voice and he stamped his foot on the tarmac. So that was the cause of the antagonism between them. Eyes couldn't help but smile slightly, though he turned his face away to hide it.

'We really need to get a move on!' Claws called down from the roof of the van.

'Quite right,' said Tar Peter. He stepped forwards and cleared his throat. Then he ran forwards, almost gliding up the rocky slope. In his wake, slick, wet tarmac appeared, as if spilling out from his black suit. He reached the summit and disappeared over it, the new road drying almost instantly.

'Nice,' Eyes said, nodding his head.

The shifters piled back into their vans. Eyes hesitated before closing the door and looked at Sparking Clank. 'Thank you for joining us.'

'Hmm, of course.' The construct lumbered up the hill and stopped at the top. Eyes set off after him, the headlights shining on the rear of their huge ally. He was more or less prepared for the sight that greeted them when he pulled up alongside Sparking Clank. But seeing it properly, rather than through Wind Talker's talisman, was still a mild shock. The Witches had created a dense forest in Hepethia, with large, gnarled trees packed close together.

Tar Peter stood at the foot of the hill, looking over his shoulder at the van perched at the top. His skin was sickly pale in the ghostly headlights of the van.

Eyes felt the van vibrating and he gripped the wheel tightly as something peeled itself away from the front. The construct friend of Tar Peter's that had taken up residence in the battering ram lurched forwards, separating himself from it. He was a towering humanoid of dense stone, with metal gauntlets on his huge fists and a helmet on his roughly shaped head. He set off down the hill, gathering pace. He spread his arms wide and crashed into the first line of trees. The thick trunks splintered and shattered. Eyes watched, gob-smacked, as the towering trees tottered and then began to fall.

The construct kept running, powering through the forest and dragging the trees over on either side of him. Tar Peter gave Eyes a wink, then set off after him, creating a rough road behind him through the trees. Eyes set off, the van bumped along, lurching up and down where the tarmac had been laid right over tree stumps and debris. It wasn't perfect, but it was certainly making it possible for them to traverse the terrain. He glanced at the clock on the dashboard and winced. It was getting late.

'It'll be okay,' Echoes whispered, barely audible over the noise of the crashing trees and rumble of the engine. 'Don't worry about them. They know what they're doing.'

'Thanks,' Eyes muttered under his breath. He willed the work to be completed more quickly. They lurched onwards slowly. Sparking Clank had fallen in behind Eyes' van, and his bulk was clearing some more of the foliage on either side of the road.

They didn't have far to go. The factory was only a few hundred yards inside the territory from this border in the human world. He clung to that as his eyes scanned the dark forest on either side of them. Shadows moved and the trees themselves seemed to be stirring.

After a torturous few minutes, the trees began to clear and Eyes could see lights up ahead. The stone construct at the head of their strange convoy came to a halt. Tar Peter stood still, the last drips of thick, black liquid oozing around his shoes. Eyes gently brought the van to a halt and looked up at the wooden fort before them. Smooth, sturdy logs stood tall and tightly packed, making an impenetrable wall with no windows or gaps. But Eyes could hear the humming inside; a low baritone melody was growing in volume.

'We need to get inside, right now,' Wind Talker hissed.

Eyes felt searing pain course through his veins. His head split open with blinding agony and he clamped the heels of his hands to his temples, his eyes squeezed tight. *Stalker!*

'Go! Now!' Eyes yelled out of the window.

Tar Peter leapt aside and the juggernaut went charging towards the fort, his head bowed. There was a sickening crunch and the sound of wood splintering. The wall lurched and swayed slightly, but didn't come down. The construct came staggering back towards the van and fixed his tiny black eyes upon it. He grabbed the battering ram and then sank down, absorbed back into the steel. Eyes slammed his foot on the gas and the van rocketed forwards. *Sorry Claws,* he thought.

The van started to shake violently as it careered towards the fort and the sound of rapid gunfire rent the air. Shells cascaded down on the roof, like metal rain. The wooden wall grew ever closer, thousands of huge splinters flying off it as the bullets made impact. When the van struck, the wall shattered like glass, bursting into millions of chips. The van skidded and Eyes fought with the wheel for a split second, before remembering to steer into the skid.

They spun sideways, the tyres squealing on the compact earth floor. Eyes opened his eyes, unaware that he had closed them until that moment. His breath was ragged and his arms ached from gripping the wheel. He looked up to see Sparking Clank crashing through the hole in the wall, making it twice as big. The Wrecking Crew screeched in behind him and skidded to a halt next to Eyes' van.

Wind Talker leaped out and clambered up onto the roof. Eyes heard both of his brothers' voices. Claws was okay, thank Luna. There was a shout and a single gunshot, not the machine gun. But it sounded so far away and his head was so foggy.

'Are you okay?' a soft voice beside him said. He looked slowly around at Last-Breath-Echoes. Her eyes shone with concern, and her slender fingers made contact with his left hand, which was still gripping the wheel. He nodded, numb with shock. 'You need to get out of the van now, bring your maul.' She spoke so softly and calmly, and yet he heard the urgency in her tone.

He could hear snarling, grunting and ripping fur somewhere in the distance. He looked at their joined hands, his gaze followed her arm up to her shoulder, and then looked into her clear eyes. He nodded solemnly and she released his hand. He snapped to his senses and reached down into the foot well for his new weapon. His fingers closed on the hilt and he lifted it out from under Echoes' feet. His door was wrenched open and Rust stood there, panting.

'You coming?' he snapped.

'Yeah,' Eyes replied, slipping to the ground. Echoes jumped out behind him, landing silently on the soft earth. He looked around. Tiny lights hung on a wire around the walls, like Christmas decorations, blinking eerily in the dark and casting their ghostly white light on the ground.

All around the fort were dozens of fae, vicious, snarling plant-based creatures with spikes and huge thorns. They swarmed towards Sparking Clank, who twisted and shuddered, his metal plates grinding as his form shifted into one with crushing fists. He opened his huge jaw and gnashed his teeth. He stomped on the smaller fae and smashed anything bigger that came within reach.

Another shot rang out and there was a *thunk* as the bullet lodged into the wooden wall on the far side of the fort. Eyes followed the trail of the bullet and saw the source of the sounds of fighting. Weaver was locked jaw to jaw with another Agrius, wrestling on the dirt.

'Stop firing!' he yelled up at Claws. 'You could hit Weaver!'

Claws reluctantly lowered his hand gun.

Eyes ran over to the fighting beasts, Rust close at his side. They grabbed hold of the struggling mass of tangled bodies and yanked them apart. Eyes took a fur-covered elbow to the nose and went stumbling backwards, clutching his face as blood trickled over his lips. He wiped the blood away and strode back to the beast as she lurched for the enemy. He jumped on her back and swiftly covered her throat with his hammer, gripping it tightly in both hands.

Weaver struggled in Rust's tight grip and slowly she shifted form, so that she stood panting in his arms. Her eyes were on fire.

Eyes still had the Witch by the throat and she struggled frantically to free herself. He didn't have time for mercy, or negotiation. He locked eyes with Weaver and gave her a nod. Rust released her and she strode over to the struggling Witch, her sister, at a guess. She raised a fist and it transformed into a clawed Agrius one. Eyes waited for the perfect timing, then swiftly released the Witch. With a single, fluid thrust, Weaver drove her huge talons into her sister's throat and ripped it out.

The beast slithered to the floor at their feet, blood cascading over her chest.

'I had to drag her across the veil to get her away from the ritual,' Weaver said coldly, not looking at her body. 'Stalker's in trouble, I felt it.'

'Me too.' Eyes nodded and put his arm around Weaver's shoulder.

Last-Breath-Echoes ran across to the centre of the room and dropped to her knees. Eyes strode over to her and saw the remnants of a detailed mural of a Green Man on the ground. It had been made of leaves, grass and twigs, which had been partially scattered by their entrance.

'We're too late,' Echoes said, looking up at him with

wide eyes. 'He's crossed over.'

'She's right,' Wind Talker said, his eyes out of focus. Without waiting, Wind Talker crossed the veil.

'Hey!' Eyes yelled at the empty space where he had been. He spun around to Sparking Clank, who was noisily finishing off the last of the fae. 'Can you cross the veil into the human world?'

'It takes effort, but yes,' the construct rumbled.

'Please do it,' Eyes implored. He grabbed Echoes and dragged her to her feet. 'Rust! Get the chains across the veil.'

Rust glanced down at the dead Witch, with a mingled expression of confusion and disgust. He ran back to his van and climbed inside, the rest of his pack followed. The van turned away from the other one and twisted across the veil, disappearing from sight.

Eyes had hold of Weaver and Last-Breath-Echoes. 'Burn it down,' he said softly.

Weaver nodded and pulled a new talisman from her pocket. It was a strange device, part lighter and part magnifying glass. She flicked it open and a flame burst out of the top. The little circle of glass captured the flame and projected it, sending a torrent of blazing fire out from it like a flame thrower. She directed it at the mural of dried leaves and twigs and they caught light easily. The fire spread quickly across the floor of leaves and rippled up the nearest wooden wall.

Eyes looked up at Claws, who was scrambling down from the van. They all climbed quickly inside and grasped hands to will themselves and the vehicle back across the veil.

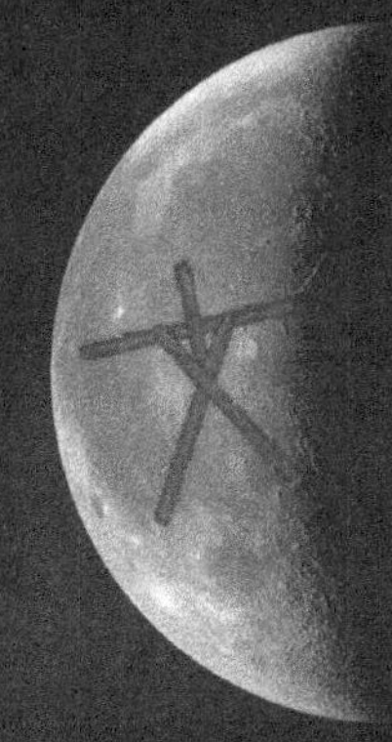

CHAPTER FORTY

STALKER-OF-NIGHT'S-SHADOW

THE FOOT CAME DOWN ON HER HEAD, sending crushing pain through every fibre.

'That's what we do with insects,' Gaze-of-Purity mocked. The others laughed.

'What do you think you're doing?!' boomed a voice behind the Witches. Stalker could feel the veil blowing as if in a breeze. Something huge had just come through it. But she couldn't see anything. Black and white spots flickered in her sight and little popping noises echoed in her ears. Her trembling hands went to her face while the Witches were distracted. There was no blood, but a hard lump was forming over her left temple where Gaze-of-Purity's boot had struck.

'My Lord,' Spinner-of-Crystal said. Stalker heard her voice as if from underwater.

'Finish the ritual!' the voice roared. 'The Equinox is upon us.'

Stalker felt their hurried footfalls through the vibrations of the floor. Her head pounded, she still couldn't see. Fear gripped her, paralysing her, and she pressed her throbbing temple to the cold floor.

'Odin,' she croaked. 'Odin, send the fire, please.' Nothing happened. She felt hot tears on her cheeks. 'I can't see. Please. Help.'

A blue light entered her consciousness: Fylgia. She saw Gudra's face amid the blue haze, she was shaking her head. It wasn't time to go to Valhalla yet either.

Chanting reached her from the other side of a vast lake, the Witches resuming their ritual. But a series of alarming sounds shattered the dull, echoing sensation in her head. Screeching tyres, shouts and then the unmistakable cacophony of what was left of the roof caving in. A heavy thud shook the floor and Stalker felt the room grow a hundred times brighter through the blue haze.

There were screams, snarls and the smell of blood. Then another ripple in the veil, and more skidding tyres and the smell of smoke. Gunshots pierced the screams. Claws was here. A smile crept across Stalker's aching face.

'Up you get.' A soft voice spoke nearby. 'Come on,' it gently urged.

'Who's there?' Stalker hissed, the smile vanishing from her lips. She reached out and caught hold of a hand, she felt rings on several thin fingers. The person's other hand was heaving Stalker's shoulders off the floor. The room spun uncontrollably and Stalker swayed as she was raised into a sitting position.

'Last-Breath-Echoes,' said the quiet voice, though it was clear and right by her ear, not far away through water.

Echoes withdrew her hand gently from Stalker's grasp and she felt two cool hands covering her eyes.

'What are you doing?' Stalker asked, her voice barely more than a rasp.

'Shh.'

Warmth spread from the hands on her face into her eyes, reaching right into her sinus and deep into her brain. She felt it running through her capillaries like warm water, soothing every ache and pain. Her eyelids fluttered, her lashes brushing against Echoes' palms. She could see slivers of bright light through the gaps between the palms and fingers, and the warm orange of the hands themselves. Echoes gently removed her hands and Stalker blinked in the bright light.

Unchained Lightning stood between them and the fight, shattered debris from the roof under his big feet. His tail swished back and forth and when he roared the whole factory shook. Two vans stood on the far side of the vast room, the laid out bodies illuminated by their headlights.

Facing Unchained Lightning was a tall, thin man made of green plant life. Hundreds of tendrils covered his stick-thin body and his bearded face was filled with fury. The Wrecking Crew were fumbling about at the back of their van, and Stalker's own pack, including Weaver, were taking on the Witches.

Stalker lurched to her feet, staggering sideways. Spots appeared in her vision again and Last-Breath-Echoes grabbed hold of her to steady her. The spots cleared quickly this time and she patted Echoes firmly on the back to let her know she was okay. She stomped forwards, drawing both of her dha.

There was a flutter of the veil right beside her and her head snapped to see Scourging Agony stepping through. His thin lips curved into a smile.

'Such delicious pain you're in my dear.'

'Not self-inflicted,' she snapped, repulsed by his close proximity.

'True, but very tasty all the same. Thank you for inviting me to the party.'

'You're welcome. Are you going to kill any Witches?'

The demon grinned, he shook his head and his bladed fingers flashed dangerously in the glowing light from Unchained Lightning. Stalker didn't hesitate. She swung one of her dha right through his long neck. His head toppled off his shoulders and rolled across the floor. His body disintegrated into thousands of pieces and disappeared back across the veil. He was really dead this time, she was sure of it.

Coolly, she looked around for her next target. The twins who should be dead were both heading for Eyes and were mid-shift when Stalker strode up behind them. She instinctively went for the one who had originally died at her hands. She drove one sword through the shoulder of the emerging Agrius, halting the shift in a grotesque mutation of their kind. A howl rent the air from the impaled Witch. Her human legs flailed around in mid-air, while her Agrius head tossed from side to side, and clawed hands grabbed at the sword.

Her sister screeched and barrelled into Stalker, knocking the odd pairing over sideways. The impaled twin went rolling across the floor, taking Stalker's dha with her. She writhed and thrashed on the floor, unable to free herself from the blade.

Stalker felt hot breath on her face and found the other twin crawling over her body, salivating. Without hesitating, Stalker shifted form, bursting into the Agrius, and launched herself off the floor, sending the Witch flying. She gripped her remaining dha and pounced forwards. Just as she reached the other twin and was about to wrap her hand around her throat, a whip-like tendril smacked her hand away. Her head snapped around to see the Green Man descending upon them. Another tendril lashed out and caught Stalker across the face. She went flying through the air, spinning over and over. She landed heavily next to a dead body. She couldn't breathe and grasped her chest.

She had dropped her dha and as she lay there, winded, all she could think about was getting her weapons back. She turned her head and saw Last-Breath-Echoes examining the bodies, hurrying from one to the next, desperately searching for something. Her lips were moving rapidly, muttering something that Stalker couldn't hear over the din of the fight echoing around the concrete chamber.

Her pack mates were all in their Agrius forms, even Claws. Wind Talker had Spinner-of-Crystal in hand to hand combat nearby. Their fierce jaws snarling and ripping at each other's fur. Weaver was chasing Gaze-of-Purity around the factory, leaping over fallen pillars and bursting through the long grass that grew up between the cracked concrete slabs on the floor.

Eyes had grabbed the other twin and Stalker watched, open mouthed as he forced her to the floor and bludgeoned her with his hammer. She had tried to kill his daughter. He had killed her once in rage, and he was going to finish the job. He pounded her skull again and again, screaming as he did. Blood splattered all over his hands and body, and flew in arcs from the swing of his weapon.

The doors from the garage burst open and Theodore appeared, an upturned car behind him. In his arms was the unconscious guard, who he tossed to one side. Vengeance-of-Steel entered the room around him, pushing the other Witch who had been in the garage with Weaver's sister ahead of her. She was handcuffed and gagged, blood trickling down the side of her face. The rest of the Glass Wolves strode into the room, surveying the chaos.

Stalker scrambled up and crawled across the floor to where Angela Carter was thrashing around, still impaled on Stalker's sword.

'It hurts, doesn't it?' Stalker snarled, though not much more than a growl escaped her Agrius snout. But the Witch seemed to comprehend her tone. She fell still, her human legs finally coming to rest. Her body slowly returned to its human form, and her cold eyes gazed up at Stalker. There was no life in them at all. And yet the girl was breathing, just. Stalker shifted form and knelt over the dying girl. Déjà vu nagged at her mind. She rolled the girl onto her side and slid her dha out of her shoulder with a disgusting squelch. 'I am sorry that I killed you before,' Stalker said softly in the girl's ear. 'It shouldn't have happened. We honestly just wanted to talk to you.'

The Witch nodded and her tongue flicked out to wet her lips.

'I know,' she croaked. 'I didn't ask to be brought back.'

'Okay,' Stalker said. The girl touched her wounded shoulder and stared at the blood on her fingers.

'Poison?'

'Venom.' Stalker could see the veins all around the wound throbbing and black through Angela's pale skin. That was Odin's gift to her, venomous blades. 'Close your eyes.' The girl complied. A moment later she drew one last shuddering breath, and then stopped. Stalker glanced over her body, she had no token to take, except for a silver claw earring, which Stalker couldn't touch without getting burned. She shook her head and stood to leave.

As she turned, she saw the Green Man heave himself up to his full height, almost as tall as the factory itself. He seemed to expand to fill the space. In one of his fists he held Terrance, of the Glass Wolves. The other Glass Wolves were gathered around, looking furious. There was a crunch as the Green Man broke Terrance in half, and then he tossed him to the ground.

One of his tendrils lashed out in Stalker's direction, but her reflexes protected her and she leaped aside. The tendril shot past her and hit a new mark with a thump. Stalker's head whipped around to see the tip spear Last-Breath-Echoes through the chest. She hung there limp on the end of the tentacle, her eyes wide. They flickered around the room and latched onto Stalker. The battle seemed to be suspended around them in that moment as they held each other's gaze. Stalker was rooted to the spot, caught on the wrong foot at the end of her leap.

The Green Man withdrew his tentacle and the vast room was filled with the sound of his laughter as Echoes dropped to the floor.

'No!' roared Eyes from somewhere in the distance.

Stalker bounded over to Echoes, dropping her sword

with a clatter. She scooped her friend up into her arms, but the light was already gone from her eyes.

'No, no, no,' Stalker mumbled, shaking Echoes by the shoulders. 'Heal,' she whispered. 'Heal yourself.'

There was a furious roar behind her, but she couldn't tear her eyes away from her dead friend. The battle was slowly resuming behind her, but it sounded so distant.

Thunder rumbled far away and heavy raindrops started to fall through the broken roof.

'Stalker!' A voice from far away penetrated her numbness. 'On your feet, soldier!' Rough hands had her by the shoulders and were dragging her up. She tried to lay Echoes down gently, but her head fell and cracked against the floor. Stalker spun to see who was dragging her away and came face to face with Fury. She shrugged her off and pushed her away.

'How dare you!' Stalker screamed.

'Not now!' Fury snapped. 'Finish the job and then grieve.'

Over Fury's shoulder, Stalker saw Eyes swinging his hammer. He was still roaring, his throat straining. The head of the hammer was glowing bright white and the Green Man stared down at him with a bemused expression on his leafy face.

Eyes released the hammer and sent it flying through the air towards the Green Man. Lightning streaked out from the head and struck the demi-god in the chest before the hammer thwacked him in the face. He stumbled backwards, and the Glass Wolves scattered out from behind him.

The rest of the Wrecking Crew charged forwards, heavy

black chains coiled in their arms. Speaker-of-Steel threw his arms into the air; the thick chains uncoiled themselves from his pack mates' arms and flew silently through the air. Speaker-of-Steel seemed to conduct the metal, guiding it with his outstretched hands, and it wrapped itself around the Green Man as he fell to the floor.

'No!' The shriek pierced the silence, and Gaze-of-Purity ran forwards, human once more.

Eyes' hammer fell to the floor with a heavy and decisive *thunk*, cracking the concrete. The crack spread rapidly across the ground, toward the Witch Alpha, and a gaping hole appeared at her feet. She fell straight through it with no time to react.

There was a muted crack of bones breaking and Stalker's gaze snapped over to Wind Talker as he tossed Spinner-of-Crystal to the ground, her head facing the wrong way. He bounded forwards and leaped into the hole after the Alpha. Eyes was right behind him, scooping up his hammer as he sped past it. Stalker grabbed her two fallen dha and raced after them. She didn't much care what happened in the main room of the factory.

The hole opened into a narrow passageway and she raced along it, barely able to see the others ahead, but she could hear their pounding feet and ragged breathing.

Don't rip her to pieces before I get there! she yelled in her mind.

There was a little light ahead and she could make out the dark shapes of running figures against it. The light drew nearer and she felt sickly warm air on her face as she sprinted towards it. She burst out into a small room. Wind Talker and Eyes stood frozen just inside, and Eyes caught

Stalker around the waist, pulling her to a halt.

In the centre of the room was a waist-high pillar in a narrow shaft of brilliant light. Stalker looked up, shielding her eyes, but there was no obvious source. Suspended there in the light, floating above the top of the pillar, was an ancient-looking piece of parchment. It had tiny writing scrawled all over it in brownish-red ink.

Gaze-of-Purity stood on the other side of the pillar, her face bathed in the mysterious light, with black shadows cast under her eyes and nose by it. Her mouth twisted into a maniacal grin.

Stalker lurched forwards, incensed. But Eyes held her fast.

'You have no idea what's coming. None,' Gaze-of-Purity cackled. She thrust her hand into the light and grabbed hold of the parchment. There was a blinding flash of light and then the room was plunged into darkness.

When Stalker's eyes adjusted, she saw that the parchment and Witch were gone. The veil was perfectly still.

'She didn't cross the veil,' Stalker murmured.

'No, she didn't,' Wind Talker confirmed.

Dust swirled in the air and the three of them stepped cautiously forwards.

'Where did she go?' Eyes snapped.

'Somewhere else,' Wind Talker replied. 'She's gone, Alpha. I think that was some sort of portal. It doesn't look like she can come back.'

Eyes roared; the sound reverberated around the small room. He swung his hammer at the pillar and it shattered, stone flying across the floor. They made their way blindly back along the passage and up into the factory. The Green Man and the Wrecking Crew were gone, the Glass Wolves were slowly moving bodies around.

'What happened to...?' Claws' question died on his lips when he saw their faces.

'She got away,' Stalker replied.

'What do you mean she got away?' Theodore said, striding over to them.

'She disappeared into another realm or something,' Stalker said, not wanting to look at anyone.

Theodore looked hard at Eyes, then turned and dropped down into the hole. One of his pack mates that Stalker didn't know went after him.

'We're going to burn the corpses,' Weaver said. Her voice was hard and formal. 'But we'll send the Witches to the Furies and bury our own properly.'

'The Wrecking Crew have taken the Green Man to Hepethia,' Claws explained. 'There's a ritual to send him back to Alfheim. Spark is going to lead it, but she'd like your help, Wind Talker.'

Wind Talker nodded and wandered slowly over to Spark, who was busy piling up corpses.

Stalker collapsed to her knees. She placed her sweating palms on the cool grass and concrete. Eyes knelt down beside her.

'We defeated them,' he said stiffly.

'You're trying to convince yourself of that,' Stalker said, smirking.

'Yes I am. But it's over. We did it. We dealt with the Green Man before he could resurrect the dead army, and most of the Witches are dead. Really dead this time, no demi-god to resurrect them.'

Stalker nodded.

'We lost a friend. She shouldn't have even been here. It was esoteric or scientific curiosity or whatever that brought her here, it wasn't her fight.'

'No it wasn't, and we will honour her.'

Theodore emerged from the hole, his face set in a grim expression. Stalker and Eyes looked up at him. He nodded, confirming their suspicions.

Movement by the door caught Stalker's eye and she looked past Theodore's bulky frame to see a dark shape flickering in the door to the garage. It moved into the room, a shifting, fluttering shadow. It took solid form, a young man with a red waistcoat, waving a white handkerchief over his head. Stalker frowned. He smelled strange, alien. Eyes followed her gaze, and gradually the room fell still as all eyes settled on the strange little fellow.

'Greetings.' His voice was warm and smooth. The two captured Witches sat tied up near the door and Stalker noticed them exchanging wide-eyed glances. They knew this figure.

Eyes got to his feet and helped Stalker up.

'Who are you?' he asked, striding forwards. He was covered in blood and his hammer was still held firmly in his hand.

'I am the envoy of the heir of Caerton,' he replied, still waving the handkerchief.

Theodore snorted, and a few of the Glass Wolves stifled laughter. Stalker failed to see the joke.

'Caerton has no heir. That archaic tradition died when we executed the last shifter styling himself "king",'

Theodore said, bitterness in his voice.

'As I'm sure you are aware, the last King was succeeded and his line has continued to thrive outside of the city. Your stewardship of the city will soon be redundant, when the heir returns to claim the throne. You all know this. Gleaming Blade will return to Caerton soon. You are to make preparations for the handover of power, in order to avoid bloodshed.'

'Is that a threat?' Eyes snarled.

'Of course,' the envoy replied, with a little bow of his head. 'I'll be taking them with me.' He pointed at the two Witches.

'Yes, I suppose you will,' Eyes replied. He didn't like the idea of keeping prisoners, though he had wanted to question them. 'The bodies of the fallen Witches too.'

The envoy nodded. The assembled shifters gathered the bodies together and lay them out at the envoy's feet. Vengeance-of-Steel ushered the captured Witches over and released them from their handcuffs.

'Make the preparations, or we can have open warfare if you prefer. It's up to you. You have three months to decide.'

The envoy shimmered and turned into shadowy smoke once more. There was a flash and he vanished, taking the Witches, dead and alive, with him.

Stalker released a shaking breath. She looked from Eyes to Theodore, and then around at the other shifters in the room. No one seemed to want to break the silence.

'Well?' she asked at last.

'Well,' Eyes replied, his gaze fixed on Theodore, who gave the smallest nod. 'I guess this means we're preparing for war.'

H. B. LYNE

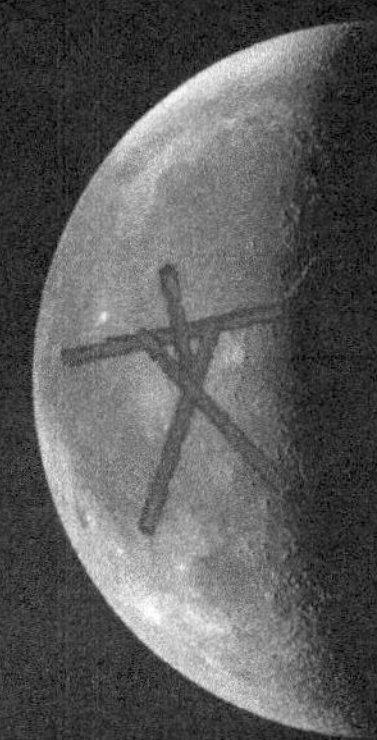

Chapter Forty One

Stalker twisted the paper napkin in her hot palms, rolling it into a thin strip then tying a knot in the middle. The café was stifling; people squeezed past her table, the hum of their voices like a busy bee hive. It was deafening. The pounding in her head wouldn't stop. She closed her eyes, trying to tune it out.

Last-Breath-Echoes was suspended on the end of the spear-like tendril, her mouth wide with shock. Dead. In an instant. Stalker couldn't shake the image from her head.

'Ariana?' Ron's voice yanked her attention back to the bustling little café and her eyes popped open. She leapt to her feet, shoving the metal chair back across the floor with a loud scrape.

'Ron, hi.' She tried to contort her face into a smile, but from his startled expression she realised she had barely managed a grimace. 'How are you?'

Ron nodded and pulled out the chair opposite,

plonking his bulky girth into it. Stalker sat back down and glanced at the matted napkin in her hands. She shoved it into her jacket pocket and picked up her coffee mug.

'Not too bad, all things considered. I'm waiting for the insurance company to do their assessment.'

'Right, of course. Have you heard anything back from the police yet?'

'They said they couldn't find any evidence of foul play and handed it over to the insurance assessors.'

'Okay,' Stalker nodded and released a shaking breath. As long as she wasn't going to be investigated, that was all that really mattered right now.

'I'm just so relieved you weren't hurt,' Ron said kindly.

'Yeah, me too.' She forced a feeble smile. Last-Breath-Echoes was dead in her arms. She sipped her coffee and shoved the memory aside. 'It was probably faulty wiring or something.'

'I suppose,' Ron said stiffly. 'I can't let the business idle any longer. I've been looking into alternative premises, short term. There's a hall not far from here that we could rent. If we could just get the kids classes back up and running it would keep us ticking over. Thing is, if we let another week go by clients might start looking elsewhere. I don't want Central mopping up our kids.'

'Sure,' Stalker bobbed her head absently. Her friend's lifeless body was dropping from her hands as Fury pulled her away. *I can't do this any more, it's too hard.* A tear formed in the corner of her eye.

Someone at the next table stood up and bumped into Stalker, snapping her out of her maudlin thoughts. She sniffed back the tear and glanced anxiously around the heaving café.

'Are you all right?' Ron asked, leaning across the table.

'Sorry, yeah, I'm just a bit worried, you know, about the dojo and the business and everything. I didn't know if I would still have a job after the fire.'

'You have a job with me as long as you want one, Ariana,' he said softly, smiling affectionately. 'As long as I can keep the business afloat.'

They drank their coffees quietly amid the hubbub for several minutes. Stalker's mind kept flashing back to the fight with the Green Man, and the run in with the Knight-of-Shadowed-Fear that had caused her to destroy her own workplace, and the loss of the Blue Moon. Everything she cared about was taken from her. Her pack, her friends, her place of work. Was it her fault? Was she at the centre of all of this? Destruction seemed to be following her. Was that why her parents had given her up? Did they know this was to come? Had one of them had a vision about her life? She should walk away. She should tell Ron right now that she couldn't work for him any more. She was endangering all of the humans that she came into contact with.

We are the chosen few who must keep humanity close to our hearts, for if we fail to do so we fall into despair. Sometimes you will need those who loved you before to remind you of all that you are.

Shadow's Step had been wrong. Trying to hold onto her humanity had endangered people and caused so much suffering. She was falling into despair now, her humanity was her weakness and she needed to be strong.

'I'd better get going,' she said stiffly. She drained the dregs from her mug and stood to go.

'Ariana.' Ron's voice stopped her. 'Don't worry, we'll get it all straightened out and be up and running again before you know it.'

She nodded and patted his shoulder. She made her way between tightly packed tables and past the queue of people at the counter. She wrenched the door open and stepped out into the cool morning, taking a deep breath and feeling the breeze on her hot skin. Cars rushed past on the busy street and pedestrians brushed past her with disgruntled scowls. She didn't care.

A vibration in her pocket startled her and she tugged her phone from her jeans. She looked at the caller ID and sighed, she had been dreading this call. She moved quickly along the street to the corner and darted into the quieter side street before answering.

'Hi. How are you?'

'Shit. You?' First Strike's voice was low and dull.

'Same.'

'Look, we're having the funeral tonight. Scribe is conducting it at Crescent Park. It's not normally the done thing to invite other packs, but Crimson said you guys should come.'

'Right, okay. I'll tell Eyes. Thanks.'

'Yeah, no worries.'

'She shouldn't have been there. I'm so sorry.'

'Yeah, I know. Whatever.'

First Strike hung up abruptly. Stalker stared at her phone for a moment, an ache in her chest. She punched in a hurried text message to Eyes to let him know, then set off at a sprint for her flat. As she rounded the corner at the end of her street she saw a man leaning against the building, one foot against the wall, his hands wedged deep into the pockets of a jacket. She stopped dead and stared at him. A painful lump had formed suddenly in her throat. It wasn't Fortune, it couldn't be. He was dead. The man looked her way, his dark hair tied back off his handsome face. She walked slowly towards Rhys, her feet dragging along the pavement. He pushed away from the wall and took a few steps towards her, a sad expression on his face. She stumbled into his arms and broke down in tears. He held her tight against his chest and stroked her hair.

'Let's go inside, come on,' he said softly. She passed him her keys and he unlocked the door, then helped her up the stairs and into her flat.

'She died,' Stalker croaked between sobs.

'I know.' Rhys calmly sat her down and took off her boots. Stalker let him look after her, too numb to resist.

'The funeral's tonight. I wish you could come.'

'Me too.' He sat beside her on the sofa and cradled her head.

'Shouldn't you be at work?' She tried to lift her head to look at him but her neck didn't want to cooperate.

'Not until this afternoon,' he said softly, still stroking her hair. 'I knew you needed me.'

'How?'

'Not sure.' She could feel a smile in his voice. He kissed her head and she let out a heavy sigh as the last tears fell. 'It's like I can feel you inside me,' Rhys said softly. 'Like we're connected at the heart.'

'Yeah,' she murmured. What he described was like the empathy she had shared with her pack before Unchained Lightning granted them telepathy. A frown creased her brow and she tugged free of his embrace to stare into his eyes. 'Yeah, it is like that. That's weird.'

She placed a hand on his face and stared into his eyes. They were totally open to her, no barriers now like their had been in the beginning. She reached into his soul, digging through darkness for a light. When she stumbled upon it it was so bright it almost blinded her; his love for her was his inner truth right now. She withdrew from inside him and managed to smile.

'Have you ever felt this sort of connection before?' he asked.

'Yes, with my pack. You?'

'Never.'

His pack were slaughtered before he ever changed, he had never been connected to other shifters the way she was.

'I wonder what it means. I don't think you've joined my pack without me realising. Have you?'

He laughed and shook his head.

'No, I haven't. I don't feel anyone else, only you.'

Stalker nodded. Her connection to her pack was intact.

'It's like I have two packs now. Them and you.'

'I think that might mean we've claimed each other,' he said tentatively. 'As mates, I mean.'

'Oh.' She nodded. *That's right.* A soft voice inside her head whispered with a gentle jingle like wind chimes. 'That's right,' Stalker said out loud, smiling. Rhys leaned in and kissed her softly. Her eyes closed and she allowed herself to fall into the moment, releasing everything else.

That evening, after sunset, the Lightning Lords made their way to Crescent Park. Gathered on the grass were all of The Hand of God; a formidable sight. First Strike stood with Crimson, both dressed all in black. Stalker didn't really know the other four, they were all muscular and fierce-looking. Last-Breath-Echoes had been something of an oddity among their number, being petite and ethereal.

Crimson nodded at the newcomers, who stood awkwardly at the edge of the lawn. Scribe-of-the-Fallen emerged from behind two of The Hand of God and made straight for the Lightning Lords. He looked drained, he was even more pale than usual and had dark circles under his eyes.

'Oh god, Scribe. Have you slept at all?' Stalker asked. She pulled him into a tight embrace and felt him shaking slightly.

'I think so, maybe a little.' She released him and he wiped his clammy hands together.

'Are you up to this?' Wind Talker asked softly. 'I could help.'

'Thank you, I think I'll be all right.'

Wind Talker nodded, but exchanged concerned glances with Eyes and Weaver.

The shifters formed a circle around a small coffin and Scribe handed everyone black candles. Stalker held back the tears that threatened to fall. The last funeral she had attended had been that of her old pack, and Last-Breath-Echoes had been there to help Scribe lead the ritual. This ritual was for her. Scribe went through the motions, his voice cold and detached. When he invited them all to place a hand on the coffin to imprint it with their memories of their fallen friend, his voice broke and a tear fell down his cheek.

The wooden box took on the impressions of those around it, covered in scrawled writing and pictures. Stalker remembered the little scratches that Echoes had left on the door frames at Grove Street and silently vowed to make sure they were never covered. She thought of the Scroll Archive and the help Echoes had given in tracing her shifter family. Scrolls and tally marks appeared on the wood around her palm.

'She was the best of us,' Scribe said softly as they all stepped back. 'She won't be forgotten.'

The coffin shone brightly before being sucked into the ground to be buried in the underworld where no one could find it.

Stalker stared at the space the coffin left. Another hole in her life, in all of their lives, because of The Witches and the Furies. Let them come, let them try and take this city. *We'll be ready.*

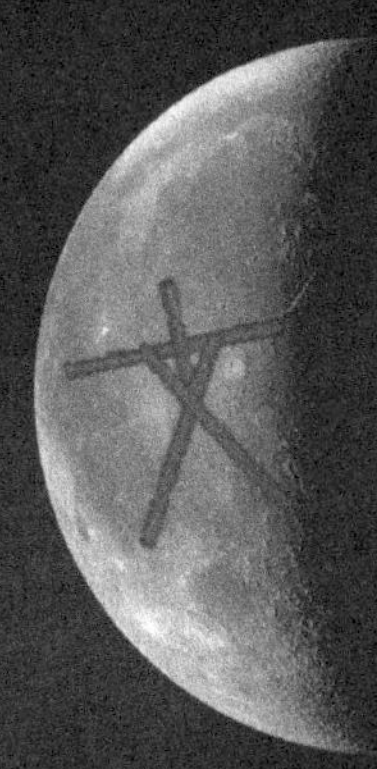

EPILOGUE

HE GRASPED THE CHARRED SKULL IN BOTH HANDS, turning it over and over, gazing into the empty, black sockets. Hidden Voice had hidden secrets. It had been close, too close. They had almost learned everything. But fate had stepped in and kept Hidden Voice quiet.

How fortuitous that he had happened upon the pyre when he did. The remains of the burned body rescued from the clutches of the sea. Poseidon had seen to it that the body was not captured, and now he had it safely in his possession. He would ensure that none of Caerton's shifters discovered its secrets.

Looking out across the stormy sea, he grasped the side of the rocking ship firmly and held the skull up against the grey sky. Lightning flashed overhead and he flinched at the reminder of his greatest threat.

He hadn't been able to find what he was looking for. Twice now he had entered their house and had even turned the place upside down looking for it, but there was no trace of it. Of course, he had framed the Witches for the break in and ransacking of 32 Grove Street. As far as he could tell, they had fallen for it.

But what was he going to do without his prize? He needed a new plan, a new way to control the King-of-Glass-and-Steel.

Rage flared suddenly in his chest and a growl rumbled from his lips. He crushed the skull one handed and watched the fragments scattering into the black water. The sea protected so many secrets, this was one more. It would be safe there.

The coast bobbed up and down on the horizon as his ship rocked on the turbulent waves. His gaze was fixed on the city. He would finish what he started. The plan to resurrect The-King-of-Glass-and-Steel was coming along nicely, soon it would be time. And when the city's soul was returned from Muspelheim, where he and the others had sent it, he would finally have the true chaos and destruction that he had always sought. His time was coming.

With that happy thought he smiled.

Please Leave a Review

I hope you enjoyed *Demons of the Past*. I would really appreciate it if you could take a few minutes now to review the book on your favourite retailer. Independent authors rely heavily on reader reviews, they really are like oxygen. Reviews help other readers decide whether a book is a good fit for them or not. Much as I want everyone to love my books, I also know that it's important to find the right readers, so just a few words from you could help me to do that and reach other readers who will enjoy my dark and twisted tales!

Thank you!

About the Author

H.B. Lyne is an urban fantasy author, podcaster and bullet journal enthusiast with a knack for organisation and getting stuff done.

She lives in Yorkshire with her husbeast, two children and midwife cat. When not juggling family commitments, she writes dark urban fantasy novels, purging her imagination of its demons. Inspired by the King of Horror himself, Holly aspires to be at least half as prolific and successful and promises to limit herself to only one tome of The Stand-like proportions in her career.

Check out my website for all the latest updates and offers
hblyne.com

Follow me on Instagram
@hblyne

And on Facebook
facebook.com/authorhblyne

ALSO BY H.B. LYNE

In the Shifters of Caerton series:

Fate of the Blue Moon

Ghosts of Winter

Demons of the Past

Rise of the Furies

Dark Echoes: Tales from the Shadows

From Ashes to Echoes

Lies the Dead Tell series:

In The Blood

JOIN MY TRIBE OF RABID READERS

Missing Last-Breath-Echoes already? Get her backstory in my special prequel novella, From *Ashes to Echoes* at **landing.hblyne.com/fate**

www.ingramcontent.com/pod-product-compliance
Lightning Source LLC
Chambersburg PA
CBHW050953180726
48291CB00006B/1807